MOST ELIGIBLE BACHELOR

BY
LAURA IDING

DOCTOR: DIAMOND IN THE ROUGH

BY
LUCY CLARK

&

HOT-SHOT SEXY DOCS!

*Two drop-dead gorgeous doctors—
a true Valentine's Day treat!*

Simon Carter will stop at nothing
to rescue Hailey Rogers in:

CEDAR BLUFF'S MOST ELIGIBLE BACHELOR
by Laura Iding

and

Can Daniel Tarvon win over
city doctor Melora's heart?

DOCTOR: DIAMOND IN THE ROUGH
by Lucy Clark

CEDAR BLUFF'S
MOST ELIGIBLE
BACHELOR

BY
LAURA IDING

First published in Great Britain 2011
Harlequin Mills & Boon Limited,
Eton House, 18-24 Paradise Road, Richmond, Surrey TW9 1SR

© Laura Iding 2011

ISBN: 978 0 263 88576 7

Printed and bound in Spain
by Litografia Rosés, S.A., Barcelona

Dear Reader

Thanks to all of you who wrote to me about how much you've enjoyed my *Cedar Bluff* trilogy. I'm always honoured to hear from my readers, and I'm glad you enjoyed the trilogy as much as I enjoyed writing it.

I'm thrilled to announce the debut of Simon's story. Simon Carter was just a secondary character at first—a friend of Jadon's—but soon I realised he deserved his own story. And deserved a strong heroine as his match.

Hailey and Simon both have guilty secrets in their respective pasts. Neither one of them is ready for a relationship when they literally crash into each other's lives. But soon they discover that only by working together can they free themselves from the mistakes they've made in order to fall in love.

I hope you enjoy CEDAR BLUFF'S MOST ELIGIBLE BACHELOR. And don't hesitate to visit my website and drop me a note.

Sincerely

Laura Iding
www.lauraiding.com

Laura Iding loved reading as a child, and when she ran out of books she readily made up her own, completing a little detective mini-series when she was twelve. But, despite her aspirations for being an author, her parents insisted she look into a 'real' career. So the summer after she turned thirteen she volunteered as a Candy Striper, and fell in love with nursing. Now, after twenty years of experience in trauma/critical care, she's thrilled to combine her career and her hobby into one—writing Medical™ Romances for Mills & Boon. Laura lives in the northern part of the United States, and spends all her spare time with her two teenage kids (help!)— a daughter and a son—and her husband. Enjoy!

Recent books by the same author:

A KNIGHT FOR NURSE HART
THE NURSE'S BROODING BOSS

Dedication

This book is for you, Olga. Always be true to yourself.

CHAPTER ONE

HAILEY ROGERS walked into Cedar Bluff's emergency department on Saturday afternoon, fluffing her blonde hair to get rid of her helmet head.

"Hi, Hailey," Rachel, one of her nursing colleagues, greeted her when she approached the desk. "You're working arena team two today."

"Sounds good." Hailey had started at Cedar Bluff hospital about two months previously, but she'd worked in the emergency trauma center at Trinity Medical Center in Milwaukee for several years, so she hadn't needed long to learn Cedar Bluff's way of doing things. Rachel had been her preceptor but they'd quickly grown to be friends.

"I'll be right next to you in team three," Rachel said cheerfully. "So if you need something, or have questions, just let me know."

"Thanks." Hailey appreciated Rachel's sincere offer. The other nurses were friendly too, but most of them were married with children so they weren't exactly anxious to stop for a bite to eat after work, or go to a movie. Rachel was single, and she and Hailey had bonded after a particularly stressful shift a few weeks back.

Moving to Cedar Bluff had been a good decision for her. She loved the homey atmosphere of the hospital and the town. Plus, her apartment was only a few miles from the hospital, making it easy to ride her bike to work every day.

Hailey glanced up at the assignment white-board and couldn't suppress a tingle of excitement when she noticed the physician leader assigned to her team was none other than Dr. Simon Carter. She knew who he was, of course. His chocolate-brown eyes, mink-colored hair and broad shoulders stood out dramatically, in her humble opinion, among the rest of the physicians. But in the two months since she'd started in the ED, they'd only worked together a few times and those had all been during her orientation, with her preceptor primarily interacting with him.

He seemed like a nice guy. And one of the few not married. Rachel had warned her that Dr. Carter didn't date any of the staff at Cedar Bluff, *ever*, but she couldn't seem to control her physical reaction to him. But it didn't matter because she wasn't in the market for a relationship either, so Hailey was more than happy to admire him from afar. She'd noticed all the staff called the doctors by their first names, but she couldn't bring herself to follow their example. Especially with Dr. Carter. Using his first name, Simon, seemed far too personal.

Heaven knew, it was bad enough that Dr. Carter's handsome face managed to invade her dreams.

Shaking off the inappropriate thoughts, Hailey quickly took report on the patients in her team from Alyssa, the day shift nurse in team two. With sixteen-month-old twin girls at home, Alyssa only worked one shift per week, and often that shift was a weekend.

"Hailey, do you have any questions?" Alyssa asked, when she'd finished her rundown. "Because if not, I need to go, I have to pick up the girls from their grandma. As much as my mother-in-law enjoys babysitting, I think it's getting to be a bit much for her now that the girls are walking."

"No questions," Hailey said reassuringly. "I can't imagine what it's like to take care of twins."

Alyssa laughed. "It wasn't too bad until Grace and Gretch learned to walk. They were preemies and a bit delayed in reaching their milestones, so they didn't figure it out until just a few days ago. Now it's like they're each on a different mission, heading off in opposite directions. Keeps us running."

"No doubt," Hailey agreed, ignoring a twinge of envy. Alyssa's husband, Jadon, was one of the ED doctors she enjoyed working with. They made a beautiful couple.

Once she'd envisioned a similar future for herself. Husband. Babies. Happily ever after. But not anymore.

Moments after Alyssa left, Leanne, the charge nurse, came over. "Hailey? I just put a new patient in room seven. Here's the paperwork." Leanne thrust a clipboard into her hand. Most of their nursing documentation was on computer, but the registration and consent for treatment forms were still on paper. "Fifty-five-year-old guy with abdominal pain."

"Thanks." Hailey took the clipboard and glanced up in time to catch Dr. Carter staring at her. The moment their gazes collided, he seemed to go still, and then tore his gaze away.

Had she imagined the flash of interest in his eyes? Most likely. Rachel had confided that she'd tried to ask Dr. Carter out several times, but he'd always politely declined.

Not that Hailey was interested in dating him, the way Rachel had been. Still, it felt good to be noticed.

"Good afternoon, Mr. McLeod," Hailey said with a

smile as she walked into her new patient's room. His wife was there too, standing next to his bed. Hailey quickly introduced herself. "Tell me what brought you to the hospital today."

The middle-aged gentleman grimaced. "We went out for lunch with my daughter, she's a sophomore at the university, and ever since we finished eating, my stomach has been hurting. The pain is cramping, and it seems to come and go. Do you think I have food poisoning?"

"Possibly," Hailey said, as she set the forms down and reached for a stethoscope. "But generally food poisoning sets in at least four hours after the meal. What did you have for lunch?"

"A steak sandwich and French fries," he admitted. His wife glowered at him and she suspected his wife had wanted her husband to pick a healthier choice.

"Hmm." She took his blood pressure, which was a bit elevated, either from the pain or because he had high blood pressure already. His pulse was tachycardic at 104 but his respirations seemed normal. "Put this under your tongue," she directed, holding out a probe for an electronic thermometer. After a minute, the device beeped. "Your temperature is normal, ninety-nine."

"Maybe it's just flu?" he said helpfully.

"Do you feel like you're going to throw up?" He shook his head no. "Have you been told you have high blood pressure?" she asked, logging on to the computer to review his medication history. "Are you taking blood-pressure medicine?"

"No." He grimaced again, and she glanced back at him in concern. Whatever was going on with him, she doubted it was food poisoning. His medical history wasn't too significant for anything other than heart disease.

"Okay, Mr. McLeod, I'm going to talk to the doctor about your case. I think we may need to do some blood work, just to make sure there's nothing going on with your heart. And then you might also need some X-rays or CT scans to see what's going on in your belly. I'll be back in a few minutes, okay?"

"Can't he have something for pain?" Mrs. McLeod asked, a worried frown in her brow.

"I'll check with the doctor. I don't know if he's going to want to wait until we know what's going on with your husband first." She pulled up a chair for the woman. "Please sit down so you're comfortable while you're waiting."

"Okay."

Hailey made a few notes on the computer and then left the room to find Dr. Carter. Mr. McLeod didn't appear too sick, but her intuition was screaming at her that something more serious was going on with his abdominal pain.

The sooner they could get tests ordered, the better she'd feel.

Simon glanced up to find Hailey striding purposefully toward him. Keeping his expression friendly but distant took more of an effort than it should have. "Dr. Carter? I need you to take a look at Mr. McLeod in room two. I'm concerned about his abdominal pain."

He frowned. "Appendicitis?"

"Maybe, but he said he doesn't feel sick to his stomach and he's not running a fever. He does have a cardiac history, and ate a steak sandwich and fries for lunch."

Hailey's expression was troubled. "His blood pressure is up a bit. One-seventy over ninety-two."

"So we'll do a full work-up, then," Simon decided. "Draw a cardiac panel, basic chemistry panel and blood count. If he has an infection, his white blood cell count will be elevated." He could feel Hailey's piercing blue eyes on his back as he headed for their patient's room.

He introduced himself to the couple. "We're going to do several types of blood test, to see if we can narrow down what's going on with your abdomen. Once Hailey gets your blood sent to the lab, I'm going to order a CT scan."

Hailey came into the room holding a fistful of empty blood tubes. "Should I put him on the cardiac monitor too?" she asked.

"Cardiac monitor? It's his stomach that hurts, not his chest," Mrs. McLeod protested.

"Yes, put him on the cardiac monitor," Simon agreed. He turned toward the patient's wife. "Sometimes chest pain can radiate to other parts of the body. We don't want to miss anything, so we're going to do a full work-up."

"All right," the wife agreed.

"I'll be fine, Myra," Mr. McLeod said, patting his wife's hand. "I'll be out of here in a jiffy. I'm sure this is nothing more than food poisoning."

Simon suspected the gentleman was downplaying his symptoms for his wife's sake. He took out his stethoscope to listen to his patient's heart and lungs. Hailey came in close beside him, reaching around him in order to put the electrodes on Mr. McLeod's chest and then reaching up to turn on the monitor. He'd picked the wrong side of the bed, since the monitor cables were on the same side he was standing. Hailey's scent, something fresh, like the scent of the ocean, teased his senses. He eased away, as far as his stethoscope would allow.

When Hailey finished getting Mr. McLeod connected to the monitor, she went around to the other side of the bed, where the supply cart was located. Simon relaxed and finished his exam, verifying normal heart and lung sounds.

He moved his stethoscope to his patient's abdomen, expecting hyperactive bowel sounds. Instead, the normal gurgling sounds were diminished.

"Tiny poke here," Hailey warned. She deftly slid a needle into his vein, filling up her numerous blood tubes.

"I'm going to call Radiology to schedule you for a CT scan," Simon told him. "You're heart looks okay so far, but I think you may have something going on with your abdomen. A CT scan is the best thing to show us what's going on."

"Do you really think that's necessary?" Mr. McLeod asked skeptically. "I'm sure I'll be fine in a while."

Simon frowned. "Yes, I do think this test is necessary," he said firmly. Hailey lifted a brow but didn't say anything as she slipped out of the room, no doubt to send their patient's blood to the lab. He sharpened his gaze on his patient. "You may have appendicitis or something worse, like a pocket of infection or an aortic aneurysm."

"Hank, please." Mrs. McLeod was practically wringing her hands at the list of potential problems. "Don't argue with the doctor. Have the CT scan, please."

"All right, I'll have the scan." A mutinous expression darkened the patient's eyes. "But I'm already feeling better. I'm sure there's nothing seriously wrong with me."

Simon wasn't so sure, but since Hank McLeod had

agreed to have the scan, he wasn't going to waste any time in getting it ordered. "Someone will be in soon to take you to Radiology," he promised.

While he was on the phone with the radiologist, he realized Hailey was standing beside him, chewing her lower lip anxiously, obviously waiting for him to get off the phone. When he finished his call, he glanced at her. "What's wrong?"

She let out a sigh. "Do you think it's possible Mr. McLeod has an abdominal aortic aneurysm? Everything about his presentation reminds me of a patient I had about six months ago back in Milwaukee. Same type of abdominal pain, same relatively stable vital signs, except for the high blood pressure, and even the same stubborn denial that anything was wrong."

Simon was impressed by her gut instinct. "It's one of my differential diagnoses, yes. And if he does have one, we'll find it on the CT scan. They're finishing another patient now, but they'll be ready for him in about ten to fifteen minutes."

"Sounds good. I'm going to give Jimmy and his mom discharge instructions and then I'll be ready to go with Mr. McLeod. I just need you to write out his prescriptions."

"Jimmy?" Simon had to think for a minute to figure out who she was talking about, and then he nodded. "Oh, yeah, the kid with the dogbite." He logged on to the nearest computer and quickly pulled up the sixteen-year-old's record. He entered in the medications and then printed the prescriptions. "Make sure he understands he has to finish all the antibiotics."

She chuckled. "I will."

Simon handed Hailey the scripts and then turned his attention to the other patients in their team. There

was a twenty-two-year-old female patient with a severe
headache that he was still waiting for Neurology to clear
before he could consider sending her home. He figured
she was suffering from migraines, since everything else
had come back negative, but wanted the specialist to see
her just in case.

Twenty minutes later, he got a call from the lab on
Mr. McLeod's blood count. The gentleman's hemoglobin
and hematocrit were on the low side, reinforcing Hailey's
suspicion that he might have a leaking abdominal aortic
aneurysm.

As Simon was on the phone with the lab tech anyway,
he took all the blood-work information, relieved that
the cardiac injury panel was completely negative. The
patient's white blood cell count was negative too, which
made the drop in his hemoglobin and hematocrit even
more suspicious.

The minute he hung up the phone, his pager went off.
He read the text message. *McLeod's BP is dropping,
come to CT stat.*

Simon didn't waste any time heading over to the
scanner, thankfully located right around the corner in
the emergency department. When he arrived, Hailey
glanced up at him, her expression grim.

"I told them to keep the IV in place. Do you want me
to start a vasopressor to bring his blood pressure back
up?" she asked.

"Yes, let's start norepinephrine titrate to keep his
blood pressure above 90 systolic." He reached for the
phone to stat page Leila Torres, the on-call surgeon
working today. He quickly punched in the number for
the CT scan, followed by a 911 so she'd know to come
straight over. "How much of the scan were you able to
complete?" he asked as he hung up the phone.

"Maybe half?" Hailey said as she pulled the IV medication out of the crash cart and hung it on the pump.

He crossed over to the reading room to look at the images. They hadn't quite been able to get half the scan done, but he could still see there was the slightest hint of blood leaking near the guy's descending aorta.

"What's happening?" the patient asked Hailey. "Is the test over?"

"Your blood pressure dropped a little too low," she explained. "We're starting you on some medication to bring it back up."

He caught Hailey's hand. "Tell Myra I love her," he said.

Simon caught the agonized look in Hailey's eyes. "I will," she assured him.

Leila strode into the room, glancing at Simon with an arched brow. "You rang?"

Simon pulled her into the reading room and indicated the worrisome spot on the CT scan. He kept his voice low so the patient couldn't hear. "The only abnormal lab test he has is a low H/H. He just dropped his blood pressure so we couldn't finish the scan. I think he has an aneurysm that's about to rupture."

"I think you're right." Leila was a petite woman with a hint of Asian heritage, and Simon had all the respect in the world for her skill as a surgeon. "I'll take over from here."

While Leila explained to Mr. McLeod what was going on, he called the OR to let them know an emergency case was on the way. Then he informed the radiology tech they needed a couple of transporters to run the patient up to surgery.

"We can't forget his wife," Hailey murmured, as they prepared to wheel Mr. McLeod down the hall.

"We've got it from here," Leila told them. "Go back to the ED. Tell his wife I'll talk to her when the surgery is over."

"All right." Simon stood next to Hailey as the team whisked the patient to the nearest elevator. This was the most difficult part of his job, giving bad news to families.

He turned and headed back to the arena. He was a little surprised when Hailey followed him into Mr. McLeod's room. Some of the nurses left the bad news up to the doctor. He appreciated her support as Mrs. McLeod looked up at them questioningly.

"Where's Hank? Have you finished his scan?" she asked, her gaze bouncing nervously between the two of them.

"Mrs. McLeod, your husband has an abdominal aortic aneurysm. What that means is that the biggest artery going from his heart down through his abdomen has a bulging section, where the artery wall is weakened."

"A weak artery is causing his pain?" she asked, her brow wrinkled in a puzzled frown.

"It's actually more than a weak artery, Mrs. McLeod," Hailey said. "This is a very serious condition that needs immediate treatment."

Simon nodded. "Your husband's blood pressure dropped while he was getting his CT scan. We started him on some medication to bring it back up, but we think the weak spot of his artery has started to give way. I'm sorry to tell you this, but he was taken to the operating room for emergency surgery."

"Emergency surgery?" Mrs. McLeod paled at the news. "But he'll be all right, won't he? I mean, you caught it in time, didn't you?"

"We acted as quickly as we could, and he has an

excellent surgeon taking care of him." No matter how much he wanted to gloss over the risks, he knew she needed to hear the truth. "As Hailey said, this is a very serious condition. A life-threatening condition. He has a good chance of making it through this surgery alive, but there is a twenty-eight percent chance he might not make it."

"No. Oh no. Hank, poor Hank." Mrs. McLeod's stoic expression crumpled. "Tomorrow is our wedding anniversary. Thirty-five years! I can't lose him. Don't you understand? I can't lose him!"

Hailey put her arm around Myra McLeod's shoulders and the woman sagged against her, sobbing as if her heart were breaking. Despite his resolve to keep a safe distance from his colleagues, a lump lodged in Simon's throat when he noticed Hailey's eyes filling with tears, several fat drops slipping down her cheeks. As she comforted the patient's wife, his gaze locked with Hailey's in unspoken, yet shared agony.

Hoping and praying Hank McLeod wouldn't die.

CHAPTER TWO

ONCE she'd managed to get the poor woman to calm down, Hailey took Mrs. McLeod to the family center waiting area, leaving her in the kind, compassionate care of the elderly volunteer behind the desk.

It was the nature of the emergency department to move quickly from one patient to the next. She loved emergency nursing but sometimes, like now, she regretted not being able to follow patients for longer than a few hours.

As she tried to get caught up with the rest of the patients on her team, she couldn't prevent her gaze from straying to Dr. Carter. Those moments when they'd stared at each other while Mrs. McLeod had cried in her arms had touched her heart—a heart she'd assumed was long frozen.

Cedar Bluff was so different from the big city trauma center where she'd worked before. Here, it seemed as if everyone took their patient's welfare more seriously. No, not more seriously, that wasn't the right word.

Personally. The staff took their patient's welfare personally. Maybe because the community was so close. Because they ran into each other at the grocery store, at church or even at the park.

"Hailey, I put another admission for you in room seven," the charge nurse informed her.

"Okay, thanks." It was just after six o'clock in the evening and she was somewhat surprised she hadn't had a new admission sooner. Not that she was complaining. The slightly slower pace made it easier to be thorough with every patient.

She enjoyed working with people, mostly because it helped her to remember that everyone had difficult situations to work through. Some worse than others.

She glanced down at her paperwork as she headed toward room two. A seven-year-old boy with a dislocated shoulder and possible broken arm. Her steps slowed as a chill snaked down her spine. One of the things every emergency nurse learned early on was to look out for the various signs of suspected abuse. A dislocated shoulder could be the result of a parent yanking on a child's arm, and abuse cases often presented with broken limbs.

Quelling her nervousness, she entered the room, mentally prepared for the worst. A young boy was lying on the cart, dried tears on his face. His mother, a pretty and obviously pregnant woman, was sitting beside him, holding his uninjured hand.

"Hello, my name is Hailey and I'll be your nurse for this evening," she said, quickly introducing herself. Deliberately focusing her gaze on the child, she crossed over to the other side of his gurney. "Ben, can you tell me what happened?"

The child glanced up at his mother, as if seeking permission, and the pregnant woman offered a strained smile. "Go ahead, Ben. Tell the nurse what happened."

"I was climbing the tree and I slipped," he said. "My arm hurts real bad."

"I know—we're going to give you something for the pain. But can you tell me what happened after you slipped? How did you hurt your arm?" Hailey sensed the boy's mother was frowning at her, but she kept her gaze on the boy. His story seemed a bit fishy.

"When I fell, I grabbed a branch, but it broke." He sent another nervous glance at his mother.

"It's okay, Ben. I'm not mad at you," the woman told him softly.

"But I wasn't supposed to climb the tree," Ben said in a wobbly voice, sniffling loudly.

"No, you weren't. But I'm not mad at you. Go ahead and finish your story."

Hailey glanced at the pretty honey-blonde-haired mother, acknowledging that she sounded sincere. But she wasn't going to let the woman off the hook yet. "What happened after the branch broke, Ben? Did you fall to the ground?"

"No, I didn't fall, I jumped. The branch didn't break all the way. I was hanging in the air when I felt my arm start hurting. When I jumped, I fell backwards on the same arm." His wide eyes filled with tears. "I'm sorry, Mom."

"Shh, it's okay, Ben." The pregnant mother sent Hailey a resigned glance. "It's not the first time Ben's had a broken bone. He's a bit accident prone."

Accident prone? The hairs on the back of her neck lifted. She highly doubted it. The way the child was so afraid of his mother's reaction didn't sit well with her at all. "All right, Ben, I need to look at your arm for a minute."

She gently palpated the extremity, reassured that there was a good pulse in his wrist. "I'm going to get the doctor to take a look at this arm, Ben. I think you're going to need X-rays. Do you know what an X-ray is?"

"Yeah. I know. It doesn't hurt." The calm acceptance in the child's eyes bothered her. No child should be that familiar with X-rays.

Hailey left Ben's room and crossed over to the closest computer, intent on bringing up the child's past medical history to look more closely at his most recent *accidents.*

"Where's Ben?" a male voice demanded. She glanced up in time to see Dr. Seth Taylor standing near Dr. Carter. The expression on Dr. Taylor's face looked grim. "Kylie told me to meet her here."

Hailey glanced at her patient's name. Sure enough, Ben Taylor. Was this the reason no one had looked closely at this child's multiple injuries? Because he was the son of a doctor on staff?

"I don't know, Seth. But calm down, we'll find him."

"Um, Dr. Taylor?" Hailey spoke up. "Ben was just placed over here in room seven."

"Thanks." Relief flared in his eyes as he headed straight for Ben's room. Dr. Carter crossed over to where she was standing.

"What happened to Ben Taylor?" he asked.

"Dislocated shoulder and possible broken arm," Hailey answered. "I'm worried about him. Hasn't anyone considered getting Child Protective Services involved?"

"Child protective services?" Dr. Carter stared at her for a few seconds and then started to laugh. "For Seth and Kylie? No, Hailey, you're way off base."

She bristled at his casual dismissal. "Oh, really? Just

because his father is a doctor here doesn't mean this boy isn't the subject of physical abuse."

Simon's laughter ended abruptly. "You're serious!" he exclaimed, his eyes widening comically. "Come on, Hailey, I know Seth and Kylie. They're not hurting Ben."

"Then why is Ben so accident-prone?" She'd pulled up the boy's medical record. Six months ago he'd had a gash to his leg that was deep enough to need stitches. And another six months before that he was admitted for hypothermia after falling into Lake Michigan. And before that he was hit by a car while riding his bike.

Accident prone was an understatement.

"Because he's a mischievous kid who's probably looking for attention now that his mother has another baby on the way," he pointed out reasonably.

"Maybe." She couldn't deny his theory made sense, if Ben was telling the truth about climbing the tree against his mother's wishes. She glanced at the boy's history again. Falling into Lake Michigan couldn't be construed as abuse. Neglect? Maybe. But his mother hadn't been the one driving the car that had hit him. More neglect?

Or was she simply overreacting?

"Seriously, Hailey, you have to trust me on this. Seth and Kylie are good people. They love Ben. They would never hurt him."

"If you're sure," she finally agreed. She didn't need Dr. Carter's approval to call Child Protective Services—anyone could make a referral. But Cedar Bluff was a small town and the more she thought about it, the more likely it seemed that if something like physical abuse was going on, others would know about it.

"Hey, don't be so hard on yourself," Dr. Carter said

quietly. "Actually, you did the right thing by raising the question. Sometimes we see these people so often, here at work and out in the community, we don't even think about the fact that something horrible could be happening behind closed doors. Having new people work here is a good way to keep us on our toes."

He was being nice, trying to make her feel better. Surely someone with integrity, like Dr. Carter, wouldn't ignore a case of child abuse. "Thanks," she murmured. "You'd better go in there to see him. He'll need X-rays for sure."

"Will do." He flashed a quick smile before disappearing into Ben's room. She followed and halted in the doorway, watching as Dr. Taylor and his pregnant wife hovered over Ben with obvious concern.

A family united.

Feeling foolish about her original suspicions, and maybe a bit envious at their closeness, Hailey turned away to check on her other patients.

After the fiasco with Ben, the rest of her shift flew by. Several times she thought about calling upstairs to the intensive care unit to find out how Hank McLeod was doing, but other issues needing her attention prevented her from following through.

But after her shift was over, Hailey couldn't leave without checking on him. She didn't call the ICU but simply walked up the few flights of stairs until she reached the third-floor surgical ICU.

Worrying her bottom lip with her top teeth, she read through the names on the census board. She didn't immediately find his name and her stomach clenched, fearing the worst. But then she found him at the bottom of the list in the very last room.

She went down the hall toward his room, only to discover he was in the middle of a sterile procedure, a central line placement from what she could tell. She glimpsed at his vital signs on the monitor, reassuring herself that he was relatively stable, before she backed away.

Not an appropriate time to check with his wife to see how things were going. Maybe tomorrow she'd stop up to see Mrs. McLeod. As Hailey walked back out of the unit, she came face to face with Dr. Carter, who was apparently on his way in.

"Hi, Dr. Carter. Guess we're both here for the same reason," she said with a sheepish grin. She was impressed he'd cared enough to come up to check on their patient. "You can go in, but they're in the middle of placing a central line on Mr. McLeod."

"Ah, then I won't bother them." He stood for a moment, his hands tucked in the pockets of his lab coat as if he wanted to say something. "Hailey, stop the Dr. Carter stuff. You need to call me Simon."

Her eyes widened and she swallowed hard. "I'll— uh—try," she hedged, stepping to go around him. "I have to run. I'll—uh—see you later."

"Wait, this is important," he called, halting her escape. "I'm not trying to come onto you or anything."

She sucked in a quick breath at his bold statement. "I never thought you were!" she said hastily, her cheeks burning with embarrassment.

Good grief, this was awkward.

Now it was his turn to avoid her gaze. Still, he continued, as if needing to clear the air. "The administration here at Cedar Bluff is working on a new initiative where we all work together as a team, keeping the patient at the center of all we do."

"Okay," she agreed slowly, trying to figure out

where he was going with all this. "I'm all for making our patients a priority—why else would we be here?" And what in the world did that have to do with calling him Simon? She could feel her cheeks reddening at the thought of being on a first-name basis with him.

"Of course, we all do. But I think you're missing the point. The most important part of achieving the goal of patient-centered care is teamwork. Cedar Bluff doesn't want us to view ourselves as a hierarchical organization. Instead, they want us to have a team approach, where everyone has an equal say in what we do for our patients."

"Really?" She couldn't help the sliver of doubt in her tone.

Now his expression seemed a bit exasperated. "Haven't you noticed how big the first name is printed on our hospital ID badge? Or heard everyone calling everyone else by their first names?"

She nodded slowly. "Yes. But I'm used to calling doctors by their formal titles. It's a sign of respect. And I figured you all knew each other well enough to use first names, but I'm still new here."

He looked a little taken aback by that statement. "Not at all. I mean, I know some of the people really well but others I don't. Regardless, it's about being a team. Not a doctor versus a nurse, or a tech versus a nurse. A team. Got it?"

What he was saying made some sense. She reluctantly agreed, "Got it."

He looked relieved. "Good." There was another awkward silence and he cleared his throat and then glanced at his watch. "I have to get home, too. Goodnight, Hailey."

His expectant gaze forced her to respond in kind. "Goodnight, Simon."

His name sounded strange when she spoke it out loud and for a moment there was a simmering awareness hovering between them. After a few moments he deliberately turned and walked away, breaking the intangible connection.

When he headed for the elevators, she decided to slip down the stairs to go to the staff locker room.

In the privacy of the female locker room, she peeled off her scrubs and pulled on her skin-tight florescent striped biking gear, reliving those few tense moments when Simon had told her he wasn't coming onto her.

Had she given him the impression she wished he would? Or that she thought he was? Good grief, talk about humiliating.

He couldn't know that the last thing she wanted was a relationship. With him or anyone else.

"I can't believe you're still here!" Rachel exclaimed, coming into the locker room and interrupting her tumultuous thoughts. "Don't tell me you rode your bike today. I know it's spring, but it's freezing outside. Not to mention dark. Why would you ride this late? It's close to midnight."

Hailey offered a weak smile. "Biking is good exercise and I don't live very far. Don't worry, this fluorescent gear keeps me safe." Despite the budding friendship she felt toward Rachel, there were some secrets that were too dark to share, no matter how strong the friendship.

After all, she'd come here to Cedar Bluff to escape the past, not dwell on everything she'd lost.

"You're crazy," Rachel said, slamming her locker door shut as Hailey pulled on her bike helmet. "Truly crazy. Are you sure you don't want a ride home?"

"I'm sure," Hailey responded firmly. She pulled on her gloves and then opened the locker-room door. She had to shut this conversation down before Rachel asked any more questions. "Bye, Rachel. See you tomorrow."

"Bye, Hailey. Ride safe."

"I will." Outside, true to Rachel's word, the cold wind cut through her sweat-wicking biking gear. She clenched her teeth together to keep them from chattering. After deftly unlocking the bike, she jumped on and followed the familiar path towards home.

She'd come a long way since those dark days after Andrew's death. In the fourteen months that had passed, she'd recovered both emotionally and physically from the accident that had stolen everything that had been important to her.

But no matter how much she'd healed, she still couldn't bring herself to get behind the wheel of a car.

Simon mentally smacked himself in the forehead as he rode the elevator down to the first floor, putting as much distance between himself and Hailey as possible.

Idiot. How could he have been such an idiot?

I'm not coming onto you or anything.

I never thought you were!

Shaking his head, he strode out to the parking structure towards his car. He'd made a complete fool of himself. But at least Hailey would know that he wasn't interested in anything more than a nice, friendly working relationship. Teamwork, just as he had said.

He shouldn't have assumed anything, he acknowledged as he drove home. Just because Rachel Connell had asked him out a few times, it didn't mean every single female would.

Hailey was beautiful enough that some other guy would surely snatch her up in no time.

And why that thought annoyed him, he had no idea. Normally he couldn't care less who dated whom.

Simon didn't live far from the hospital, so he made it home in less than fifteen minutes. He walked inside his small ranch-style home and tossed his keys on the counter.

The blinking light on his answering-machine gave him pause. Most of his friends used his cell phone. He only kept the land line because of the need to be on call for the emergency department. He'd started out using just his cell phone, but he'd slept through the first call he'd ever received because the ringer on his phone, even at maximum volume, just wasn't loud enough.

Maybe his parents had called? He hadn't talked to them in over a month, he realized guiltily.

He pulled a beer out of the fridge, twisted off the cap and took a long drink before walking over to look more closely at the answering-machine.

Three messages, all from a blocked phone number. He frowned. Not his parents. Unless they'd changed to a blocked number for some reason? He pushed the play button.

The sound of a dial tone echoed in the room.

He deleted that message and played the next. More dial tone. The third one was also nothing but dial tone.

Three hang-up phone calls. All from blocked numbers.

Dread painfully twisted his stomach.

Erica had left hang-up messages. Especially in those final weeks before he'd finally picked up and moved, without telling anyone where he was going. Not only had he kept quiet about his true destination, he'd claimed he was moving to Arizona to be closer to his parents. He'd even gone as far as applying for an Arizona medical license.

No one, outside his parents, knew he'd come to small-town Cedar Bluff in Wisconsin instead.

Almost two years had passed. Surely Erica hadn't found him. Why would she even bother after all this time? She must have moved on with her life by now.

Hadn't she?

CHAPTER THREE

BY THE next morning, Simon had convinced himself that telemarketers had left the three hang-up messages. It was the only explanation that made sense. He needed to remember to update his number on the national do-not-call list.

He sipped at a mug of coffee, thinking about his plans for his day off. He found he was oddly disappointed that he wouldn't be seeing Hailey.

Stupid, since nothing would ever come of it.

He was through with relationships. After everything that had happened with Erica, he couldn't imagine allowing anyone to get close.

To this day, he still felt guilty for what had transpired between them. He'd had no idea she was the clingy type of woman when they'd started to see each other. She'd been a nurse working in the same Chicago Children's hospital emergency department he had been. The way she'd call him if she hadn't heard from him had seemed nice at first, complimentary. Deep down, he'd been thrilled to know how much she liked him. And she was sweet, too.

But then, when he'd tried to pull back a little, needing a little breathing space, Erica had got upset. She'd been so upset that he'd gone back to seeing her, thinking that perhaps he'd overreacted.

All too soon he'd known it wasn't going to work. So he had broken things off again. And then circumstances had changed and things had gone from bad to worse.

He closed his eyes for a moment, wishing desperately that he'd handled the situation differently. His actions had caused both of them to suffer. And then there was...

No. He shoved thoughts of Erica aside. Two years was a long time. She'd moved on and so should he. Maybe a tiny part of him would never be the same again, but he had created a new life in Cedar Bluff. New friends. And he was being considered for a promotion, the open ED Medical Director position.

He was happy with his new, if lonely, life. And he'd finally realized there was nothing he could do if Erica wasn't happy in hers.

Nothing he could do to change what had been lost.

While mowing his lawn, a job he liked for the sheer mindlessness of the work, Seth Taylor called him. He had to shut off the lawnmower in order to hear him.

"Simon, I need a favor."

"No problem."

There was a slight pause on the other end of the line. "I haven't told you what the favor is yet," Seth protested.

He chuckled at Seth's incredulous tone. "Doesn't matter, Seth. But go ahead and ask me, if it makes you feel better."

"I need you to cover my three-to-eleven shift in the trauma bay tonight. Kylie has to cover a sick call for the paramedic unit and I don't want to leave Ben with a babysitter as he's still having some pain in his broken arm."

"No problem," Simon repeated, glancing at his watch. He had a couple of hours until three o'clock. "I'd be happy to cover you."

"Thanks, man. You know I'll return the favor some time," Seth said gratefully.

"I know," he agreed. Since he was one of the few single guys on staff, he had less reason to need anyone to cover him, but he didn't mind.

Work was his salvation.

When Simon walked into the ED a few hours later, controlled chaos reigned.

Apparently several staff members were sick with flu, so they were working short-handed. Even with the tight staffing, he was surprised to see that Hailey had been assigned to work trauma with him.

Not that Hailey wasn't a capable nurse. She'd certainly proved herself with the McLeod case. But Cedar Bluff's policy was not to put their new nurses into the trauma bay until after six months. Hailey had come to them with trauma experience, though, and from a level-one trauma center to boot, so maybe that was why they'd made an exception in her case.

Secretly thrilled to discover he was working with Hailey after all, he crossed over to talk to Quinn Torres, the day-shift physician in the trauma bay, to find out what was going on.

"Hey, Simon," Quinn greeted him. "It's been steady all day, but nothing too overwhelming. The biggest issue is staffing. For second shift the trauma team is also covering team one."

Double duty. He grimaced at the news, knowing there would be delays with patients in team one if emergency cases arrived. There was nothing they could do, though, other than their best. "All right. What's the disposition with this guy?" he asked, glancing at the patient who was currently in the trauma bay, hooked up to a cardiac monitor and a ventilator. He noticed Hailey was there getting a report from Claire, the day-shift nurse.

"Fifty-eight-year-old guy with a GI bleed. We've dumped several units of blood and fresh frozen plasma into him, so he's stable for the moment. We're waiting on an ICU bed—hopefully should get one within the next fifteen minutes or so," Quinn replied. "They're moving someone out to make room."

"So are all hospital beds tight or just critical care beds?" he asked. Without open-floor beds and ICU beds, patient dispositions took much longer, causing back-ups in the ED. Not good on a day when they were already short-staffed.

"Just critical care," Quinn assured him. "And I think they're moving a couple of patients out, so you should be fine."

"Okay. Anything else about this guy I need to know?"

"Not really," Quinn murmured, glancing over at the patient. "We have an H/H pending and there are four units of PRBCs and four units of fresh frozen plasma on hand if you need them."

"Sounds good."

"Excellent," Quinn said, slapping Simon on the back. "Have a good night, because I know I will."

Simon had to laugh. "Is that your way of saying Leila is off tonight, too?"

"Yes, and Kane Ryerson is the surgeon on call tonight. Don't you dare page Leila unless you have a code-yellow situation," Quinn threatened.

A code yellow was a disaster call, something they'd never had to implement in time he'd been there. "Don't worry, we won't."

After Quinn had left, he went over to stand at the foot of the patient's gurney, taking note of the most recent vital signs flashing across the screen. Hailey was performing a physical assessment, her head bent down as she listened to his heart and lungs. His fingers itched to tuck the silky strands of blonde hair behind her ear.

He dragged his gaze away with an effort. So what if he thought she was incredibly attractive? Just the fact that she was a nurse on staff made her off-limits.

"Ah, Dr—I mean, Simon?"

He inwardly cursed when just the sound of his name in her voice made his gut tighten with awareness. *Get a grip! She's off-limits!*

"What do you need?" he asked, glancing up from the computer screen and keeping his expression neutral.

"His hemoglobin hasn't come up much—it's 7.8 now and was 7.5 before the blood transfusion," Hailey informed him. "Do you want me to start another unit?"

"Yes, that should work. Hopefully he'll be transferred upstairs to the ICU shortly," he decided.

"Sounds good."

Hailey smiled, but he noticed a strange wariness in her blue eyes as she crossed over to the nearest phone to order the unit of blood.

He told himself to be glad Hailey seemed content to keep a professional distance between them.

Because heaven knew, if she were to come on to him, he wasn't sure he'd be able to turn her down as easily as he had Rachel.

* * *

Hailey eagerly transferred her patient up to the medical ICU, thankful for the momentary reprieve from being stuck in close proximity to Simon.

She'd tried to get out of working in the trauma bay for her shift but Theresa, the ED manager, hadn't given her a choice. The two trauma-trained nurses had both called in sick, leaving her to pick up the trauma shift.

Another reason she'd left Trinity Medical Center had been because she'd lost the thrill of working in a level-one trauma center. She liked ED nursing overall, but had told Theresa there was no rush in getting cross-trained to trauma. Hailey had planned on settling in for at least another few months before having to face her first shift there.

Guess not.

She could do it, she told herself for the fifth time. Of course, having Simon on duty with her served as a distraction from her past.

She didn't linger upstairs, as much as she wanted to, but hurried back down to the trauma bay, knowing another patient could arrive at any moment. Besides, there were still a few patients in team one to follow up on.

Her trauma pager remained silent, though, so when she returned to the department, she left the tech, a new woman named Bonnie, to clean up and restock the trauma bay while she headed back over to team one.

She double-checked on the patient they were treating for flu. The poor woman had thrown up right after getting settled into her room, just missing Hailey's feet. Hailey glanced up at the IV bag, satisfied to see it was nearly empty. "How are you feeling, Christy?" she asked the young college student.

"Better," the girl murmured with a wan smile. "At least I don't feel as much like I'm going to throw up."

"Well, that's a relief," Hailey said in a light, teasing tone. "Good to know my shoes are safe. Let's have you try to eat something, hmm? I'll get you some crackers and white soda."

Christy wrinkled her nose and put a hand over her stomach. "Do I really have to?"

Hailey nodded. "If you can keep the crackers and soda down, I'll get Dr. Carter…er…Simon to discharge you."

"Dr. Dreamy's name is Simon?" Christy asked with a heavy sigh, running her fingers through her limp brown hair. "He's not wearing a wedding ring. Does that mean he's single?"

She chuckled and shook her head. "I'm not answering that, you'll have to ask him yourself." She left the room to get the promised crackers and soda, returning in less than a minute. "Here you go."

"Thanks." The girl's eyes brightened despite her pasty complexion and Hailey wasn't surprised when she heard Simon enter the room behind her. "Hi, Dr. Simon. I'm feeling much better after that IV you gave me."

"I'm glad to hear it," Simon responded, his deep voice sending a shiver down Hailey's spine. She didn't so much as glance at him, concentrating on disconnecting the IV tubing from the pump. "Looks like you're well enough to leave, Christy."

Leave? Hailey tossed the bag and tubing in the garbage and turned toward him. "I told Christy she had to eat the crackers and drink the soda first, to make sure everything stays in her stomach."

There was a slight hesitation before he gave a brief nod. "Good. I'll get the discharge orders started."

After Simon left, the young woman let out another sigh. "Maybe I should throw up again, just so I can stay longer."

"I wouldn't recommend it," Hailey said dryly. "A better plan would be to get healthy, and then come back to visit when you look smashing. Doctors aren't overly impressed with sickly patients."

"Good idea," Christy said, with such enthusiasm Hailey knew the girl was starting to feel better.

Barely three seconds after Christy Drummel had been safely discharged, Hailey's trauma pager went off.

She read the text message with a sinking heart.

Male victim, MVC, pulse 130, BP 80/40, long extrication, suspected chest injuries. ETA three minutes.

"Hailey?" she glanced up when Simon called her name. "We have a trauma on the way. Are you ready?"

No. She wasn't ready. But she nodded anyway, praying she wouldn't throw up the way Christy had. "Of course."

Hailey finished with her other patient's labs and then took her place in the trauma bay as the paramedics wheeled in the new arrival. The patient was a young seventeen-year-old male, who'd run his stolen car into a tree while being chased by the police.

He'd been wedged inside the car, to the point where it had taken the firemen over forty-five minutes to get him out.

The first glance at his pale and lifeless face made her blood run cold.

Not Andrew.

She kept the mantra running in the back of her mind as she concentrated on getting the new patient connected to the heart monitor. His vital signs were dangerously low.

The monitor began alarming. "I'm losing his blood pressure," she said sharply, with a worried glance at Simon.

Simon looked up at the monitor, his expression grim. "PEA. Probably a hemothorax with his crushing chest injuries. I need a chest tube."

Hailey grabbed the chest tube tray at the same time Bonnie, the ICU tech, did. Bonnie stared at her for a moment, and Hailey readily let go, realizing setting up and assisting with the chest tube was something useful the tech could do.

She vaguely heard Simon give Bonnie instructions on prepping the guy's chest. She hung IV fluids and performed a quick assessment, noticing the young man's abdomen was taut.

Their patient rebounded as soon as Simon placed the chest tube. Bright red blood came pouring out, though.

"Call Kane Ryerson," Simon said to Bonnie. "This guy needs the OR."

Bonnie headed for the nearest phone, but almost immediately the patient's blood pressure bottomed out again.

"He's bleeding into his abdomen," Hailey said, watching in horror as the patient's belly grew larger right before her eyes. "Simon? Do you see his belly?"

"Yeah. We're going to have to open him up here." Simon didn't look very happy with the prospect.

She tugged the peritoneal lavage tray from the

bedside, but before Simon could get the guy's abdomen opened, his heart rate slowed and then stopped.

"No!" Hailey shouted, unwilling to believe they were going to lose him. She climbed up on a stool to start chest compressions. One and two and three and four and five. Breathe. One and two and three and four and five. Breathe.

We're not going to lose him. We're not. We're not…

"Hailey!" Simon's sharp tone finally registered. She stopped CPR and glanced up at the heart monitor.

Asystole.

"It's over," Simon said quietly. "Time of death, six-forty-two p.m."

She thought she could handle it. But without warning her eyes filled with tears. "Excuse me," she mumbled, nearly falling off the stool in her haste to get away.

"Hailey!" she heard Simon shout behind her.

But she disappeared into the staff lounge, shutting the door firmly behind her.

CHAPTER FOUR

SIMON followed Hailey as soon as he could, but by the time he arrived at the staff lounge she appeared to have pulled herself together. But her red, puffy eyes and stuffed-up nose betrayed how she'd been crying.

"Are you all right?" he asked, concern in his voice. He took a step forward, instinctively wanting to offer comfort. What in the world had happened in there? Did she know the young man?

"Yes. Sorry for running off," she muttered, avoiding his gaze and moving to brush past him.

He caught her arm to prevent her from leaving. Immediately, a sizzle of electricity zinged up to his shoulder.

Quickly, he let go and took a step back. What in the world was that? "Hailey, there's no rush, if you need a few minutes yet," he began.

"I'm fine." Her tense tone was not at all reassuring. "I shouldn't have left like that. I need to get back to work. And we have to make sure his family gets notified of what happened."

He stared at her for several long seconds. Logically, he knew it would be best to leave her alone. Maybe Hailey always reacted like this after losing a patient.

Especially a young man who'd had his whole life ahead of him.

And even if there was something more going on with her, it had nothing to do with him. So why was he so reluctant to leave well enough alone?

"All right," he agreed, stepping away from the door. She hesitated only a moment, before walking past him to return to the trauma bay.

Letting her go was harder than he'd anticipated. With a resigned shake of his head, he followed her back to the trauma bay.

The rest of their shift flew by quickly, but while they had several trauma calls, none of them were as serious as the young man who'd died.

Simon kept a close eye on Hailey, but she seemed fine as they cared for a seemingly endless line of patients. He sought her out at the end of their shift, intending to talk to her again, but she'd apparently left without saying goodbye.

He headed home, uncharacteristically frustrated that he hadn't been able to spend a few minutes alone with her.

The next day he locked his front door before heading outside to his car for his shift, ducking his head in the rain. A crack of thunder made him jump as he climbed into the front seat. He pulled slowly out of his driveway, the rain coming down in sheets making it difficult to see the road in front of him.

Lightning flashed and more thunder rolled as he made his way to work. He slowed his speed, peering through the deluge of rain hammering against his windshield as he headed to Cedar Bluff hospital.

Maybe they did need the rain after nearly a month of

drought, unusual for April. But with the force of the rain coming down, flooding was a definite concern. Water pooled on the roads and he carefully rolled through the deep puddles to avoid stalling his car.

As he approached an intersection with a four-way stop, a cyclist came out of nowhere, not stopping or slowing down at the junction, instead racing across the street directly in front of Simon. Startled, and a bit freaked out by the fact that someone was crazy enough to be riding a bike in this downpour, Simon slammed on his brakes.

Too hard!

He wasn't going very fast at all, but his car started to hydroplane on the slick street, heading diagonally in a path straight for the cyclist. Simon's heart hammered in his chest as he gripped the steering-wheel tightly, keeping his foot firmly planted on the brake as the antilock brake system bucked the car, praying he'd miss the slim figure on the bike.

No such luck. He grimaced as his car bumped the cyclist with a soft thud, just loud enough to hear over the pelting rain.

His tires finally gripped the road, stopping the car abruptly. He grabbed his cell phone and dialed 911 even as he jumped out, heading for the cyclist who was sprawled on the pavement not far from the bike, which lay crumpled beneath Simon's front bumper.

He could barely hear the operator asking about the nature of his emergency over the sound of the storm. "Injured cyclist, hit by my car. Send a paramedic unit. We're at the intersection of Grover and Howard. Hurry!"

Snapping his phone shut, he tucked it in his pocket as he knelt beside the crumpled heap of aluminous yellow cycling gear. His breath caught in his throat nearly strangling him when he realized it was Hailey.

Thankfully, a helmet covered her chin-length blonde hair, but her eyes were closed and her face deathly pale, despite the rain coming down.

"Hailey? Can you hear me?" He sheltered her from the rain with his body as much as he could as he felt for a pulse. Relieved when he found one, he turned his attention to the rest of her potential injuries. Her body was lying at an awkward angle halfway on her side, and he was loath to move her without a neck brace at the very least.

"Hailey? Open your eyes," he said, running his hands along the arm and leg that he could easily reach, trying to ascertain if she'd broken anything. "Hailey, please open your eyes. I need to know if you can hear me."

Her eyelids fluttered open and she groaned as she tried to turn over onto her back. She still had a backpack looped over her shoulders.

"Easy," he cautioned, halting her movement with his hands. He unhooked the backpack from the one arm and twisted it up and out of the way. "First, tell me what hurts."

"Everything," she whispered. Her blue eyes were wide and frightened as she gazed up at him. "But mostly my arm and the leg beneath me."

The naked pleading in her eyes did him in. He quickly unlatched the strap of her helmet and supported her head with his hand. "Okay, you can roll onto your back very slowly but don't twist your spine or your neck."

She let out a whimper as she log-rolled onto her back, his hands cradling her neck and head for stability. He slid off the backpack, tossing it aside.

"You're going to be okay," he told her reassuringly. "A paramedic unit will be here any minute."

"Andrew?" Hailey whispered, looking at him oddly. A chill snaked down his back. Had she managed to sustain a head injury despite the protection of her helmet? "Andrew, is that you?"

"No, I'm Simon, not Andrew." He took her hand in his and she grasped it like a lifeline, her fingers cold in the rain. Her apparent confusion scared the hell out of him. "Hailey, do you know where you are?"

For a moment she looked confused. "On the road. We had a car accident."

Somehow he didn't get the impression she was talking about this most recent accident but a different one. Suddenly her reaction the day before with the young trauma victim made sense. The sounds of sirens split the air. He was glad, very glad, to know help was on the way.

"Yes, I was in the car, but you were on your bike." He held her gaze with his, willing her to remember.

She seemed to accept that, or else she couldn't hear him clearly as the sounds of the sirens were growing louder. The rain lightened up a bit, although they were both soaked through to the skin.

The ambulance pulled up and he loosened his grip, intending to let go of Hailey's hand, but she tightened her hold on him. "No! Don't leave me," she pleaded.

He couldn't ignore the panic in her eyes. "I won't," he promised, feeling a little sick at the thought of how he'd made the same promise to Erica.

Different situation entirely, he told himself harshly. Hailey needed his support right now. Considering how he'd caused her injury, it was the least he could do.

Kylie Taylor was the first paramedic to reach them.

He was surprised she was still working at nearly six months pregnant. "Simon! What happened?"

"I skidded on the road and hit her." The reality of what had happened made his throat swell with guilt. The roads were slick, but he knew he should have had control of his vehicle. Maybe if he hadn't stomped on his brakes quite so hard...

Kylie's gaze flashed with sympathy but she turned her attention to Hailey. "Oh, my gosh, she's the nurse who took care of Ben."

"Yes." Simon hadn't told Kylie or Seth of Hailey's suspicions about child abuse. "We need to get her out of the rain."

"We will, don't worry. She needs a neck brace, but first I want to check her vitals."

A second paramedic joined them, a muscular guy by the name of Mike, and soon they'd checked Hailey's vitals, fitted her with a neck brace and then slid a long board beneath her.

Simon wanted to help lift her up and onto the stretcher, but Hailey clung to his hand as if he were the only stable thing in her universe. The way she kept murmuring *Don't leave me, don't leave me* ripped his heart. He couldn't bring himself to let her go.

"I'm riding in the ambulance with you," he told Kylie in a tone that warned her not to argue.

Kylie looked like she wanted to protest, but she'd noticed Hailey's death-like grip on his hand and gave a brief nod. "You'd better get your car and her bike out of traffic first," she told him.

He fished his keys out of his pocket, knowing Kylie was right but hating to upset Hailey by letting go, even for a few minutes.

"I'll get it," Mike said, grabbing the keys. Mike

yanked the bike out from beneath the car, tossed Hailey's backpack and helmet into the backseat and then slid behind the wheel of Simon's car. He parked the vehicle on the furthest edge of the road and put the hazard lights on. He'd arrange for a tow truck to bring them both back to the hospital as soon as he could.

The bike wasn't mangled as badly as he'd thought, and he hoped that meant that Hailey's injuries weren't as bad either.

Soon they had Hailey loaded into the back of the ambulance. Simon stayed out of Mike and Kylie's way as much as possible, while continuing to hold Hailey's hand. Her vitals were relatively stable, a little shocky but not bad. Being drenched in the cold rain hadn't helped.

Hailey didn't have any obvious signs of injury, but she easily could have several broken bones. They'd need a slew of X-rays to know for sure. She was dressed head to toe in some sort of biking gear that had protected her skin fairly well, although there were several holes in the fabric through which small, bloody abrasions could be seen.

He momentarily closed his eyes as his adrenaline rush began to fade. Dear God, the outcome of this accident could have been worse. So much worse.

Hailey would be fine. He'd make sure of it. And he planned on doing whatever was necessary to help her get through this.

Hailey stared into Simon's dark eyes, trying to keep herself focused on the present. There were lots of other healthcare professionals around her now that they'd reached the Cedar Bluff trauma room, and they kept asking her questions that she answered easily enough, but truly she could only see one man.

Her brain knew he was Simon Carter. Simon. Not Andrew.

But when she closed her eyes, she saw her fiancé's face. The open cut on his forehead starkly red against his pale skin, his eyes wide and unfocused.

Dead.

Her fault. It was all her fault.

"Hailey?" Simon's face hovered closer. She knew she was being totally irrational but she couldn't let go of his hand. If she did, she'd get lost in the nightmares of the past again. And what if she couldn't find her way back? "Are you sure your head doesn't hurt?" he asked for what seemed like the tenth time. Had she been confused? Lost consciousness? She couldn't remember.

"I'm sure," she responded. "I was wearing my helmet."

"All right, Jadon has ordered several X-rays for you. They're going to take you to Radiology now, okay?"

Radiology? Alone? "No, don't leave me. Please?" She hated the way she sounded, like a pathetically scared rabbit afraid of its own shadow, but just the thought of being alone made her shake uncontrollably. "I'm s-sorry," she whispered, her teeth chattering as the sudden coldness overwhelmed her. "B-but if you could just s-stay with me for a while longer…"

"She's cold," Simon said, a harsh edge to his voice. "Someone get her a warm blanket." Then his face appeared in her line of vision, and he was gazing down at her with a relaxed smile. "I'll stay right beside you the entire time," he vowed. "I promise I won't leave you alone, Hailey, not for a minute."

"Thank you," she whispered. The warm blanket that

Bonnie threw over her felt wonderful, but she was more grateful for Simon's unwavering acceptance of her irrational fear than anything else.

She should have felt embarrassed, knowing these people she worked with had seen her nearly naked, having cut off her biking gear before covering her with a hospital gown. But she couldn't seem to care. Simon had kept his gaze locked on hers the entire time.

It seemed they were in Radiology for ever, getting X-rays of her entire body. She couldn't suppress a twinge of guilt at how Simon had remained true to his word, staying right beside her and holding her hand, wearing a lead apron to help protect himself against being overly exposed to the various X-rays.

She needed to get a grip here and stop clinging to the poor man. With the rain in her eyes, fogging up her goggles, she hadn't even seen his car. Normally she was a defensive cyclist. But today she'd been preoccupied.

She needed to let him know the accident wasn't his fault.

As soon as she could find the strength to relinquish her hold on his hand.

"Tibia fracture?" she overheard Simon say as the radiologist came out to talk to him. "Nothing else? Are you absolutely positive?"

"Yep. She'll have plenty of bruises, I'm sure, but overall she's incredibly lucky," the radiologist allowed. "I've sent them to Jadon to see, but you can read them for yourself, if you like. Everything is clean, including her spine."

"Thank God," Simon murmured. He gave the radiologist a nod and then swung his gaze down to hers. "Hailey, I need to tell you that you have a non-displaced right tibia fracture. No other broken bones, thankfully, but we'll need to get your right leg in a cast. After that, all we need to do is watch you for a while to rule out any internal bleeding."

Considering her minor injury, she felt even worse at how she'd been acting. For heaven's sake, she was an ED nurse—a measly broken leg was nothing. "I'm sure I'll be fine. My muscles ache a bit, but I don't have any other sharp pains. Mostly bruises, like he said."

"I'll feel better once we get a CT scan of your head and abdomen," Simon said, his expression grim. "There was another trauma who was already in the CT scanner so we decided to go with regular X-rays first."

For a moment the panic at being alone hovered, but she thrust it away with steely determination. Enough already. She was not going to expose Simon to any more radiation. Somehow she'd deal with the CT scan, and whatever other tests and treatments she needed, alone.

Or she could ask Simon to find Rachel. Surely Rachel wouldn't mind coming down to sit with her for a while. Although she'd no doubt give Hailey a piece of her mind for riding her bike to work in a thunderstorm.

Her bike. Heavens, how was she going to ride her bike with a broken leg? For that matter, how was she going to work with a broken leg?

She took a deep breath and tried to keep calm. There was no point in worrying over things she couldn't change. She needed to pull herself together, starting right now.

Two transporters arrived to push her gurney back to the ED, while Simon walked alongside.

"Thank you," she said finally, prising her fingers from his hand. She forced a smile she was far from feeling. "I'll be fine. I'm sorry I got so worked up over nothing." She wondered if her face was as red as it felt.

She couldn't imagine what he thought of her. First the awkwardness last night and now this. Talk about adding insult to injury. "Honestly, I'm usually not so pathetic in a crisis."

"Don't," Simon said in a low, rough tone. She'd let go of his hand but he'd kept his fingers lightly wrapped around hers, refusing to relinquish the skin-to-skin contact. "You have nothing to apologise for, Hailey. I'm the one who needs to apologise to you."

For a moment she was confused. "For what?"

"Don't you remember?" His face wore an incredulous expression. "I'm the driver of the car that hit you. I could have killed you, Hailey."

CHAPTER FIVE

"No!" HAILEY stared up at Simon earnestly, hating the shadow of self-loathing in his eyes. She needed to make him understand. "It was my fault, not yours. I couldn't see anything in the rain. I never saw your car."

"Don't bother trying to let me off the hook," Simon said grimly, in a low tone. "It's always the driver's fault when losing control of the vehicle." He shook his head impatiently. "Why am I arguing with a concussed woman?"

She scowled. "I don't have a concussion. I was wearing my helmet."

"You were confused at the scene," he said firmly. "I'm reserving judgement until we see the results of your scans."

She didn't remember being confused at the scene, except for the flashback. Had she said something weird to Simon? She didn't have time to ask because the transporters wheeled her into the CT scan.

"Hi, there," the tech greeted her cheerfully. "We're going to move you onto this table here, okay?" The radiology assistant paused and then asked, "You're not pregnant, are you?"

"No, I'm not pregnant." She could feel her face flushing again with embarrassment. It was a legitimate question, but that didn't mean she had to like it. There was an odd expression on Simon's face when she tugged on her hand, the one he still held captive. "You can let go now. I'm fine."

The enigmatic look in his eyes was a bit confusing, but eventually something in her gaze must have reassured him because he released her hand slowly, before stepping back. She looked over at the radiology tech. "I'm ready."

"Be careful of her right leg," Simon warned as the radiology tech and the two transporters began to slide her from the gurney over to the CT table. They managed to get the task accomplished without jostling her leg too much, although she couldn't help wincing a bit as the throbbing in her right leg made itself known.

How she'd ignored the pain up until now was a miracle. Must have been the effect of holding onto Simon's hand.

She closed her eyes, pushing away the ridiculous thought as the machine whirled and the table began to slowly move her through the opening. First they took pictures of her head and then of her chest and abdomen. Overall the entire process took a good twenty minutes, and she fully expected Simon would be gone once the scan was finished.

But he surprised her by staying. Hovering at her side again, as the staff slid her back onto the gurney.

No doubt he'd stuck around out of guilt. And because she'd clung to him like a limpet. She was such a wimp.

"We need the radiologist to review the scans for the official read," Simon informed her. "But I didn't see anything major. No bleeding in your head, chest or abdomen."

She forced a smile. "Good. See? I told you I was fine."

He scowled, but didn't say anything else as the two transporters took her back to the emergency department. Based on the nature of her seemingly minor injuries, they took her into one of the rooms in the arena, rather than back to the trauma room. Simon took a few minutes to make a phone call out in the hall, before following her into the room.

"Thanks for staying, Simon," she said finally. "But you must have much better things to do than to hang around here. I'm sure you're probably working tonight." Actually, she knew he was working second shift because she'd checked the schedule before going home last evening.

But how could she tell Simon she'd been preoccupied with thoughts of working with him again, when she should have been paying attention to her surroundings on the slick roads?

Guilt threatened to choke her again. She really needed to learn to concentrate while traveling.

"I was scheduled to work but Jadon is going to stick around for a couple of hours until Seth can get here to cover my shift."

For long moments she stared at him. Was he still feeling guilty about hitting her? "I told you, I'm fine, Simon. I don't want you to rearrange your schedule just for me."

"Trust me, I'm doing this for myself as much as I'm doing it for you," he corrected in a low voice. He pushed his fingers through his hair. "It's not every day I hit a cyclist."

She suppressed another sigh. "You're going to make me feel bad if you keep up that attitude," she warned. "I highly doubt you were expecting to find anyone riding in the storm in the first place, right?"

She saw the flash of acknowledgment in his gaze before a knock at her door interrupted them. An older gentleman poked his head inside the door. "Hello. May I come in?"

"Sure." She stared at him, thinking he looked familiar, but she couldn't quite remember his name.

"I'm Dr. Maxwell," he said kindly, coming inside and dragging a plaster cart behind him. He reached over to take her hand. "I'm here to examine and cast your right leg."

Oh, yes, Dr. Maxwell was the orthopedic surgeon, she remembered now. Simon eased back, obviously willing to give her some privacy. "I'll check back with you in a little while," he assured her.

"Thanks," she murmured. There was no need for Simon to check back with her, but she suspected nothing she could say was going to convince him of that.

Guilt. Wasn't she all too familiar with the emotion?

"So I hear you had a run-in with a car?" The older doctor gently smoothed his hands over her right leg and she couldn't hide a wince. "Luckily for you, this is a clean fracture and shouldn't put you out of commission for too long."

She bit her lip anxiously, mentally calculating how much money she had in her savings account. Not nearly enough to be off work for any length of time. She needed to talk to her boss, Theresa, as soon as possible. "How long?" she asked, bracing herself for the news.

"Well, I'd like you to stay off it completely for two weeks. You'll need to follow up with me in the clinic and if the bone is healing well, we should be able to switch over to a walking cast."

Two weeks? She tried not to let her dismay show. Two weeks would seem like for ever, sitting around at home. There was no way in the world she was going to be able to ride her bike with a cast. "But I can get around on crutches, right?"

"Absolutely," he assured her. "We're going to put a cast on this leg, from your knee down to your foot." He turned toward the cart and pulled out a stocking. "How are you doing as far as pain medication?"

"I'm fine," she said, lying through her teeth. She wasn't exactly fine, but she didn't want to take anything that would make her groggy. Or loopy. She was afraid the flashbacks would return.

Besides, narcotics made her itch.

The orthopedic doctor chatted while he applied the cast, probably trying to divert her attention from the task at hand. The pain quadrupled when he lifted her leg off the bed to wrap the wet cast material around it. She gritted her teeth, feeling faint as waves of pain washed over her.

She was immensely relieved when he gently eased her leg back down on the pillow. He checked the circulation in her toes and the pulse behind her knee one last time before declaring he was finished.

"Remember, come back to see me in two weeks, sooner if you're having any problems, all right?"

"I won't forget," she promised weakly, wiping the sheen of perspiration from her upper lip. Maybe she'd have to break down and take some pain medication after all, because the throbbing had only become horrendously worse instead of better.

Dr. Maxwell left and she closed her eyes, breathing deeply in an effort to get a grip on the pain.

"Hailey!" Her eyes flew open at the sound of her

name. Rachel rushed into the room, with Simon following behind her. "My God, Hailey, what happened?"

"I ran into Simon on my bike," she said quickly pre-empting his response. "I couldn't see a thing. My goggles were totally fogged up."

"You rode to work in a thunderstorm?" Rachel said, her tone rising incredulously. "A car crash was the least of your worries. What if you'd been struck by lightning? Why on earth didn't you call me? I would have driven you to work even on my day off."

In hindsight, that would have been a smarter thing to do. But she'd already dodged Rachel's questions regarding her decision to ride her bike everywhere. She hadn't wanted to outright lie to her friend.

She'd come to Cedar Bluff to forget the past. Not be reminded of it on a daily basis. Yet here she was, reliving it anyway.

"I should have called," she acknowledged, glancing at Simon. "See? This really was my fault. Even Rachel thinks I'm stupid."

"Why were you riding your bike in the thunderstorm?" Simon asked, his intense gaze unwavering. "Did your car break down?"

She hesitated, not sure how to answer that one. But she needn't have worried.

Rachel rolled her eyes. "Car? What car? Hailey doesn't *own* a car. She rides everywhere on that bike of hers. And I mean everywhere!"

Simon couldn't believe what he was hearing. Hailey didn't own a car? Because she couldn't afford one? Had to be. He couldn't imagine anyone not wanting the ease of car transportation.

"Thanks for blabbing, Rach," Hailey muttered.

Simon lifted a brow, but let the comment go. "I'll drive you home," he announced.

Hailey's eyes widened. "That's not necessary," she started to say.

But Rachel cut her off. "Yes, it is necessary. I'm covering your shift, so I can't drive you home. And I don't care what you say, there's no way on earth you're going to be able to crutch-walk three miles to your apartment."

Simon bit back a curse at the image. What was wrong with her? Why was Hailey being so stubborn? "I'm driving you home," he said again, in a steely tone that left no room for argument.

Rachel flashed an odd glance at him, but then nodded. "Good. So that's settled." She turned back to Hailey. "I have to go take care of my patients, but call me later, okay?"

"Okay," Hailey agreed, resigned acceptance in her tone.

When Rachel left, a heavy silence hung over the room. Simon scrubbed his hand over his jaw, searching for something to say.

She shifted her weight on the cart, sucking in a quick breath when she moved her right leg. Her face was whiter than the hospital bed sheets and when he looked closely, he saw a faint sheen of sweat covering her brow.

"Have you taken anything for the pain?" he asked. She looked awful. Worse than awful.

"No." She worried her lower lip between her teeth in a habit he shouldn't have found endearing but did. "I was thinking of asking for some ibuprofen but I don't want to take it on an empty stomach."

Ibuprofen? For a broken leg? "Do you have something against narcotics?" he asked warily.

She gave a small shrug. "They make me itch."

Since itching could be an early sign of an allergic reaction, he sighed and nodded. "Okay, there is non-narcotic pain medication too, you know. I'll talk to Jadon, see what he's ordered."

"I'd really rather wait until I get home," she said, when he moved toward the door.

"Getting in and out of a car and then from the car into your apartment is going to hurt," he told her bluntly. "I suggest you have something now."

He took it as a good sign that she didn't argue. Taking control of the situation, Simon arranged for her to get a dose of the medication now and a prescription filled by the outpatient pharmacy here at the hospital. Jadon was happy to write her discharge orders after getting the official all-clear on her CT scans from the radiologist.

Simon still couldn't believe Hailey didn't own a car, but didn't ask about it as he pushed her wheelchair out to the ED surface parking lot, where the towing company had left his vehicle. The tow-truck operator had told him there wasn't a scratch on his car. That made him feel even more guilty.

Of course Hailey and her bike had sustained the brunt of the damage.

The torrential rain had tapered off to an annoying drizzle. Hailey was wearing a pair of scrubs Rachel had dug out of her locker and a borrowed windbreaker to help keep her warm.

After setting the brakes on the wheelchair, he went over to open the passenger door. Hailey didn't wait for his help, though. She pushed herself up on her good leg, balancing precariously as she reached around for her crutches.

He muttered an oath under his breath and tucked his arm around her waist. "I've got you," he murmured. "Don't worry about the crutches for now. All you need to do is to pivot around and I'll get you into the car."

Her breath was warm and moist against his neck as he held her close, supporting the bulk of her weight so she wouldn't have to do anything.

Hailey reached up to wrap her arm more firmly around his shoulder, bringing her body even closer to his. He could feel every sensual curve pressed against him, and he froze, alarm bells clamoring in the back of his mind.

Holding her close like this felt good. Sinfully good. For a moment he was tempted to breathe deeply, basking in her fresh scent.

He yanked his mind away from that train of thought. Hailey would not appreciate knowing he was thinking along these lines when she was in terrible pain from a broken leg he'd caused, no matter what she'd claimed about who had been to blame.

Grimly, he concentrated on the task at hand. Somehow he managed to swing her around so that she was close to the passenger door. He ignored his physical response to her nearness, tucking one hand behind her thigh to support her casted leg and the other around her shoulders as she lowered herself into the passenger seat.

"Thanks, I have it now," she murmured breathlessly. He could see she was breathing rapidly, as if she'd run a marathon instead of simply getting settled in the car. The way she avoided his gaze made him think she was embarrassed.

Hell, if anyone should be embarrassed, it should be

him. For thinking with the lower part of his anatomy instead of his brain. Hadn't he learned his lesson the hard way?

He tucked the crutches into the backseat. After closing the door, he walked around to the driver's side, momentarily turning his face up to the rain, welcoming the coolness.

He needed to stay in control. No matter how his body managed to betray him, he would not act on his feelings.

Not now.

Not ever.

As he slid behind the wheel and started the car, Simon did his best to think of Hailey as a patient. She'd latched her seat belt, he saw with approval, but had leaned back against the headrest, her eyes closed.

"Are you okay?" he asked, as he backed out of the parking space. He knew she had the prescription bottle of non-narcotic pain pills tucked in the pocket of her windbreaker.

"Fine," she whispered, keeping her eyes closed.

He could appreciate how exhausted she must be, but he needed to know where to go. "Hailey? What street do you live on?"

She turned her head and cracked one eye open to look at him. "The Rose Glen apartment building, off Howard."

"Got it," he said, turning right to head in that direction.

Hailey didn't move, but her hands were clasped tightly in her lap, so he knew she wasn't sleeping.

No, not sleeping. More likely, she was fighting the pain. It would take a while for the full effect of the pain medication to work.

He pulled into the parking lot behind the apartment complex, somewhat relieved to notice it was only a two-story building. He was willing to wager, however, that Hailey lived on the second floor.

"I can do it," she said testily, but in the end she needed his arm to help her get out of the car. He reached for the crutches, offering them to her once she was standing.

"Which apartment?" he asked, pulling her backpack out of the backseat, where Mike, the helpful paramedic, had left it.

"Two-eleven," she answered, confirming his suspicions she was on the second floor. She swung her crutches forward and took a slow step forward. He stood right beside her, hating how her face went pale as she made her way slowly toward the apartment door.

He was sweating more than she was, just from watching her struggle. Ten times over he had to stop himself from just scooping her into his arms and carrying her in.

"Keys in the front pocket of my backpack," she said in a strained voice as she came to a halt in front of the main apartment door.

He found the keys, opened the lock and then held the door open for her. Thank God there was an elevator, so he wouldn't have to helplessly watch her attempt to maneuver the stairs.

When they reached her apartment door, he unlocked and opened it, holding it for her. She went inside, pausing in the tiny foyer.

"Thanks for the ride. I can take it from here," she said calmly, drumming up the most pathetic excuse for a smile.

Like hell she could. He ignored her, coming inside and closing the door firmly behind them. As he looked around at the inexpensive but neat furniture in the apartment, he asked, "How much food do you have?" Walking further into the room, he looped the strap of the backpack over the edge of a chair. How she managed to go grocery shopping on a bicycle was beyond him. "I'll run out and get you whatever you need."

Hailey eased herself onto the sofa with a low groan. He crossed over, helping her to lift her leg onto a pillow, elevating it. "I'm not sure," she said tiredly. "There's probably not much in the cupboards. I was planning to go shopping tomorrow.

She was clearly losing steam, not that he could blame her. He reached into her coat pocket and took out the pain pills. "You might need to take another one," he suggested, settling beside her on the sofa. "You can take two of them every four hours, as needed, and you only took one."

"Because it was a big horse pill," she muttered. But when he opened the bottle she held out her hand and took the tablet. He went to the kitchen, filled a glass with water and brought it back to her. She downed the second pain pill without hesitation.

He figured she'd be out like a light as soon as the second pill was absorbed into her system. And while she was sleeping, he'd take inventory to find out what she needed food-wise so he could shop for her.

But before that there was one question that had been burning in the back of his mind ever since the moment he'd tended to her at the side of the road. Maybe it wasn't completely fair to ask her now, when she was so clearly not herself, but he needed to know.

"Hailey?" When he sat beside her on the sofa, she opened her eyes and gazed up at him. Before he could talk himself out of it, he asked, "Who's Andrew?"

CHAPTER SIX

In a heartbeat Hailey's exhaustion vanished. Every muscle in her body went tense, as she stared at Simon in stunned surprise.

How on earth had he known about Andrew?

Her flashback, she realized slowly. She must have said something to him during the moments at the side of the road when she'd been gripped in the horror of the past. She'd seen Andrew's face so clearly.

His pale, lifeless face. Streaked with blood.

Quickly she blocked the memory. No, don't go there. She needed to stay focused on the present.

But how to respond? Unfortunately, she couldn't bring herself to lie to Simon. Not after everything he'd done for her. Without his steadying presence, at the scene of the accident and in the emergency department, she knew the nightmares would have sucked her down into the whirling vortex of blackness that had characterized the last fourteen months.

She swallowed hard and tried to keep her voice from betraying her by trembling. "My fiancé."

Simon's eyes widened and she noticed he glanced at her ringless finger. "Why didn't you say something sooner?" he asked in a rush. "I didn't know you were engaged. We need to call Andrew to let him know you're all right."

She fought the urge to close her eyes and bury her face in the pillow, avoiding the painful subject. But she'd learned the hard way that hiding your head in the sand didn't make things go away. Simon wouldn't let her off the hook that easily. "No. I meant he was my fiancé. Andrew—he died a little over a year ago."

Fourteen months, to be exact. And she'd spent three of them recovering from the injuries she'd sustained in the accident in which he'd died.

But nothing would ever heal her heart. Or ease her conscience.

The usual sympathy darkened his eyes. "I'm sorry," he said simply.

Her stomach tightened painfully. She wanted to shout at him not to apologize. Why did everyone keep saying that? She was the reason Andrew was dead. She'd insisted on driving that night.

She didn't want Simon's sympathy.

Or anyone else's.

"I feel sick," she murmured, changing the subject as she put a hand over her abdomen. She wasn't lying, she really did feel sick. Throwing up would only make a bad day even worse, so she fought the urge and drew an uneven breath. "Would you mind bringing me a few saltine crackers?"

Instantly, he rose to his feet. "Of course not. Stay put, I'll find them."

"Third cabinet on the right," she murmured as Simon headed for the small kitchen. She took several shaky breaths. He rummaged around for a few minutes, and then returned with water and the promised crackers.

"You don't have any white soda," he said. "But don't worry, I'll run to the store and pick up a few things."

"There's no need," she began, but he cut her off.

"Don't argue. I'm going. It's not like you can live on jail fare," he said, gesturing to her water and crackers, "for the next few weeks."

"Rach can pick up some things for me," she pointed out stubbornly.

He didn't even look at her or acknowledge her statement. He simply stuck her door keys in his pocket and walked back to the kitchen. From her position on the sofa, she could hear him opening and closing the cupboard doors and her fridge, muttering to himself. Good thing she couldn't hear what he was saying, because it was no doubt something scathing, considering the bare state of her cabinets.

Old Mother Hubbard, went to the cupboard...

She wasn't destitute, but she did tend to buy sparingly because she had to lug everything on her bike. Or walk, which was actually much harder. At least on the bike she could cover the distance more quickly.

But she wasn't about to explain that to Simon.

After a good five minutes he returned, holding a list in his hand. A long list. "I'll be back in a little while. Take a nap," he suggested. "The best thing you can do right now is to rest."

Before she could think of a response, he left her apartment, softly shutting the door behind him.

She scowled at the closed door.

Sure. Take a nap. She grimaced as she tried to move into a more comfortable position. Except she couldn't find a more comfortable position.

Wearily she closed her eyes and did her best to ignore the throbbing pain in her leg. Why hadn't she called

Rachel for a ride to work that morning? What idiot rode a bike to work in a thunderstorm? Her ridiculous need to remain independent had cost her dearly.

Now she'd be dependent on others for help over the next who-knew-how-long. Two weeks for sure. Hopefully not longer. And as a new employee she didn't have any sick time to cover the time she'd need off work.

Maybe once she had a walking cast on, she could manage to ride her bike. At least well enough to get to work and home. If the hospital would let her work with her walking cast on.

With a sigh she decided not to worry about that now. First she needed to get through the next two weeks.

Surprisingly, she must have dozed because she awoke to a more intense throbbing in her leg. And the mouth-watering scent of chicken noodle soup.

Dusk had fallen. Her living room faced west, so it was easy to see through the window that the sun had set. She estimated the time must be somewhere close to seven o'clock.

She stretched, working the kinks out of her neck. Had Simon left some soup for her? She propped herself up on her elbow and leaned over to reach for her crutches standing upright against the edge of the end table nearby.

"Hailey, you're awake?" he asked, coming into the living room and startling her so badly she jerked like an epileptic and knocked the crutches to the floor with a crash.

"Cripes, don't do that!" she admonished, clutching a hand to her hammering heart. "You scared me to death."

"Sorry," Simon said with a grimace. "I didn't mean

to startle you. I didn't think you were sleeping very soundly because you kept muttering in your sleep."

"I did?" She could feel her face flush. Talk about embarrassing. Although it could be worse. He could have told her she snored.

"Are you ready for more pain medication?" he asked. "It might be helpful to eat some soup first, so that your stomach doesn't get upset."

She wasn't sure which need took higher priority—her mouth watering and stomach growling for the soup or the throbbing in her leg.

"Soup," she finally decided, leaning over to pick up the fallen crutches from the floor. She narrowed her gaze when he swooped down to snatch the crutches before she could grab them. She sighed. "Look, Simon, I appreciate your help, but you don't need to stick around any longer. I'll be fine."

He stood holding the crutches, and lifted a sardonic brow. "Don't worry, I haven't exactly moved in yet," he said dryly, making her flush all over again. "Relax, all I did was pick up a few groceries and heat up some soup. Why don't you let me bring it in on a tray, so you don't have to get up?"

"Because soup would be easier to eat at the kitchen table. I'd prefer not to wear it." Somehow, she knew that once she got up and moving, she'd prove to Simon once and for all she was fine. And then he would leave.

At least, in theory.

Because surely that crack about moving in was a joke.

Wasn't it?

Yes, it was. She was losing her mind to think anything else. She gritted her teeth and swallowed a groan as she swung her leg over the edge of the sofa. Simon set the crutches aside and bent over to put his hands around her waist. Before she could squeak out a protest, he lifted her up on her good foot, supporting most of her weight.

She gripped his upper arms, momentarily distracted by the bulging muscles beneath her fingertips. His musky scent filled her head, making her dizzy.

Good heavens, she could stay here with him like this for the rest of the night without needing a single dose of pain medication.

"Let me know when you're ready," he murmured, his mouth dangerously close to her ear.

Ready? For what? To fall into his arms? To be swept down the hall to her bedroom?

"I'm—uh—ready," she said breathlessly, forcing herself to concentrate. She needed to move away. And fast. "You can—uh—hand me the crutches now."

For what seemed like endless moments neither one of them moved. She held her breath, waiting for what she had no idea, but every nerve in her body was tingling in awareness. The throbbing pain in her leg was nothing compared to the blood rushing through her system.

But then Simon moved one of the hands at her waist to bring over the crutches. He tucked one beneath her arm, and she reluctantly let go of his biceps to grasp the crutch. Then he handed her the second crutch.

When he was sure she was steady on her feet, he backed away. She kept her gaze on trained on the floor as she cautiously swung the crutches forward, moving slowly toward the kitchen.

There was an empty bowl on the table sitting beside the small bottle of pain medication and a fresh package of crackers. As she lowered herself into the chair, Simon filled her bowl from the steaming pot on the stove and set it back down in front of her.

"Do you need anything else?" he asked, when she took a sip of the soup.

She nearly scalded her tongue. "No, Simon, this is perfect. Just what I needed. Thanks. For driving me home, shopping and cooking for me."

A ghost of a smile flirted with his lips. "You're welcome."

As much as she wanted him to leave, for her peace of mind more than anything, she gestured to the empty seat at the table beside her. "Please, join me. I'm sure you're hungry, too."

He moved as if to do just that, but then stopped abruptly. "Ah, no, thanks. I should probably get going. Are you sure you'll be okay here alone? I could wait until you've finished eating if you think you need help getting settled for the night."

This time she did scald her tongue and she took a sip of white soda to cool the burning. The thought of Simon anywhere near her bedroom made her break out into a cold sweat.

Not because she didn't want him there.

Just the opposite.

"I'm sure I'll be fine," she said firmly, tearing her thoughts from that traitorous path. She was not going to wonder what it would be like to kiss Simon.

Not. Going. There.

"I'm not helpless, you know," she said tartly. "I'm not the first person with a broken leg and I won't be the last."

She caught a glimpse of his grim expression before it vanished. "Okay, then. Here's my cell phone number." He slid a slip of paper across the table toward her with his number scrawled on it in his bold script. "I want you to promise me you'll call if you need anything."

"All right," she agreed, knowing she wouldn't. If she'd call anyone it would be Rachel. Not Simon.

No matter how tempting.

"Thanks again, Simon." She took another sip of her soup, hoping he'd take the hint.

He did. "Goodnight, Hailey." He stared at her for several long seconds before turning on his heel and walking toward the door.

She held her breath until he shut the apartment door quietly behind him.

Letting out a ragged sigh, she dropped her spoon and buried her face in her hands.

And fought the overwhelming urge to call him back.

Simon left Hailey's apartment, calling himself every kind of fool.

Hailey would be fine. He was being a total idiot for overreacting like this. She would be absolutely fine.

A broken leg wasn't the end of the world. Logically, he knew that.

But he couldn't help feeling responsible. It was his fault she was laid up for the next two weeks at least.

He didn't need to keep checking on her. Unless she called. Which he knew she wouldn't.

Hailey was perfectly able to take care of herself.

Shoving his hands in his pockets, he ducked his head against the drizzle and walked out to his car. As he headed home, the thought of sitting around in his empty house made him restless. Normally he yearned for some quiet time. He'd just bought a new book but tonight the idea of losing himself in a great story did not hold any appeal. In fact, he didn't want to go home.

He'd wanted to stay with Hailey.

Not an option, he reminded himself harshly. Then what? Call Jadon? Or Quinn? Nah, both men had families of their own.

Executing a safe and legal U-turn, he turned the car around to head back toward Cedar Bluff hospital.

"What are you doing here?" Seth asked, seemingly exasperated when he strolled in. "Hell, Simon, I'm here covering you so you can have the night off."

"I know, but things have changed." Simon forced a smile. "I'm here to finish my shift, so you can go back home to your pretty pregnant wife and son."

"I don't think so," Seth argued lightly. "For one thing, you don't look as if you've really recovered from hitting Hailey. Not that I blame you, that had to be horrible. But honestly? I could really use the money as I missed that shift the other day. Kylie really wants to move into a newer and bigger house before the baby is born. We're scraping up some money for a decent down payment."

Damn. The one argument he couldn't fight. He'd never take a needed shift away from a colleague, much less a friend.

Seth could finish off the shift if he wanted to.

But Simon still didn't want to go home to his empty house. He glanced around, almost desperate for something to keep his mind occupied. With a frown, he noticed the census board wasn't overly filled with patients. "I could still help out—if things are crazy. Free of charge," he added hoping he didn't sound as pathetic as he felt.

"Nope," Seth said cheerfully. "No worries, we have everything under control. Seriously, man, it's just not that busy."

It figured. Monday nights were generally one of the quietest days of the week.

"How's Hailey?" Seth asked with a keen glance.

Simon wasn't fooled by his friend's deceptively casual tone. The last thing he or Hailey needed was for rumors to start flying. And considering how he'd held her hand during her examination in the trauma bay, he figured the rumors were already brewing. "Fine, considering I slammed into her with my car and nearly killed her."

Seth arched a brow. "I don't think a broken leg qualifies as nearly killing her. But, hey, glad to hear she's doing all right."

"Yeah, well, she made it pretty clear she wanted me gone, so I don't think she shares your view of the accident," Simon countered.

But Seth only grinned. "And that's bugging the hell out of you, isn't it?"

Simon was about to tell him to shut the hell up when he saw, out of the corner of his eye, that the new unit clerk, Mary something or other, was blatantly eavesdropping on their conversation. Her eyes, dramatically green from colored contacts, shifted under his gaze and she turned away.

He grimaced. Great. More fuel for the gossip mill. He loved living in Cedar Bluff, but compared to the blissful anonymity he'd experienced in Chicago, living in this place was like living in a bubble where everyone stuck their noses into everyone else's business.

Which normally wasn't a problem for him. People in Cedar Bluff usually left him alone, because obviously he'd never given them anything to talk about.

Until now.

"Hardly," he said, narrowing his gaze on Seth, silently warning him to drop it. "And if you don't need my help, fine. I have some paperwork to finish in my office, anyway. There are several quality cases that need to be reviewed."

"You're hopeless, my friend. Truly hopeless," Seth muttered, shaking his head in mock dismay. "What a lame way to spend your night off."

Simon ignored him. Seth couldn't know that tossing and turning in his bed, thinking of Hailey, would be far worse than any torture imaginable. "If you get slammed with patients, let me know."

"Sure," Seth said, glancing down as his trauma pager began to vibrate. "No worries."

Simon did his best to concentrate on the cases he needed to review, but after reading the same case three times without comprehension he shoved it away with a disgusted sigh.

Seth was right. He was truly hopeless.

He shut off his computer and stood. When he dug in his pocket for his car keys, he realized he still had Hailey's apartment keys.

For a long agonizing moment he wondered if he'd subconsciously kept them on purpose.

Because now he had a good excuse to see Hailey again.

CHAPTER SEVEN

THE next morning Hailey crutch-walked the short distance from her bed to the bathroom, groaning under her breath with each clunky step.

Every muscle in her body was sore. Muscles she hadn't known she possessed hurt. But the good news was that her leg didn't throb as badly as it had yesterday.

From here on, she'd probably start feeling better each day.

It took her much longer than normal to get showered and dressed, especially as her cast had to be wrapped with plastic for the shower, and then afterward the bulky covering didn't fit into the pants leg of her jeans. She had to rip out the side seam out of an old pair of sweats, topped with an equally ragged T-shirt, so she wouldn't have to walk around in her underwear.

She ate a bowl of cereal for breakfast and then cradled a mug of coffee in her hands, the day looming endlessly before her. Often she'd wished for a few days off to get caught up on errands and such, but not like this. Not wearing a cast that prevented her from doing anything.

The scrap of paper with Simon's number was still sitting on the kitchen table, mocking her. Last night she'd actually tossed the note into the garbage, but had then changed her mind and dug it back out again, smoothing out the crumpled edges.

Stupid, because she didn't plan on calling him.

But it had been sweet of him to leave it for her. In fact, Simon had been wonderful, in many ways.

She gave herself a mental shake. There was no point reading anything but basic kindness in his motives for helping her. She knew that even though she'd taken the blame for what had happened, he still felt responsible.

Simon was honorable that way. And maybe a bit stubborn.

Just because she found him devastatingly attractive, it didn't mean he felt even remotely the same way about her.

And even if he did, they were colleagues. Maybe even friends. Nothing more.

Anxious for something to do, she headed for her bedroom and the looming pile of laundry waiting for her there. Of course, if she'd known she was going to break her leg, she would have made sure her laundry was caught up.

Where was that crystal ball when you needed it?

She had to leave her mug of coffee on the kitchen table as she couldn't crutch-walk and carry it at the same time. Neither could she carry her laundry basket.

Muttering a naughty word under her breath, she used her crutches to shove the laundry basket piled high with dirty clothes across the carpeting and down the hall, until she reached the kitchen.

Doing the laundry would take her twice as long on crutches, but it wasn't like she had other burning plans anyway. Watching television was sure to get boring. Maybe Rachel would stop at the local video store to pick her up some movies to watch.

While seated on the kitchen chair, she split her laundry into two loads, and then went back to the hallway closet to get the bottle of laundry soap, dangling it from her two fingers while manipulating the crutches. Thank heavens her apartment was small.

Crutches were really a pain in the butt.

Once she had the clothes divided and a load in the laundry basket, she looked around for her keys.

Of course, she couldn't find them.

After ten minutes of looking, she gave up. The last time she'd seen them had been when Simon had taken them to go grocery shopping.

Had he inadvertently taken them with him last night?

Possibly. Maybe she should call him. Her heart leaped at the idea. But she just as quickly shut it down.

Pathetic. She was truly pathetic.

The building manager had a spare key. She could just as easily get it from him. She had, in fact, done that very thing the last time she'd accidentally locked her keys inside the apartment while doing laundry.

There was no need to bother Simon.

But she needed to prop the door open somehow, so she jammed a pair of dirty scrubs beneath the apartment door to keep it from closing. From there, she pushed the laundry basket full of clothes down the hall in front of her until she reached the elevator.

Once she had the load into the washer, she was able to grab the empty laundry basket with the edge of her fingers and carry it back up to her apartment. She made better time, although the empty basket was bulky and kept bouncing against the wall along the way.

When she reached her apartment, though, the tip of her crutch got tangled up in the scrubs she'd jammed beneath the door. For a moment she teetered precariously as she tried to regain her balance while untangling the tip of the crutch, but then she toppled over. And hit the floor.

Hard.

More bruises, she thought with a weary wince as she tried to catch her breath.

"Hailey? My God, are you all right?"

Sprawled inelegantly on the floor just inside her apartment, with the empty laundry basket on lying on top of her, she glanced up to find Simon standing in the doorway. He looked incredible in a long-sleeved denim shirt and well-worn blue jeans. She shoved her hair out of her eyes.

Seriously, the man had the absolute worst timing.

Simon scowled as he tossed the empty laundry basket aside and looked Hailey over, assessing the damage. He saw the scrubs stuffed under the door and figured they'd gotten tangled in her crutches, causing the fall. His fault for taking the stupid keys in the first place. He should have dropped them off late last night before she'd gone to sleep. "Are you sure you didn't hurt yourself?"

"Only my pride," she muttered, pushing herself upright.

"Here, grab my hands and then bend your good leg," he instructed. "I'll help lift you up."

"I swear I'm not usually this clumsy," she said, as he hauled her upright with a smooth motion. Once she was standing on her good foot, he put his arm around her waist to steady her.

"I know," he said reassuringly.

"You seem to have a knack for seeing me at my

worst," she grumbled, as he helped her over to the kitchen chair.

"Hailey, you look fine. I'm glad I was here to help."

Once he had her safely seated, he pulled the scrubs out from beneath the door and then closed it. He picked up the rest of the clothes scattered across the floor, tossing the items into the empty basket.

"Please, just leave them. I'll pick them up," she protested.

He ignored her, finishing the task while taking care not to examine the frilly, lacy items too closely. He pushed the basket out of the way and glanced at her. "I guess you realize I accidentally took your keys," he murmured, pulling out a chair to sit next to her. He was somewhat surprised to see his phone number still sitting on the kitchen table. "Why didn't you call me? I would have brought back your keys and hauled your stuff down to the laundry room, too."

She avoided his direct gaze. "I needed the door to stay open anyway, because it's too hard to maneuver it along with the crutches. And the keys were no big deal. I would have borrowed a spare set from the manager."

"I see." He stared at her, trying to figure out why she seemed to be going out of her way to avoid him. He blew out a heavy breath. "Hailey, I'm sorry about hitting you and causing all this. I feel awful. I wish there was something I could do to make it up to you."

"Simon, you have to stop acting like I'm badly injured," she said, clearly exasperated. "You've already helped me a lot. More than anyone else would have done. You wouldn't even let me pay you for the groceries."

No, he wouldn't. And now that he was here, he didn't plan on leaving anytime soon. She was obviously too stubborn for her own good. She was lucky she hadn't hurt herself worse with that earlier stunt.

Why on earth she'd had the burning need to do laundry first thing this morning was beyond him. No lounging around and resting for Hailey. He reached over to lightly grasp her hand. "I'm not working today, so my entire day is free. Just tell me what you need. I'm all yours."

Her head jerked up, her surprised gaze colliding with his. A sizzling awareness shimmered in the air between them. For long seconds neither one of them said anything. Belatedly, he realized how his last words might have sounded.

I'm all yours.

For the first time since Erica, he wished they were true. After the constant emotional drama, and the subsequent loss, he'd been more than content to live his life alone, without the entanglement of a relationship.

Yet looking down into Hailey's bright blue eyes, he understood what he'd been missing. Until now, he hadn't realized the restlessness he thought he'd been feeling might actually be pure loneliness.

When the silence stretched to the point where it became downright uncomfortable, he let go of her hand and cleared his throat. "So what are your plans for the day? Aside from laundry," he added, glancing at the basket. "I'd be happy to finish up the loads for you, but that won't take long."

"No plans, really," she said with a careless shrug. "What can I do? I don't have a lot of money, especially now that I can't work for the next two weeks. I was actually thinking of calling Theresa to see if there was any way I could do something to get a few hours in. But other than that, I'm pretty much stuck here. There isn't a whole lot of things to do within walking distance."

He made a mental note to approach Theresa himself to plead Hailey's case. Surely there were some chart audits for their upcoming joint commission survey she could do. And he could actually use her help with the quality-of-care cases that he'd only just begun to review.

"Okay, then, let me ask you this," he said. "What would you do today if you could get out of here for a while?"

"Go to the park," she answered, seemingly without thinking. "Maybe stop at the library or the video store to rent a few movies. But you certainly don't have to be my babysitter, Simon. I plan to give Rachel a call later. I'm not totally helpless, you know."

He stared at her for a moment. He didn't want her to call Rachel. Or anyone else for that matter. "Hailey, I never once thought you were helpless. Quite the opposite."

Her smile seemed a bit sad. "Well, thanks for stopping by to return the keys. I'm sure you have better things to do with your day off."

He understood that she'd continue to shove him away unless he made her understand how he really felt. Opening himself up wasn't easy. But neither was walking away. "What if I told you I didn't want to spend the day alone?" he asked softly. "What if I told you I'd much rather spend time with you?"

There was another pause, and he almost wished he'd kept his big mouth shut.

But she smiled. "I'd say I'm glad to hear that, because I'd like to spend the day with you, too."

He grinned, a feeling of relief sweeping over him

rather than the usual sense of dread that normally curled in his gut whenever he'd considered seeing a woman on a personal level.

Hailey was different. Or rather his feelings toward her were different. And right now he couldn't find the energy to care if he was walking along the edge of a slippery slope as long as Hailey was beside him.

Hailey watched Simon haul her laundry bag of dirty clothes out of the apartment, wondering if she had rocks for brains.

Why had she agreed to let him help? Especially with something as personal as her laundry? Just the thought of him looking at her intimate wear made her blush.

But even worse, why had she agreed to spend the entire day with him?

She wanted to think he'd simply caught her in a weak moment but, in truth, she'd agreed because she wanted to spend the day with him.

Treading into dangerous territory? Maybe. But she shoved her misgivings aside. For too long her response to men had been non-existent, and now that her emotions had thawed, she found she liked having them. And the thought of being cooped up inside the tiny apartment wasn't at all appealing, so why not take advantage of Simon's generosity?

He didn't have to know how much she admired him. She'd treat him like a friend. Surely everyone could use a few friends?

Thankfully, Simon didn't insist on doing everything. He brought the clean clothes up from the basement laundry room and gave her the opportunity to fold the items and put them away.

He was on the phone when she emerged from the

bedroom. He quickly finished his call and snapped the cell phone shut when he saw her.

"I'm sorry, but I don't have much to wear other than this," she said, gesturing to the slit-up-the-side-seam sweat pants.

"That's okay," he said, waving away her concern. "We're only going to the park, to the library and to the video store."

She rolled her eyes. "I don't think we have to cover everything I mentioned."

He simply cocked a brow. "Well, as the sun is shining and it's a balmy sixty degrees outside, why don't we go to the park first? If you're up to it we can make another stop or two at the library or the video store on the way home."

"Sounds good." She went over to her purse to pull out her sunglasses. She followed Simon down the hall, going through the doors he held open for her.

"I can't believe how nice it is outside after the storm yesterday," she said, squinting in the glare of the sun.

"I know. Good thing the storm didn't do any major damage." Simon held the passenger door open for her.

She hesitated just for a moment. Riding in a car as a passenger wasn't her favorite pastime, but she'd managed to get over her fear to a certain extent. And she didn't have much of a choice now that she'd broken her leg. This would be the beginning of many car rides.

She could do this. No problem.

Taking a deep breath, she slid into the passenger seat, extremely conscious of Simon's hand under her elbow. His touch, even as light and impersonal as it was, helped distract her from being in the car.

She could get used to having his hands on her.

Giving a mental eye roll, she stared forward through

the windshield, determined not to let her idiotic fantasies ruin the day.

When they arrived at Cedar Bluff park, there were two paths, one that climbed up to the top of the bluff and one that lead down to the lakefront. If not for the crutches she would have preferred to go up, but when Simon started out along the path leading down to the lake, she fell into step beside him.

The sun was warm on her skin, and the light breeze coming off the lake felt refreshingly wonderful. She loved the rhythmic sounds of the waves crashing over the rocky shore.

"I'm so glad we came," she said, pausing for a moment to tuck her hair behind her ears to keep it out of her eyes. "I didn't realize how much I needed to get out of that stuffy apartment."

"I'm glad we came too," Simon murmured. He walked slowly alongside her, keeping pace with her awkward gait, his hand resting lightly on the small of her back.

She imagined that anyone watching them would think they were a couple. The thought caused a tingle of awareness. She glanced around, thinking it was a good thing the lakefront was deserted on a Tuesday in the middle of the day.

"Hailey, do you mind if I ask you a question?"

She glanced at him in surprise. "Of course not."

"The day we took care of that young seventeen-year-old motor vehicle crash victim, you seemed to take his death pretty hard. Was that because he reminded you of your fiancé, Andrew?"

They'd reached the lakeshore so she stopped, staring out at the rippling water for a moment. "Yes."

"Because he died in a car crash too?" Simon asked persistently.

"Yes." She turned toward Simon, suddenly tempted to tell him the truth. All of the truth.

Even the parts she'd never told anyone.

But the words stuck in her throat.

"Is that why you don't drive a car?" he asked. "I mean, I had this brilliant idea to offer to share my car with you, but even if I did, you wouldn't drive it, would you?"

Obviously, he had all the answers, so why bother with the questions? She blew out a breath, amazed that he'd nailed the truth. She'd already told him about Andrew so it wasn't much of a stretch to put two and two together and come up with four. "No, I wouldn't," she finally admitted. "But thanks for the kind offer."

"Why not? You seemed fine riding as a passenger. Why not drive a car?"

"I can't," she said helplessly, avoiding his gaze. "I don't enjoy riding in a car as a passenger, either. But the reason I go everywhere on my bike is because I haven't driven a car since the accident. Because I was driving that night. The crash—Andrew's death—was my fault."

"Hailey," he murmured, and suddenly he took one of her crutches out of the way so he could pull her into his arms. His musky scent intermingled with the fresh air coming off the lake. "No, don't say that. Sometimes things happen. Like you and me colliding in the rain. Didn't you tell me that hitting you wasn't my fault? It's the same thing."

No, it wasn't. He didn't know the whole story. How she'd insisted on driving that night because Andrew had had a few drinks. They'd argued, heatedly. And in the end her decision had cost him his life. If she'd let him drive, she would have been in the passenger seat.

She didn't want to relive the painful memories. She could feel Simon's intent gaze. It was tempting, so tempting to hide her face in the hollow of his shoulder. To simply give herself over to his warm embrace.

Gathering her courage, she forced herself to meet his compassionate chocolate-brown gaze.

But before she could say anything to make him understand, she was distracted by his mouth, dangerously close to hers. And whatever thought she was about to voice flew right out of her head.

She must have been a little too obvious because he murmured her name again, almost like a plea, before his mouth came down to capture hers.

CHAPTER EIGHT

THE urgency of Hailey's response, the way her lips parted invitingly, made it impossible for Simon to pull away. Instead, he broke every one of his rules by deepening the kiss.

He wanted her. More than he could ever remember wanting anyone else. Her taste was like a drug and he was willing to suffer any consequences in order to have more. In some distant part of his mind he remembered to be careful of her broken leg, although he crushed her close, enjoying the way her soft curves pressed against him.

She fitted in his arms perfectly.

Reluctantly, he broke off the kiss when he heard a dog walker approaching. They were standing right in the middle of the narrow path so they needed to get out of the way. He steadied Hailey with one hand and bent over to pick up her discarded crutches from the ground.

Hailey gripped his arm like it was a lifeline, balancing her weight on her good leg. The dazed expression in her eyes only made him want to kiss her again.

How would she look if they made love?

His pulse skyrocketed at the mere thought. He pulled himself together with an effort, ignoring his body's physical response. Even this kiss shouldn't have happened.

He couldn't take things between them any further. Giving in to his libido had cost him more than he could bear with Erica.

"Sorry about that," Simon murmured, tucking each of her crutches beneath her arms.

She grasped the handles of the crutches and moved out of the walker's way. She looked up at him, her expression uncertain. "I'm not sure I understand what you're apologising for," she said.

He swallowed a curse. This wasn't Hailey's fault. It was his. He didn't know what in the hell he'd been thinking to kiss her like that. And no matter how much he wanted to avoid the topic, Hailey deserved the truth. "I—uh—shouldn't have kissed you."

Her gaze dropped to the ground. "I see." Without saying anything more, she pivoted and continued walking down the path toward the lakefront.

Dammit. Now he'd made her feel bad. He quickened his pace to catch up to her. "Hailey, I'm sorry."

"Yeah. You already said that." Her clipped tone and hurried pace were the only outward signs of her anger.

"Let me explain, please?" She was crutch-walking at a fast pace and he had to lengthen his stride to keep up with her. "It's not that I didn't want to kiss you—" he began.

"Don't." Her sharp tone interrupted him. "Don't bother giving me the *it's not you, it's me* speech, okay? I get it. I already heard from Rachel how you have a rule about not dating women you work with."

He couldn't completely hide his surprise. "She told you?"

She flashed him a disgusted look. "Yes, she told me. And, really, it's no big deal. We'll just forget that this—uh—interlude ever happened." She grimaced and kept her gaze purposely away from his.

Forget about their kiss? Not bloody likely.

Although maybe she wasn't as affected by what had happened as he was. The thought was sobering.

He sighed, and found himself wanting to explain. He'd never told anyone about Erica. He'd been too embarrassed to admit how far over the top she'd gone.

And the role he'd played in the fallout. The memory still tortured him.

No, he couldn't tell her everything. Not his deepest, darkest secret. But he had to tell her something.

"It's not a bad rule," he muttered defensively. "If you date people you work with and then something doesn't work out, it's a mess. Everyone ends up affected, not just the people who were in the relationship."

She stopped so abruptly he almost knocked into her. She swung around to pierce him with her direct gaze. "Is that what happened to you?"

The fiasco with Erica was so much more than that, but it was easier just to nod. "Yeah. And it was bad. So I made up my mind not to repeat that mistake ever again."

She continued to stare at him for several long seconds. "You're right," she agreed softly. "It's not a bad rule."

His mouth dropped open in surprise, and disappointment stabbed deep. For a ridiculous moment he wanted her to argue with him, to reassure him that things between them could work out. That even if their relationship didn't last, they'd always be professional enough to work together without dragging their personal lives into the mix.

What a load of rubbish. He really had it bad to even attempt to rationalize this.

Hailey resumed walking and he followed more slowly, scrubbing his hand over his face, knowing he should be glad she wasn't making this difficult for him.

Yet irrationally annoyed that she could drop what had just transpired between them so easily.

When they reached the lakefront, Hailey stopped and gazed silently out at the rhythmically rolling waves. For several long moments neither of them said anything.

"Thanks for bringing me out here, Simon," she finally said. When she turned to face him, her earlier irritation seemed to have vanished. "I…really hope we can remain friends."

Friends? Was she kidding? The urge to sweep her into his arms again, to kiss her senseless, was overwhelming. Every cell in his body protested the idea of simply being friends.

But he forced himself to nod. "Of course, Hailey. I value you as a friend."

Relief flooded her gaze. "I'm glad. Now that we have that settled, do you mind if I sit on one of these rocks to rest a minute? I'm exhausted."

Without waiting for a response, she made her way over to a large, flat rock.

And despite knowing she was right, he couldn't ignore the devastating sense that he'd just lost something precious.

Hailey kept up the pretense of being Simon's friend throughout the events of the day—the trip to the library, where she discovered they had identical taste in fiction, to the video store, where she discovered they had completely opposite tastes in movies, and throughout the impromptu dinner at a small Italian restaurant that seemed a little too cozy and romantic to be just a dinner for two friends.

Not until Simon had dropped her off at home did she collapse onto the sofa and close her eyes in despair.

There was no way in the world she could do this again. Pretending to be just friends with Simon was too difficult.

And painful.

Despite her exhaustion, images of their day together continued to flash in her mind, like a slide show. Simon intensely discussing the latest novel he was reading. His grimace when she'd picked out a couple of romantic comedies from the video store. The blatant desire in his eyes after he'd kissed her.

She did her best to block them out, especially that last image, but when she opened her eyes and stared up at the ceiling she felt like crying.

Maybe she didn't deserve happiness. After Andrew's death she'd truly believed she'd suffer for ever. She had punished herself for what she believed had been her fault.

But then she had learned that life really did move on. And the bouts of self-pity came less and less frequently. She'd even found herself laughing on occasion.

For a few minutes there on the path, when Simon had kissed her, she'd begun to believe she might be ready for another relationship.

Only to have that hope brutally squashed.

Okay, enough self-pity, she told herself sternly. One kiss did not a relationship make.

The fact that she'd responded to Simon at all was good news. If she was attracted to Simon, surely she could be attracted to someone else?

Of course she could.

The role she'd played in Andrew's death had changed her. But maybe she'd been changed for the better?

Taking a deep breath, she pulled herself upright, groaning under her breath as her aching muscles protested painfully.

No matter how sore she was from being out all day, she refused to regret one moment. At least in Simon's arms she'd felt truly alive.

The next two days were excruciatingly long and boring for Hailey. Despite the books she'd picked up at the library and the movies she'd watched with Rachel, the two days seemed like a lifetime.

How she'd get through two full weeks, she wasn't sure.

On the third day her cell phone rang and her heart irrationally leaped in her chest as she grabbed the phone, peering at the screen.

Her hope deflated. Not Simon.

Her boss. She forced a cheerfulness she didn't feel into her tone. "Hi, Theresa. Did you get my leave-of-absence paperwork?"

"Ah, yes, I did." Theresa cleared her throat on the other end of the line. "But, Hailey, I'm afraid I have some bad news. I don't think your leave of absence will be approved because you've only been working here two months. Normally, you have to be working for a full twelve months in order to get approved for a leave of absence."

She sank into her kitchen chair, her crutches dropping to the floor with a crash. It took a few minutes to find her voice. "What does that mean?"

"I don't know for sure," Theresa admitted. "I'm

waiting to hear back from Human Resources. The good news is that your health insurance will cover the costs of your treatment for the accident. But normally we have a return-to-work program for staff on medical leave so they can do light-duty functions, and I'm afraid you won't qualify."

"Does that mean I have to leave?" Ironically, the first thought that entered her mind was that if she was forced to quit her job, she wouldn't be Simon's coworker any more. His rule wouldn't apply.

But on the heels of that, practical logic kicked in. When the full realization hit, her stomach sank.

"No, you don't have to quit. But you won't get any payment for being off work either."

No payments. And no way to return to work for the full time her leg was in a cast? "Theresa, please, isn't there some way I can qualify for returning to work on light duty? I need to be able to pay my rent. I'd be willing to do anything—paperwork, or even a triage nurse..."

"No, not as a triage nurse," Theresa said firmly. "Hailey, you can't be on crutches and take care of patients. If a patient's condition suddenly deteriorated, you'd need to be able to respond immediately. And if you hurt yourself in the process, we'd be responsible from a worker's compensation perspective."

She couldn't argue against her boss's logic. "Okay, paperwork, then. I can't be hurt doing paperwork. I could do chart reviews. The schedule. I'll be your assistant. I'll function as a unit clerk. Anything you want me to do." She halted, realizing she was close to begging.

"I'll see what I can work out with Human Resources," Theresa hedged. "We have work you can do, but the problem is that you don't qualify for the program because you haven't been here long enough."

Hailey swallowed hard. "Is there anything I can do to help plead my case?"

"I'll see what I can do," Theresa promised. "Maybe if I explain how we badly we need some chart audits done before our joint commission visit, they'll give in."

Hope flared. "I can do chart audits," she quickly interjected. "You tell me when and where. I'll do a hundred chart audits."

"I need to get approval from the vice president of Human Resources first," Theresa cautioned. "But I'll ask and let you know, okay?"

"Today?" She grimaced at her pathetically hopeful tone.

"Soon," Theresa promised. "Give me a day or two, all right?"

"All right. Thanks, Theresa." Hailey snapped her phone shut and tried to quell her rising panic.

Surely they'd let her do something. Wouldn't they?

She buried her face in her hands and battled the irrational urge to call Simon. She hadn't seen or spoken to him since the day of their kiss. The day she'd pretended to feel nothing but friendship toward him.

No, she couldn't call him.

She tried Rachel, and ended up leaving a message. Maybe she could help sway Theresa, as Rachel had worked here in Cedar Bluff for a few years.

Of course, Simon might be willing to put a good word in for her, too.

Maybe.

She tried to lose herself in a book, but after reading the same few pages several times she gave up.

Instead, she decided to balance her checkbook. She had a banking program on her computer, so she turned on her laptop and went meticulously through her financial situation.

The news was grim. She would only be able to hold onto her apartment for another six weeks without a paycheck and the rent was due in two weeks.

This time, when her cell phone rang, she held her breath and closed her eyes as she answered it, hoping Theresa wasn't calling with bad news.

"Hi, Hailey, how are you?" The deep voice was Simon's. She was so surprised she didn't answer immediately.

"I'm okay." She mentally winced at her lackluster response. She tried to brighten her tone. "How are you? Busy at work?"

"What's wrong?" Simon asked. "You sound upset."

So much for her attempt to sound cheerful. Since she was feeling desperate, she put her pride aside. "I am upset. Apparently the hospital won't approve my leave of absence because I haven't worked there for a full year. My boss told me I don't qualify for the return to work light-duty program."

"What? That's ridiculous." Simon's outrage on her behalf made her smile. "So what if you haven't been here a year? There are plenty of things to do. In fact, I need help with some quality reviews. I'm going to talk to Theresa."

"Really?" She couldn't hide her flash of excitement. "Oh, Simon, it would be great if I could help out. Even part-time hours. Anything."

"I'll call you right back."

Simon didn't call right back, and in the hour that passed she convinced herself he'd been unable to plead her case. A good hour later, Theresa called.

"Hailey? I managed to convince Human Resources

to cut you a break and bend our policy. You're approved for light-duty work but only part-time hours. You'll do chart audits for us and quality review cases for Simon Carter. Do you think you can start with a few hours this afternoon?"

"Yes!" she exclaimed. "Absolutely! Thank you, Theresa. You don't know how much this means to me."

"All right, be here about one o'clock and we'll go over what needs to be done."

Hailey had been so excited about working she'd forgotten she didn't have a bike. "I'll be there," she rashly promised.

She'd crutch-walk the three miles if she had to.

But, of course, Simon called her back almost immediately after her conversation with Theresa. "Hailey? I'll be there at twelve-thirty to pick you up."

"I'll be ready," she assured him. "And, Simon? Thanks for going to bat for me."

"Anytime," he said gruffly.

Wearing scrubs, the wide pants legs just barely fitting over her cast, she couldn't hide her relief as she and Simon walked into the busy emergency department. Because Theresa was busy trying to fill a sick call, Simon took her into his office.

"Here's a list of cases I'd like you to review." He handed her a slip of paper with ten patient names on it. "Go through the computer records and let me know if you think the medical staff and nursing staff provided appropriate care."

"All right," she agreed. "Is there a reason to believe the care wasn't appropriate?"

He hesitated. "I'd rather not answer that until you've reviewed them with fresh eyes."

She could see his point. If she knew his opinion, she'd likely look at each patient's record differently. He was asking for a nonjudgmental approach. "Where would you like me to work?"

"You'll have to find a workstation out at the main desk by the unit clerk," he said, glancing toward the arena just a stone's throw from his office. "I have some things I need to do in here."

"Okay." She ignored the flash of disappointment that they wouldn't be working more closely together. What did it matter where she worked? She was truly grateful for the paperwork assignment that would help pay her rent.

She sat down at the only empty computer, not far from the unit clerk. There was so much activity, though, that she quickly became distracted by the orders that came flying toward the poor woman. Orders for labs, X-rays, consultants—it seemed like the list was never ending.

"Would you like some help?" she asked Mary, the unit clerk on duty. The woman was close to her own age, but looked older because of her bleached blonde hair, which was cut short and was spiky with gel. Her green eyes were too bright to be real, so they had to be from colored contact lenses. She'd tried to befriend the woman, as Mary was also relatively new to Cedar Bluff.

"No." The rude response took her by surprise, especially when the woman pretty much ignored her. "I don't need your help."

Okay, then. With a shrug, Hailey turned her attention back to the task at hand. She made a Herculean effort to block out all the noise around her, concentrating on the notes in the patient's chart.

Her elbow was roughly jostled by someone next to her and she looked up in time to see the tech, Bonnie, trying to reach around her, holding a full glass of water. One moment the cup was in Bonnie's hand, the next it had been dumped into her lap, soaking her scrubs and the computer monitor.

Hailey leaped up from her seat, trying to shake off the water pooling in her lap, but forgot about her cast until pain shot up her leg as she put her full weight on it. She fell against the edge of the desk with a cry.

Pain reverberated down her hip to her leg, her scrub pants were soaked and the computer screen had gone completely blank.

"I'm so sorry!" Bonnie exclaimed in horror.

CHAPTER NINE

SIMON overheard a ruckus out at the main desk in the arena, and as he couldn't concentrate, thanks to distracting memories of kissing Hailey, he came out to investigate.

Hailey was leaning heavily against the edge of the desk without her crutches, her expression a pained grimace as she tried to shoo several well-meaning staff members away. The dampness of her scrubs and the upended cup of water lying on the computer keyboard bore testament as to what had happened.

"I'm fine," she insisted, using the paper towels someone had brought over to mop up the mess. "But we need to call a tech from IT to fix the computer."

He came over at the same time Theresa approached from the opposite direction, her brows pulled together in a deep frown. "Hailey? You don't look very good. Are you sure you didn't injure yourself?"

Hailey's smile was strained and he suspected the pain was far worse than she was letting on. "I didn't hurt myself, Theresa, but unfortunately the water took out the computer monitor."

For a long moment Hailey and Theresa stared at each other, until Theresa finally glanced away. "Maybe this wasn't such a good idea."

Hailey paled, her blue eyes standing out starkly against the rest of her features. Simon had the uncharacteristic urge to reassure her that everything would be okay.

"Theresa, please," she said a bit desperately. "I swear this wasn't my fault. It was an unfortunate accident with a bit of spilled water, nothing more."

Simon readily jumped to Hailey's defense. "I'm the one who told Hailey to come out to the front desk to work. I should have let her use my office."

Theresa looked torn. He understood. As the nurse manager for the area, she shouldered a heavy responsibility. "I don't know, if Hailey hurts herself while working here…" She didn't finish the thought but he knew exactly what she meant. He'd learned all about worker's compensation laws when one of the residents had been injured on duty.

Theresa didn't want the hospital to be legally responsible for adding to Hailey's injury. He could respect that.

"She won't hurt herself doing chart reviews," he said firmly. "I'll get the computer fixed and from now on Hailey can sit in my office to complete the reviews." He was determined to make this work out, so Hailey would have some sort of income, as it was primarily his fault that she was unable to perform her normal duties as an ED nurse.

He'd find something to occupy his time elsewhere. Heaven knew, his office was not big enough for the both of them.

Another long silence hung in the air, before Theresa finally nodded. "All right. I guess she can do the chart reviews in your office."

"Thank you, Theresa," Hailey murmured, her relief

and gratitude evident. "I promise you won't regret this."

The wry expression on Theresa's face betrayed how she pretty much already regretted the arrangement, but she didn't say anything.

"Call the IT department," Simon instructed Mary, who seemed to be watching the interaction with frank curiosity rather than pitching in to help. Maybe someone needed to explain the teamwork concept to her. "Tell them to replace this unit and send the invoice to me through the medical staff office."

"Simon, that's really not necessary," Theresa interjected. "The ED budget can handle the replacement of a keyboard and monitor. Hopefully the hard drive is still intact."

"Let me know if it isn't." He turned toward Hailey. "Come on—let's get you settled in my office."

Hailey picked up the list of names, which were now barely legible as a result of being soaked with water. She wiped the list against the only dry spot on her pants leg, and then followed him back through the ED arena.

In the privacy of his office, he urged her to sit down in his chair behind the desk. "How bad is it?" he asked.

She momentarily closed her eyes. "Hurts a little," she admitted.

"I can tell that your leg hurts much more than just a little," he argued. "You stood on your injured leg, putting all your weight on it, didn't you?" When she didn't respond, he leaned forward earnestly. "You can be honest with me, Hailey. I'm on your side."

"I appreciate that, Simon. But I really am fine." She tilted her chin stubbornly and he had the wild urge to kiss her again. "Like I told Theresa, spilled water isn't the end of the world. I feel bad about the computer, though."

He could tell she was determined to downplay what had happened. He sighed and straightened. "Fine. I'll be right back with a hefty dose of ibuprofen and a dry pair of scrubs." He left before she could try to argue with him again.

As he made his way back through the ED, Bonnie came up to him, putting her hand on his arm. "I'm so sorry, Simon. I hope Hailey is all right."

For a split second the way she put her hand on his arm with such familiarity reminded him of Erica. But he quickly dismissed the unfair comparison, as he'd noticed most patient care providers had a touchy-feely approach to people. He couldn't help leaning back, as she was too close to his personal space. "She's fine, don't worry. Could have happened to anyone."

"Good. I'm so glad." Bonnie smiled and he was relieved when she dropped his arm and walked away.

He returned to his office with the promised ibuprofen, water and fresh pair of scrubs, to find Hailey already logged onto the computer, reviewing one of his patient's charts. He set the pain reliever and the water a good distance away from the keyboard. No sense in pushing their luck! She paused long enough to take the medication, reinforcing his belief that she hurt worse than she was letting on.

"Do you need anything else?" he asked.

"No, thanks." She flashed another strained smile, but then immediately turned her attention back to the chart. "I'll have these chart reviews finished as soon as possible."

"Hailey, take your time. There's no rush." He stood

there for a moment, but as he couldn't come up with any other reason to hang around, he turned to leave.

"Simon?"

The way Hailey said his name caused an immediate physical response. One he really needed to get control over, and quickly. He paused at the doorway, and then turned to glance at her over his shoulder. "Yes?"

"Thanks for supporting me with Theresa," she said slowly. "If you hadn't, I don't think she would have let me stay on. I owe you one, Simon, big time."

You owe me, Simon. Don't leave like this. You owe me!

He blanched, echoes of his disastrous relationship with Erica reverberating through his mind. "No! You don't owe me anything," His tone came across more harshly than he'd intended. "Nothing! Understand?"

She stared at him in shock. "No, Simon. I don't understand. If you don't want my gratitude, why did you bother sticking up for me in the first place? Out of guilt? I already told you the accident wasn't your fault. I don't need your pity. I can handle things just fine on my own."

"I'm not helping you out of guilt," he protested, even though he suspected that it was, in fact, part of the reason. He struggled to get a grip. His issues with Erica and his mistakes of the past had nothing to do with Hailey, none of this was her fault. He tried to soften his tone. "I shouldn't have snapped at you. Chalk it up to lack of sleep."

She arched a brow at him, as if she didn't believe a word he was saying.

He tried to smile but his face felt frozen. "I'll come back to check on you later, all right?"

"Don't bother," she muttered.

He opened his mouth to argue again, and then realized he should quit before he only made matters worse. "I'll see you later," he said. He left, closing the office door behind him with a sense of relief.

When he walked back into the arena, he became keenly aware of several curious pairs of eyes focused on him. He stifled the urge to shout at them to mind their own business. But he knew, better than most, how working in the emergency department was equivalent to living in a fishbowl.

That was exactly why he needed to stay away from Hailey.

No matter how desperately he wanted to see her again.

Hailey managed to get some work done, although it wasn't easy. Simon's scent permeated the office and while she was undeniably annoyed with him, she couldn't seem to prise him out of her mind.

Thanks to the ibuprofen he'd brought for her, the sharp pain in her leg had receded to a dull ache. After he'd finally left her alone, she'd gratefully changed into dry scrubs, wincing with the effort. Stupid of her to forget about her broken leg when she'd jumped up from her seat like that. Maybe she was cursed. It certainly seemed as if she was experiencing an unusual run of bad luck.

Once she was dry and feeling a little better, she went back to work, completing several of the chart reviews. One in particular bothered her. It seemed as if one of the physicians had totally missed several key symptoms on a patient, who had returned to the emergency department a couple of days later, only to end up emergently intubated and in the ICU. She placed her notes for that chart review on top, so Simon would see them right away.

When her four hours were up—Theresa had made it clear she could only work four hours a day and not a minute more—she logged off Simon's computer, feeling at least somewhat of a sense of accomplishment. Certainly completing chart reviews was better than sitting around at home all day, doing nothing.

It wasn't until she picked up her purse that she remembered Simon had given her a ride to the hospital. And she needed a way to get back home.

After the odd reaction he'd had when she'd tried to thank him earlier, she was loath to seek him out now.

He was obviously afraid she expected something from him. After that kiss down by the lakefront her attempt to thank him for his efforts had freaked him out.

She might be having a run of bad luck, but she wasn't pathetic enough to think that one kiss between two adults carried any sort of importance.

No, there was no way in the world she was going to wait around for Simon. And because Rachel was working too, her friend wasn't able to drive her home either.

Mentally she debated her options. Crutch-walking three miles to her apartment was not a smart choice. She'd thought she was in relatively good shape but soon discovered going long distances on crutches made her upper arms ache. She could call a taxi, but taking taxis to and from work each day would defeat the purpose of saving up money in order to pay her rent and the rest of her bills.

Before she'd bought her bike, she'd mapped out the bus routes to and from the hospital. The biggest problem with the bus routes in Cedar Bluff was that they weren't at the most convenient locations. At least, not for her. The closest bus stop to her apartment was a good four blocks away. And the bus stop here at the hospital was also several blocks down the road. At the time, riding her bike had been the best answer all around.

However, the bus was probably her only viable option now that she couldn't ride her bike. Surely the more she used the crutches, the more strength she'd gain in her arms?

For a moment she considered going to find Simon to let him know her plans, but she instantly dismissed the idea. He'd said he'd come back to check on things, but he hadn't.

No doubt, he was looking for ways to avoid being alone with her. She understood he didn't want her to get the wrong idea about their...*friendship*.

She was a capable adult, one who could certainly find her own way home.

The bus stop was located at the farthest corner of the road that came right up to the main lobby, so she left the emergency department through the back way, taking the long, winding corridor down to the main lobby. From there, she slowly made her way down the street to the bus stop. Thankfully it was nice outside, if a little breezy, and not raining.

Impossible to carry an umbrella and use crutches at the same time.

After glancing at her watch, she realized she had no idea when the bus was due to arrive. With a sigh she lowered herself down onto the bus stop bench, grateful to take the pressure off her arms even for a short while.

She had no idea how much of a time lag there was

between buses. Thirty minutes? Forty? Surely not more than an hour?

She should have brought something to read. Sitting around doing nothing was going to drive her crazy. An hour would feel like an eternity.

Ten minutes into her wait, a familiar low-slung black car pulled up in the bus lane. The passenger window was lowered, revealing Simon's dark scowl as he leaned over the passenger seat from the driver's side to talk to her. "What in the world are you doing out here?"

"Isn't it obvious?" she asked mildly. "Can't you see this is a bus stop? If you're looking for the quality review report, I left it on top of your desk."

If anything, his scowl deepened. "Hailey, don't be ridiculous. I'm not here for the stupid report. Get in the car. I'll drive you home."

"No, thanks."

The way Simon scrubbed his hands over his face would have been comical if she weren't so annoyed with him.

"Hailey, please. I'm going right past your house on my way home. Let me give you a lift."

She knew she should simply ignore him, but there were already a couple of cars coming up behind Simon, waiting impatiently. Simon completely ignored them, as if he couldn't care less how he was blocking the lane. One of them leaned on their horn.

Simon didn't even glance behind him, but waited patiently, looking at her expectantly. When the driver hit the horn the second time, she caved in. "Fine." She stood up, grabbed her crutches and crossed over the sidewalk to yank open the passenger door. Simon took the crutches from her and tucked them into the backseat as she slid in beside him.

Neither one of them spoke, not a single word, as he

drove the few miles to her apartment building. Hailey had to admit that somehow riding in a car with Simon wasn't bad at all.

Maybe she was slowly getting over her stupid fears.

Even once they'd arrived, Simon simply hauled the crutches out of the backseat, before coming around to help her out of the car.

"You know I would have been fine on the bus," she said, when Simon followed her up to the front door of the apartment building. "But thanks for the ride."

She was surprised when he followed her inside and up the elevator to the second floor. When they reached her apartment, he waited patiently as she dug out her keys and then held the door open for her.

She blocked the doorway. "Thanks, Simon, but I'll be fine from here."

"I'd like to stay, just for a few minutes, if you'd give me a chance to explain," he said, finally breaking his prolonged silence.

Exhausted mentally and physically, she was half-tempted to tell him to take a hike. But obviously something was bothering him. She knew, both from personal experience and from Rachel, that Simon was the most even-tempered of the emergency physicians on staff at Cedar Bluff.

Reluctantly, she made her way over to the sofa, sinking gratefully onto the soft cushions. She lightly massaged her upper arms. Simon closed the door behind him, and then took a seat on the opposite end of the sofa, as far from her as possible.

"I'm sorry that I've been a jerk," he said, staring down at his feet. "You already know how I was in a relationship that ended badly."

"Yes." Hadn't they already covered this issue? She

wasn't in the mood to regurgitate the past yet again. "And I already explained that I don't expect anything from you, Simon."

"I knew you didn't wait for me because you were mad. And I can't blame you."

She held up a hand to stop him. "I'm not mad. And there was no need for you to come and pick me up from the bus stop. I'm perfectly capable of taking the bus to and from work every day."

"Hailey, give me a moment to explain, would you?" He sounded exasperated.

She rolled her eyes and waved a hand, indicating he should continue.

His resigned gaze met hers. "The relationship I was in before, the one that didn't end well, involved a nurse. A nurse I worked with closely in the emergency department at Chicago's Children First Hospital."

She nodded in understanding. A nurse, a coworker, it explained a lot. She could see why he might be hesitant to go down that route again.

"The worst part of all was that when things ended badly between us," Simon said slowly as if the words were torn from somewhere deep in his soul, "we didn't just lose on a personal level, although that was bad enough. But, at least for me, I lost on a professional level as well. Because the horrible way things ended cost me my career."

CHAPTER TEN

THE moment the words left Simon's mouth he inwardly swore and wished he could call them back. He'd only intended to make Hailey feel better about why he'd been such a jerk. He hadn't planned on telling her all the gory details about his past relationship with Erica.

He hadn't told *anyone* the full extent of what had transpired.

"What? Your career? How?" Hailey demanded, her beautiful blue eyes snapping fire with outrage on his behalf. The way she jumped to his defense almost made him want to smile. "Just because you broke some sort of no-fraternising policy? That's ridiculous!"

He hesitated. How much should he tell her? Keeping his dark secret had been an ingrained habit for so long he wasn't even sure where to begin. Or where to stop. He couldn't tell her everything, just enough to help her to understand, to explain his behaviour.

"Not because of a policy," he finally admitted. "I was being groomed for the medical director position, a job I coveted. But one disastrous night my personal life became center stage in the middle of the ED."

"Oh, no," she whispered in horror. And she didn't know the half of it. The personal loss was hard enough, but to have everyone else know about it was far worse.

"The scene was pretty ugly and afterwards my career suffered irreversible damage," he continued, determined to finish. "My boss pretty much came right out and told me I should look for another position at a different hospital if I wanted to move into a leadership role." Even now, that painful discussion grated on him. As much as he'd understood where his boss had been coming from, he'd found it impossible to believe his four years of hard work hadn't counted for more.

Erica had blown his dreams away in a fit of anger.

No, that wasn't fair. The entire mess had been his fault and no one else's.

Hailey's brow puckered into a frown. "I'm surprised you allowed yourself to participate in a fight with your girlfriend in the middle of the unit," she said frankly. "That's not at all your style."

Simon dropped his head and rubbed the back of his neck. He hadn't participated in the fight, other than to try to get Erica out of there when she had started screaming at him so they could talk someplace private. But that had been when she'd turned on him like a wildcat, hitting and scratching, striking out in anger. He'd defended himself the best he could without hurting her, but in the end several nurses had been forced to step in, dragging Erica off him. Just thinking about the humiliation of that night made his gut knot painfully.

He'd handled it all wrong, he could see that so clearly now. Erica hadn't been emotionally stable, and his breaking things off had only been one issue sending her over the edge. Getting his life back on track had been hard enough, but he hadn't been given the chance to recover once Erica had resorted to other means to make him pay.

In some respects, he was still paying for his mistake.

Would he be forced to pay forever?

"Simon?" Hailey said his name, dragging his thoughts back to the present. "What happened?"

"I was caught off guard," he admitted. "I wasn't expecting her to start yelling at me in the middle of the unit, dragging our personal life into the public eye. But in the end it didn't matter who started what. I took accountability for what happened because I didn't handle things well enough with her from the very beginning."

"I see," Hailey murmured, although he could see dozens of questions reflected in her eyes that showed she really didn't.

He didn't want to go into details about Erica with Hailey. Mostly because he was too embarrassed at how far things had spiraled out of control. And the role he'd unwittingly played.

He could see now how his good intentions had only made things worse instead of better.

But the past was over and done with. He just wanted to move on. "I came to Cedar Bluff to start over. It's a great hospital and a warm, welcoming community. And for once my timing was right on target because the medical director here, George Hanover is about ready to retire and I've made it clear I'm interested in replacing him."

"I'm surprised Dr. Taylor, Dr. Reichert or Dr. Torres aren't fighting you for the spot," she pointed out, naming the other younger attending physicians on staff. Seth, Jadon and Quinn were his colleagues but he also considered them his friends. "They've been here longer than you and have more seniority."

Talking about his career was much easier than talking

about his personal failures. "They have more seniority here," he agreed. "But being a medical director is more about management experience than just tenure and I have far more management experience than they do, thanks to my years at Children First in Chicago. I'm already the chairman of the ED quality review committee, which means I work closely with Theresa on cases where we could have done better either from a medical or nursing perspective."

Hailey smiled warmly. "It's no wonder you're such a great doctor. I can tell you really care about your work, Simon."

He shrugged, pleased with the compliment. Because she was right. His patients were important to him. Although somewhere along the line, his personal life had become important too.

"I do. Very much." Which was why he was trying so hard to keep his distance from Hailey. To ignore his unwavering physical attraction to her. His expression turned serious. "I'm sorry Hailey, but I hope you can see where I'm coming from. I can't afford to screw up this opportunity."

Her smile faded and she dropped her gaze. "I understand, Simon. Although, I've already tried to explain that I'm not interested in having a romantic relationship with you."

Her blunt statement stabbed deep. He ignored the pain, telling himself this was exactly what he wanted. So the kiss they'd shared didn't mean as much to her as it had to him. Fine. Better for both of them. "Good. Then we're in agreement. I hope we can remain friends."

The expression in her gaze was difficult to read but she readily agreed. "Of course. Friends."

There was a long, awkward silence. Time to change

the subject to something neutral. He glanced around. "Ah, what time do you work tomorrow?" he asked.

She lifted a shoulder. "I can go in anytime, as long as I get the work done. Theresa made it clear I could only work four hours a day, regardless. Apparently they don't want me to overdo things."

"Sounds reasonable to me."

She grimaced. "I'd rather work full-time, but after that mess today, I'm just grateful Theresa is willing to keep me on at all."

He could relate. "I work day shift tomorrow, but I could come over right after work to pick you up," he offered.

But she was already shaking her head. "No, thanks, I would rather take the bus in."

He didn't understand the flare of panic. Was this it then? Was she going to stop seeing him completely? He'd been banking on the fact that they'd continue to spend time together at least as friends.

Quickly, he considered his options. "Actually, that would work out great, Hailey. Why don't you come in around eleven? You can use my office since I'll be staffing in the department, caring for patients, and then I can drive you home after my shift is over."

For a moment she looked like she might argue, but then she slowly nodded. "Sure, that might work. I'll see how I feel in the morning."

For a moment he wondered if she was just stringing him along, but then he pushed the idea aside. Surely Hailey wasn't looking forward to riding the bus. While she was on crutches he wanted to help in any way possible.

His stomach rumbled and he realized they'd missed

lunch. "Are you hungry? There's a Chinese place nearby that delivers."

She looked taken aback by his suggestion. "I was planning to relax and watch a movie tonight. Really, Simon, you don't have to stick around to entertain me. I'll be fine."

"I need to eat too and I don't have any plans for the evening," he assured her, getting up from the sofa and pulling out his cell phone. "And luckily I have Chang Lee's number in my cell phone directory. Chang Lee's has the best Chinese food in town. Anything in particular you want to eat or should I get a variety?"

There was a pause and he waited, hoping she wouldn't tell him to get lost. "A variety."

He couldn't help but grin. It was nice to have a woman who shared his taste in food. Erica had been the queen of eating salads. Except she hadn't eaten them, she'd picked at them. Had driven him nuts. "Perfect."

He gave their order to Mrs. Chang Lee herself, and then picked up the movies she had sitting on top of the DVD player. They were both romantic comedies, but as he'd invited himself over, he wasn't about to complain. "Which one did you plan on watching?" he asked.

"*The Princess Bride*," she said instantly. "It's my favorite."

He'd never watched it, but tried not to grimace at her selection. He was sure he wouldn't like the chick flick, but staying there with Hailey for a few hours watching something he didn't like was better than going home to sit in his empty house all alone.

His cell phone rang, and he glanced at the screen, wondering who was calling. He frowned when he saw *Unidentified number* on the display.

Every day for the past week he'd had hang-up

messages on his answering-machine at home. Up to five a day. He figured the telemarketers would give up sooner or later.

But would telemarketers call on his cell phone? He pushed the button to send the caller to voice mail. The caller with the unidentified number could just leave a message.

A few minutes later his phone chirped again, announcing he had a voice mail message. Planning to listen to it later, he tucked his phone away.

He loaded the movie into the DVD player. Ten minutes into the movie, their food arrived. They ate while they watched, and he hated to admit that the movie wasn't nearly as bad as he'd anticipated.

Sappy, sure. But enough action to make up for it.

There was only about six inches of space between them on the sofa as Hailey had stretched out in her search for comfort, her broken leg propped up on several pillows. Her eyelids drooped, as if she was exhausted.

He seriously considered pulling her into his arms, knowing she'd be far more comfortable, but instantly rejected the idea. He was the one who'd set the boundary of friendship. So he kept his gaze on the movie, subtly watching her out of the corner of his eye.

Very soon her head dipped down to the right, her chin practically resting on her chest.

Her breathing evened out and he realized with an amused grin that she'd fallen asleep. When she slid further toward him, he debated only a moment before drawing her close, so she could rest without suffering a crick in her neck.

She turned her face into the hollow of his shoulder. He held his breath, waiting. Was she awake? When she didn't move for several long moments, he bent to lightly rest his cheek on the top of her head. Her scent filled his senses and he nearly groaned when his body tightened with need.

He ignored the urge to kiss her awake. Maybe, if the stars were aligned in his favor, she'd stay close to him like this for a while.

Pathetic, sure, but he was willing to take what little bit he could get.

When the movie was over, he didn't want to disturb her so he used the remote to change the channel to a ball game. Luckily, there was a double header playing. He put the sound on mute and watched the action silently.

But he couldn't have told anyone who won the game. Soon he closed his eyes, and held Hailey in his arms as she slept, secretly wishing things could be different.

Wishing he deserved a personal relationship—a future with someone like Hailey.

Hailey gradually became aware of her surroundings, realizing very quickly from the deep rumble beneath her ear that she was not alone.

Sucking in a quick breath, she froze and became instantly wide awake, blinking in the dimness of the room.

Simon was holding her in his arms. A soft snoring sound filled the air, confirming he'd fallen asleep. There was some old black and white sitcom flickering across the television screen and from what she could see out of her living-room window the night was pitch black.

She guessed the time to be well after midnight.

How on earth had this happened? The last thing she remembered was watching *The Princess Bride*. But not the end, she realized with a frown. Darn it, she'd missed her favorite part.

Holding herself still, she breathed in Simon's musky scent, enjoying the feeling of being pressed up against him a little too much.

She should wake him up and send him on his way. Sleeping in Simon's arms was not in keeping with their deal.

Friendship. All he wanted from her was friendship.

After hearing about what had happened in his previous relationship, and how his personal life had ruined his career, she really couldn't blame him for not wanting to get personally involved.

There had been a tiny part of her that had wanted to protest, telling him she was not like his ex-girlfriend. She'd never start a fight with him in the middle of the emergency department.

After all, she worked there, too.

Since the flashbacks after her bike accident hadn't returned, she'd hoped that she'd successfully put the past to rest. Although, if she was honest, she'd admit the familiar cloak of guilt remained.

She wasn't the right woman for Simon. He could do far better. She knew he could easily find someone else. Someone worthy of his love. Possibly someone who didn't work with him in the emergency department.

But maybe, just for a brief time, enjoying what they had would be heavenly. Because being with Simon like this, in his arms, however accidentally, made her feel alive.

Steeling her resolve to get up, putting an end to the ridiculous fantasies, she placed her hand on his chest and gently pushed herself upward.

Simon's arm tightened around her, holding her in place. "Hailey," he murmured.

Her breath lodged in her throat. Was he dreaming about her? The way she'd dreamed about him?

No, maybe he was awake. "Simon," she whispered. "We have to get up. We fell asleep."

In the dim light of the TV she saw his eyes were open and he was staring at her intently. He shifted and suddenly she was lying more fully against him.

She sucked in another breath, acutely aware of the rigid hardness of his groin pressing against her.

"Hailey," he said again, his tone husky and pleading at the same time. Before she could respond, he lowered his head and kissed her.

She fisted her hand in his shirt to push him away, but when he angled his head to deepen the kiss she lost the battle with her common sense. With a groan she returned his kiss, eagerly pressing against him, desperate for more.

She didn't want to be Simon's friend.

She wanted him like this. Holding her and kissing her like he'd never let go.

The heat of his hand scorched the bare skin of her back when he slid it beneath the thin fabric of her loose top. She nearly wept with intense pleasure.

Too long. Fourteen long months since she'd been held like this. Kissed like this.

Made love to like this.

She shifted to the side, giving him better access to her breasts. Her hand lowered and caressed the rock hardness straining against his zipper.

He groaned again, pressing deeper into her caress, but when she stroked him again more firmly he froze. She sensed he was about to pull away.

"Simon, please," she whispered, stroking him and eliciting another low groan. "Don't stop."

There was a long silence, and she hoped she'd gotten through to him, but then suddenly he pulled his hand from beneath her shirt and grasped her wrist, halting her caress. "No, Hailey. We can't do this."

For a moment she wanted to rail at him. Why was he doing this to her? First he'd said no, then he'd invited himself for dinner and then he'd fallen asleep on her sofa, holding her in his arms.

One minute he'd been kissing her and the next he was telling her they couldn't do this.

She resented feeling like a yo-yo.

With a spurt of anger she pushed away from him. She swung the leg that had the cast onto the floor and sat up, putting as much distance as possible between them. She grabbed her crutches and levered off the couch, crossing the room so she wouldn't be tempted to smack some sense into him.

"If you remember, I didn't ask you to stay, Simon," she said in a clipped tone. "You're the one who over-stayed your welcome."

He let out a heavy sigh. "I know. I'm sorry."

His apology only made her angrier. "I don't want you to be sorry, Simon! I want you to make up your mind. Are we friends? Or are we something more? Because quite frankly the signals you're sending out are so damn confusing I can't figure them out." She gripped the hand rests of her crutches tightly. "What do you want from me?"

He rose to his feet, stumbling a bit before he got his balance. "I want to be your friend, Hailey. I wish I could... But it doesn't matter. All I can offer you is friendship."

She stared at him. "I can't do this. I changed my mind," she said abruptly, swinging away and walking toward the kitchen, flipping on the light as she went. Too bad she didn't have a bottle of whiskey because right now she could use a shot. She put her crutches aside and opened the fridge, settling for a glass of orange juice instead.

"Changed your mind about what?" he asked, following more slowly. The way he limped and kept stamping his foot on the floor made her suspect his leg had fallen asleep.

Too bad. She was too upset with him to give a damn. She downed the orange juice in one gulp and then leaned against the edge of the counter, crossing her arms over her chest defensively. "I changed my mind about being your friend, Simon." Her words stopped him in mid-step. "I think it would be best for both of us if we stopped seeing each other completely."

CHAPTER ELEVEN

"No Way." Hailey was surprised at the vehemence in his tone and the stark anguish on his face. "Please don't do this. I want to help while your leg is healing. Don't throw me out of your life completely."

She stared at him. And suddenly she was tired of arguing. Obviously the only thing that was going to get through to him was the blunt truth. "I can't do this, Simon. I can't treat you like a friend when I want more from you." She took a deep breath and let it out slowly, searching for the courage to bare her soul. "I want more than friendship. I want what just happened on the sofa. And since you've made it clear you can't or won't return my feelings, it's better for me if I don't see you at all on a personal level."

For a long moment he didn't answer, myriad emotions playing across his features. But then he came closer, the rest of the way into the kitchen. She would have taken a step back, but she was already up against the kitchen counter.

"Okay," he said finally.

Okay what? He was going to leave her alone? Fine. That was exactly what she wanted. She ignored the sharp stab of disappointment, swallowed hard and tilted her chin, determined to see this through. "I'm glad you understand."

"Oh, I understand exactly where you're coming from, Hailey. Because I want you, too."

Nonplussed, she stared at him. He came closer, lightly grasping her shoulders in his hands. She opened her mouth but nothing came out.

"So you're basically telling me that it's all or nothing between us, right?" His dark eyes pierced hers. She nodded, unable to speak. His expression twisted wryly. "In that case, I choose all. Everything."

"What?" She found her voice, but it was her turn to backpedal. She'd thrown out the challenge but hadn't expected him to actually take her up on the offer. And what about his determination not to get involved with someone he worked with? She tried to gather her scattered thoughts. "But…on the sofa, you stopped…"

"I was stupid. I panicked. Give me another chance, Hailey." He nuzzled her hair, his voice low, husky. "This time I promise I won't stop."

When she pulled back to stare at him, he took her silence for acquiescence and kissed her again. Urgently. Desperately. Showing her without words how much he wanted her.

And, heaven help her, she wasn't strong enough to push him away. She slipped her arms around his neck, drawing him closer. The endless kiss was only broken by the all-too-human need to breathe.

"I can't let you go after all, Hailey," he murmured. "Don't ask me to."

His confession made her heart swell with hope. When he swung her into his arms she gasped, realizing his intent. "Simon, are you sure about this? I won't—I won't quit my job for you."

"We'll need to be discreet," he said, planting a kiss on her temple as he strode confidently down the hall to her bedroom. "And careful. Neither one of us is going to quit our jobs, but we need to keep our personal feelings out of the workplace. But no matter what, I can't walk away, Hailey. I can't imagine leaving you."

"But—" she tried again.

"Don't. Let's just take this one step at a time, hmm?"

Making love seemed like a giant leap rather than a single step, but when he gently set her on the bed and began to strip off his clothes, she couldn't find the strength to protest.

Naked, he was simply amazing, all hard sculpted muscles and lean hips. When he reached for the hem of her scrub top, drawing it slowly up and over her head, she quelled a spurt of panic. She hadn't been with a man in years, not since Andrew.

"God, Hailey, you're so beautiful," he whispered huskily nuzzling the valley between her breasts after he tossed her bra aside. "I don't deserve you."

That made her laugh. If only he knew. "Oh, Simon. I don't deserve you, either."

His eyes glittered in the darkness. "I guess that means we're perfect for each other."

She wasn't so sure that was true, but when he kissed her again, following her down onto the mattress, their naked limbs entwined, she gave herself up to the wonderful sensations. When he kissed his way down her body, exploring every inch, she stopped thinking at all.

No matter what happened between them, she wouldn't regret one moment of being with him like this.

Simon prised his eyes open, instinctively knowing it was time for him to get up. His internal alarm clock never failed him and when he blinked the sleep from his eyes, glancing at Hailey's clock on her dresser, he saw it was five in the morning. Just enough time to get home, shower, change and then get to work.

Hailey murmured in protest when he untangled himself from the bed. "Shh," he murmured. "Go back to sleep." He soothed her with a gentle kiss.

She nodded, obviously half-asleep as she snuggled deeper beneath the covers, and he had to fight the urge to join her. He stood staring at her for a long time, knowing he was crazy to have stayed to make love to her but unable to deny a surge of satisfaction.

No matter what, he couldn't regret making love to Hailey. She'd been so good for him. No, actually, they'd been good for each other. For the first time in what seemed like for ever, the future didn't seem quite so bleak. Or lonely.

Only the knowledge that he'd see her in a few hours made it possible for him to turn away and pull on his wrinkled clothes, moving quietly as he let himself out of her apartment.

He made it to work early, heading to his office so he could review the quality report Hailey had left for him. When he used the key in the lock, though, his door opened easily.

With a frown, he realized Hailey couldn't have locked it behind her. Probably because he'd promised to return to check on things.

When he flipped on the light, his desk was neat and tidy. But there was no report. Hadn't Hailey told him she'd leave it on top of his desk?

He opened the top drawer and the side drawers, wondering if she'd meant to leave it out but had, in fact, tucked it away instead. But he didn't find anything.

Not even in the garbage.

Perplexed, he sat at his desk, staring at the computer screen. He didn't know what had happened to the report, but all he could do was to wait for Hailey to come in. No doubt she'd know where to find it.

He quickly reviewed his email, responding to the various issues before heading back into the trauma bay for the start of his shift.

"Hey, Simon. How are you?" Quinn Torres greeted him when he walked in.

"I'm good, thanks. How was your night?"

Quinn shrugged. "Not bad. Leila and I didn't have too many trauma admissions."

Simon had been a bit surprised to discover that Quinn often matched up his shifts in the ED with the nights his wife, Leila, who was one of the trauma surgeons, happened to be on call. Apparently they weren't worried about working together. In fact, they seemed to enjoy it.

A kernel of doubt gnawed at him, but he shoved it aside. Hailey was the complete opposite of Erica. She was fiercely independent and adorably stubborn. They'd both been on the exact same page last night. He flat out refused to regret taking their relationship to the next level. "How's Danny?" he asked, focusing on Quinn.

"He's good," Quinn responded with a broad grin. Once his son Danny had had emotional issues that had prevented him from talking, but not any more. "He's thrilled because we let him spend the night with Ben Taylor."

The two boys had been inseparable, even in those early days when Danny hadn't been talking. He remembered how Hailey had suspected Seth of hurting Ben.

If only she knew how much they were all like one big family.

One in which he'd often played the outsider, looking in.

"I bet they had a blast," Simon agreed. He glanced up at the census board and the dozen or so names that were still listed there. "Give me the rundown on the patients so you can get out of here."

When Quinn had finished going through the patients that were still in the ED, Leila arrived, walking toward them and wrapping her arms around her husband's waist in a tight hug. "Ready, darling?" she asked.

"Absolutely," he responded huskily, and the way the two gazed into each other's eyes made it clear they were heading home to bed but not to sleep.

Simon flashed a wry grin, for once not experiencing the pang of envy he usually felt when watching the married couples around him. Maybe because he'd spent a rather satisfying night with Hailey?

And he hoped they'd have many more. The mere thought made him grin.

"Get out of here," Simon said, shooing them away. "I have work to do."

The four hours dragged by with excruciating slowness as he examined and treated patients. He was standing in the arena when Hailey walked in.

"Good morning," she greeted him in a reserved tone, abiding by her promise to keep things professional while they were at work. "Do you have a list of patients you need reviewed today?"

"Actually, I need the reviews you did yesterday," he told her.

Her eyes widened in surprise. "What are you talking

about?" she demanded with a frown. "I left the details of my review right on top of your desk."

Several employees, two nurses and the unit clerk were watching their interaction with open curiosity. His face tightened and he gave a jerky nod toward his office. "Let's discuss this in private," he said in a clipped tone.

She followed him into the office, and then stopped abruptly when she saw the empty desktop. "I don't understand. I swear, Simon, I left the report right there on the top of your desk."

He let out a sigh. "Well it's obviously not here, Hailey. Go and check your locker. Maybe you intended to leave it here but took it with you by mistake."

"I didn't take it with me." Her blue eyes flashed fire and he couldn't help thinking about how beautiful she looked, even when she was angry. "Carrying things with my crutches isn't exactly easy. I didn't take the report out of the office. I know I left it here, Simon. Someone must have taken it. I left your door open because I wasn't sure whether you had your keys and I didn't want to lock you out."

He remembered how his office door hadn't been locked. In his haste to find Hailey last night, he'd simply closed the door behind him without checking. "You're right, my door wasn't locked. But I've searched everywhere, in the desk drawers, even in the garbage, and it's not here."

"Someone must have taken it."

He snorted. "Oh, sure, that makes sense. Why on earth would someone take it, Hailey? What's the point? The report isn't irreplaceable. You can re-create it easily enough."

She slowly shook her head. "I don't know, Simon. But

I still think it's odd. I can't help but wonder if someone took it to make me look incompetent."

Hailey stewed over the missing report long after she'd re-created it and moved on to the next few cases.

She wasn't losing her mind. She'd left the report in plain view. Someone had to have taken it on purpose. To make her look bad?

She couldn't help remembering the way the ED tech, Bonnie, had tripped and spilled water all over her the day before. Had that been on purpose too? But if so, why? Bonnie was relatively new to Cedar Bluff, just like she was. Why would the tech dislike her so much? She couldn't remember having had any sort of run-in with the woman.

Hailey hadn't been in Cedar Bluff long enough to make enemies. She'd barely had time to make friends in the two months since she'd started.

She pushed the paranoid thoughts aside. Maybe the answer was something simple. Like the papers had fallen on the floor and the cleaning staff had tossed them out because they'd thought they were garbage.

That must be it. There wasn't some sort of conspiracy against her.

She focused her attention on completing the list Simon had given her. Even when her four hours were up, she kept working. At a quarter to four Simon opened the office door. "Hailey? Are you ready to go?"

"No. I need to finish this report first."

He leaned against the doorjamb, frowning at her. "I thought Theresa didn't want you to work more than four hours?"

"I'm not counting the first thirty minutes it took me to re-create the missing review. As far as I'm concerned, the clock started at noon." She barely glanced at him, intent on getting the last chart finished. "Go ahead and leave if you want. I'll take the bus home."

She heard him sigh. "Finish your report, then. I'll give you fifteen minutes." Her shoulders dropped in relief when he stepped back and closed the door.

For a moment she allowed herself the luxury of dropping her head into her hands and massaging her temples. Treating Simon like a stranger at work was more difficult than she'd imagined.

Last night, making love with Simon had been incredible. Better than anything she could possibly dream up. But now, in the cold light of day, nagging doubts threatened to choke her.

Maybe they were moving too fast. Maybe they needed to take a step back and really think about what they were doing.

Already, it seemed as if keeping their personal lives separate from their professional lives would be next to impossible. From the moment she'd come into the unit, she'd been able to feel Simon's terseness as he'd asked about the report. She'd been taken completely off guard at his annoyance after the wonderful night they'd shared.

With a deep, cleansing breath, she lifted her head and went back to reading the electronic chart. She made several notations and then sat back, rubbing the back of her neck.

She was finished, with five minutes to spare.

It was tempting to leave now, before Simon returned. But when she glanced down at the stack of papers containing all her notes, she scowled.

No way. This time she wasn't leaving until Simon had the reviews safely in his hands.

While she waited she gazed curiously around his office. He had his medical school diploma and his undergraduate diploma mounted proudly on the wall. But other than those two items, there was nothing personal that she could see.

Not even one photo of his family.

She frowned. Did Simon have family? Surely he had parents somewhere. But the question bothered her. She'd slept with the man but she didn't really know much about him.

Other than the fact that he had a former girlfriend who'd started a huge fight in the emergency department, which had cost him his job.

Why was the lack of knowledge about Simon's family bothering her now? She'd thought she'd known Andrew very well, had met his family numerous times, but in the end the way he'd started to drink heavily had been a surprise.

The office door opened, startling her. "All finished?" Simon asked.

"Yes." She leaned on the desk to stand, balancing her weight on her good leg. She held out the stack of paperwork she'd compiled. "You might want to put this someplace safe."

He came into the room, taking the paperwork from her and leafing through it quickly. "Very comprehensive, Hailey," he commented. "Thanks."

"You're welcome." She reached for her crutches.

Simon edged behind her—the office really wasn't very big—and opened his desk drawer, putting the paperwork she'd handed him into one of his files.

"Aren't you going to lock it?" she asked, when he slammed the drawer shut.

"No. I'll make sure the office door is locked."

Hailey frowned. "Humor me. Lock the desk, too. The cleaning people have a key to your office, right?"

"Yeah, probably."

"If the cleaning staff has a set of keys, then pretty much anyone could get one if they really wanted to. Maybe someone on staff doesn't like the idea of me reviewing the care of our patients. Maybe they're afraid we might find something they'd missed."

He paused, but then slowly nodded. "I'd thought of that possibility too," he admitted. "Okay, I'll lock the desk."

She stood by the doorway as he searched for and found the keys to the desk. Once he'd locked everything up, he put the key on his keyring.

Awkwardly, she leaned on one crutch to open the door. Simon came up behind her, and placed his hand in the small of her back. "I'll get it," he said, his voice close to her ear.

His touch, even as light as it was, sent fissures of awareness tingling down her spine.

She blushed, wondering if he had any idea what he was doing to her. "Simon, maybe you should wait here and let me go first, so it doesn't look so obviously like we're leaving together."

"Don't be ridiculous," Simon responded, but he dropped his hand from her back as he opened the door wider. "Everyone knows I hit you on your bike. It's no secret that I feel responsible. Giving you a ride home isn't a big deal."

She swallowed her argument, her expression annoyed as she swung out of the office on her crutches. Why the man was so stubborn was beyond her.

Maybe it was just her imagination, but it seemed like everyone in the arena stopped what they were doing and blatantly stared at her as she came out of Simon's office and walked across the unit.

This was exactly what she'd been afraid of. She imagined the rumors about Simon and herself were flying fast and furious.

"Hailey, watch out!"

Too late. She belatedly realized water was on the floor when the crutch in her right hand slid out from beneath her.

CHAPTER TWELVE

SIMON leaped forward as Hailey leaned heavily on one crutch, precariously teetering as she struggled to keep her balance.

The crutch clattered to the floor.

"I've got you," he said, catching her and hauling her close in time to prevent her from falling.

"Thanks," she murmured, her voice muffled by his shirt.

For a moment he almost forgot they were standing in the middle of the arena, so overcome was he by the urge to kiss her. But he managed to loosen his grip and take a safe step backward. "Okay now?"

"Of course." Hailey pointedly averted her gaze as she stood leaning on one crutch. Simon bent down to pick up the other one, which had crashed to the floor. She took it wordlessly.

"Call Housekeeping and get someone over here to mop up the spill," Simon directed the unit clerk, the one with the weird green eyes. "And throw me a towel, please."

"I already called them," Mary assured him, her expression one of concern. He grabbed the towel from Bonnie and placed it over the spill.

"Good thing you're so quick," Bonnie said, "otherwise

poor Hailey might have fallen and hurt herself even worse."

"Yeah." He carefully stepped around the wet spot on the floor, wondering why it seemed Hailey was suddenly so accident prone. Especially when the accidents were not the result of anything she'd done.

If you didn't count riding her bike in a thunderstorm.

Simon hurried after Hailey as she'd continued crossing the arena, heading for the hallway leading to the staff locker rooms. He caught up with her right before she disappeared inside. "Hailey? Are you all right?"

"I'm fine." Her low voice was difficult to read. "I'll meet you outside in the parking lot in a few minutes."

He stepped back, frowning as she disappeared into the woman's locker room. Had she hurt herself but was afraid to say anything? He was tempted to follow her inside, but forced himself to head out to his car.

True to her word, Hailey came out less than five minutes later. She had her purse slung over her shoulder, and this time she put her crutches in the back herself, before sliding into the passenger seat.

He didn't immediately drive away. "Are you sure you're all right?" he asked. "Did you wrench your arm or your shoulder?"

"No, luckily my arm strength has improved over the past week." Hailey relaxed against the seat with a sigh. "But I swear I'm cursed."

"I doubt you're cursed, Hailey," he muttered. "But it does seem as if you've had a run of bad luck. I'm glad you didn't hurt yourself."

"Me, too. Where are we going?" she asked, when he turned left instead of right toward her apartment.

"I thought maybe we'd go out for dinner," he said,

keeping his tone casual with an effort. He felt guilty for not taking her out on a proper date before spending the night in her apartment. He glanced over at her, trying to gauge her reaction. "Is that all right with you?"

"Ah, sure." Hailey flashed him a tentative smile. "Dinner sounds good."

He relaxed a bit. At least she hadn't told him to take a hike. "There's a nice restaurant, Stephen's, that overlooks the harbor."

"Would you mind if we took a walk first?" Hailey asked, when he pulled into the parking lot of Stephen's. "I really need to stretch my muscles. I'm not used to sitting so much. I miss my bike," she said in a forlorn tone.

He almost laughed, but then realized she was serious. "So you really enjoy riding your bike everywhere?" he asked curiously. He couldn't imagine functioning without a car.

"Yeah, I do." Hailey turned onto the sidewalk that ran along the lakeshore. "I don't particularly like exercising in general, especially running, but biking helps to keep me in shape."

He thought of the bike he'd purchased last summer. He'd only ridden it once, and that had been for a charity ride that a group of the ED doctors had participated in. His butt had hurt for almost a week after a measly twenty-five-mile ride. "I have a bike," he told her. "Maybe once you're off your crutches we can ride together."

She threw him a surprised glance and nodded. "Sure."

The wind kicked up, bringing a cool breeze off the lake. When Hailey shivered, he suggested they turn around and head inside.

Since they were still rather early, they had their

choice of seating. Simon asked for a table overlooking the harbor.

"It's so beautiful," Hailey murmured, staring through the window at the purple and pink sky. He took the crutches from her, propping them against the wall, and then held the chair for her. "Thanks."

"Would you like something to drink?" Simon asked, opening the menu to review the appetizers.

"Just water for me," Hailey said as she read through the menu.

"Not a glass of wine? Or a cocktail?" he asked. Didn't she realize he was trying to make up for his lapse of not asking her out sooner? "I'm driving," he teased.

She frowned and shook her head. "Actually, Simon, I don't drink. At all. And if you don't mind, I'd rather you didn't drink tonight either as you are driving."

Surprised, he stared at her. Was she joking? Surely one drink couldn't hurt either of them. But then he understood. "Because of the accident?"

She stared at her menu for so long he thought she wasn't going to answer him. Finally she dragged her gaze up to his. "Yes. Andrew had had several martinis that night and I could tell he wasn't in any condition to drive, so I told him I would. Unfortunately, he didn't think he was impaired and kept insisting he wanted to drive. We argued, not just in the parking lot but even after he finally gave me the keys and we started driving home." There was a brief pause. "I couldn't let it go."

She looked so stricken his heart went out to her. "And then what happened?"

Her voice had dropped down so low he was forced to lean forward to hear her. "On the way home, a truck came out of nowhere. I was so busy arguing with

Andrew I didn't see the truck until it was too late. He ran a red light, striking the passenger side of our car."

She looked as if she was about to burst into tears. "It's okay, Hailey," he said, reaching across the table to take her hand. He wished they were at home so he could hold her in his arms. "I'm here for you."

"I don't think you understand. Andrew died because of me." Hailey raised her anguished gaze up to his. "Don't you see? If I hadn't argued with him, if I hadn't made such a big deal out of it, he'd be alive right now."

"No, you don't know that," he argued, tightening his grip on her hand when she tried to pull away. "Hailey, listen to me. So you argued. So what? The guy ran a red light! How is that in any way your fault?"

"I didn't see him. I wasn't paying close enough attention to my surroundings," she said.

"And you think if Andrew had been driving, the outcome would have been any better? That's crazy. For sure he wouldn't have been able to pay close attention to his surroundings, not after all those drinks. No, I think if Andrew had been driving, both of you would have probably died."

She was quiet for a long moment. "I've replayed those seconds before the crash over and over in my head. I just can't help thinking I should have seen that red truck sooner."

"And if you had?" he pressed. "Was there really a way to avoid the guy running a red light? Seriously, Hailey, where could you have gone? You had the right of way, didn't you?"

She shrugged helplessly.

He couldn't stand to see her hurting like this. Why had he brought up the painful past? But then a horrible thought occurred to him. "You did have the right of way, correct? I mean, you didn't get a ticket or anything, did you?" he asked cautiously.

"No." Hailey let out a deep heavy sigh. "He got the ticket, not me. But just a few weeks later I heard about another woman who was having an argument in the car and caused a serious accident. She got cited for reckless homicide. Ever since then I've wondered if I got off too easy."

Hailey couldn't believe she'd told Simon her deepest secret, but now that it was out in the open, she couldn't deny feeling relieved.

"Trust me, Hailey, a guy running a red light trumps an argument in the car every time." Simon stroked his thumb over the back of her hand, the caress sending tingles of awareness up her arm. "I heard about that case where the woman was cited for reckless homicide for not paying attention to the road because it made national news, but that was a completely different situation. Don't you see? It wasn't your inattentiveness that caused the accident, the way it did with that woman. The guy who ran the red light broke the law and caused the accident."

She licked her suddenly dry lips. What he was saying did make sense. But she'd lived with the guilt for so long she was afraid to believe. "I wish I could believe that for sure, Simon. Every time I think of that night, I think of how I might have punched the gas pedal, shooting forward enough to avoid the crash if I hadn't been so busy arguing with Andrew about his drinking."

"Don't torture yourself like this," he pleaded. "I'm sorry you had to go through that but you can't feel guilty for the rest of your life. I've felt guilty over things I've done in the past, too, but sometimes I think bad things happen for a reason. Because they teach us a lesson. Or because they somehow make us stronger."

He wasn't telling her anything she hadn't already told herself. Because there were times that she wondered how Andrew would have turned out if he had survived. Would he have continued to drink? Become an alcoholic? Or would he have turned his life around? Could she have helped him?

It was the not knowing that hurt the worst.

But one thing she did know for sure. In her heart, she knew that she and Andrew hadn't been destined to stay together.

"I guess you're right," she agreed slowly. For the first time she considered how the accident might have made her stronger. For one thing, she'd learned how to overcome adversity in a big way.

Was it possible Simon was right? That things happened for a reason?

It occurred to her suddenly that if she hadn't been riding her bike in the thunderstorm because of her fear of driving, she and Simon might not be sitting across from each other right now.

Fate? Maybe.

The waiter interrupted them, asking if they'd decided on what they wanted to order. She was very glad when Simon turned down the happy-hour cocktail two-for-one specials to order the tomato and mozzarella appetizer instead. He also told the waiter to keep their water glasses full.

"Thank you, Simon," she said, after the waiter left.

"For what?" he asked, reaching for her hand again.

"Not drinking," she clarified. "I know I'm probably

overreacting, but after everything that happened with Andrew, I can't help how I feel."

"Hailey, you are far more important to me than a measly drink," he said in a low, husky tone. "Of course I'm going to honor your wishes. Why wouldn't I?"

She had to blink to keep sudden tears from welling up in her eyes. She remembered, with sudden clarity, how she'd pleaded with Andrew to stop after the third martini, especially because his voice had become more boisterous and his gait unsteady, indicating he'd had enough. But he'd brushed aside her concerns as if they'd been unimportant.

She shouldn't doubt her decision not to let Andrew drive. But maybe she should have called for a taxi. Although there was no way of knowing if the taxi would have been hit by the red truck instead.

"Hailey, don't. Please." She glanced at him in surprise. And the expression in his gaze confirmed he knew exactly what was going through her mind. "Don't keep playing the what-if game. It's a game that's impossible to win."

She couldn't help but smile. "You sound like you're speaking from experience."

He nodded, his expression grimly serious. The shadows in his gaze surprised her. "I am. I've played that game too many times to count. And I lost every time."

Because of the fight with his girlfriend that had cost him his career? "Simon, you're not responsible for what's-her-name's actions. Really, what could you have done differently?"

There was a long pause. "Erica," he said finally. "Her name was Erica. And I know I'm not responsible for her actions, but I am responsible for my own."

Before she could ask him what he meant by that,

the waiter brought their appetizer. From there, the conversation turned to food and the choices of possible entrées.

They each decided to try something different and to split the meals to share. Hailey was glad when Simon kept the mood of the evening light.

She couldn't remember the last time she'd had fun spending time with a man. How long since she'd been out on a date? Not since those early months with Andrew.

And she wasn't going to think of her former fiancé now.

For once she was going to be selfish and only think about herself. And Simon.

She was going to learn from her past mistakes and move forward with her life.

"Are you all finished?" he asked, when she set her fork down and pushed her plate away with a sigh.

"Yes, the food was delicious but, honestly, I can't eat another bite."

His plate was, of course, completely empty. "Neither can I. Although I can't decide which meal I liked more. Your swordfish or my veal."

She laughed. "They were both fabulous. And it looks like your mother taught you to always clean up your plate," she teased.

"She did." Simon handed over her crutches when she stood. "My parents chose to retire in Arizona, which is great for them, but unfortunately I don't see them as often as I should."

Secretly pleased he was opening up about his family, she responded in kind. "I don't see my parents much either, but for different reasons. My parents split up when I was young, and I bounced back and forth between households until I was sixteen, when I finally put my foot down and insisted on staying with my mother. It was awkward, especially after they both remarried."

She tensed a bit when Simon rested his hand in the small of her back. The way he was always touching her caught her off guard. Andrew hadn't been one to display overt gestures of affection. She couldn't deny how she loved the way Simon touched her, with the barest hint of possessiveness.

"That must have been difficult for you," Simon murmured as they headed out of the restaurant and back out to his car. "Did both of your parents have more children?"

"Yes," she admitted. "I have three half-brothers and two half-sisters, but they're all much younger than I am."

"I bet that didn't help in making you feel welcome," he said astutely.

She wrinkled her nose. "Yeah, pretty much. Don't get me wrong, it wasn't as if I didn't have a good childhood, because I did. Yet once I moved out to attend college, I knew I'd never go back." Which was why she was teetering on the brink of debt now. Between the car accident and moving to Cedar Bluff to start over, she'd used up the majority of her savings.

Simon drove to her apartment, pulling into the parking lot and then glancing over at her, his expression uncertain. "I had a great time, Hailey, and I have to confess, I'm not ready for the evening to end."

She caught her breath at his frank admission. "I'm not ready for the evening to end, either. Do you want to come up for a bit?"

He stared at her for a long moment. "Yes. And I don't want you to be offended, but I have an overnight kit in the trunk."

Her jaw dropped open in surprise. An overnight kit? So he'd planned to spend the night with her again? She wasn't sure if she should be flattered or upset. So much for thinking that they should slow things down a bit. "I honestly don't know what to say," she admitted.

"Don't be mad," he said, opening the driver's-side door. "I wasn't taking anything for granted, Hailey. I only threw some things together because I was hoping and praying you'd invite me up."

She climbed out of the car and reached into the backseat for her crutches. "And if I hadn't?"

He paused and shrugged. "I would have understood. It's your decision, Hailey. I can't say I wouldn't be disappointed, but if you've changed your mind about this—about us—then I'll leave you alone."

The ball was in her court and for the life of her she couldn't remember why she'd thought it would be best to slow things down. Maybe keeping her relationship with Simon on a professional level at the hospital was more difficult than she'd imagined but wasn't being with him worth the effort?

Did she really want him to leave?

"Please don't go," she said, reaching out to him. He came closer and folded her into a warm embrace.

"Are you sure?" he murmured, trailing a string of hot kisses down the side of her neck. "If you need more time, I'll understand."

More time? Wasn't it a bit late for that? They'd already made love once and she desperately wanted to be with him again. Had she ever felt this insatiable need with Andrew? If she had, she didn't remember it.

Enough of punishing herself for the past. She wanted this. She wanted him.

"I'm sure. Come inside with me, Simon." She flashed him a cheeky grin. "And don't forget your overnight bag."

He held her purse for her as Hailey opened her apartment door and flipped on the lights. Simon followed right behind her, carrying his small duffel bag.

For a moment there he'd prayed he hadn't been overconfident in telling her about the overnight kit he'd packed. Thank heavens Hailey hadn't taken offense.

"I'll, uh, just be a few minutes," she said, heading down the hall toward the bathroom. "Make yourself at home."

He took her at her word, heading into her bedroom, tossing his bag onto the closest chair and setting her purse on the bedside table. In his duffel he had a change of boxers, his shaving gear and, of course, condoms.

Hailey had told him she was on the Pill, but he wasn't about to take anything for granted. Considering he didn't have to work until second shift the next day, he figured—or at least hoped—they could take their time and really enjoy themselves.

When Hailey emerged ten minutes later, dressed in a filmy nightgown that was so sheer it gave him an enticing view of her breasts, he nearly swallowed his tongue.

How had he gotten so lucky? Hailey was beautiful, sweet, sexy, smart and funny.

The whole package. Everything he'd always wanted in a woman. And more. For the first time in years he realized he could trust his gut instincts about her.

She wasn't Erica. Not by a long shot.

"You're so beautiful," he said as he crossed over to

meet her. He tossed the crutches aside and gathered her into his arms. Lifting her up, he carried her to bed.

"So are you," she murmured, kissing his neck in a way that made him groan. She tugged at his shirt. "But I think you're overdressed."

"I think so too." He set her down and then quickly stripped off his clothes. As he joined her in bed, her cell phone rang.

"Ignore it," he whispered, suckling a rosy-tipped breast.

She gasped and arched beneath his kiss. "Okay."

He lifted up the sheer fabric, desperate to see all of her. Every glorious inch. And when her cell phone started ringing again, he swore under his breath and levered up to grab her purse with the phone inside and hand it to her. "Shut it off," he said huskily.

She chuckled and dug the cell phone out. She glanced at the screen. "That's odd," she murmured.

"What?" he could barely hide his impatience. He didn't care who was calling, he wanted to make love to Hailey. Now. Without any more interruptions.

"Both calls are from an unknown number," she said as she shut off the cell phone.

He froze, a chill running down the length of his spine. He swiftly took the phone from her hand, turned it back on and stared down at the screen.

The familiar words screamed at him.

Unknown number? Just like the non-stop hang-ups at both his home phone and his cell phone?

Dread twisted in his gut like a snake. This couldn't be a coincidence. All the calls had to be from the same person.

CHAPTER THIRTEEN

"SIMON?" Hailey put a hand on his arm. "What is it? What's wrong?"

He pulled his gaze up from the phone to look at her. What should he tell her? He couldn't be certain who the unknown caller was. Maybe the same telemarketers that hounded him were bothering everyone that owned a cell phone.

But even as the thought formed, he knew he was lying to himself. There was no way the caller was a random telemarketer.

Two years. He'd been in Cedar Bluff for *two years*. Surely Erica had moved on by now. No woman in her right mind would keep trying to track someone down for two years.

But then again he couldn't say Erica had ever been in her right mind. She was far from emotionally stable.

His fault. This was all his fault.

"Simon?" Hailey said again. "Tell me what's wrong."

He slowly shook his head, knowing he couldn't do that. He couldn't explain and he definitely couldn't stay to make love with Hailey.

"I'm sorry." Regretfully, he pulled the sheet up to cover her bare breasts, before rolling off the bed and reaching for his discarded boxers. "I can't."

"What? You're leaving? *Now?*" Her incredulous tone made him wince and he felt a hundred times worse than she could ever know.

He was screwing this up badly, and he knew it. But he needed to know if he was just being paranoid or if it was even remotely possible that Erica was the one calling him.

Calling Hailey.

The hairs on the back of his neck lifted and the sick feeling in his gut twisted to the point that he almost doubled over in agony. How could Erica even know about Hailey? Even if she'd found his address and his phone number, he'd never once taken Hailey to his place.

Was Erica following him again? The way she had back in Chicago? And if so, why suddenly start calling Hailey?

Was she going to start stalking Hailey the way she'd continually come after him? And ruin her career as well?

The very thought made him want to slam his fist through the wall. None of this was Hailey's fault. None of it! Dammit, hadn't he suffered enough? What more did Erica want from him?

Whatever it was, maybe he deserved it, he thought with a tired sigh. But Hailey sure as hell didn't.

He glanced at Hailey, knowing he'd do anything to protect her. Because this was his mess to clean up, not hers. He needed to put an end to Erica's out-of-control behavior once and for all.

"I'm sorry," he said again, as he finished pulling on his clothes. "But I can't do this."

She wasn't about to let him off the hook so easily. "What can't you do? This? Us? Our relationship? Talk to me, Simon. You're not making any sense.

I'm sure whatever the problem is, we can work it out. Together."

He reached for his duffel, steeling himself against the need to tell her everything. He shouldn't have let things go this far. Not until he'd dealt with Erica. Dragging Hailey into the mix wasn't fair.

How had he even thought he could have a future without settling the past, once and for all?

"I'm sorry," he repeated. "But I can't do this Hailey." Not yet anyway, he thought to himself.

Her gaze narrowed. "You're breaking up with me? Again? Just like that?"

"Yes." He forced himself to look her directly in the eye and lie. "This isn't working for me. I can't see you any more." The words felt like they had been wrenched out of him, each one more hurtful than the one before. But he was doing this to protect her. Because none of this was her fault.

"But—"

"Let's not make this worse than it already is. I made a mistake. I have to go." While she gaped at him, he quickly left, before she could say anything else.

And before he changed his mind.

Stunned, Hailey stared at the doorway long after Simon had closed it behind him.

Her thoughts swirled, a chaotic mass of confusion. What had she done to push him away? What had caused Simon to swing from one extreme to the other?

He was the one who'd taken her out to dinner. He was the one who'd told her he didn't want the evening to end.

He was the one who'd packed an overnight bag!

Her heart squeezed in her chest, his words echoing over and over in her mind.

I made a mistake.

None of it made sense, but the loss devastated her. She buried her face in her hands, fighting tears.

She'd fallen in love with Simon. Forgiving herself for the accident had given her the freedom to fall in love. She loved Simon with a depth that she hadn't felt for Andrew.

But obviously Simon didn't feel the same way.

The ringing of her cell phone interrupted her pity-party. Sniffling, she reached for the instrument that Simon had tossed on the bed, suddenly hopeful. Was he calling her back to apologise? To explain he hadn't meant what he'd said?

Unknown number was displayed on her screen. Annoyed, she pushed the button to answer the call. "Hello?"

No response. But she could tell someone was on the other end of the line because she could hear breathing.

"Hello?" she said again. "Who is this?"

Still no response. She was just about to hang up when she finally heard a soft voice say, "Stay away from him."

"What?" Hailey wasn't sure she'd heard the female caller correctly. At least, she thought it was a female caller. "Who is this? What do you want?"

"Stay away from him. Or else…"

The softly spoken warning sent a fissure of apprehension down her spine. "Or else what? Are you threatening me?"

She listened intently, but all she could hear was the sound of a dial tone buzzing loudly in her ear.

The caller had hung up.

Hailey flipped her phone shut, feeling more confused than ever. She'd never in her life been threatened. Stay away from him? From who? Simon?

Of course Simon. And suddenly she knew why Simon had left so abruptly. Why he'd broken up with her out of nowhere.

Because he knew who the unknown caller was.

His former girlfriend, Erica. The one who'd cost him his promising career at Children First in Chicago.

Erica must be here in Cedar Bluff. And she clearly wanted Simon back or she wouldn't have warned Hailey to stay away from him.

But the question remained. What did Simon want? Had he left her because he planned to go back to Erica?

Or because he'd given up on personal relationships for good?

Simon had stewed about the problem of Erica all night. And first thing in the morning, he'd known what he needed to do.

So he'd driven straight to the Cedar Bluff police station. But he hadn't gone in. Instead, he sat in the parking lot, inwardly debating the best course of action.

He closed his eyes and pressed his fingertips against his pounding temples. He knew his story would sound crazy. Totally nuts. Not to mention he had absolutely no proof, other than his gut instincts telling him that Erica had found him.

What could the police do with an unknown number? Probably not a hell of a lot.

Years ago, when he'd first realized Erica's attachment had grown to the level of stalking, he'd shied away from involving the authorities. Partially because he felt like an idiot. He'd been stupid enough to go out with her in the first place. And, besides, what guy couldn't handle a woman who'd become a little too attached? He'd thought he'd had everything under control. His pride had prevented him from asking for help. Instead, he'd kept trying to reason with her, over and over again.

But that approach hadn't worked.

So he'd simply done his best to avoid her, hoping the situation would resolve on its own. That she'd get tired of harassing him, coming over to confront him. Calling him.

And when that hadn't worked either, he'd picked up and moved his entire life, breaking off all his friendships, not telling anyone other than his parents where he'd gone. Cedar Bluff had been the perfect place to start over. Small enough and remote enough that Erica would never find him.

Maybe he should have called the police. But even then he'd known that Erica might have been arrested. And considering her fragile state, emotionally and physically, wasn't that adding insult to injury?

But now, two years later, the situation was well beyond the level of a nuisance.

For Hailey's sake, he needed to report it.

With renewed resolve he climbed from his car and strode into the police station. The place was buzzing with activity. He asked to speak to one of the detectives, and was taken over to a small office no bigger than a broom closet.

Detective Arnold had listened attentively while he'd explained the entire situation from start to finish. Even to his own ears, the story sounded unbelievable.

At least the detective hadn't laughed at him.

"So you think this unknown caller is this woman who's tracked you down over the course of two years?" Arnold said, summarizing his story in one sentence.

"Yeah. I do."

"Have you seen her in Cedar Bluff?" Detective Arnold asked.

"No. But I haven't seriously looked for her either," he admitted. Erica was pretty enough, with her shoulder-length dark brown hair and hazel eyes. She was rather tiny in stature, only five feet two inches tall and as thin as a rail. She wouldn't stand out as noticeable in the crowd unless you were looking for her.

The detective scratched his chin. "I guess we'll have to assume she's here somewhere. Unfortunately, women change their hair color on a whim, so your description of her isn't likely to do us any good. Maybe you've seen her but you just didn't recognize her?"

"Maybe." Simon had racked his brain all night, trying to think of anyone he'd seen around his neighborhood who looked even remotely like Erica. There hadn't been anyone who'd even come close to fitting her description.

He'd wondered if Erica was working at Cedar Bluff, and had called the human resource office, asking about her, but he'd confirmed there were no nurses working at the hospital with that name. It wasn't likely Erica could fake a nursing license.

But maybe she was working in a nearby nursing home?

"We can put a trace on your home phone number," Arnold said, interrupting his thoughts. "But other than that, there isn't much we can do. You might want to consider changing your phone numbers."

Simon stared at the detective, his worst fears coming

to fruition. "You need to understand, this woman is emotionally unbalanced. And she's calling Hailey Rogers, the woman I'm—er—was dating."

Arnold spread his hands helplessly. "Until you can give me something more to go on—a car, a place where you think she's staying, something concrete—there's nothing more I can do."

"What about searching all the hospitals, clinics and nursing homes in the area to see if she's working there as a nurse?"

The detective tapped his pencil on the table, looking thoughtful. Then he jotted down a few notes and slowly nodded. "Yeah, I can make a few phone calls. But in the meantime I suggest you pay attention to your surroundings. My guess is that she's somewhere close by, watching you."

Yeah. That's exactly what he was afraid of. Simon let his breath out in a heavy sigh. "Okay, thanks. If I do see her, I'll be sure to let you know."

"You do that," Arnold said as Simon stood and walked toward the door. "And you might want to warn your lady-friend, too."

Simon paused, swinging back to face the detective as the implication of that statement took a moment to sink into his brain.

Arnold was right. He shouldn't have left Hailey without explaining what was going on. If Erica had gone so far as to call Hailey, there was no telling what else she'd do. He'd been so panicked by the thought of Hailey being affected by this mess that he hadn't been thinking clearly.

"I will. Please let me know if you find anything out about Erica, too."

"I'll be in touch."

Satisfied he'd done what he could, Simon left the police station and walked outside into the bright sunlight. He paused and slid his sunglasses on, sweeping a gaze around to see if he saw anyone. Of course there was no one in sight. Shaking his head at his stupidity, he slid into the driver's seat of his car and headed back to the other side of town, toward Hailey's apartment building.

He needed to take the detective's advice to warn Hailey.

Simon pulled into the parking lot of Hailey's apartment building, once again glancing around curiously as he walked up to the door.

Being on edge like this was already driving him nuts. He pushed the buzzer for Hailey's apartment and waited for her to respond.

He hit the buzzer again and again, still with no response. The manager of the apartment building came out to get his newspaper, saw Simon standing there and opened the door. "Can I help you?"

"Have you seen Hailey Rogers in apartment 211?" Simon asked.

"She left about twenty minutes ago, wearing scrubs, so I think she was planning to go to work," the elder man informed him.

"Okay, thanks." Simon headed back out to his car, glancing at his watch. Ten in the morning. How long would it take her to walk to the bus stop? Would she still be there?

He drove the couple of blocks to the bus stop, disappointed to find that Hailey wasn't sitting there, waiting. Maybe she was already at the hospital. For all he knew, she'd gone in early.

He relaxed, the tension easing out of his shoulders. The hospital was probably the safest place for Hailey right now. At least at work she was surrounded by plenty of people.

Besides, he sincerely doubted Erica would go as far as to attempt to harm Hailey. More likely she'd just continue to call her, doing nothing more than being a general pain in the ass. Erica was obsessed with him, not with Hailey.

He pulled over to the curb and called the hospital, asking to speak with Theresa. When the emergency department manager answered the phone, he quickly identified himself. "I hate to bother you, but would you mind telling me what time Hailey came in this morning?" he asked. "I want to come in to work on some paperwork, but wanted to wait until Hailey was finished with my office."

"Ah, sure, let me see what time she swiped in." He could hear the click of the keyboard as Theresa worked on the computer. "I'm sorry, Simon, but Hailey hasn't punched in for her shift yet."

"Oh, okay." Now he really felt like an idiot. "I must have just missed her. Sorry to bother you."

"No problem. Bye, Simon."

He snapped his phone shut and drove home. He had a few hours yet before he needed to pick up Hailey from work. In the meantime, he planned to make a few phone calls himself.

Maybe he'd find Erica before Detective Arnold did.

After a restless night of broken sleep, Hailey had decided to go into work early, so that she could get her four hours of light-duty work out of the way before she confronted Simon.

It wasn't until she'd arrived at the hospital that she'd realized she wasn't sure what to work on as she'd been doing his quality review project.

She walked over to Theresa's office, poking her head in just as she hung up the phone. "Theresa? Do you have the list of chart audits you wanted for the joint commission?"

"Hailey, you startled me." Theresa put a hand over her heart. "That was Simon on the phone, asking if you were here. I told him you hadn't punched in yet."

Was Simon checking up on her? Because he was concerned about her? Hope lightened her heavy heart. "Really? Did he ask to talk to me?"

"No, he just wanted to know what hours you were working so he'd know when he could get into his office." Theresa rummaged around on the messy piles of paper scattered across her desk. "Here's the list. Do you have a key to Simon's office?"

"No, I don't." She took the list of charts, stung by the knowledge that Simon wasn't concerned. Rather, he was trying to avoid her. "But it's no big deal, I'll find somewhere else to work."

"Okay. Good work on the quality reviews, by the way," Theresa said as she turned to leave. "Simon showed me your results and I think you're right on. We're going to discuss the signs and symptoms of sepsis at the next staff meeting. And Simon has already sent the same message out to all the physicians."

"Great, I'm glad I could help." Despite her sorrow over her break-up with Simon, Hailey was pleased that she'd been able to contribute to the unit, even in a small way.

"You have. And if you get all those audits done too, I'll be grateful. We expect the joint commission to show up in the next few weeks. If there are gaps in our documentation, I'd like to know about it now."

Hailey smiled. "I'll get them done," she promised.

When she walked out to the arena, the activity level was as high as usual. Remembering the last time she'd tried to work in the midst of the chaos, she decided to find the quietest work station she could.

She settled on the tiny computer workstation that was usually used by the ED educator. Since Joanne wasn't around, she figured no one would care if she used it. She could always move if Joanne needed her computer.

The chart audits were painstakingly slow, much worse than the quality reviews she'd completed for Simon. Her mind kept wandering, replaying those moments when Simon had broken things off. The more she thought about it, the more she became determined to confront him about his actions.

She realized, she hadn't really confronted Andrew about his actions until that fateful night. And, really, his drinking had been bothering her for weeks before that.

She needed to learn from her past mistakes once and for all. Why wait? The sooner she could talk to Simon, the sooner she could get to the bottom of what was going on. Besides, she was exhausted. Her lack of sleep was already causing her eyes to burn with gritty fatigue, the words on the computer screen reduced to a senseless blur.

She rubbed her eyes and pushed away the keyboard. There was no point in trying to work today. Not until she'd ironed out this issue with Simon. She could make up the hours tomorrow, as long as she didn't go over the amount that Theresa had approved.

Satisfied, she felt energised by her course of action. She would find Simon, and she would confront him about Erica. It couldn't be a coincidence that the moment her phone had rung, he'd suddenly changed his mind about being with her.

He must have broken things off because he was avoiding relationships altogether. But it was too late. They were already in a relationship.

She just needed to make him see that as well.

She walked into the female staff locker room to get her purse. Leaning on her crutches, she quickly opened her locker, took out her purse and shut the door.

When she turned, Mary, the unit clerk with the bleach blonde spiky hair and the freaky green eyes, was standing in front of the door. Hailey was surprised as she hadn't heard her come in. "Hi, Mary. What's up?"

The clerk stared at her across the room, without smiling. "I tried to warn you. You should have stayed away from him."

Dear heaven. A sick feeling curled in her stomach as realisation dawned. "Erica?"

"Yes. My real name is Erica. Mary is my sister. She let me borrow her identity so I could get this job. Wasn't that nice of her?"

Hailey stared at the woman blocking the doorway, all the seemingly insignificant details suddenly falling into place. "You bumped Bonnie, causing her to spill water in my lap on purpose," she accused. "Did you take the report from Simon's desk? And leave water on the floor? That last stunt was risky—you're lucky I didn't seriously hurt myself."

"I tried to warn you." Mary's expression didn't show

one iota of remorse. "You were supposed to stay away from Simon."

Hailey sucked in a harsh breath when Mary, or rather Erica, reached behind to lock the door.

CHAPTER FOURTEEN

HAILEY swallowed nervously and watched Erica warily, trying to assess her options. The woman was blocking the doorway, but surely there was no reason to panic. Someone would come into the locker room sooner or later. Erica couldn't possibly keep her locked in here indefinitely.

Could she?

Obviously, this woman had seen her and Simon together. All the way back to that day he'd hit her bicycle and had then had stayed by her side, holding her hand.

She almost winced, realizing how much that would have bothered Erica.

But she wasn't going to apologise. Not for being with Simon. Or for loving him.

"What do you want, Erica?" Hailey finally asked, leaning heavily on her crutches. Maybe she could bluff her way out of this mess. "You want me to stay away from Simon? Okay, fine. He broke up with me anyway, so you have nothing to worry about."

Erica's blank, emotionless expression was eerie, to say the least. She just kept staring, acting as if she hadn't heard a word Hailey said. The weirdness of the entire situation was starting to get to her.

"Did you hear me?" Hailey said impatiently, in an

attempt to break through the other woman's iron mask of indifference. "Simon is all yours! Take him with my blessing."

Another long pause. "We had a baby together. Did you know that? Did Simon tell you about our son?"

A son? Hailey couldn't prevent her jaw from dropping in shock. A baby? Simon hadn't said a word about a baby. "No, I'm afraid he didn't."

Erica reached into her scrub pocket, pulling out a small photograph. She smoothed the crumpled edges with her fingertips in a slow, overly deliberate way that suggested she performed the task often. "I have a picture. Do you want to see him?"

Hailey almost started to shake her head as she was still struggling with the idea of Simon and this woman having a baby together, but she sensed that making Erica more upset wasn't going to help. She'd already pretended she didn't care one bit about Simon. Maybe she needed to play along with this, too.

The sooner this poor woman got everything out of her system, the sooner they'd get out of the claustrophobic locker room. "Sure."

Erica held up the photograph. It was a grainy picture of a sonogram with the barest outline of a fetus. "See? Isn't he beautiful?"

"Ah, yes. He is. Beautiful," Hailey murmured, glancing briefly down at Erica's non-pregnant stomach. Was it remotely possible Erica was pregnant now? No, more likely she'd been pregnant in the past while she'd gone out with Simon.

Nothing in the world would make her believe Simon had been with Erica three months ago.

"His name is Joshua, just like Simon's father." Erica

turned the photograph around and stared at it again for several long minutes. "Joshua Simon Carter," she murmured.

The way Erica was talking about the fetus, as if it were still alive, gave her the creeps. "That's a wonderful name. I'm sure Simon was very proud."

"Yes." She carefully tucked the photo in the pocket of her scrubs.

"Does Simon know you're here?" Hailey asked cautiously. "Have you spoken to him?"

"Not yet." A scowl crossed her features but then disappeared so quickly Hailey wondered if she'd imagined it. "He didn't recognize me because I've changed my hair color, eye color and padded my underwear. But I know he'll be glad to see me once he realizes it's me."

Hailey wasn't sure what to say about that. Her only option at this point was to agree with Erica, no matter how much she wanted to stake a claim in Simon for herself. "I'm sure he will."

"I'm glad you understand. Because Simon and I are going to have another baby together. To make up for the son we lost."

"I'm sorry for your loss, Erica." Hailey couldn't imagine how awful it must have been for Erica to lose the baby she'd obviously wanted very much. No wonder the woman had gone a little crazy. Could she really blame her?

"Oh, yes." Surprisingly, Erica nodded, and pulled out a syringe filled with a clear substance topped with a needle. "I do believe you will be sorry, Hailey. Very sorry that you had the audacity to come between me and Simon."

* * *

Simon spent a good two hours trying to find out if Erica was working as a nurse somewhere close to Cedar Bluff. But he soon gave up in frustration.

Because the more he spoke to the various human resources departments of the medical facilities he'd pinpointed as possibilities within a thirty-mile radius, the more he believed he was searching in vain.

What if Erica wasn't working as a nurse, especially since she'd need to go through the hassle of obtaining a Wisconsin nursing license? Erica could just as easily be working in some other capacity.

Hell, she could be a waitress or bartender for all he knew.

He glanced at his phone, wishing the detective would call with some news. And when he found himself glancing at the clock for the tenth time in half as many minutes, he gave up any pretense of working. He headed out to his car, determined to go to Cedar Bluff hospital to find Hailey.

He really needed to tell her the entire story about Erica. Something he should have done a long time ago.

When he arrived at the hospital, he strode quickly through the arena, searching for Hailey amidst the chaos. His office door was closed, and he grimaced as he realized he hadn't given Hailey his key.

He caught sight of Theresa and hurried over. "Where's Hailey?"

"I don't know, Simon. She was here a couple of hours ago. It seems our new unit clerk disappeared too, so if you find Hailey, see if she's willing to sit and answer phones for a while."

"Where was she working?" he asked, glancing

around again, not seeing her at any of the workstations in the arena.

"Honestly, I have no clue." Theresa flashed him a harried smile before crossing over to answer a ringing phone. "Emergency Department, may I help you?"

He couldn't believe he'd missed Hailey. By his estimation, she should have at least another hour and a half of work yet to complete her allotted four hours. Perplexed, he crossed over to the locker room, thinking she was taking a break. When he tried the handle, he discovered the door was locked. "Hailey? Are you in there?"

"Simon?" He thought he heard Hailey cry out his name, but then there was the sound of a scuffle followed by a loud thud.

"Hailey!" Extremely worried now, he pounded on the door and tried the door handle again. "Open up!"

"I'm sorry, Simon." A sing-song voice that definitely wasn't Hailey. "I'm afraid Hailey is indisposed at the moment. You'll have to settle for me."

In that second he remembered what Theresa had said about the unit clerk disappearing. The new one? What was her name? Mary? With the bleached blonde short spiky hair? And the colored contact lenses?

No, not Mary. Erica. Dammit, he should have figured it out, despite the drastic differences. He'd never looked twice at the unit clerk, honestly hadn't paid the woman the least bit of attention.

He never should have assumed, even for a moment, that Erica would take a job somewhere else rather than here at the hospital.

He pulled out his cell phone and called Detective Arnold. Thankfully, the detective answered on the first ring. "Erica's here at Cedar Bluff hospital and she has Hailey locked in the woman's locker room."

"I'll send a team right away."

Simon snapped his phone shut and tried to think of what to do next. He wasn't going to attempt to reason with Erica, since that had never worked in the past. Better to find Theresa and someone from Security.

He had to get a key for the locker room.

"Simon? Are you still out there?" Erica called.

He'd managed to flag down Theresa, without going too far away. "Get Security up here with a master key, stat," he whispered urgently. In a louder voice he responded to Erica. "Yes, Erica, I'm here. Why don't you open the door so we can talk?"

"I told Hailey all about our son, Simon. She understands why you can't stay with her now."

This was nothing he hadn't heard before, but somehow knowing Hailey was locked inside made the entire situation much worse. Erica's miscarriage had been awful. He'd mourned the loss of their baby, too. He never should have left the birth-control responsibility to Erica alone. And then the miscarriage had sent Erica over the edge.

In the past, whenever Erica had talked crazily like this, he'd gently tried to ground her in reality.

But right now it seemed better to play along. No matter how much it pained him. "I broke up with Hailey," he told Erica. "I'm ready to get back together with you. Open the door, Erica. Please?"

"You are?" The cautious hopefulness in Erica's tone made him feel lower than sludge for raising her hopes, even for a moment. "Really?"

He closed his eyes and rested his forehead on the cold wooden door. "Yes. Open up, Erica. You don't need Hailey. Let's go away and talk, just the two of us. Alone."

Erica didn't respond right away, and he was getting more and more worried, especially when he couldn't hear Hailey. What had happened in there? Where in the hell was Security with that master key?

The seconds ticked by with excruciating slowness until finally a tall, dark-haired security officer came up behind him, waving a key.

Simon put a finger up to his lips, indicating the security guard should remain silent. The guy nodded to indicate he understood. Slowly, he slid the key into the lock.

The guard met his gaze questioningly, and Simon nodded. "Go!"

The guard twisted the key and threw his weight into the act of opening the door in case Erica had blocked it with something heavy on the other side. The door opened surprisingly easily, but when he came in behind the security guard, he saw Hailey crumpled on the floor, her casted leg stuck out at an awkward angle.

"Simon!" Erica cried as she rushed toward him.

Thankfully the security guard caught her before she reached Simon and quickly grabbed hold of her wrists. "Ma'am, you need to come with me."

"No!" Erica screamed, struggling against the security guard. "Simon!"

He flicked her a brief glance, feeling nothing but pity for her, before he knelt beside Hailey. "Hailey? Wake up, honey. Are you all right?"

At the sound of his voice, her eyelids fluttered open. She tried to say something, but he couldn't make it out. Her eyelids drifted back down.

Had she hit her head? He was about to lift her head

to examine it for wounds when he spied the needle and syringe on the floor.

Dear God. *Erica had drugged Hailey!*

Simon sat beside Hailey's bedside, his head bowed over their clasped hands, listening to the reassuring sounds of the dialysis machine and the heart monitor beeping over her head. Jadon had told him she'd be fine, but he wouldn't believe it until she woke up.

Detective Arnold had arrived and arrested Erica. Simon knew he should have gotten the police involved much earlier.

Like two years ago, when she'd vandalised his car.

And had started following him everywhere, calling him day and night. Begging to have another baby with him.

His stupid pride had nearly cost Hailey her life. Erica had given her enough of the drug to stop her breathing. Luckily, they'd caught her before her respiratory rate had fallen too low.

He never should have left her last night. Hailey hadn't done anything wrong. She didn't deserve this.

When Hailey stirred, tugging at his hand, his head shot up, his gaze searching her face. "Hailey? Are you all right?"

"Simon?" she frowned and glanced around the room in confusion. "Where am I?"

One side effect of Versed, the drug Erica had used, was an amnesic affect. "You're in the hospital, getting dialysis. Do you remember being locked in with Erica?"

Instantly her confusion cleared. "Yes." With her free hand she reached for a cup of water, taking a long sip before resting back against the pillow with a sigh. "She told me about the baby."

Cautiously, he nodded. "I didn't know she was pregnant when I broke off our relationship, Hailey. She was so clingy, so needy, constantly going wherever I was, calling me non-stop. But I swear to you I didn't know she was pregnant. And when she told me she was expecting our child, I agreed to support her and the baby financially. I wanted to be a part of my child's life. But she would settle for nothing less than marriage."

He paused as memories of the past clouded his mind. Especially the deep fear that Erica would take off with his child and disappear. "When I told her I wasn't going to marry her, she went a little crazy. She took a steel-pronged rake to my car, gouging the hell out of it. I should have called the police then, but she was pregnant with my child. I couldn't do that to her. Not when her pregnancy was as much my responsibility as hers. So instead I kept trying to reason with her, even though she kept insisting that we had to be a family." He scrubbed a hand over his face in a weak attempt to erase the past.

"What happened then?" Hailey asked.

"I was working when she called me, completely hysterical, crying because she was bleeding." For several seconds he stared at their clasped hands, before dragging his resigned gaze up to hers. "She lost the baby. I couldn't believe how much that loss hurt. Yet as bad as I felt about losing the baby, I can't deny I was also a little bit relieved. For her sake, more than anything. I figured losing the baby was somehow meant to be. I thought she'd be able to move on with her life. Make a fresh start. But unfortunately losing the baby only pushed her further over the edge of sanity."

"So she started stalking you."

Even now, after all this time, he shied away from the ugly term. But he couldn't deny the truth. Lying to himself about the seriousness of Erica's obsession was how Hailey had ended up on the wrong side of a hospital bed.

"Yeah. She began stalking me. Kept showing up at my house, at work, at the gym, begging me to take her back, to make another baby." He sighed. "It was awful. After the big scene in the middle of the emergency department, when she literally attacked me physically, I took the easy way out. I packed my gear, quit my job and moved out of Chicago." At the time he'd thought he was doing the right thing. "But what I should have done was reported her to the police. I'm sorry, Hailey. I'm so sorry you had to go through that."

"Yeah, I wouldn't recommend it." She gave a wry smile and shifted restlessly on the bed. "But you know—I don't hate Erica. I actually felt sorry for her, Simon."

He couldn't hide his surprise. "Even after she locked you up and drugged you?"

Hailey grimaced. "Well, not that part so much. But I'm sure losing the baby was hard on her. And I think, in her own way, she really did love you."

Simon slowly shook his head. "No, you're wrong about that, Hailey. She was only in love with some fabricated image of what she wanted me to be. That's one of the things I regret the most. I knew, almost from the beginning, that things weren't going to work out between us, but I allowed our relationship to get intimate. That was one of my biggest mistakes."

"Don't torture yourself, Simon," Hailey murmured, turning his own words to her during their dinner at

Stephen's against him. "You can't play the what-if game, remember?"

He refused to be sidetracked. "I'm surprised you don't resent Erica for what she's done. You're an amazing woman, Hailey."

"You're not so bad yourself, Simon," she said, flashing a sleepy smile, her eyelids sliding closed.

He loosened his grip on her hand, intending to leave her to recover in peace, but her eyes flew open the moment he let go. "Where are you going?"

"I thought maybe you'd rather be alone." He wouldn't blame her for not wanting to see him, a constant reminder of the horror she'd gone through.

She clung to his hand, her glassy gaze focused on his. "Were you serious last night, when you said our relationship was over?"

His heart swelled with hope at the uncertainty in her gaze. "No, Hailey. That was just a misguided attempt to spare you from all this…" He waved a hand in disgust. He tried to read her facial expression. "Are you telling me that after everything that's happened, you're still willing to give me a second chance?"

"Do you want a second chance?" she asked, instead of answering his question.

"Yes, Hailey. God yes." He pulled her hand up and pressed a kiss in the center of her palm. "When I saw you lying on the floor, I was afraid I hadn't arrived in time." He took a deep breath and decided to bare his soul. "I love you, Hailey. More than you can possibly know."

Her eyes widened at his declaration. "You do?"

"Yes. I do." Just saying the words gave him a sense of freedom. For too long he'd refused to let anyone get close. Had been afraid of commitment. And the possibility of a family.

Now, Hailey could never be close enough. "I think I knew, right from the start, that we were meant to be together. But I understand if you need time to get used to the idea," he added when she didn't say anything more. "Take as much time as you need. But know this, Hailey. I'll be ready and waiting for you, no matter how long it takes. I'm in this for the long haul. There's no rush. We have plenty of time."

Hell, was he babbling?

He seriously needed to get a grip.

"That's very sweet, Simon, but I don't need any time. I already know how I feel." Her mouth curved into a sweet smile and yet he found himself holding his breath, almost afraid to hope. "I love you, too."

"Oh, Hailey." He bent over the bed and gathered her as close as the dialysis machine would allow. He buried his face in her hair, knowing he was the luckiest man alive. "You've forgiven me way too easily."

She let out a muffled laugh. "Oh, yeah? Are you complaining?"

"Never," he vowed. "I swear I'll make it up to you."

"Ah, Simon." She lifted her face and gently kissed him. "Don't you know? You already have."

EPILOGUE

HAILEY rejoiced with a little skip as she started up the steps to her apartment on the second floor, her first time since getting the bulky cast off her leg.

Freedom! Who would have thought that walking up stairs could be so fabulous?

Her cell phone rang and she knew the caller was Simon before she glanced at the screen. He'd already surprised her with a brand-new bicycle, to replace the one he'd crunched under his bumper. She'd taken her first ride on it today, while he was finishing up his day shift.

"Hi, Simon."

"Hailey, we're celebrating tonight, so put on your dancing shoes and be ready by six."

Even though he couldn't see her, she raised her hand in a mock salute. "Yes, sir."

He chuckled. "Okay, sorry. I didn't mean that to sound like an order."

"I know." She giggled as she put the key in her lock and opened her apartment door. "Don't worry. I'll be ready by six. Where are you taking me?"

"It's a surprise."

Her grin widened. "I love surprises." And she had a surprise for Simon too. She was ready to get behind the wheel of a car. She'd been practicing, without his knowing. She couldn't wait to tell him.

Hailey took her time, lingering in a bubble bath that was nothing short of heavenly. Her right leg looked a little pale and small compared to her left, but she didn't care. She pulled on the slinkiest red dress she owned and was ready and waiting when Simon showed up.

He whistled when he saw her, frank admiration in his gaze. "You look amazing."

"Thanks, so do you." His dark shirt and slacks were casually elegant. He was by far the most handsome guy in the universe, in her opinion.

Simon drove to a restaurant on the outskirts of town, and she could hear the band playing from the parking lot. The thought of dancing with Simon made her pulse skip with excitement.

She barely had time to put her purse on the chair before he was tugging on her hand, drawing her out onto the dance floor. She would have sworn he'd paid the guy off, because the music immediately slowed to an intimate pace. When he stroked his hand down her back, lingering low on her waist, she shivered.

They danced three songs in a row, before he deemed it break time and escorted her over to a cozy table off to the side.

She tensed, just for a moment, when the waiter came over, but once again, Simon told him they'd stick with water. "Go ahead and bring out the first course," he said.

The waiter bowed and disappeared.

She flashed him a mock frown. "What's the first course? Don't I have a choice as to what I want to eat?"

Simon shrugged. "You always have a choice, Hailey.

Wait to see what it is first, and if you don't like it, we'll send it back to the kitchen for something else."

She sighed, reminding herself that she loved surprises. She took a sip of her water, gazing at Simon. He was so handsome he made her heart ache. The past five weeks with him had been wonderful.

"Thank you, Simon. This is the perfect way to celebrate getting my cast off."

"You're welcome, Hailey."

At that moment, the waiter came out with one silver-dome-covered tray that he set in front of Hailey.

"Don't you get one?" she asked.

Simon gave a tiny shake of his head, his gaze surprisingly wary. "I'll share yours."

The waiter paused dramatically, and then lifted the cover. Instead of a mouth-watering appetizer, a small black velvet ring box sat on the middle of the plate.

She sucked in a quick breath, raising a shocked gaze to Simon. "What is this?"

He looked tense, his gaze searching hers as he said, "Open it."

With fingers that threatened to tremble, she picked up the box and opened it. A beautiful emerald-cut diamond glittered inside. "Oh, Simon!"

"Hailey, will you marry me?"

Tears threatened, and she blinked them away furiously. They'd only been together for six weeks, but she didn't for one minute doubt her feelings for him.

Or his feelings for her.

"Yes, Simon. I'd be honored." And since she wasn't hampered by her cast any longer, she picked up the ring and jumped up from the table, and went over to wrap her arms around him in an exuberant hug.

He took the ring and slid it onto the third finger of her

left hand. "Come on," he murmured, nudging her once again toward the dance floor where the music instantly turned to a slow, romantic number. He'd definitely paid off the band leader.

"I'd like to dance with my fiancée," he murmured softly, nuzzling her ear.

"For the rest of our lives," Hailey agreed with a sigh as she rose up on her tiptoes and captured his mouth in a heartfelt kiss.

DOCTOR: DIAMOND IN THE ROUGH

BY
LUCY CLARK

MILLS & BOON

First published in Great Britain 2011
Harlequin Mills & Boon Limited,
Eton House, 18-24 Paradise Road, Richmond, Surrey TW9 1SR

© Anne and Peter Clark 2011

ISBN: 978 0 263 88576 7

Harlequin Mills & Boon policy is to use papers that are natural, renewable and recyclable products and made from wood grown in sustainable forests. The logging and manufacturing process conform to the legal environmental regulations of the country of origin.

Printed and bound in Spain
by Litografia Rosés, S.A., Barcelona

Lucy Clark is actually a husband-and-wife writing team. They enjoy taking holidays with their children, during which they discuss and develop new ideas for their books using the fantastic Australian scenery. They use their daily walks to talk over characterisation and fine details of the wonderful stories they produce, and are avid movie buffs. They live on the edge of a popular wine district in South Australia with their two children, and enjoy spending family time together at weekends.

Recent books by the same author:

THE DOCTOR AND SOCIETY'S SWEETHEART
THE DOCTOR'S DOUBLE TROUBLE
A BABY FOR THE FLYING DOCTOR

For my wonderful mother—Glenda—
who is a constant source of support and inspiration
and who fervently hopes that one day I'll learn
the difference between 'affect' and 'effect'.
Thank you—for everything.

Ps 63:1

CHAPTER ONE

MELORA WASHINGTON slipped her sunglasses onto her face, hefted her large carry-on bag over her shoulder and gave the flight attendant a polite smile. She stood in the doorway of the small twelve-seater Cessna, looking out into the bright Tarparniian daylight.

This was it. She'd made the decision, had done the mound of paperwork required to apply, passed the interviews, completed her medical checks and had been approved to work for Pacific Medical Aid for the next two weeks.

The need to take a break from her life as a general surgeon working at a busy teaching hospital in Sydney was something she was definitely looking forward to. Coming here, to a world so different from her own, with the promise of adventure and excitement—*anything* that was new and out of the ordinary was what she was looking for.

It had been her close friend Emerson Freeman who had been the one to suggest Tarparnii as the 'take a break from my life' destination.

'You've been through too much in the past few years, Mel,' Emmy had implored. 'Taking a break, a complete getaway from the path your life has been forced down, would definitely benefit you.'

'Tarparnii?' Melora had been stupefied at the suggestion. 'That's a jungle. I was thinking of a nice quiet resort in Far North Queensland.'

'You'd be bored within twenty-four hours,' Emmy had pointed out. 'You've been through an emotionally draining physical experience, not to mention all the drama associated with the nullification of your engagement.'

'But a jungle?' Even the word 'jungle' had made Melora wonder whether this could really be possible.

'What could be more different from your present lifestyle here in Sydney than a jungle? Trust me. You'll love it. The people are wonderful, the scenery is to die for and PMA offers you the opportunity to help out in a practical sense. Besides, it's only for two weeks.'

Emmy had made some valid points and at that point in her life, after the upheaval she'd lived through, Melora had been almost desperate to get away, to try something different, to *be* someone different from the woman who'd felt as though the walls had been closing in on her. Her world may have been blown apart, crashing down around her in an array of disappointment, disillusionment and discouragement, but that hadn't meant she had to stand for it.

'Tarparnii will help you to heal,' Emmy had said softly. 'Trust me on this.'

Melora had looked at her friend, had seen the concern in her eyes and heard it in her voice. 'You really think it's the right thing to do?'

Emmy had smiled brightly and reached for her phone. 'I do. Let's call PMA now and get this show on the road.' As Emmy had made the phone call, Melora had felt a buzz of rejuvenation flood through her.

Could she really do this? Take more leave from the hospital, take some time out of her everyday world and try another? She'd heard Emmy and her husband, Dart, talk about Tarparnii for years but never in her wildest dreams had she thought that she, herself, would go.

Then again, she'd also thought that her future had lain with Leighton, with marrying him and starting a family, and look at how badly that had turned out. Add that to her recent surgery and multitude of tests, and she had been more than ready for something new.

As Emmy had finished making the phone call to arrange an appointment for Melora to go to the PMA offices, excitement had burst forth from her friend. 'You'll love Tarparnii, Mel, and April is a beautiful month to go. It's always humid and sticky and it rains almost every day but it's still stunning. Oh, and the people you'll meet. Meeree and Jalak are like loving, caring parents to anyone who enters their village, and then there are the doctors and nurses who live there, like Belhara and Bel and Tarvon.' Emmy nodded enthusiastically. 'It'll be great. You'll love it. I promise.'

Melora blinked, bringing her thoughts back to the present, amazed that she was finally there, finally taking that tenuous step away from everything she'd known in order to try something so completely different. She smiled again at the flight attendant in eager excitement.

'Your PMA contact is over there, Dr Washington.' The flight attendant pointed in the direction of a man leaning by an open-top old army Jeep, his arms folded over his chest, his legs crossed at the ankles. The man had dark hair, dark skin and was dressed in khaki shorts and a pale blue striped cotton shirt, which appeared to be mis-buttoned. There was a hat on his head, sunglasses covering his eyes and hiking boots on his feet.

He didn't look anything like a doctor! He looked rugged and wild and unruly.

She swallowed over her suddenly dry throat and looked from the man back to the attendant. '*He's* my contact? Are you sure?' He most certainly didn't look anything like a doctor. 'I'm to be met by Dr...' She stopped and dug into the pocket of her linen trousers for the piece of paper she'd printed out. 'Dr...er...' She consulted the page. 'Tarvon? Daniel Tarvon?'

The attendant's eyebrows hit her hairline. 'Is that his first name? I never knew. Everyone always calls him Tarvon.'

Melora pointed to the man who looked as though he hadn't had the opportunity to shave that morning. It gave him a dangerous but exciting look and she couldn't stop the butterflies from churning in her stomach. This was it. She was here. Her adventure was about to begin...with a real-life jungle man as her guide. 'And *that's* Tarvon?'

'It is indeed, Dr Washington.' The attendant appeared to be looking at Dr Daniel Tarvon as though he was the best thing since sliced bread. The woman sighed with longing, as though she wanted nothing more than to head on over to Daniel Tarvon and press her lips eagerly to his own. Melora let her gaze rest on the overall package the man made and from where she stood she had to admit that he appeared quite trim, taut and terrific. Then again, looks weren't everything, as she'd already figured out with Leighton.

The woman beside her quickly straightened, as though only just realising she'd been caught ogling the Tarparniian doctor, cleared her throat and turned back to face Melora, a polite smile pasted in place.

'On behalf of Pacific Airways, I'd like to thank you

for flying with us today, Dr Washington, and hope you have an enjoyable and safe time in Tarparnii.'

Melora nodded. 'Thanks.' Feeling her excitement bubble to the surface, she dragged in a deep breath, watching Dr Tarvon as he leaned against the old green Jeep, which appeared to have known better days...*much* better days. It was as though she'd stepped out of reality and into some strange, world with lush green trees, high humidity and relaxed doctors. She was used to the crisp efficiency of a large teaching hospital, overbooked clinics and operating lists, and doctors who wore three-piece suits. Dr Tarvon appeared to be a far cry from any of that.

Hefting her bag once more, she alighted from the plane and walked across the open tarmac towards the Jeep, which was parked next to the large shed that served as the airport's terminal. Dr Tarvon didn't move, his arms still crossed, his legs still crossed, his reflective sunglasses making it impossible for her to see his eyes.

It was now that she could see more clearly the stubble indicating he probably hadn't shaved for a few days. It also appeared that he was sporting a little ponytail and that surprised her even more. As far as a contrast to Leighton, Dr Daniel Tarvon was the complete opposite. Both were good looking but there was something about the indolent man before her that seemed to radiate sensuality.

Melora breathed it in, the warm humid Tarparniian air filling her senses along with an earthy, muscular scent from the man before her. He was much taller than he'd looked from the doorway of the plane. Probably about six feet four inches. Far taller than the average Tarparniian, or, at least, so her research had led her to believe. After her initial meeting with PMA, Melora had spent quite a bit of time researching the island, its customs and its people. While she might be looking for a change, for a bit of adventure, she also liked to be prepared.

Even though she stood right in front of Dr Tarvon, he still didn't move. Arms crossed, legs crossed, reflective glasses shining her image back to her. She'd dressed with the humid climate in mind, wearing a pair of comfortable walking boots, linen trousers and a large cotton shirt, tied with a scarf at her neck. She'd read about the large sandflies and ticks and other insects Tarparnii was infamous for and was eager to avoid them wherever possible. She'd been poked and prodded enough during the past twenty months to last her a lifetime and she knew there was still more to come. The last thing she needed now was to get sick during her time there.

She continued to stand there, feeling highly self-conscious, and Dr Tarvon's silence making her rather apprehensive. Perhaps he wasn't her contact? Perhaps the flight attendant had been wrong? She looked around but there really was no one else about.

'Hello?' When he didn't immediately respond, she began to wonder if he really was all right. She reached out a finger, edging closer, and gave him a little poke in his upper arm. 'Hello?' she said at the same time, her tone a little louder.

'Huh? What?' Dr Tarvon jolted as though she'd startled him. He sprang upright, knocking his hat from his head, his sunglasses skewing slightly. 'What? Oh. Sorry. Must have dozed off. Rough night.' His tone was deep and his words were crisp, indicating a strong British accent, which surprised her given Emmy had led her to believe he was a native Tarparniian. Dr Tarvon bent to pick up his hat and shifted his sunglasses to the top of his head before holding out his hand to her, a tired yet jovial smile on his face. 'Dr Washington?'

'Yes.' She took off her sunglasses so she could greet him properly.

'I'm Tarvon.'

'Daniel Tarvon?' Melora confirmed, slipped her hand into his, noting the way his large, warm hand seemed to envelop hers completely. He really was tall, dark and handsome and just the brief touch of her skin against his was enough to give her a tingle of awareness.

'Yes. Great to meet you.' He actually shook her hand, up and down, rather than a polite clasping squeeze as she was used to back home. 'Actually,' he continued, letting her hand go for a brief moment before clasping both of hers in his, 'we should greet like this.' He moved their hands in small circles and she experienced the traditional Tarparniian welcome that she'd read about on line.

'Yes. Of course. When in Tarparnii…' She let the sentence hang as she tried to calm the way her body seemed to have become electrified by his touch.

He chuckled as he slowly let go of her hands. 'Exactly.' Her skin had been so soft, so tender and so completely different from his own callused hands. 'OK, then.' He took his hat off and tossed it into the back seat of the old Jeep, which she now saw had several rust spots, a broken taillight, no rear-vision mirror, and the corner of the front windscreen held together with some sticking tape. 'Ready to go?' He stepped forward and took the bag from her shoulder, placing it into the Jeep with ease. 'Or do you have more luggage to come?'

As he moved towards her, she caught a glimpse of something hanging off the belt at his waist. Her eyes widened as she realised it was a sheathed hunting knife.

A knife? She was about to get in a car with a man who had a knife strapped to his waist.

'Dr Washington?' he prompted, and she immediately lifted her gaze from the knife to meet his. 'Any other luggage?'

'Er...no. That's it.'

'Excellent.' He noticed her gaze drop back to the hunting knife and saw her wariness at getting into a car with him. He couldn't blame her. He was sure that in Sydney not many people walked around with hunting knives on their belts. He put his hand on the knife then looked at her. 'Out here, we use these for protection. There are a lot of predators, such as poisonous snakes, *ha'kuna*—which is like a cross between a dog and a wolf—and other nasties, roaming in the jungle.' He patted his knife. 'It is a necessity.'

Melora, somewhat appeased by his explanation, nodded. 'Fair enough.'

Daniel indicated the passenger side. 'I'd hold the door open for you if there was one but as there isn't, please have a seat.'

Melora eyed the vehicle. 'Are you sure it's going to hold together long enough to transport us to where ever it is we're going?'

He laughed, a rich, deep sound that washed over her with delight. 'I'm sure.'

She sat down and held up a piece of thick rope. 'And this is?'

'Your seat belt. Even though it doesn't look like much, it will do the job of keeping you secure as we drive along.'

'Really?' Her lips twitched in disbelief.

'Really. We'll be encountering some rather rocky terrain between here and the village.'

'OK. I'll take your word for it.' She did as he'd suggested, positive that this particular car had been used in the Second World War it was so decrepit. Dr Tarvon came around to the driver's side, touched two wires together to start the engine, and after they'd both put their sunglasses back on turned to look at her again.

'Ready?'

She grinned at him and nodded, holding on to the side of the front windscreen as the car jolted into motion, the excitement at her jungle adventure actually beginning bubbling through her.

The buildings of the small Tarparniian town that straddled the airport disappeared within the blink of an eye and before she knew it, they were driving along a dirt road, lots of lush green trees surrounding them. The scenery was beautiful and very soothing.

As they drove along, Dr Tarvon had continued to impress her further by pointing out different areas of interest and giving her details of his country.

'Have you lived here long?' she found herself asking, mildly intrigued by him. He most certainly didn't fit into the mental picture she'd drawn of the typical Tarparniian, given that he was taller, broader and had that exciting rugged edge to him.

'I was born here, although educated in England.'

Well, that explained his accent and the fact that he was a qualified medical doctor. Her friends Emmy and Dart had had nothing but praise for Daniel Tarvon but Melora was eager to make up her own mind, although he was most definitely off to a good start. If she had to work alongside this handsome colleague during her time here, that would be a hardship she'd just have to bear.

She was here for adventure. She was here for an escape from reality, an escape from her life, and while she knew nothing serious would ever happen between herself and her new colleague, or any of her colleagues for that matter, it was great just to let loose and step outside her comfort zone.

After a pause, Dr Tarvon asked, 'What's your first name, Dr Washington?'

'Oh. Sorry. You don't know? I would have presumed it was on the paperwork PMA sent.'

Daniel's smile was instantaneous and natural. 'It most probably was, Dr Washington, but unfortunately I didn't have much time to prepare for your arrival. You see, we spent most of yesterday in a clinic on the other side of the island. We only arrived back in the village two hours ago. I had just enough time to have a quick wash before driving out to the airport to meet you.'

'Oh. Do you often travel to the other side of the island?'

'Yes. Quite often. Luckily, for you, the rest of today is considered as time off so you'll have the opportunity to settle in and relax before tomorrow, when we'll take you to the waterhole, throw you in and see if you swim.'

'Swim?' Melora's eyes widened in absolute horror, her mouth went dry and nervous heat settled over her. She swallowed. 'I'm afraid I don't swim, Dr Tarvon. In fact, I didn't even pack a bathing suit.' Of course she *could* physically swim but given that she'd had major surgery, her body shape changing drastically, she didn't feel at all comfortable with the concept.

Daniel looked over at her for a moment before a wide grin split his face and he chuckled. 'I didn't mean it literally, Dr Washington. I simply meant we have a long clinic day ahead of us tomorrow. It'll be extremely hectic but I'm sure you'll do fine.'

'Oh.' Melora closed her eyes, glad she was still

wearing her sunglasses so he couldn't see the embarrassment written all over her face. She took a few deep
breaths, forcing herself to relax, to let go of the tension
that had instantly gripped her at the thought of swimming. Although she was here for adventure, there were
some things she needed to leave until later...such as
after her breast reconstruction surgery.

'But it is a shame you don't swim. The waterhole is
lovely this time of year, Dr Washington—and you still
haven't told me your first name. We're very informal
out here,' he continued. 'There's no room for Dr this or
Mr that.'

'My name is Melora.'

'Melora,' he repeated, and then smiled, his straight
white teeth gleaming in the midmorning sunlight. 'A
very pretty name.'

'Thank you.' Although she couldn't see his eyes, she
was surprised and a little touched at his words. No man
had ever said that to her before. 'It was my aunt's name.
She died not long after I was born.' Now, why had she
just told him that?

Usually, she didn't volunteer personal information
until she knew people a lot better rather than the twenty
minutes she'd known Dr Tarvon. Still, there was something about him, perhaps his easygoing nature combined
with his jovial humour, that made her feel more relaxed
in his presence.

'I'm named after my father.'

For the first time since they'd met, Melora detected
the veiled hint of censure in his words. Was it his name
he didn't like or was it the mention of his father? 'The
flight attendant on the plane didn't know your first
name. She said she only knew you as Tarvon. Emmy
and Dart always referred to you as Tarvon as well.'

He raised an interested eyebrow. 'Ah…you know Emmy and Dart. Great. They're such wonderful people and they do always call me Tarvon. Most people around here do. My mother is Tarparniian and my father was British. When I'm in England, which isn't very often, I'm known as Daniel. Here, I'm usually known as Tarvon.'

She thought on this for a moment. 'Tarvon sounds like a Tarparniian name. Am I right?'

'Correct. Tarvon is my mother's family name.' He passed on the information but could see in advance where this conversation might lead.

'Oh. So even though your father was English, is it the Tarparniian custom that any children take the mother's surname?' She hadn't read about that in her research but, then, she doubted the internet covered *everything* about this magnificent country.

Daniel clenched his jaw but kept his smile in place. 'No. My father's surname is Knightsbridge but as we never got along, when I was old enough, I legally took my Tarparniian ancestral name.'

She absorbed this information, realising it told her a lot about the relationship he'd shared…or more correctly *hadn't* shared…with his father. 'You took the trouble to change your name and yet you didn't change your first name—the name that was the same as your father's?'

'My mother was the one to name me Daniel and she is the one I kept it for.'

Melora nodded, hearing the softer tone in his voice when he spoke of his mother.

'You're close to her? Your mother?'

His natural smile returned to his face. 'I am.'

'That's nice. Do you have any siblings?'

'Yes. Two sisters. You are certainly full of questions, Melora Washington.'

'Sorry. I'm not usually this nosy about my colleagues. I simply find your country and its customs extremely interesting. I apologise if I've caused you any discomfort.'

'It's fine.' He waved her words away, his tone more calm and relaxed, as it had been when they'd first met. 'Question away. If you get too personal, I'll let you know.'

'OK. So, Dr Tarvon, tell me how long have you been working with PMA?'

'Many years—far too many to count. I am a permanent member of their Tarparniian staff. Unlike you and a lot of other doctors who volunteer to come and help here for a period of time, as I'm classified as a native Tarparniian, I don't have time restrictions placed on me.'

'I see.' There was silence for a few minutes before she asked, 'So…do I call you Daniel or Tarvon?'

Daniel slowed the vehicle and turned off the graded road into what appeared to be a very loose track. 'Take your pick. Which do you prefer?'

Melora thought for a moment, feeling quite strange at being able to choose what she would call this man who was her main contact. Choosing to call him Tarvon might help to keep things on a more medical footing. However, he'd already told her that out here they were all very informal and, therefore, it might actually be better to call him by the name his mother liked. Besides, he *looked* like a Daniel.

'I like Daniel,' she finally decided.

'You gave that a bit of thought.'

'Why wouldn't I? It was an important decision. After all, you are the PMA team leader, are you not?'

'I am.'

'Then it's always good to be perfectly clear on how

to address your boss.' As she spoke the words, her mind jumped instantly to Leighton. He'd been her last boss, he'd also been her fiancé and neither of those things had ended well. She shook her head to clear the thoughts away. She was in a new place now, a new country, having a new experience. She didn't need to be dwelling on Leighton or her past.

He grinned at her words. 'Agreed.'

As they were now driving in the shade of the trees, Melora lifted her glasses to the top of her head and glanced over at him. She found his smile to be so fresh, so encompassing it was causing a slight shift in the walls she'd built around herself. Just because Daniel Tarvon was tall, dark and extremely handsome, it didn't mean she couldn't appreciate it in a nice, friendly manner.

'So are you the type of person who likes everything to be neat and organised?' he asked.

'I used to be.'

'And now?'

'Now…who knows? My life has been jumbled up and turned inside out but where work is concerned, I confess I do like things to be clear. As a surgeon, when I operate, I prefer staff to ask me ten questions and get something right than to ask one question and get it wrong.'

'Surgery is all about absolutes,' he agreed.

'Are you a surgeon?'

'I'm a GP and a physician and a dentist and an obstetrician and a bit of an orthopaedist.'

'So I take it you get to see quite a variety out here?'

'Yes, and so will you.' He glanced over at her. 'I wonder if you know what you've really signed up for, Melora.'

She laughed but she was certain both of them heard the excited nervous tension. 'I've been wondering that myself ever since I stepped off the plane.'

'So what did prompt you to come to Tarparnii? I'm guessing it was the need to do something completely different, to recharge your love of medicine and to escape your own life for a spell.'

'How…how do you know that?' Had Emmy or Dart contacted him? Given him a precise of her situation?

He shrugged. 'It's a strange ability I've inherited from my mother, to sort of be able to see into people, to get a sort of sense from them.'

'Are you telling me you have psychic powers?' Melora looked at him in disbelief.

Daniel laughed, the sound washing over her with delight. 'Hardly. I leave that to Meeree. She's a woman who sees far more than you know and she's *always* right. In my case, though, it's more of a sense about someone. A gut feeling, I guess you could call it. I sometimes get…a feeling about someone or something. That's all.'

'Wow. I wish I had that ability. Would have saved me a lot of heartache.' She mumbled the last part, thinking that perhaps, if she'd had a smidgen of Daniel's ability, she might have realised that Leighton had been cheating on her.

'Sounds as though you've been through a bad time,' Daniel remarked, and it was only then she realised he'd heard her.

Not wanting to talk about it, she sat up straighter, holding on tighter to the side of the vehicle as he manoeuvred them out from the overhanging trees and back into the sunshine. 'That's all in the past. I'm here to have a new experience.'

'Ahh…the glass is half-full, eh?'

'Exactly.' She slipped her sunglasses back on and turned her face towards the sun, eager for the cobwebs to be removed from her life as she headed towards her new adventure.

They drove in silence for the next few minutes, back on a graded road that actually seemed to have more 'traffic', for want of a better word, travelling on it. There were several army-type trucks, most with big red crosses painted on them. There were bicycles, handcarts and other vehicles, just like theirs but in far worse condition, usually carrying far more than two or four passengers as had been the original car's design.

One car passed them with at least twenty people either sitting or hanging off the sides, the tyres almost flat from the weight. Everyone waved and called out greetings in the native Tarparniian guttural language. Daniel waved back, smiling brightly or beeping his horn jovially.

'Everyone seems so friendly,' Melora commented, mentally taking in everything around her. When they passed another such laden car, she found herself smiling and offering a very tentative wave.

'Not necessarily everyone,' Daniel remarked as they came around a corner to be faced with a barricade across the road. He slowed the Jeep and soon came to a complete stop. With the engine still running, he leaned over towards Melora and opened the glove-box, the flap of which flicked down and hit the tops of her knees.

'Sorry,' Daniel said, and before she knew what he was doing, he'd rubbed the tops of her knees where she'd been hit.

'It's fine.' She straightened her legs as best she could and scrunched herself as far away from him as possible. The warmth from his impromptu touch had filtered through the linen of her trousers, causing heat to spread from her knees up throughout her body. Thank goodness she hadn't worn a skirt today.

He found the papers he was looking for and closed the compartment, straightening as he did. When he turned to look at her, Melora felt for certain that she was blushing. 'Do you have your papers?' he asked.

'Pardon?' She was watching his mouth move but the words weren't sinking in due to the fact that she was still affected by the caring way he'd rubbed her knees. The action had been that of a parent, the touch, though, had definitely been one between a man and a woman. No colleague had ever penetrated her comfort zone so effortlessly, not even Leighton. Dr Daniel Tarvon, she was quickly coming to realise, really wasn't like any other man she'd ever met before.

'Your papers?' he asked again, and then pointed to the men who were standing next to the roadblock. It was then that Melora realised what he was saying as the men had rifles slung over their shoulders and were checking the papers of all who wished to pass through the block.

'Oh! My papers.' She was pleased to focus on something other than trying to figure out just why Daniel seemed to be causing her mind to flounder. Melora undid the piece of rope and climbed from the vehicle. Bending into the back seat to retrieve her bag, she rummaged around for her PMA papers. As she did so, she couldn't help but glance over at where Daniel was warmly shaking hands with the soldiers.

He knew them? Melora straightened, papers in hand, and looked over to where Daniel was laughing at something one of the soldiers had said. She felt highly self-conscious and completely out of her depth and for a moment the old Melora, the one who had needed to understand and have some semblance of control over every situation, returned.

What was she doing here? In this jungle country, with soldiers and guns and fighting going on somewhere near them? She tugged at the hem of her untucked shirt then checked that the collar and her scarf were still in place, keeping her well covered.

Just that morning she'd woken up in her apartment, had a shower, dressed, had finished packing her bag and caught a taxi to Sydney airport. It had still been dark, the sun not yet risen. She'd flown to Cairns where she'd switched planes to the small Cessna, which had flown her to Tarparnii. Then she'd climbed into a car with Daniel Tarvon and now was standing before men with guns. Daniel—a perfect stranger—was really the only person she knew.

It was all too…rudderless.

How had her world moved from knowing what she'd be doing every hour of every day of every week of every year to this? Standing at a checkpoint, about to hand over papers to a man with a rifle! When Emmy had suggested a complete change of scenery, she'd really meant a *complete* change.

For the past twenty months, Melora's life hadn't been her own due to the cancer that had attacked her body, but after lifesaving surgery, chemotherapy and the return of her hair she was now determined to find the control that had been rudely taken from her with that first diagnosis.

She was different now. Not only mentally but physically as well. She'd made the decision to join PMA, she'd accepted this job here in Tarparnii, and now that new and, albeit, scary events were unfolding around her, she was determined to see them through.

She'd survived Leighton's betrayal. She'd survived cancer. She could survive this!

Feeling a surge of determination and strength return, she straightened her shoulders, lifted her head high and headed over to where Daniel stood talking to the soldiers. With her smile pasted firmly in place, she held out her papers to the man Daniel was talking to…the man with the gun. 'Here you are.'

'Thank you.' The soldier spoke with an educated lilt to his tone, much the same as Daniel's.

'Melora, this is my second cousin, Paul.'

'Paul?' She was startled for a moment at such an English name. She put her smile back in place and nodded politely. 'Nice to meet you, Paul.' He checked over her papers and handed them back all neatly folded.

'Everything's in order,' Paul remarked. 'Have a great day.' He motioned to some of the other soldiers to lift the boom and as Melora and Daniel headed back to the Jeep, Paul called, 'Will I see you on Sunday at the bonfire?'

'Probably not. Depends on work,' Daniel replied, and gave his second cousin a high five as they drove past.

'Well, that was a little surreal,' Melora commented a few minutes later as they continued down the road.

'Going through a checkpoint? You'll get used to it. Just always make sure you have a set of papers with you. Usually the papers are for the vehicle, rather than just a single person, but as this was your first time, you needed to show your personal papers. Paul will make a record that you are officially in the country and working with PMA.'

'What happens if you don't have papers? Do they detain you? Hold you captive?' There was an edge of concern and disbelief in her voice.

'They detain you until someone can head back to the village, get the papers and bring them back to the checkpoint. Forgetting your papers usually results more in inconvenience rather than anything else.'

'Why did you need to show Paul your papers when he's your cousin? Surely he can vouch for who you are.'

'True, but, as I said, the papers are more for the vehicle logs than anything else. It's a strange system but it's a system that works.'

'It's so different.' Melora spoke softly and didn't think Daniel had heard her over the sound of the car's engine and the reverberation noise of the tyres on the graded road.

'That's what I thought the first time my father took me to England. So different.'

'You spent quite a bit of time there?' As he'd opened the subject again, she didn't feel as though she was prying.

He nodded. 'I was educated there. Did my medical training there but always came back to Tarparnii for my holidays.'

'To spend time with your mother?'

'Exactly. She didn't like England that much so most of the time she preferred to stay here in Tarparnii with her village. My father was a doctor and one of the first to work here in Tarparnii. I was sent away to boarding school for many years.'

'You mentioned that you had sisters. Do they live here, too?'

'Yes they do. They're both married and so live in the villages of their husbands.'

'And your parents?' He really was quite a fascinating man. 'They're still together after all this time?'

'No. My father passed away six years ago.' The tone in his voice when he spoke of his father, however, was crisp and brisk, as it had been when he'd previously mentioned his father. It was clear the two had been at odds. 'My mother still lives in her village. She is the headwoman there and as such is needed to guide and care for her people.'

'Wow. I'm presuming being headwoman is important?'

His mouth creased into a smile. 'Very.'

'Do you see her often?'

'Quite often.' Daniel nodded. 'It depends on where I'm needed.'

'Work first?'

'Exactly.' He changed gear. 'Ready for a bit of cross-country?' This time, when he turned off, there didn't even appear to be tyre tracks on the ground.

'Do you know where you're going?' she couldn't help but ask as she held onto the windscreen with one hand and the bottom of her seat with the other as they bumped along the uneven terrain. This was very odd, very different, very…not normal.

Daniel laughed. 'This is my country, Melora. I know exactly where I am. This is my favourite short cut.'

'Short cut? Why…do…we need to take…a short cut?' The old car jolted up and down, jarring her words.

'Relax. Once we get through this area of dense forest, you'll have the most spectacular views.' There was a rumble from above them and she looked up to see clouds starting to gather, and quite quickly, too.

'Oh…well there's…no…need to go to…too…much trouble…for me…' she stumbled as she continued to bounce up and down in the Jeep. Her answer was more of Daniel Tarvon's easy laughter. 'Is…it going to…rain?' she asked.

Daniel glanced up. 'More than likely.'

'Do we…need some sort…of shelter? A roof…of

sorts on the…car?' He didn't seem to be slowing down for any of the bumps.

'Why bother? It rains for about five minutes straight, we all get wet and then ten minutes after the rain has finished, we're all dry again. You'll get used to it.'

'I hope so.' She glanced over at him, at his strong profile. His nose was slightly crooked, indicating a break, and she idly wondered how it had happened. His unshaved chin and jawline were square and proud and she could tell by the smile on his lips that he was enjoying himself immensely. His large hands on the wheel were completely in control of the vehicle and his broad shoulders were strong and powerful as he continued to drive them through the dense forest.

When the rain came a few minutes later, the heavens literally opening up to emit a torrential downpour, Melora told herself to relax, to enjoy, not to worry about every little thing. So she was getting soaked. That was OK. Daniel was getting soaked, too.

She'd spent so much of her life playing by the rules, doing what was right, following the guidelines set down by society at large, and she'd been incredibly successful at it. She'd been dux of her high school and medical school, had passed her general surgical training with full marks and was now a highly trained, highly competent surgeon.

But society at large had not prepared her for the upheaval cancer would bring into her world and now, having had enough of living by the rules, she was here, to have adventures such as driving in an old Jeep through a jungle while getting soaked.

The car swerved slightly to the side, the ground becoming more slick and slippery to drive on. Still Daniel didn't slow down and she knew that sometimes going faster over such ground was actually safer than slowing down.

They were almost at the top of the small mountain, the car's engine straining but not complaining as Daniel steered them ever onwards and upwards.

'How are you doing?' he called, glancing at her, his face, his hair, his body dripping with water. Melora blinked through the rain that had settled on her lashes, wanting to wipe her hand over her face, but was positive that her fingers had welded themselves to the sides of the Jeep in her effort to hold on.

'Good,' she called back, but no sooner had she spoken than a loud crack sounded behind them. 'What was that?'

'Uh…' Daniel gritted his teeth and put his foot down on the accelerator. 'You may want to hang on tight.'

'I *am* hanging on…tight.'

'Then hang on tighter,' Daniel remarked with a wild laugh as they crested the hill, the rain still pelting down on them. Another loud crack sounded and Melora's eyes widened. She hadn't seen any lightning in the sky so what on earth was making that noise? Another rumble and then the car started to slide again, Daniel instantly attempting to correct the direction of the tyres.

'Why? What's happening?' she called, but in the next instant the car lurched forward, and it had nothing to do with Daniel's driving.

He grinned at her, his brown eyes alive with the thrill of their situation.

'Daniel?' she called again as the car started to pick up speed. 'What is it?'

'Woo-hoo. *Mudslide!*'

CHAPTER TWO

'Wha?!'

There was panic in her tone, even though she was trying her hardest to stay calm. She'd wanted this, hadn't she? She'd wanted to step outside of her comfort zone, to step out of her normal life, to do something different. Well, this was different but a little *too* different. 'What?'

'Mudslide!' Daniel laughed again even as he concentrated on trying to control the steering-wheel as best he could. The rain was still pouring and they were heading down the hill at an even greater speed than Melora had expected...not that she'd expected, in her wildest dreams, to be trapped in a mudslide inside a car feeling more helpless than when she'd been diagnosed with cancer.

'Daniel!'

He glanced at her briefly, delight all over his face. 'Don't worry, Mel,' he called over the roar of nature around them. 'This happens all the time. It's quite a tame one. Just hold on and enjoy the ride.'

'Tame?' The disbelief in her tone went unnoticed as Daniel continued to appear as though he did indeed have some sort of control over the vehicle. There was nothing left for her to do but trust him and hang on. Of one thing she was sure, her heart was pounding wildly against her chest with a surge of adrenalin. Exhilaration wasn't far behind and when the rain stopped, just as Daniel had said it would, she began to relax a little.

'I'm going to turn the wheel sharply and hopefully disengage,' he called rapidly, Melora only hearing every second word. She was about to ask him to repeat himself when he yelled, 'Hang on!'

She tightened her grip, her knuckles white and wet, all feeling in her fingers having long since gone because she was holding on so hard. Then, with a quick full lock of the wheel and pressing down on the accelerator, the car jerked a sharp left and bumped its way over even rougher terrain than before.

'Ahh... Daniel! Watch out for that tree!' Melora yelled, but she needed not have worried as within another second Daniel had once again swerved before bringing the Jeep to a stop.

Neither of them moved for half a minute, Daniel being the first to recover. 'Whoo-ee. What a ride!' He undid his piece of rope-belt and stepped from the vehicle, his feet crunching down on leaves and twigs as he shook the rain from himself. She watched as he pulled his dark hair from its ponytail and pushed his fingers through the wet strands.

It gave him an even wilder look than before, like he really was a jungle man. The style didn't make him look at all feminine—in fact, it had quite the opposite effect. With his unshaven face, slightly crooked nose and his dark wet hair framing his face, he looked powerful, as though he could do anything, take on anything, such as navigating a car through a mudslide, and come out the winner.

She shook her head in wonderment as she watched him make his way around the front of the car to her side.

She hadn't moved anything but her head, her arms still outstretched, her body still rigid, her heart thudding so loudly and powerfully throughout her body she was certain he could hear it.

'Are you all right?' he asked, coming to stand beside her.

'I…uh…' She swallowed and this time the powerful thudding of her heart had nothing at all to do with the roller-coaster slide they'd just finished but everything to do with the man before her. So strong, so virile, so masculine.

It was a shock for her to realise that she really was attracted to this man…to this man she barely knew but one who had probably just saved her life by his amazing ability to steer them through a mudslide. What woman in her right mind *wouldn't* be attracted to Daniel Tarvon? The fact that she wasn't at all in the market for any sort of romantic relationship was something she would do well to remember, but it was the way he was so easygoing, so relaxed, so personable that had made her instantly like him.

'Melora?' Daniel stepped closer and placed his hand over hers, gently prising her fingers from their clenched positions. 'Blood in the extremities?' He held her hands in his, rubbing his thumb and fingers over them, stimulating blood circulation. The intent was medical, the touch was personal.

She pulled her hands away from him and clenched them tightly together in her lap. 'It's fine. They're fine.' She fumbled with the piece of rope across her lap, which had indeed performed its job and kept her secure. 'I'm fine. Thank you,' she added, belatedly remembering her manners. She would be fine, would be able to get her heart rate back to a more normal and steady rhythm so long as Daniel kept his distance.

'Hop out and stretch your legs. Sorry about not being able to stop at the amazing view I'd previously promised but the mudslide obviously had different ideas.'

She laughed nervously, needing distance from him, and fast. 'I don't care much about the view right now. I'm just glad to be alive.' In more ways than one, she realised. It would have been ridiculous to have survived breast cancer only to be swept away down a hillside by a large mass of mud.

Melora carefully shifted her legs, making sure they were going to work before swivelling to the side and climbing from the vehicle, shaking her head politely at the hand Daniel stretched towards her to offer assistance. 'Thanks, but I'm fine.'

'As long as you really are and you're not just saying that so I'll leave you alone. The last thing I want to do is to deliver you to the village already in need of medical attention.'

She smiled, trying to control her reaction to this man. Good looking, charismatic and funny. Definitely a lethal combination and one she had to confess she hadn't really expected to encounter here in Tarparnii.

'That would not be good.' Melora looked away from him as he pulled his hair back into a ponytail. She didn't need sexy visions of her new colleague penetrating her mind. She would need to put personal protocols in place to control her reaction to him. She was here to work, not flirt. She needed to remember that. Instead, she peered through the thin tree trunks around them. 'Exactly how far are we from the village?'

'It's about another ten minutes north-west of where

we are now,' he replied as he started to inspect the car, making sure that it was still in working order.

'Oh. So not that far at all?' Melora decided to test her legs, to get them moving, and walked a little further away from the Jeep and away from Daniel Tarvon's powerful presence. 'Wait. Is that ten minutes by car or by walking?'

'Car.'

'Oh. Right.' She self-consciously pushed her hands through her short blonde hair, fluffing it out, surprised to find it already partially dry. She continued to pick her way through the fallen bark and bits of branches and leaves and goodness knew what else on the ground. The sounds of insects filled the air, birds flew high above them through the trees, water droplets hung from leaves and branches, the sun's rays peered through the clouds. It was definitely another world but it was an extremely beautiful world...and Daniel only enhanced it.

Having realised she was attracted to Daniel, she now found it difficult to look at him. It didn't matter that the attraction wouldn't—*couldn't*—go anywhere because at the moment her life wasn't technically her own. She still had to wait for results, results that would confirm or deny that she was cancer free. Who knew what sort of time bomb might be waiting to drop into her life? And to that end she was here to step outside her comfort zone and what she'd just come through—a mudslide in a Jeep—most definitely counted.

Something rustled in the bracken to her right and she stopped moving, peering closely, wondering if it was a pretty bird. 'Wait.' She peered further into the bushes, edging forward.

'Something wrong?' Daniel asked, standing up from where he'd been surveying the undercarriage of the car for damages. He brushed his hands together as he headed in her direction.

'I don't know. I thought I saw something.' She peered through the branches and tree trunks, listening carefully.

'What? Where?' Daniel was instantly by her side.

'Over there,' she pointed. 'I think I saw someone.'

'What did you see?' His voice was calm but firm. 'Was it a group of men? There usually aren't soldiers in these parts of the forest because it's too densely populated.'

'Soldiers? No. It looked like one person. I think it was a woman or a girl. She was just over there. I promise you I'm not making this up.'

'I have no doubt you're telling the truth.' His gaze remained glued to the surrounding area.

'There!' She pointed. 'Daniel. Through there.' Melora pointed again and this time Daniel could see exactly where she meant.

There, in the scrub, were three women, all of them wet, one of them lying on the ground in pain. Daniel called out to them in his native language and Melora could see the two women who were trying to help their friend look around at him in fright. He said more words as they made their way towards them, the younger woman rushing forward to him.

'Dokta! *Qah*. Dokta.' She spoke in a rapid-fire way but Melora didn't need to hear what was going on. She could see it. The woman lying on the ground was in the last stages of labour, in the middle of a forest in the middle of nowhere.

'Melora.' Daniel turned to face her. 'Back in the car, down behind the back seat, is my medical bag,' he said.

'I'll get it,' she called needlessly, and hurried back to where he'd stopped the car. She found his medical bag but it was wedged beneath the seat. Grumbling when she realised she couldn't move the front seat forward to retrieve it, she climbed into the old Jeep and leaned over the seat, tugging the bag as best she could without causing any damage. Why was nothing ever simple?

Finally, she had the barely wet bag in her hands and headed back to where Daniel was now crouched down at the woman's feet, talking to her in calm, soothing tones.

'Here.' Melora put the bag down beside him and opened it up. She rummaged around for a second before pulling out gloves. 'Put these on.'

'Thanks.' He did so and on performing an examination found that the woman, who looked to be about seventeen years old, was fully dilated. 'Contractions are only a few minutes apart.'

'What's her name?' Melora asked, and Daniel turned and asked all their names.

The older woman was answering Daniel, the stress and panic gone from her face now that the 'dokta' was here. Melora waited patiently for him to translate.

'The mother is P'tanay, the young daughter is K'hala and this brave woman...' he indicated the woman in labour '...is J'tana.'

'A mother and her daughters?' The mother, P'tanay barely looked old enough to have her own children let alone about to be made a grandmother. K'hala, the other girl, looked to be about thirteen. 'Isn't K'hala a little young to be witnessing a birth?' she asked quietly.

'No. K'hala would have seen many women giving birth since she was very young. It's part of the culture that young girls learn the ways of women from the older women. Childbirth is an important part of life for a Tarparniian woman and it's an honour to be asked to assist. The only men who are allowed around birthing women are doctors and even then they prefer the doctors to be female.'

'Oh. Does that mean I need to take over?'

Daniel raised an eyebrow. 'Have you delivered many babies? I thought you were a general surgeon.'

'I am and…uh…I delivered a few during my internship.'

'Many years ago, no doubt. Well, consider this birth a refresher course, Melora, because you're bound to see a few more during your time in Tarparnii. Today you can be my assistant.' He smiled up at her and Melora felt the full effect of his handsome face, his bright twinkling brown eyes, his perfectly straight teeth and his slightly crooked nose. Sunlight was shining down through the trees onto his dark hair, almost giving him a halo effect. Daniel Tarvon? A saint? Well, she was sure these three women thought him so.

Melora swallowed and forced herself to look away from the man before her, forced her mind to concentrate so she could be of assistance to him rather than an imbecile who stood there ogling him. So he was handsome. That didn't mean a thing. She'd dated handsome doctors before, she'd even been engaged to a handsome doctor, but her life had changed and she was no longer the woman she'd once been. End of story.

Pushing that thought and all others from her mind, she put on her game face. 'OK, *boss*. What do you need me to do?'

'While we're waiting for the baby's head to crown, which should happen any time within the next few contractions, I need you to find something to wrap the baby in. While it's quite warm today, we need to keep the baby as warm as possible.'

'Right. I'll check the Jeep.' But even as she headed back to the vehicle, she knew exactly what she'd find in the back seats. Her bag. As she circled around the car, she noted the spare tyre, a jerrycan full of petrol and another full of water locked into the very rear of the Jeep. She managed to unlock the jerrycan with h2o written in bright letters on the outside and put it on the ground. Next, she unzipped her large bag and began rummaging for something they could use to wrap the baby in after its birth.

She'd been told by PMA that all bedding would be provided but she'd still packed her own things. She'd packed two travel towels so pulled out one to use now. She found a large cotton shirt she used for painting, which she could tear up if necessary. Next, she pulled free her very compact sleeping bag, which would be perfect for keeping the baby warm.

Where she ordinarily liked her things to be packed neatly and tidily, she gritted her teeth, shoved everything back into her bag and zipped it closed. Now was not the time for fastidiousness but rather for helping out in an emergency. Gathering her things and the jerrycan of water, she headed back to Daniel and the women.

'Ah, good. You found the water,' he said. 'I had meant to ask you to bring it down. Well done, Melora. We'll make a jungle doctor out of you yet.'

'Thanks.' She tried not to show how pleased she was at his praise. She was a surgeon, she was out of her depth and she hadn't been praised by a peer in years, and yet it still felt wonderful to hear those words. While she appreciated the seriousness of what they were doing, knowing that anything could go wrong at any given moment, she couldn't ignore the fact that she was also excited about being able to help out at such a special time. She guessed that jungle doctors needed to practise jungle medicine!

She showed Daniel the other things she'd brought down to assist with the delivery as they sat on the ground at J'tana's feet. P'tanay and K'hala were muttering soothing words, helping J'tana through this difficult time.

'Great. We'll wrap the baby in the towel and keep it warm with the sleeping bag.' J'tana moaned again, gritting her teeth against the pain, trying not to call out, and Daniel checked the status of the baby. 'Head is definitely crowning.' He spoke in Tarparnese and even though Melora couldn't understand him, she could see through his expression and hear in his tone that his words were of encouragement.

Melora took another look through Daniel's medical bag and noticed he'd already used the stethoscope as it was lying on top of other things. Below it, she saw a portable sphygmomanometer. She pulled both out and once the contraction had finished, she shifted around with her equipment, getting into position to do the observations.

'Thanks, Mel. I was just about to suggest you check her blood pressure for me.' He rapidly explained to the women what she was going to do and they moved aside so Melora could do her job.

'Blood pressure is slightly elevated but within normal range,' she reported as she hooked the stethoscope into her ears and pressed it first to J'tana's heart and then to her abdomen. 'All within normal range,' she announced.

'Good. Thanks. While this is J'tana's first baby, it's

coming quickly, although her mother did say that J'tana had been in labour on and off for the past few days.'

'Poor girl.'

'They thought they'd be able to make it to the clinic but apparently the baby was impatient to make its entrance into the world.'

'They were almost there, almost made it to the village. What strong, brave women they are.' Melora smiled at all three of them and P'tanay smiled back. She said something to Daniel and he quickly translated.

'She says thank you.'

'She can understand me?'

'She said she's heard the English phrase "strong, brave women" before and she thanks you for thinking it of her and her daughters.' Daniel's smile increased. 'Looks as though you've made your first new friends in Tarparnii.'

This news made Melora feel incredible.

It made her realise that out here it didn't matter what degrees she held or what research projects she'd undertaken. Careers were important within hospital walls, not in the jungle. Out here, she was a doctor who had come to help and the Tarparniian people were extremely grateful for that help.

J'tana gritted her teeth and pushed again, and with this contraction the baby's head came out completely. As they waited for the shoulders to rotate, Melora once more did the observations and then started to prepare for the next stage of labour. She found locking forceps, ready to clamp the cord, scissors for cutting the cord and a small container she could use to put water into.

As she continued to get set up, Melora watched the way Daniel was interacting with his patient. He was all ease and friendliness. There was no falseness about him and again she compared him to the crisp, by-the-book surgeons she'd been working with for the past few years.

She compared him to some of the doctors she'd had during her mastectomy surgery and while they had been top in their field, Melora had quickly realised that bedside manner did indeed count a lot towards a patient's level of recovery. Daniel Tarvon seemed to have an amazing bedside manner and her opinion of him increased.

'Shoulders have rotated,' he announced. 'Just a few more good pushes, J'tana.' He said the words in English but then broke into Tarparnese halfway through. The young mother didn't cry out but gritted her teeth and pushed as hard as she could, sweat on her brow, breath held, pain in her eyes. This was hard labour.

Soon Daniel was lifting the healthy-sized baby boy and Melora held out her towel, accepting the child. She wrapped him loosely, rubbing his little body, stimulating him to breathe while cleaning off the vernix. She could feel the cord pulsating and silently counted the beats, watching his chest for any sign of movement.

'He's bradycardic. We have to get him breathing.' She looked around, feeling helpless without any sort of medical equipment. 'We need suction and oxygen, Daniel. What do I do?' There was veiled panic in her tone.

'Relax, Melora. All you need to do is put your mouth over his mouth and nose and suck any obstruction out of the way. That should do the trick.'

'What?' Disbelief was written all over her face. Was he joking or serious?

'That's all you need to do. It'll work. Trust me.'

Trust him? She'd known him for less than an hour!

Well…what else was she supposed to do? The baby wasn't breathing.

'Here goes,' she mumbled quietly to herself, and did as Daniel had suggested. Thankfully it worked and within another few seconds the baby gurgled, his little face contorted and he gave a hoarse cry.

Everyone exhaled. J'tana smiled and collapsed back into the bracken, her eyes closed, fatigue starting to wash over her. The baby was OK.

Daniel stripped the cord as best he could with his fingers before reaching for the locking forceps and the scissors. He clamped and cut the cord and Melora re-wrapped the crying baby boy, ensuring he was dry and warm.

J'tana accepted the baby with pride, mother and sister speaking and cooing rapidly at the baby, showering him with love. Melora smiled, surprised to find tears misting her eyes at the sight.

'Gets to me every time, too,' Daniel murmured, and when she looked at him she realised he mirrored the look of wonderment that no doubt was on her own face. The miracle of life, the amazing healthy delivery of a perfectly formed human being. The world was indeed an awesome place. 'We just need to deliver the placenta and then we can get everyone into the Jeep and head for the village.'

'What do you usually do with the placenta? I mean, we're out in the middle of nowhere and I don't have anything you can put it in. Do you bury it?'

'Can't. *Ha'kuna* will dig it up and eat it. That gives them a taste for human flesh.' Daniel looked around them at their surroundings then pointed. 'Over there. See those large dry leaves from the trees.' Melora nodded, the trees looking a lot like banana trees with long, wide leaves. Daniel continued. 'Gather a few of those and we'll wrap the placenta in that, take it back to the village and burn it.'

'It really is a different world,' she muttered as she went to do as she was told. Once the placenta had been delivered, Daniel checked it then wrapped it as securely as he could with the leaves. While he was doing that, Melora used the shirt strips and water, mixed with disinfectant, to help cleanse J'tana.

When next she looked at the mother, she had the young babe to her breast, the child suckling hungrily. Melora swallowed, the natural sight bringing an instant pain to her heart. It was what breasts were meant for, to feed and nourish a child.

For her, though, that wasn't the case.

One whole breast had been removed, as well as the cancerous lymph nodes. Part of her body, a vital part that expressed her femininity, had been cut from her in order to save her life. She knew she was fortunate, she knew that her prognosis was considered favourable, and she really couldn't ask for more than that.

She knew she was privileged to live in a time where treatments such as radiotherapy and chemotherapy could assist in keeping patients cancer free for the rest of their lives and she desperately wanted that to be the case. The fact that she'd left it too late to have children, to nuzzle a baby to her breast, just like J'tana, was something she would have to live with. She'd concentrated on her career, pushing the thought of marriage and children into the 'later' box. Now, though, that box was out of reach and she envied J'tana the natural ability to breast-feed her child.

'Melora?'

At the sound of her name, she turned quickly to look

at Daniel, unaware there were tears streaming silently down her cheeks until it was too late. He'd already seen.

'Melora? What is it?' he asked quietly. 'What's wrong?'

Melora bit her lip and shook her head, breaking her gaze away from his expressive brown eyes, which were filled with concern. He watched as she continued to roll up the strips of her shirt she'd been using to help cleanse J'tana, tidying things up and then pulling off her gloves, tying them into an enclosed ball.

She brushed a hand across her face and concentrated on controlling her breathing. Daniel wasn't at all sure what had just happened but the look he'd seen on her face had been one of utter desolation. He knew people came to Tarparnii for many different reasons. Some wanted a break from their lives, some were running away from something, some simply wanted to forget.

He'd learned that it didn't really matter why these professionals came to help, just that they *came*. The people and the lifestyle in Tarparnii had helped many of his friends in the past and as he'd witnessed the pain on Melora's face as she'd watched J'tana feed the baby, he hoped Tarparnii would have the same healing effect on her as it had had on others.

As they continued to pack everything away, Melora having taken J'tana's blood pressure again and listened to the baby's heartbeat, pronouncing herself satisfied, Daniel assisted the new mother into the Jeep. J'tana was positioned in the back seat, lying as best she could, leaning up against her sister. Melora had insisted P'tanay sit in the front but the new grandmother had declined and squeezed into the back with her daughters.

Sitting in the front seat, with her large bag on her

lap, which almost obscured her vision, was how Melora finally arrived in the village. Daniel beeped the horn as they drove up and soon they were surrounded by several people, all coming out to see what the ruckus was about. When they realised what had happened, J'tana and her baby were whisked away, the rest of her family following.

'Welcome to our village.' The greeting came from a small but slim Tarparnii woman with grey hair, wise eyes and a heartfelt smile. 'I am Meeree and this is my husband, Jalak. He is the headman of the village.' Meeree held both of Melora's hands in hers, turning them in a small circle, as was the customary Tarparniian greeting.

'Thank you. I am very honoured to be here.' Melora smiled politely, greeting Jalak as well. 'Your country, what I've seen of it so far, is beautiful and…energetic.' She added the last word as she recalled the mudslide adventure she'd experienced. She looked over her shoulder, expecting to see Daniel close by, but was surprised to find he'd disappeared.

'He has gone to take care of other matters,' Meeree said, and it was then Melora remembered the placenta. Daniel was obviously doing what needed to be done.

'Of course. Yes.'

'Please. You will come and have something to drink. You must wash and become refreshed.' Meeree put her arm through Melora's and started leading the way. Melora quickly bent to pick up her bag but found that Jalak, a man she gauged to be in his late seventies but still appearing very sprightly, had hefted it up onto his shoulder and was carrying it with ease.

As she walked further into the village, Melora was charmed by what she saw. There were quite a number

of bamboo huts with woven leaves for screens and walls
and all had cone-shaped thatched roofs. The huts were
raised from the ground and in many places there were
slatted walkways that joined the huts together. This was
obviously to keep them above the mud that would no
doubt gather in the wetter months but for now everything
was quite dry.

Many of the huts also had little gardens out in front,
filled with native flora, the bright flowers and non-
deciduous bushes bright with a mix of colours. There
were also gardens devoted solely to specific vegetables
and Melora knew that somewhere else would be even
bigger areas of food production.

There were chickens, a few ducks and some goats
roaming about the place, mixing in with the plethora of
children who seemed to be running about, chasing each
other, laughing, clapping and having a good time. There
was a large fire area where a lot of their food would be
cooked, and also a well, both situated near the centre
of the clearing for all to use.

Some women were crouched on the ground, using a
crude form of mortar and pestle to grind things; others
were mixing and some were kneading a large doughy
mass on a flat bamboo-style mat, their guttural language
surrounding them as they talked.

'What a wonderful community you have here,' she
found herself saying as she stood next to Meeree and
drank it all in. 'It's so vibrant and alive.'

'I thank you most humbly,' Meeree remarked, waiting
patiently for Melora to finish looking at the new sights
before her. When Melora was ready, she was welcomed
into Meeree and Jalak's hut, thankful to pour some water
into a basin and wash her hands, face and arms. What
she really wanted was a hot shower but knew that wasn't

on the cards for the next two weeks. She'd done her research. She knew what to expect.

Except for Daniel Tarvon, a quiet voice inside her head remarked, and she realised it was true. She hadn't expected to like what she'd seen in him, and where she'd initially been wary, the way he'd handled the vehicle during the mudslide, the way he'd kept them both safe, had definitely made her drive from the airport to the village a bonding experience. Add to all of that the shared assistance in delivering a child, working together in the face of an emergency, needing to trust each other instantly in a medical capacity…yes, Melora had come to trust him in a personal sense as well.

Even after she'd had a drink and eaten some delightful exotic fruits, one which tasted like a cross between a pear and a banana, she couldn't help but wonder where Daniel had disappeared to. Was he checking on J'tana? Should she go, too? Was there something else happening? Something medical? Did he require her services somewhere?

'He is seeing to his duties,' Meeree said softly, standing and walking to her front door. Melora wasn't sure what the other woman was talking about at first but when Meeree motioned for her to follow, Melora headed outside to stand on the top step, looking out into the village clearing.

There she saw Daniel, surrounded by several children, laughing and enjoying a joke with them, but there was one little girl, with big brown eyes and little blonde pigtails, who was held securely and protectively in his arms.

'His duties?' She found herself asking, unable to take her eyes from him.

'It is the duty of a parent to greet their family when

returning to the village. Daniel Tarvon is greeting his daughter, Simone.'

'His *daughter*?' Melora asked with incredulity, her eyes wide with surprise as she took in the sight of father and daughter.

CHAPTER THREE

HE WAS a father?

As she looked across at him, holding his daughter, laughing and kissing her sweet skin, Melora's heart softened. It looked so natural—father and daughter—and it was evident that he loved her a great deal.

The hollow pit inside her, the one she'd vowed not to think about, started to make itself known. She had been looking forward to starting a family with Leighton, to finally becoming a mother, and now that part of her life was definitely over. She knew it was almost impossible that she would one day feel the same parental love that she could see written on Daniel's face. He was, most definitely, a lucky man.

She could feel Meeree studying her and it was then she remembered Daniel saying that Meeree was a woman of insights. Even though they'd only just met, did Meeree have insights into her? Could the woman see the pain and anguish that had previously made up Melora's life? It made her feel self-conscious and she tugged at the hem of her shirt and then checked the top buttons were still securely in place, her fingers fussing with the edges of the scarf around her neck.

She had come here to Tarparnii to search out a newness that her life had been missing. Too much had gone wrong and where she'd wallowed, feeling as though she'd been walking through the season of winter, her life bleak and hopeless around her, once her chemotherapy had ended she'd decided that enough had been enough.

Tarparnii and the experience she would have here offered her hope. Already today she'd been on a scary but exhilarating mudslide ride, had assisted with the birth of a newborn babe and made friends with the locals. While the opportunity to have children may have passed her by, she'd been blessed in other ways, and finding the silver lining in her situation was what she was trying her hardest to do. She watched as Daniel tickled his daughter, the child's laughter ringing out across the village.

'He's a lucky man,' she murmured.

'He would say he makes his own luck but, yes, he has been most fortunate in having such a wonderful child,' Meeree remarked. 'He is a caring father. That is who Daniel is. He is always bright and smiling, caring for everyone, but his heart has known great sadness and the child in his arms brings him comfort.'

She was thoughtful as the woman's words floated around her. 'His wife has passed away?'

'Yes. She died. They were not here but back in the other country belonging to Daniel. B'lana, his *par'machkai*—his wife—was ill. She was a woman raised in two countries, this one and another one, like Daniel. When her sickness became too much, he took her there for stronger medicines but they would harm the babe. B'lana said no. The babe must remain strong and now look at the child today. Simone is bright and strong, as was the wish of her mother.'

'It can't be easy for Daniel to raise her on his own.' Her admiration for the man increased yet again.

'Not on his own. She is here.' Meeree spread her arms wide. 'With a large family who love her. Every child here belongs to the village and the village belongs to them.'

Melora instantly smiled. 'That's so great for the children.'

'You do not have a large family?'

'No.' She looked away from Daniel and his daughter. 'I'm an only child and one who generally prefers the company of a good book to the company of others, but I'm trying to change.'

'Coming here is something new for you.'

Melora laughed. 'Yes, exactly.'

'Then I am glad you are here.' With a brief touch of warm welcome on her arm, Meeree smiled before turning away and heading over to where a young child of about two had fallen over and was crying.

Melora returned her attention to where Daniel and his daughter had been playing and was almost startled to find him standing before her, his gorgeous little girl still firmly in his arms, her hands wrapped lovingly around his neck.

'Melora, this is my daughter, Simone.' At his words, Simone smiled.

'I'm four and three-quarters, nearly five,' she said with a perfect English accent.

'Wow. You certainly look very much like an almost-five-year-old,' Melora remarked, smiling at the child.

'How old you are?' Simone wanted to know.

Daniel grimaced. 'Simone. You know it's not polite to ask grown-ups their age.' He gave Melora an embarrassed smile. 'Sorry. Lately she's become highly fascinated with everyone's ages.'

'It's all right. I don't mind.' Melora met the little girl's gaze directly. 'I'm forty-one.'

'So is my daddy!' Simone sat up straighter in his arms and unwound her hands from his neck, clapping them with delight. 'You're the same.'

'It appears we are,' Melora agreed with a bright smile.

'And *we* are the same.' Simone pointed between the two of them and then touched her blonde pigtails. 'We have yellow hair but mine is lots longer. Nobody else has yellow hair in the village. They all have black.' The child tipped her head to the side and raised a finger to her chin as though she was thinking. 'Emmy has red hair but she's not here now and Gloria has lots of different colours but she's not here now, too.'

'All right,' Daniel interjected. 'Enough about hair colours, *Separ*. We need to show Melora around the village.'

'Sounds good.' Melora nodded, already half in love with the gorgeous four-year-old.

'This way.' When he inclined his head, she descended the few steps to the ground and followed him. 'How's the acclimatisation process going?'

'It's a lot to take in,' she remarked. 'This world is so different from my own, especially the notification and charting of age and hair colour.' She smiled at Simone.

Daniel chuckled. 'Especially *that*.' He shifted Simone to his other hip, grumbling about how big his daughter was getting. The little girl giggled and it was clear that the two of them were very close. A father having a close relationship with his daughter. It was so nice to see, especially as Daniel had already mentioned that he hadn't connected with his own father.

'Quick layout, just so you can get your bearings. Over here,' he said, pointing, 'are the huts the PMA staff share. They're all quite full at the moment so we're not exactly sure where you'll be sleeping.'

'Oh.'

'Don't stress. We'll find room.' He smiled reassuringly at her and Melora found herself responding with a small smile of her own.

'Thank you.'

'That hut at the end,' he continued, 'is the food hut so if you're hungry at any time, head in there and you'll be able to find something to eat and drink. Cold meats, fruits, breads, that sort of thing. And over here is the brilliant and wonderful medical clinic. Only two years old and still very precious.' Daniel walked over and stroked the mud-brick building, making Melora laugh.

'Ah, yes. Emmy has told me about the clinics. I hear they have running water.'

'Such a luxury,' he confirmed with a nod. 'It was Emmy and Dart who commissioned them and while it may have taken a while to actually have them built, we're all forever grateful. We have four clinic rooms, two treatment rooms and a small six-bed area that serves as a recovery and general ward.'

He put a jiggling Simone down and within seconds she'd run off to join her friends, her blonde hair making her easily stand out amongst the rest of the children.

'Do I stand out that much?' Melora absent-mindedly touched her short, blonde hair.

'Yes.' The one word was soft and quickly spoken and when she turned to look at him, it was to find him regarding her with an intense expression. 'But that's not necessarily a bad thing.'

Their gazes held for a long moment and she felt as though Daniel had just reached out and caressed her cheek. It was the oddest sensation. Melora dropped her hand back to her side and swallowed, desperate to ignore the frisson of awareness that seemed to spring up between them.

'Uh…how are J'tana and the baby?' She glanced at the building behind them, thankfully breaking the contact. Now all she had to do was to ignore the residual tingles that were still flowing through her body. Had Daniel Tarvon just implied she was beautiful? If only he knew the truth about her. No. She wasn't beautiful.

'Both doing very well.' He gestured that they should go inside and again she found herself following him.

'When will they start to head back to their own village?'

'Not for a few more days, possibly a week. It depends how long it takes J'tana to feel up to walking all that way again.'

'Can't they be driven back in a car?'

Daniel shook his head. 'Only to a certain point, and we'd have to go through about five checkpoints to get there. Some villages don't have access by any roads. There are places here that are more easily accessed on foot. That's one of the reasons why we do clinics in different places, the larger villages or ones with other smaller communities around them, to provide easier access for more people.'

'Fair enough.' Talking about their patient and shifting the conversation back to a medical-related focus had helped Melora to feel more calm, more in control, rather than being aware of the man beside her.

Inside the clinic, Daniel pointed things out and even turned on the taps for her. 'I know you probably think it's next to nothing, given that back in Australia you can turn on taps without thinking about where the water's coming from, but here—it really is like a miracle.'

'Daniel. I understand,' she said with a smile. 'You don't have to explain. I think it's brilliant that there's running water and that it makes you feel like a child in a candy store at Christmastime.'

He returned her smile. 'Yes. Yes, it does.' As they stood there in the small examination area, he couldn't help but admire how Melora seemed to be taking everything in. Over the years, he'd seen numerous people come here to help and take weeks, if not months to settle in. Some *never* settled in but apparently Melora Washington wasn't one of them.

While it was clear she was out of her comfort zone, Daniel had the sense that it didn't have all that much to do with being in a completely foreign environment. Something had made her cry as she'd stood and watched J'tana feed her newborn baby. Whatever had caused that reaction was no doubt the real reason why Melora had seemed upset.

As they went through to check on J'tana, he decided to hang back a little, watch how she handled the situation, but as soon as P'tanay saw her, she rushed over and, speaking rapidly, touched Melora's blonde hair.

Melora smiled, feeling highly self-conscious at being touched. She looked to him for a translation and he nodded.

'You're quite right, P'tanay,' he said in Tarparnese, before looking at Melora. 'She says that with thanks to the "bright" woman who was there for the delivery of her first grandson, they're going to name the baby J'torek, which means child the bright light shines on, or child of good fortune.'

'My hair?' She looked astounded, pleased and almost fit to bursting with excitement. 'They're naming the baby after my hair?'

'Yes.' Daniel stepped closer. 'It's better than them naming him after your nose.' He winked at her and she felt a thrill of delight pass through her. It was odd how a bit of teasing, a bit of joking around with her new colleague could give her such a feeling, but as she usually worked with up-tight, stiff doctors back in Sydney, his words had been refreshing.

'What's wrong with my nose?' she asked quietly, a glint of appreciation in her eyes.

His grin increased. 'Nothing. However, your hair, now, that is really something. People here are fascinated by it. P'tanay says that the "bright" woman brought good fortune on her daughter, that it was you who saw them, you who helped with the delivery and that is why you should have the honour.'

Melora was almost fit to bursting with pride. 'Me? I am touched. I'm so grateful.' She said the words to P'tanay. 'Oh, Daniel. Will you please translate that for me? Please?'

Melora's excitement was highly contagious and Daniel translated her words, watching as she clutched her hands lovingly to her chest as though she was accepting an imaginary award. And in some ways she was…accepting the award of having a child named after her.

'I'm touched. I'm so…well…apparently I'm speechless.' Melora turned to the mother and bowed a little. 'Thank you,' she said. Daniel translated her words and then, to her surprise, P'tanay embraced her. Melora was momentarily stunned but carefully returned the embrace, patting the grandmother on the shoulder. P'tanay drew back, talking and smiling and touching Melora's hair one last time.

'Congratulations, Melora,' Daniel remarked placing

his arm around her shoulders and drawing her close. The instant he touched her he realised he might have made a mistake as her entire body tensed. He quickly broke the contact and stepped back. It had been a natural reaction to embrace her as that was simply how the staff here reacted to good news.

Sharing the highs and lows of this job could only really be done by those who were in the thick of it with you. As such, the friendships formed between staff usually became very strong. They would often link arms when walking, or they'd hug—either for comfort and support or for encouragement or even for celebration. Platonic physical contact was very high between the staff members.

Daniel was curious to observe Melora's reaction to her other colleagues. The big question was *why* didn't she like being touched? What had happened to her in her past to make her withdrawn? Perhaps her childhood hadn't been all that happy? Maybe her parents hadn't been the demonstrative type? His own father had been cold and sometimes rejecting, especially when it had come down to showing vulnerable emotions. His mother, on the other hand, was warm and inviting and always had been.

Melora insisted on taking J'tana's blood pressure and listening to her heartbeat, pronouncing herself satisfied that the readings were all within normal limits. He also watched as she checked the baby, listening to his chest and checking the range of movement of his legs and arms. J'torek looked robust and healthy but was starting to make his impatience known at being poked and prodded by the 'bright' doctor.

'He's going to get stroppy with you in a minute, Melora,' Daniel remarked good-naturedly.

She laughed and the soft tinkling sound washed over him, warming him through. He stopped at that thought, watching as she swaddled the babe once more and gave him a little cuddle. Her laughter had warmed him. That was odd because the last woman who had evoked such a reaction had been B'lana, his wife.

Daniel shook his head, as though to clear it, realising he must have imagined the sensation. B'lana's death had left a large hole in his life, one that had taken almost four years to patch over. He wasn't sure the area was strong enough for him to mentally walk on and, besides, he wasn't sure he wanted to. Naturally, he found Melora attractive, but there wasn't a red-blooded male who wouldn't.

She was about five feet eight inches, had honey-brown eyes which he'd already realised were highly expressive whether she was excited, scared or simply happy. Her cheekbones were defined, her nose was straight and her lips were a natural plump pink…the kind of lips that were perfect for kissing.

'Whoa!' The word sprang from his lips.

'Something wrong, Daniel?' Melora asked as she held little J'torek while his mother found a position comfortable enough to be able to feed the baby once more.

Daniel quickly cleared his throat, reminding himself he had no need to be embarrassed because Melora couldn't read his thoughts—thankfully. 'No. Fine. Carry on.'

What was wrong with him? What had he been thinking? He must surely be insane to be actually wondering what Melora's lush pink lips would taste like! It was definitely out of the ordinary for his thoughts to head in that direction, especially about a colleague. Being friends and keeping relationships happy and amicable was part of his job as PMA team leader so he definitely had no business thinking about those plump lips of hers.

He also had other things, more private things, on the boil in the back of his mind, and top of the list was Simone. Now that she was getting closer to the age where she should be attending school, he had some big decisions to make. Having been given every opportunity by living in two very different countries, even if he'd garnered a lot of resentment back then, Daniel knew the importance of a good education.

However, he couldn't bring himself to 'post' Simone off to boarding school and then leave her like a forgotten letter—just as he had been. He wasn't barbaric like his own father and was determined to be a major part of his daughter's life.

J'torek started to cry, bringing Daniel's thoughts back to the present. He watched as Melora cuddled him close before pressing a kiss to his head and handing him back to his mother. 'I think he's getting mighty impatient.' She looked at J'tana, touching her bunched fingers to her mouth, indicating food. 'He's a very healthy boy.' She put two thumbs up to show her approval but Daniel quickly translated her words for her.

J'tana smiled tiredly and settled down to feed her child. Melora felt that same tightening of her insides at watching woman and child, in the way they'd been designed for each other. It was good. It was right, and the fact that it wouldn't happen to her was completely beside the point. She was happy for J'tana and clenched her jaw, ignoring the hollowness that once more rose within her.

Feeling as though the walls were starting to close in on her, Melora smiled politely at the three women before excusing herself and heading out into the fresh air. Once there, she dragged in a few deep breaths, focusing her thoughts on the positives in her life. She had good, supportive friends and an exciting adventure ahead of her.

She heard a sound behind her and quickly looked over her shoulder, not surprised to see Daniel standing there.

'Everything all right?' he asked as he walked to her side. She looked at him, nodded and smiled.

'I'm fine. It's just wonderful to have a happy ending for J'tana and her new son. He has a good set of lungs on him, that's for sure.'

Daniel nodded but looked at her closely. Melora wondered what it was he could see and just as she was starting to squirm inside, he took a step to the side and beckoned her closer. 'Come with me.' He indicated a well-worn path that led away from the village. 'There's something I'd like to show you.'

'Oh. OK.' Once more, Melora found herself following him, trusting this man she really didn't know all that well, but as he was the person she knew *most* in this country, she did as he asked.

Without a word, they walked along the path. It was fairly open, not surrounded by dense scrub but with enough foliage that Daniel had to hold back a few bushes for her to pass by. Neither of them wore a hat, nor did they wear sunglasses, but thankfully the sun wasn't too hot. She swatted at an insect as they headed along, looking around her and drinking in the very different scenery to the city buildings she was used to.

In the past, she'd been quite content with her life. She'd studied hard, worked hard, built her career and attained the position as a general surgical consultant.

She'd found a man she'd wanted to spend the rest of her life with, had become engaged and planned to live happily ever after.

She shook her head. That wasn't how life happened. It wasn't how things had turned out and during the past two years she'd changed into a woman who'd been desperate to find a way to gain some control over her life. Out here, in this lovely scenery, she felt the tension and stress that had plagued her begin to ebb. She imagined herself sitting out here with her sketchpad or, if time permitted, her water-colours. The problem, she soon realised, was choosing which glorious landscape to capture. She was spoiled for choice.

They continued on and within another few minutes Daniel left the path and beckoned her over. 'Come take a look at this,' he encouraged.

Melora followed him and then gasped as they came to a thick, large tree trunk, but the tree had been split in two, the trunk wide open. The detail in the bark, the gnarly twists of the knots, the thickness of the roots—it was utterly exquisite. 'Lightning?'

'Yes. Well over twenty years ago now but this tree always reminds me that out of bad things, good things can grow.' He pointed to the new growth, the small tree that was growing right in the middle of the split trunk. The original tree still had foliage on it, its roots sunk deep into the ground.

'My wife died,' he ventured, hoping that if he opened up to her a little, just a little, she'd open up to him. He wasn't asking for massive revelations but something was obviously bothering her and as PMA team leader, he wanted to help. Telling her a bit about B'lana might help her to trust him a little more. It was definitely worth a shot.

'Meeree mentioned it.'

Daniel didn't seem annoyed at Meeree having told her. 'B'lana was like me. Raised in two different countries but where my father was British, her father was Tarparniian and insisted that his daughter be raised in the ways of her country. She was Tarparniian first, British second, whereas for me, my father made sure it was the other way around.' Daniel reached out and stroked a hand down the tree, the tactile sensation providing importance, providing physical connection.

'This tree has always held such significance for me. I often felt as though I was split in two, raised loving two different cultures.'

'And your life here with your daughter is that the new little tree, that new growth growing right in the middle?'

Daniel's smile at the mention of his daughter was automatic. 'Yes.' He paused. 'When B'lana died, I felt as though I'd been struck by lightning again, that my life had been ripped open and I was exposed…raw.'

Melora nodded, knowing that sort of sensation all too well. She felt as though she'd been struck by lightning, that her life had been ripped apart by forces beyond her control.

'I don't want to pry, Melora, but out here, working in such a small community and in an often stressful environment, it's paramount that we're able to keep ourselves focused. Seeing J'tana with her baby affected you deeply. Over fifty per cent of our patients are pregnant women, some younger than J'tana, some in their forties having their tenth or eleventh child. On a strictly work-related basis, I need to know that you're going to be able to handle seeing them with their children.'

Anger and heat started to rise within Melora and

she clenched her teeth together. 'I'm a professional, Dr Tarvon. I'll do my job.'

'I'm not saying that you won't.' He hadn't missed the way she'd called him by his title and surname. He'd angered her with his words, not what he'd meant to do. He simply wanted her to open up a little so he knew how best to guide her while she was there. 'What I am saying is that I get the feeling that your life has been split in two, just like this tree. I don't know what might have happened to you but I have the feeling that it has something to do with babies.'

She straightened her shoulders, pushing aside the emotions of her heart and pulling on her professionalism. 'No. Not babies, per se.' Slowly, she met her new colleague's gaze. 'I don't think my past, whether my life has been split in two or not, is of any relevance at the moment.'

'It is if it affects your work,' he countered.

'It won't.'

'You can't know that for sure, Melora.'

'I can. I've been a highly competent, fully qualified general surgeon for quite a number of years. Medicine has been my main focus for over half my life and learning to control my own personal feelings has been part of that training, as I'm sure you well understand.'

'But out here, out in the middle of a jungle...' Daniel spread his arms wide, indicating the fact that they really were, for all intents and purposes, standing in the middle of nowhere '...emotions have a way of sneaking up on you and slapping you fair in the face.

'You've come here for a change, Melora, and for that alone I applaud you. However, the majority of people who come to provide medical aid in Tarparnii are usually trying to escape from something. It might be that they need to recharge their batteries, to remember why they decided to pursue medicine in the first place, or it might be because their ordinary life has dealt them a cruel blow and they feel so at odds with their life that they simply want to run away.'

He raked both hands through his hair, needing to get through to her. 'Dart, Emmy's husband, came here regularly for six years before he was even able to face the tragedy of his past. Another friend, Eden Montgomery, who I first worked with in the Ukraine, literally ran away from home, but instead of joining the circus she joined PMA and was able to work through her personal pain by helping others. And let's face it, the need to be able to help others, to make a difference in their lives, is what no doubt leads most of us into the medical profession in the first place.'

'But…?' she prompted, knowing he wasn't going to let this subject drop until he'd made his point.

'But out here, working with a very close-knit group of people, providing care for literally hundreds and hundreds of people on a weekly basis, means that we need to be open with each other, that we need to rely on each other, to trust each other. Relationships in big teaching hospitals can take years to evolve, but out here they take a matter of days, sometimes…' he spread his hands wide as though to indicate the two of them '…a matter of hours, especially if there are mudslides involved.' His lips twitched into a smile at the last words. 'My point is that we're all in this together and you need to know that not only are we here as a team to provide medical care to those who need it, we're also here to help one another.'

'So you're saying that working here has helped you get over your wife's death?' She sounded sceptical but he didn't pursue it.

'Not "get over" her death but to at least come to terms with it, to accept the finality of it, yes, and I couldn't have done that without the support of those around me.' He paused, hoping he was getting through to her. 'I miss B'lana. That will never change. But I've managed to move on with my life, and I did it in stages. I'm not ready to move on in a romantic sense but time and understanding friends do go a long way to help heal the gaping holes in my life, especially when I feel raw from being split in two.' He indicated the tree beside them. 'Coming to Tarparnii has been the next stage in your life and you've done it so you can start to deal with the pains of your past.

'I'm not asking for a complete rundown of your entire history, Melora, but it's clear you're hurting, it's clear that your life has been fractured in some way. The areas of your life that can have a direct impact on your job here are what I'm asking you to be open about. If I know, I can help. If you have difficulties being around babies, I'll make sure your case load contains a lot of old men.'

He smiled and she nodded, knowing he had a point but not at all sure she could actually just blurt out the truth and tell him what was really wrong.

Melora's previous anger towards him started to fade. 'You're right that people in big teaching hospitals can take years to form any sort of lasting relationships.' Her throat went dry and she swallowed a few times and licked her lips. 'I feel as though I know you better than half the people I've been working with for years,' she said, thinking directly of Leighton. She'd been engaged to the man for two years and in the end she'd realised she'd never really known him at all. 'It's a very strange sensation.'

'Out here, we're all each other has,' he agreed, and knowing that he'd nudged her enough for the moment took a mental step back to wait. He'd watched the defensive anger she'd pulled around her start to vanish but in its place came a hesitant wariness.

A few minutes ticked by and when she didn't speak he wondered if he'd backed off too far. He was just about to talk again when she bent and picked a wild flower and started plucking the petals from it.

'My life has been split in two, just like that tree, and sometimes it feels as though it's in even more pieces than that. It's as though someone has plucked all of my petals, just like this flower. Different parts of me, the *old* parts of me, have been crushed up and scattered in the wind and I don't know if I'll ever get them all back, no matter how hard I strive for normality.'

Daniel waited, surprised at the elation he felt that she'd decided to trust him, that she'd started to open up. He knew she wouldn't tell him everything, but it was a first step, the tip of the iceberg, and at the moment that was all he needed so they could both do their jobs properly.

'I just want you to know, though, that I've passed all my medicals, that PMA and my surgeons have cleared me to come and work here.'

Her surgeons? That startled him a little. 'You were sick?'

'Yes.' She was still looking at the destroyed flower in her hand, feeling as though it really did signify her life. 'This morning I was in Australia, getting ready to embark on a new and very different adventure, which has brought me here—standing on a valley floor, next to a tree with so much essence and character, trying to find the right words to describe what's happened to me without boring you with all the nitty-gritty details. It's been the strangest, most exhilarating and emotionally draining day I've ever had.'

'I can believe it and, just for the record, it's not every day that we get large mudslides. I know you're probably tired and want to lie down for a while and rest, but this is important, Melora. You're only here for two weeks and I'd like those weeks to be full of healing, for both you and the patients, but also for it to be enjoyable as well.'

Melora nodded, knowing all she needed to do was to tell Daniel enough of her turmoil so that he could structure the PMA workload while still maintaining an overall level of privacy and control. If she told him too much, too soon about her obliterated life, he'd end up feeling sorry for her and would probably remove her from the duty rosters all together.

He was looking at her now, watching her closely as she plucked another flower, blowing the petals into the wind. Was that really what her life felt like? As though she'd been plucked, her life broken up into pieces and scattered on the breeze?

Being a diagnostician, he mentally worked through a few different scenarios in his mind, watching as she tried to find the right words to tell him what had been upsetting her. She'd been sick. Perhaps she'd lost someone close to her, a child maybe. No. He dismissed that because he'd seen the way she'd eagerly held baby J'torek, kissing the child's forehead with heart-felt love. Besides, she was the one who had been sick. She'd had surgeons.

He looked at her hair. It was still short. Not extremely short but from the light, feathery way in which it was styled, he did wonder whether her present hairstyle had something to do with chemotherapy.

'I didn't mean to cry,' she ventured. 'Earlier, when J'tana was first feeding the baby,' she quickly clarified. 'The emotions caught me completely unawares.'

'Understood.'

'I thought I'd dealt with a lot of this.'

'Sometimes emotions do tend to catch us on the hop.' She was stalling. He could see it and as she tugged at the hem of her shirt, her other hand flying to ensure the collar was down and the scarf was secure, he thought about letting her off the hook. After fidgeting, she crossed her arms protectively over her chest and he wondered why such a beautiful woman with such a slim build hid herself behind such baggy shirts.

'I can do my job, you know.' She was starting to clam up, to batten down the hatches, and Daniel's thought processes sped up. He'd taken her to the edge of the cliff and she'd thought about jumping off, of opening up to him, but now she was backing away, deciding she didn't want to do this at all. He hated to push, but he felt compelled to do it in this instance—one of his famous gut reactions he'd learned to trust over the years.

'Have you had cancer?' he asked almost before she'd finished speaking.

The colour instantly drained from her face and she felt as though the world had started to spin in the opposite direction.

'You can tell!'

CHAPTER FOUR

'OH, MY goodness!' Melora found it difficult to breathe. 'You can *tell*?' Her hands started to tremble and she clasped them together. It didn't do any good.

How could he tell? Had her prosthetic breast slipped out of line beneath her shirt? Had she accidentally knocked it? Panic and mortification continued to rise within her. She was still so new to this, was still coming to terms with everything that had happened to her during the past twenty months, but she'd also thought she was getting better at dealing with the emotional angle. Obviously not.

She shook her head and bit her lip. Daniel was talking to her, saying words, but she couldn't hear him, couldn't make out what he was saying because the drumming of her heart was reverberating around her body. Even though she was standing out in the middle of nowhere, she felt as though the world was closing in on her.

Looking up at the sky, it started to swirl around, making her feel sick. She looked down at the ground but it was doing the same thing. How had this happened? How could he tell? Could he see? Was it that obvious? Bile rose in her throat. She squinted and tried to focus but nothing seemed to be standing still. Not the sky, not the ground, not the split-in-two tree. She felt herself pitching forward and blindly put out a hand to try and stop herself from falling over.

'Whoa, there,' she heard Daniel say, and then felt his warm arms come around her body, holding her close. 'Steady there, Melora.' His words were close to her ear, deep and rich and soothingly nice. She closed her eyes, starting to feel a bit better as she leaned into him. He adjusted his hold on her, shifting so she rested her head against his chest.

She knew she should tell him to let her go but she didn't. Standing there, waiting for the world to stop spinning, she felt secure and protected in Daniel's arms. It was an odd sensation, to feel protected by someone she really didn't know. She'd spent years with Leighton, their relationship gradually moving from colleagues to friends to a much deeper friendship before he'd proposed, and yet she'd never once felt protected by him.

Of course, that had been BC—before cancer—when her world had been under her complete control. Now, though, it felt as though it was completely out of control. Daniel could tell she'd had breast cancer! She had no idea how he knew but as the world stopped spinning and her mind cleared from her instant panic, she knew she had to face him.

With her thoughts gradually returning to normal, Melora breathed slowly and deeply, her senses tantalised by Daniel's earthy, spicy scent. It teased around her, mixing easily with the sweet fresh fragrance she wore, blending into an exotic combination.

He smelled so nice and even though her breathing was almost back to normal and she was sure her legs would support her once again, Melora lingered for a few seconds longer, allowing his protective warmth to flood through her body.

Leaning into him, feeling calm and protected for the first time since her world had been turned upside down. For this brief snatched moment, Melora felt as though it was possible to get her head above water. It was long enough for her to take a much-needed breath and it was all because her new colleague had made her feel safe.

'You smell really nice,' she murmured, knowing it was time to pull back, to let this brief moment go.

'So do you,' he replied, his tone deep, rumbly and sexy. It wasn't until his words penetrated her mind that she realised she'd actually spoken out loud. She instantly pushed herself away from him, his arms falling back to his sides as she stepped back, horror swamping her that she'd actually spoken those words out loud!

She stood there, staring at Daniel, her hands coming to her cheeks to feel the heat gathering there. Why had she spoken out loud? She swallowed, unsure what to do or say next.

'It's amazing that after travelling, assisting with an emergency and the lack of running water in the village, you still smell as fresh as a daisy,' he said into the temporary silence, picking up on the fact that Melora was feeling rather out of her depth at the moment.

For some reason, the fact that he'd guessed she'd had cancer had put her into a tailspin. It had just been a guess and, sadly, not a difficult one in this day and age. Even then, he was still unsure exactly what type of cancer she'd had.

Physically recovering from cancer was one thing but dealing with the emotional side-effects was something completely different and could take years to overcome. Any long-term, terminal illness could have the same effect. That was something he knew all too well, having nursed B'lana through her own terminal illness. For

Melora to come to a new country, intent on new experiences, showed gumption.

Without a word, she started walking, heading away from the tree, back to the trail. Unable to look at Daniel, knowing his words had been an effort to try and bring their worlds back onto a more even keel, Melora simply wanted to get back to the village where there were other people about.

'Melora?'

He reached out a hand to her but she managed to evade his touch, her body still heated from before. Furious with herself for letting him see her like this, angry that he'd brought her out here in the first place, embarrassed that she'd almost fainted and that he'd saved her, she simply wanted to return to the village.

She reached the well-worn path and started to pick up the pace.

'Melora?' he called again, coming after her and putting his hand on her elbow to stop her. She spun around to pin him with a glare.

'What is it, Daniel?' she demanded, trying to call on the cool, calm and professional demeanour she usually wore.

'You're going the wrong way.' He pointed in the direction she was headed. 'This path takes you to the waterhole.' He jerked his other thumb in the opposite direction. '*That's* the way back to the village.'

'Oh.' Closing her eyes and clenching her teeth together, unable to believe she was behaving so irrationally, Melora took a steadying breath before looking at him. 'I'm sorry, Daniel. I don't usually act this way.' She shook her head. 'I'm usually quite poised and in control but…'

'Cancer has a way of changing all of that,' he offered.

'Yes. I've come here to Tarparnii because even though it's almost two years since I had the initial surgery and even though I've returned to work at the hospital, I have since discovered that my life, the life I had before the cancer, just doesn't seem to fit me any more.'

She paused for a moment. 'It's not really a big secret, I guess. I'm just a private person and for a while I was number one on the hospital gossip hit parade with everyone knowing I'd had breast cancer. I guess you just... took me by surprise when you guessed.'

Daniel kept his expression neutral. Breast cancer? She'd had breast cancer! His mind played back over her earlier mortification when he'd 'guessed' why she'd been sick. Had she thought he could *see* that she'd had a mastectomy? That hadn't been the case at all. Now, though, wasn't the time to tell her that. She was on a roll. She was talking and he wasn't about to stop her.

She looked down at the baggy shirt she was wearing. 'I don't know *how* you could tell. Maybe you're a superhero doctor with X-ray vision.' Her attempt at humour fell flat and she cleared her throat.

'Coming here, to this beautiful country, I thought I'd be able to get away from everything. To get away from being talked about, from everyone knowing my business, like how I coped with the last lot of chemotherapy, or that my platelet count was low this week, or that today Dr Washington's having a blood transfusion.

'It's very difficult,' she continued, 'to try and get on with your life when you have a constant barrage of "How *are* you, Melora?" being asked everywhere you go.'

'People care about you. That's good.'

'I guess.' Melora sighed heavily.

'But when everyone continually asks you "How are you?" it can become very draining,' he continued, and she turned to look at him more closely. His dark eyes were filled with sadness.

'Exactly.'

Daniel nodded. 'The same thing happens when someone you love dies.'

'Of course. So you know how it feels to not really *know* where you fit within your own world?'

'I do.'

'My world felt as though it was starting to implode. It came to the point of me not wanting to go to work, not wanting to see patients, not wanting to practise medicine any more. I felt as though I was turning into an ice queen, distancing myself from everyone, unsure who to trust, unable to find any sort of satisfaction with my life.'

'PCS. Post-cancer stress.'

'Yes. I realise that now but before Emmy suggested I come to Tarparnii, I wasn't sure what to do. So I guess I need to confess that I'm not only here to work with PMA but also to find out who I am.'

Daniel smiled. 'A noble quest.'

Melora felt the tension and earlier anxiety seep from her and sighed. Daniel knew what had happened to her and it appeared not to concern him. She was here to work, to do a job, and that was what she would do.

'Feel better?'

'Surprisingly, yes.'

'Shall we?' he asked, indicating the correct way back to the village.

'Yes. Thank you.'

As they walked, Daniel pointed out other different

things. Chatting to Melora, sharing more of his land with her, meant he didn't have to think about the intense couple of moments they'd shared—of seeing the mortification cross her face, of seeing the panic in her eyes just before she'd almost fainted and ended up in his arms. Holding her close, supporting her, feeling the pain emanating from her, Daniel had wanted to help her, to hold her, to protect her. She was a woman who'd been through a lot and yet she was still soldiering on.

He admired her for that.

'Everything out here is so incredibly different.' There was utter delight in her tone. 'The colours, the smells, the—'

Daniel put his arm out in front of her to stop her walking. 'Wait.'

'Daniel?'

'Shh. Don't move.' His words were quiet but direct and Melora's alarm bells instantly started to ring. She quickly looked around them, trying to figure out what was going on…and then she saw it. A large, thick, snake crossing the path not too far from where they were. A cold sweat settled over her and her mouth went instantly dry.

'What do we do?' She clutched at his arm, needing the security of being close to him.

'Just stay right where you are. Don't move.'

Melora kept her eyes fixed to the snake, unsure in which direction it was travelling as she could see neither the head nor the tail. 'Is it…deadly?' In her research she had come across information about snakes and the different types that were indigenous to Tarparnii but right now, for the life of her, she was unable to recall any of the information as fear had become her dominant emotion.

'Very.'

'Do we just wait for it to go?'

'No.' There was determination mixed with a hint of regret in Daniel's tone. 'It's too close to the village.' He dropped his arm and she immediately clutched her hands together, holding them close to her chest as her heart pounded wildly.

Shivers ran down Melora's spine and as Daniel moved away from her towards the snake she instinctively reached out a hand to stop him. 'Daniel,' she whispered, her concern more than evident in her tone.

He glanced back at her and smiled. 'Relax. I've done this hundreds of times.'

'Done what?' Her eyes widened as she watched him head off the path and into the scrub, pulling the hunting knife, which she'd completely forgotten he wore, from the pouch at his waist. 'Oh, my goodness.' She swallowed over the terror in her throat and stood exactly where she was, following his instructions to the letter.

Her eyes were almost bugging out of her head, and her hands now up at her mouth as Daniel disappeared completely from her view. She could hear him, his gentle and careful footfalls before the sound of a loud *thwack* reverberated around them.

She screamed at the sound, shoving her hands almost into her mouth in an effort to keep herself quiet. The length of snake still visible on the path started to wiggle and squirm and although Melora wanted nothing more than to close her eyes, to be anywhere except where she was, standing still on a slightly overgrown path in the middle of a jungle, she kept her gaze firmly fixed on the reptile. There was another thud and then the snake's body moved extremely fast towards the direction Daniel had taken.

Her heart rate was all but off the chart with fear and trepidation as she stood there, waiting. A minute later, she couldn't take the suspense and uncertainty any more. 'Daniel?' she called.

'It's fine. I'm fine,' he returned, and instantly appeared at the edge of the path. 'Sorry. Didn't mean to frighten you.' He had his hunting knife in his hand, the blade tinged with what she presumed to be bits of snake.

'Ugh.' Shuddering again, she looked at him. 'Can I move now?'

'Yes. It's all safe. No more snake. Well…' he said as he stepped over a fallen tree branch onto the path, the snake's body in his free hand, 'no more *alive* snake. It won't be bothering the village this evening, except as an accompaniment to tonight's meal.'

Melora shook her head in utter astonishment and swallowed over the bubble of hysteria she could feel rising up. 'Oh, well…that's OK, then,' she remarked with a nervous laugh.

'Shall we head back?' He inclined his head towards the village.

'You're not dull to be around. I'll give you that,' she said, walking quickly past him. He stayed a few steps behind her, dragging the snake's dead body after them. Melora glanced at it more than once.

'What type of snake was it?'

'Green-belly ringed snake. Sort of the Tarparniian equivalent to the boa constrictor. They don't usually come this close to the village but when they do, we need to get rid of them quickly. Also, they're the ones that taste best.'

Melora laughed in disbelief. 'You're wild, Daniel Tarvon.'

'Actually, I'm just your typical Tarparniian-Englishman who has vowed to protect new PMA staff from snakes, mudslides and anything else that might come along.' He chuckled, the sound washing over her, relaxing her previous tension and giving her that same light-heartedness she'd experienced after the mudslide adventure had ended.

As they entered the village, Daniel's green-belly ringed snake instantly became the centre of attention, Melora wondered who was going to protect her against the awe and sensual attraction she most definitely felt for her new colleague.

That night, as it turned out, was a special night in the village.

'It's a welcoming banquet,' Daniel told her after he'd washed up from handling the snake. They were sitting in the food hut, chopping up fruit. Simone and two other children had insisted on helping and were putting the chopped fruit onto wooden platters. The little girl declared that she would sit next to Melora while they worked.

''Cos we're yellow girls.' She giggled, referring to the colour of their hair, and that was that.

'What's a welcoming banquet?' Melora asked. 'Is someone important coming to the village?'

'Yes.' Daniel glanced across the table then pointed to her. 'You.'

Melora stopped chopping and met his gaze. '*Me*? Oh, no. I don't need a big welcoming banquet. They don't need to do that. There doesn't need to be any fuss for me.'

'It's their custom, Melora. The village welcome all new PMA doctors, on behalf of the Tarparniian people, as a small token of their thanks. It would be extremely ungracious of you to refuse and they would take great umbrage.'

'And they do this for everyone who comes?'

'Yes. They don't have much but what they do have, they're more than willing to share.'

She looked around the food hut, seeing women preparing food, kneading a bread-type dough and generally getting things ready. She shook her head slowly, amazed at the generosity of these people. 'They make me feel very humble. I'm sure I don't deserve it.'

'I'm sure you do.' Daniel smiled. 'Usually, we have a group of people arriving from PMA to help out and they all get welcomed in just the same way. As it turns out, this time it's just you coming into this little world and, as such, you deserve the official welcome. Of course, that doesn't mean you get out of helping.' He pointed to the fruit in front of her. 'Now chop, Dr Washington!'

As the sun started to set, Melora found it difficult to believe so much had happened to her since she'd risen early that morning back at her apartment in Australia. In some ways, it felt as though she'd been here in Tarparnii for much longer than just today. While exhaustion was starting to set in, she was eager for the celebrations to begin.

The bonfire was lit, food was passed around, children clapped and laughed, singing songs with the help of one of the PMA crew, Sue, who played the guitar. Meeree and Jalak officially welcomed her to their village and where she thought she'd feel highly self-conscious, standing out from the crowd with her blonde hair and inexperience of their way of life, she didn't feel at all like an interloper but rather as though she'd just been accepted into a loving family.

It warmed her heart and humbled her at the same time.

Throughout the evening Daniel was attentive by her side, introducing her to the other PMA staff members, some of whom had come from the United Kingdom and New Zealand and some who, like Daniel, lived in the village, such as Belhara, their resident anaesthetist, and Bel, a Tarparniian nurse.

Daniel was her anchor in this foreign world and she would turn to him with questions and comments and he would always provide whatever answer she needed.

'How are you feeling?' he asked as Melora sipped at her drink. 'Tired?'

'Yes, but it's a good tired.' She nodded. Simone ran past them at that point, laughing and playing games with her friends. The young girl had been particularly attentive towards Melora that evening, often telling anyone who would listen that there was someone else in the village just like her—someone with yellow hair. The child seemed happy, relieved in some ways, to no longer be the odd one out, and the hair colour connection had instantly bonded them.

'Simone is simply gorgeous, Daniel. She's a credit to you.'

'Thank you, Mel. That means a lot.'

'Mel?' It wasn't the first time he'd called her that today.

'Do you not like it?'

'I don't mind it. It's what my closest friends sometimes call me.'

He shifted on the wooden bench they sat on, coming physically closer to her. 'Is this close enough?' he joked, his voice laced with ironic humour.

'It's too close.' She gave a nervous chuckle and edged

away, wishing he wouldn't do things like that because it only served to remind her of how incredible he really was. Although, when she thought about it, could he really be as wonderful as he appeared? Everyone had flaws but she was yet to discover what Daniel's were.

'Fair enough,' he murmured, and eased back. 'But I can still call you Mel, right? I mean, we've shared quite a bit today.'

'We have.' She nodded as Simone came running up to them.

'Melora?' she began in that sing-song tone of hers, clambering up onto Melora's knee.

'Yes?' She put her arms around the little girl and held her close, loving the feel of the small body against her own. She was still astonished that this child, a stranger, had taken such a shine to her. It was incredibly nice as well as flattering, and with the way her ego had been dented in the past, she would take all the flattery she could get.

'Will you…' Simone yawned '…read me a story?'

'Oh.' She was a little surprised at the request. 'Uh… of course.'

'Good.' Simone leaned into her, shifting to put her legs out along the bench, her feet resting on her father's knee. 'I'll get the book soon.'

'OK.' Melora rested her chin on Simone's head and looked over at Daniel. 'What were we talking about?' As she asked the question, she felt a yawn begin to rise and quickly smothered it.

'Simone's started you off,' Daniel joked. 'You must be exhausted, Melora.'

'I don't know, between mudslides, births and snakes, you would have thought I'd have an extra barrel of energy somewhere.'

'I think you've already used it up.' He looked at the two of them, the 'bright' girls with their shiny blonde hair. 'You've really made her day. Thank you.'

'For having the same colour hair? I assure you, I didn't plan it.'

His soft chuckle washed over her. 'Thanks all the same. As a doting father, I like seeing my daughter happy. It doesn't take much to put a smile on her face but when it's there, it's as though all is right with my world.' There was a wistfulness in his tone.

'How long ago did your wife die?' she couldn't help but ask.

'Just after Simone turned one.'

'Meeree mentioned you were in England?'

'That's right. B'lana had been diagnosed with a Tarparniian disease known as *Olhano Sigdesh*.'

'I've never heard of it.'

'I wouldn't expect you would. Even here in Tarparnii it's not all that common. It's a disease that attacks the immune system, much like leukaemia or Mediterranean fever. By the time I was able to pinpoint what was wrong she was already pregnant with Simone. Treatment would have cured her but killed the baby. B'lana refused to let anything happen to our child. It was a difficult decision for her to make…but now, almost four years later, only now am I starting to feel as though I have my life back on firmer ground.'

And that, more than anything, was the perfect reason why Melora knew she had to keep her distance from this man who was interesting, intriguing and incredibly sexy. He was handsome, rugged and had a fantastic sense of humour. After everything that had happened today, she trusted him, and her trust was not something she gave away willy-nilly.

'Simone helped to get you through the toughest times?' Melora asked before smothering another yawn. The child in her arms hadn't moved, hadn't run off to get the story book and instead was deadweight, obviously sound asleep.

'She did. If I hadn't had Simone to concentrate on during those first few months after B'lana's death, I most certainly wouldn't have coped. Here, let me take her. She can get quite heavy.' He shifted Simone's feet off his knee and stood to take his sleeping child from Melora.

'Time to turn in,' Daniel announced. 'You have a busy day ahead of you tomorrow, Dr Washington, and you're going to need all the rest you can get.'

Melora put her hand across her mouth as she yawned again, relieved he'd taken Simone from her but sad that her cuddle had come to an end. She twirled her wrists and stretched her arms as she stood. 'Earlier on, I did wonder whether I'd be able to sleep tonight but the fact that I'm now completely exhausted will no doubt assist in that area.'

Daniel shifted his daughter so her head lay on his shoulder, her arms about his neck. 'You'll sleep. Most definitely.'

'Great. Has anyone figured out exactly where I'm supposed to sleep?' she asked as they walked quietly towards the huts. 'I'm presuming my bag is wherever I'm headed.'

'Yes.'

'Great. I'm looking forward to changing out of these clothes. So which hut is yours?' she asked as they strolled along.

'The one down the end. Simone and I share with the supply hut.'

Her smile was instant. 'Oh, how delightful for you both.'

'It's not that bad. Supplies are at the front, Simone and I are at the back. We'll shift some boxes and crates around and make some room for you.'

'I'm to sleep in *your* hut?' She was gobsmacked. 'I uh…I hadn't realised.' And why was she getting all jittery about it? It was a hut. Somewhere to sleep. She needed to be practical about it but all she kept thinking was that she didn't want to share a place with Daniel for the next two weeks. The man was affecting her far more than she liked and now she was going to have to deal with sleeping in the same hut as him, with only a four year old girl as chaperone? Not that they needed a chaperone, she added quickly, mainly because nothing was going to happen between them.

Attractions could be fought. Exhaustion couldn't—at least, not now. Melora yawned again. She would start fighting tomorrow.

CHAPTER FIVE

THERE was pain. She had pain and it didn't seem to be going away.

Although Melora had been exhausted after her exceedingly full day, she was roused from her sleep due to pain in her left arm. When she tried to sit up, to figure out why her arm had no blood flow, she was astonished to find Simone had snuggled close to her and was resting her heavy little head on Melora's arm. She lay back down and sighed, wondering how to extract the child without waking her up.

'Something wrong?' Daniel's tone on the other side of Simone had been bleary, indicating he was half-asleep himself.

'No. Sorry. Didn't mean to wake you.'

'I was dozing. Are you not comfortable? The sleeping mats and bedding do take a while to get used to, especially if you're used to a soft mattress with lots of cuddly blankets on top.'

'No. It's all fine.'

'You're warm enough? Or cool enough?'

'I'm in a perfect state of warmness.' She smiled at his words. 'It's not that.'

Daniel eased up onto his elbow, the sheet which had been across him sliding down to reveal a dark, naked chest. There wasn't much light in the room, only that afforded by the half-moon outside, but even amongst the shadows Melora could tell that he was a man who definitely kept in good shape. 'What's the problem?'

No sooner had he propped himself up on his elbow and looked across at her than he realised what had happened. Without worrying about waking his daughter, he reached out and shifted the little body back towards him, resting Simone's head on the frilly pink pillow that was, no doubt, Simone's pride and joy.

'Sorry about that. She's a real cuddler. I often wake up with dead arms and quite a few times she either has her head on my chest or right up against my face.' He chuckled into the darkness, still looking over at Melora. 'It's a bit disconcerting when the first thing you see when you open your eyes in the morning are two big brown eyes staring directly into yours only a hair's-breadth away.'

Melora was rubbing her arm, trying to get blood flow back into it. 'I wasn't sure if I could move her or not. I thought she might wake up.'

'Ha! Once Simone's out she's out for the count, but be warned, she wakes very early. It's almost as though she can sense the first rays of the sun hitting the earth. Half the time I think it's Simone who wakes the birds up, rather than the other way around.' He pushed his long, loose hair back from his face, highlighting the angles and rugged jaw, and she found it difficult not to stare.

Melora smiled at his words and turned to lie on her side, the pins and needles in her arm now starting to settle down but the butterflies in her stomach starting to take flight. What was it about this man that seemed to send her hormones off into a right old tizz? 'It's nice to see a father who's so close to his daughter.'

'Thanks.' He reached out a hand and brushed hair back from Simone's face. 'She's my world.'

His words were so rich, so deep, so powerful that Melora's throat instantly choked over. Daniel slowly shook his head. 'She's my world and yet I need to destroy hers.'

'What?' She frowned. 'Why?'

Daniel exhaled slowly. 'She's getting older. She'll need more soon. More than just running around the village enjoying the carefree existence she thinks is her life.'

'School?'

'Yes.'

'Don't they have schools here?'

'They do…' Daniel lay back and laced his hands behind his head, looking up at the thatched roof '…but academic excellence isn't all that important to Tarparniians.'

Melora shifted up onto her elbow so she could see him a little better, then immediately wished she hadn't as the outline of his arm muscles was intense. 'It's normal…' she started, and had to clear her throat as her words had come out all sleepy and husky.

'It's normal,' she tried again, 'for a father to want the best for his child. Of course you want Simone to have a good education. Think of all the different ways she'd be able to help out here in Tarparnii when she's older if she's been properly educated.'

'But is it really *that* important? Why can't she be like the other children here? Like Belhara's children? Going to the local school, learning the basics and also being a functioning member of this village—*her* village?'

'Because you have the means, the knowledge and the understanding to know there is more for her. Belhara told me he was trained by PMA staff to be an anaesthetist, that he'd studied tribal medicine but that through PMA training him, he can help out more for his people.'

'He told you that?' Daniel was a little surprised.

'Yes. At the welcome banquet.'

'Where was I?'

'I think you were off getting me another drink, which you didn't need to do, by the way. I was more than capable of looking after myself.'

'I was being a polite host,' he countered.

Melora smiled. 'And I thank you for it, kind sir.'

'I should think so,' he muttered, but she could hear the humour in his words. They fell silent again and Melora lay down again, looking across at Simone and Daniel.

'I don't know if I can send her away to school. My father did that to me. Ripped me away from my mother, from my life here, and dumped me in a boarding school.' There was pain and anguish in his tone and he shook his head. 'That first year, so young, so alone, so terrified...' He trailed off, not bothering to finish his sentence because the desolation in his voice was evident and enough to convey into the silence how much pain he'd experienced. 'I can't do that to her.'

'Then you'll find an alternative, Daniel. Simone *is* your world. That's clear even to me and I've only known you both a day. You're right to be really thinking things through and you'll find a solution.' Simone shifted again and this time turned towards her father, cuddling in close, his arms coming about his child in a firm and protective manner. 'You'll do what's right for both of you.'

They were silent for a while and Melora had just
closed her eyes when he spoke again.

'Thanks, Melora. I needed to hear that.'

She kept her eyes closed but smiled, sighing con-
tentedly as sleep once more started to claim her. 'Any
time.'

With that, Daniel heard her breathing even out, indicating she'd gone back to sleep. He lay there, in the still-
ness of pre-dawn, unable to believe how much better he
felt after talking to Melora. She had confidence in him,
confidence that he would make the right decision, that
he would do what was best for himself and Simone.

It was a nice feeling to have, given that since B'lana's
death he'd simply seemed to muddle through from one
day to the next, learning as he went. Toilet training, manners, feeding times, teething, inquisitiveness. Although
he'd had help from those around him in the village,
although he knew that Simone belonged to everyone,
as did all of the other children in the village, the adults
always caring and teaching and protecting their own,
he was her father and at the end of the day *he* was the
one to make the hard decisions.

'You'll do what's right for both of you.' Melora's
words hung in the air and slowly Daniel closed his eyes.
This woman, this new woman who had herself been
through a very traumatic time, believed in him and it
made him feel great.

True to his word, Daniel had his team up and ready to
work well before seven o'clock the next morning. Melora
was surprised to see patients emerging from the forests
surrounding the village at such an early hour, lining up
in an orderly fashion outside the clinic building.

'P'Ko-lat is our receptionist-cum-triage nurse so she's

the one making sense of the variety of patients we'll see,' Daniel said as they exited the food hut with Keith, an orthopaedic Maori doctor from New Zealand hard on their heels. Richard, an obstetrician from the UK, had already gone into the clinic with Sue, an Australian nurse from Perth.

She was keeping her distance from Daniel this morning, his powerful presence only adding to her awareness of him. Melora had been talking to Bel when Daniel had first entered the food hut that morning, surrounded by Simone and her friends. He'd organised the children, sitting them down at the long wooden tables and making sure they all had something to eat before finally sitting down with his own breakfast.

He'd glanced her way once and smiled, his brown eyes deep and expressive, but then Simone had accidentally spilt her drink and he'd quickly set about cleaning it up. As she'd watched him talk to his daughter and the rest of the children, she'd been able to see what a wonderful, caring father he was. Although he had help from the rest of the village, there was something about the way he held Simone, the way he pressed a kiss to her head, lingering slightly and closing his eyes as though he wanted to capture that single moment in time. He loved his daughter It was plain for everyone to see and Melora had been touched with his dedication as a father.

'If you need any help with translating,' Daniel continued, bringing her thoughts back to the present, 'ask P'Ko-lat—or Meeree is usually around, helping out. Everything you need should be in the examination area but I'll quickly go over things now with you so hopefully you won't feel as though we're throwing you in at the deep end...especially as you didn't pack a bathing suit,' he couldn't help but tease, and his words went a long way to helping ease her nervous tension.

'Very funny, Tarvon. Are you always this witty with your newest recruits? Trying to make them feel less flustered by teasing them a little?'

'It's working, isn't it?' They entered one of the small examination rooms, Daniel grinning his gorgeous, heart-stopping grin at her. 'Bathing suit or not, I think you're going to do brilliantly, Melora. Right.' He put one hand on the cupboard and opened the door. 'Supplies. What you have in here should last you the entire clinic. You'll have plenty of people needing immunisations, others requiring debridement and bandaging of wounds, mostly general first aid.

'I tend to get most of the eye cases as I've become an expert over the years, Richard will take most of the pregnant women, Keith will have any patients with broken bones but we all see a general mix. P'Ko-lat is good at recognising our individual strengths and tailoring the patient's needs with the necessary health-care provider. If you *do* get a case you're unsure of, interrupt whoever you need. We're all here to help each other help the people. We're a team.'

'No "I" in team. Got it, boss.'

Daniel smiled and shook his head. 'Sorry. Didn't mean to get carried away with the pep talk. Just want you to know your parameters.' He quickly pointed out a few more things in the room before walking to the door. 'All right, Mel.' He nodded then gave her a mock salute. 'See you on the other side of clinic!'

'Once more into the fray?'

Daniel's spontaneous laughter vibrated through her and she couldn't help but smile in return, desperately ignoring the way her world seemed a little brighter when he was around. 'Precisely.' With that, he headed off to his own examination room. No sooner had he left than P'Ko-lat came through with a patient, explaining to Melora the problem.

That set up the rhythm for the rest of the clinic, with Meeree and P'Ko-lat working together to make sure she knew what each patient required. Melora wrote notes for every patient, as was the clinic's practice, and just when she thought there couldn't possibly be any more patients who required attention, another wave seemed to appear from nowhere and in they'd come.

At some point someone brought her a warm drink and some fruit, for which she was very grateful, and later that night she literally fell into bed, doubly exhausted from two very hectic days. Where she'd felt a little self-conscious sleeping in the hut with Daniel and his daughter the night before, tonight she didn't feel nearly as concerned. It was a great sensation and when Simone asked for a cuddle, Melora instantly opened her arms, delighted to have been accepted so easily by this child.

'She really likes you,' Daniel murmured, both of them yawning with exhaustion.

'The feeling's mutual.'

'She's never really bonded with any of the other women in this way. Of course she likes them and cuddles them but with you it seems to be different.'

Melora breathed in Simone's scent and relaxed. 'It's the hair colour.' She yawned, her words a little slurred, indicating she was on the verge of sleep. 'It has the power to make me stand out from the crowd, to have babies named after it and attract other blonde little girls.' She chuckled at her own silliness and Daniel smiled.

'Mel?' he said a few minutes later, but received no

reply. 'Melora?' He looked over at the two blonde-haired beauties and wondered whether he should be concerned. Simone had attached herself to Melora within minutes of meeting her but there was something else... Was Simone trying to tell him that she needed a mother? That although she was well cared for within the village that she still wanted a mother of her own?

Melora would be gone in just two weeks' time, out of their lives for goodness knew how long. Would she ever come back to help again in Tarparnii? Would she settle down to her life in Sydney, having found the level of inner peace she was searching for? Was it right for him to allow Simone to become close to this woman who would leave?

Daniel knew he couldn't protect Simone from every pain the world would throw at her but as a father it was his job to be concerned.

Melora was up bright and early, and she and Simone were able to tiptoe out of the hut without waking Daniel, the two of them giggling together as they ran to the food hut. That's where Daniel found the two of them about twenty minutes later. Melora was sitting next to Simone, reading a book out loud while nibbling on some fruit and honey mixed with goat's milk yoghurt. He stopped before they saw him, watching the two fair-haired beauties engrossed in the story he must have read to Simone over a hundred times.

She loved that book. It had been one of the ones B'lana had bought as they'd prepared the nursery together at his apartment in Bath. The story was about a little girl who wasn't afraid to go to school, to take a step outside her comfort zone, because she had support from her family and friends.

'You'll read it to her when she's older,' B'lana had said to him as she'd caressed her belly.

'Don't talk like that,' he'd answered. 'You'll make it through. We'll find a cure.'

B'lana had merely shaken her head and smiled at him in that indulgent way that said she knew he was wrong but she was more than willing to humour him.

'Find someone.' Those had been some of the last words his wife had said to him, almost four years ago. 'There is someone else out there for you to love, Daniel. Someone who will be good for you and for our Simone.'

'No!' The word had been wrenched from him and tears had filled his eyes as he'd held her close, willing the life that he could feel slipping from her body to instantly return.

Simone giggled and clapped her hands, bringing Daniel's thoughts back to the present. He blinked away the past and watched as his daughter looked up at Melora.

'Again?'

Melora's only response was to raise a stern eyebrow, indicating Simone had forgotten something.

'Please, Melora?' Simone batted her eyelashes as well, hoping that sweet and cute might work as well as manners.

'Ah, Miss Manners, there you are. Of course I'll read it again.'

Excitement bubbled through Simone and she opened the book to the first page. 'I like the way you read it. It's different from the way Daddy does it.'

'That's because we're different people with different experiences in life, so we read the same book differently.'

Simone giggled and pointed eagerly to the first page. Melora began to read, quietly but with resounding inflection. At present they were the only two in the food hut, sitting there, absorbed in their own little blonde world, and Daniel wished he'd brought his camera with him so he could capture the two of them in a photo.

When Simone turned the page, the two of them discussed the pictures drawn to illustrate the words and Melora popped a piece of fruit into her mouth. She was reaching for her second piece when she glanced up and saw him standing there.

Their eyes met across the empty food hut, neither of them moving, both of them staring and neither of them looking away. The rotation of the earth seemed to slow down and time seemed to stand still.

He was freshly washed and clean shaven, his hair pulled back into its usual ponytail. He wore a cotton shirt, a pair of shorts and his comfortable boat shoes, the belt, complete with hunting knife, at his waist. It was his clean, fresh face that definitely caught her attention as since she'd arrived he hadn't shaved, giving him that dark and rugged and slightly dangerous look that had definitely appealed to her.

Now that she was able to see his square jaw, the clear angles of his cheekbones and the full effect of his mouth, her heart seemed to be thumping faster. If he had been wearing a three-piece suit, he'd fit right in at any high-powered hospital in the world, and yet still there was a heated sensuality to him that only enticed her further.

He really was incredibly handsome, and he appeared to be looking at her as though she were unique and wonderful and precious. It was an odd sensation, and one Melora couldn't remember ever feeling before, even when she'd been engaged to Leighton.

It brought back the memories of being held close to Daniel's firm body when she'd been in his arms, the warmth surrounding them, the world disappearing so only the two of them were left. The same sensations seemed to be surrounding them again and she was confused about what she should do next. The way he was looking at her made her heart-rate increase, made her mouth go dry and her body instantly react with a mass of tingles.

How could he evoke such a reaction with one simple look? And even then he'd accomplished it from the other side of the hut. What did it mean? It made her feel so special and very feminine, something she hadn't felt in such a long time.

Was it real or was she simply imagining things? Perhaps he wasn't looking at her at all but rather was looking at his daughter? No. Even though her mind was working three times as fast as normal to try and make sense of the multitude of girly emotions buzzing through her, Daniel was most definitely looking directly at her... as though she was really special to him.

'Mel-ora.' Simone's sing-song tone beside her burst the bubble and Melora instantly whipped her head down to look at the little girl.

'Yes? Sorry? Yes?'

'Did I scare you?' she asked with a little giggle.

'Uh...yes. Yes, you did.' Melora closed her eyes and willed her body to stop trembling with excitement and to focus on the child beside her. She didn't want to open her eyes in case she came face to face with Daniel. Maybe he'd decided against having some food and had headed off to the clinic with an empty stomach. Maybe she'd find that he hadn't been standing there at all and that she'd simply been hallucinating. One could only hope.

'Daddy!' Simone squealed, and Melora tensed for a moment. It had been real. The whole 'eyes meeting across an uncrowded room' thing had been real. Daniel had stared at her and she'd stared back at him. She hadn't imagined it at all and now she had to face the man who was starting to rattle her nerves more than she cared to admit.

'Good morning, *Separ*.' Daniel greeted his daughter. 'What are you two doing?'

When Melora opened her eyes, it was to find that Daniel was now sitting down on the opposite side of the large wooden table. The large bench seats often accommodated about eight to ten people on either side but at the moment the three of them seemed to be here in a pocket of time where there was no one else around.

'Melora is reading to me, Daddy.' Simone patted her book lovingly.

'Isn't that nice of her?' Daniel's gaze slowly travelled from his daughter, who was once more engrossed in the story, to encompass Melora. 'Thank you, Mel.'

'It…it's no big drama,' she said, cross with herself for stuttering. 'It's a great book.'

'It's my favourite,' Simone added. 'My mummy bought it for me before she died, didn't she, Daddy?'

At the mention of Daniel's wife Melora started to feel a little uncomfortable yet she wasn't quite sure why.

'She did and she would be so happy to see that you and Melora are enjoying the story together.'

'That's nice.'

'My mummy was nice, wasn't she, Daddy?'

'She was very nice,' Daniel agreed, winking at his daughter.

'And she was pretty, just like me, wasn't she, Daddy?'

Simone smoothed a hand down the blonde hair Melora had combed that morning.

'Very pretty,' he confirmed, and from his indulgent tone Melora had the feeling this wasn't the first time he'd had this conversation with his daughter. It was good that he reminisced with Simone about her mother. It was right.

Simone looked seriously at Melora. 'She died when I was one.' The little girl's lilting words indicated she'd had those same words spoken to her by someone else and was parroting them. 'She got really sick and didn't want to take the special medicine because it might hurt me, because I was in her tummy and she said she wanted her baby to be big and strong, and I *am* big and strong, just like my mummy wanted, and she did all that because she really loved me, didn't she, Daddy?' Simone nodded as though she already knew the answer.

'She *really* did,' he confirmed.

Melora was listening intently to everything Simone was saying and Tarvon wondered what she might be thinking. He looked across at her and once more their gazes seemed to meet. This time, though, there wasn't the heat or recognition of awareness he'd seen before but instead her honey eyes reflected that she was happy.

'My daddy loves me, too,' Simone told Melora, her tone still earnest.

'I can see that. You're very special to him.'

Simone tipped her head to the side. 'Am I special to you?'

Melora's heart turned over with pride at being asked such an important question. 'Of course you are. We're the girls with the yellow hair, remember?'

'Yes. We are special to each other.' Simone clapped her hands joyfully, happy to have received approval from her Melora. Daniel heard alarm bells ring somewhere in the back of his mind, warning him that it might not be all that good for Simone to form a permanent attachment to Melora, but he suppressed them.

Instead, he clapped his hands together, needing to move things along. There was another busy day ahead of them. 'Right, *Separ*.' He fixed his daughter with a look. 'If you've finished your breakfast, I suggest you go along and see Nandi. She's waiting to show you and your friends how to make bread dough today.'

'Yay.' After more clapping of the hands Simone slid down from the bench, shimmying beneath the table to pop her head up beside her father. After giving him a quick hug, she was about to break into a run when Daniel stopped her.

'Excuse me, missy. Manners, please?' He held out her book to her and inclined his head towards Melora.

'Uh? Oh, sorry.' Simone faced Melora. 'Thank you for reading to me. I did love it.'

'You're welcome. Any time.'

'How about tonight?' Simone instantly asked.

'You've done it now,' Daniel remarked in an under-tone that made Melora smile.

'Sounds wonderful.'

'Yay.' Simone took the book from her father before skipping out of the food hut, leaving the two of them alone.

'I'm not sure if you fully realise what you've just com-mitted yourself to, Melora. My daughter is a bookworm and loves to have stories read to her. You're just lucky that for the past two nights she's been too exhausted to bother reading.'

'That's good that she likes books so much, especially for someone her age, and as I'm a bookworm, too, I think I'll cope.' She paused and then asked, 'Is this part of your plan to further her education? She speaks both Tarparniian and English fluently, she loves stories, and in loving stories she'll find reading easier to cope with.' Melora paused for a moment. 'You said there are schools out here. Why couldn't you send her to one of the village schools and then have other schoolwork sent over?'

'I've thought of that but with all the work I do with PMA, I simply don't have the time to devote to her studies, not properly, and I also don't want her to have a half-hearted education.' He shook his head. 'She has a passion for learning.'

Melora agreed. 'Children her age are usually like little sponges, all too eager to soak up knowledge.'

'True, and that's why Meeree and Jalak are also encouraging the children here to learn English. Most times they can speak it better than their parents.'

'It's great that they want to learn. You'll sort it out,' she encouraged him again. 'She's four and three quarters, almost five, Daniel,' Melora pointed out with a cheeky smile, recalling how Simone liked her exact age to be known. 'You've got some time to figure things out.'

'The boarding school in England can take her in six months' time or else she has to wait another year.' He put his elbows on the table and covered his face with his hands, dejection in his shoulders, lifelessness in his tone.

Melora could see how badly the thought of being separated from his daughter was affecting him and desperately wanted to shimmy beneath the table herself so she could pop out the other side and comfort him. Sanity, thankfully, kicked in and she stayed where she was but couldn't resist reaching out a hand to him, touching his arm gently. 'Would it be so bad for her to go?'

'I don't want her to have the horrible time I had,' he mumbled into his hands.

'How do you know she will? You've told me that you didn't really get along with your father, and maybe that's the main difference here. You and Simone are very close, like peas in a pod, and nothing—not boarding school, not having experiences in other countries—is ever going to change that. You're not "posting" her off to boarding school to get her out of your hair, you're giving her the opportunity to have a wonderful education because you want her to have a rich and full life.'

Daniel was silent and for a moment Melora wondered whether she'd overstepped the lines of new friendships. 'Maybe that's what your father wanted to give you as well,' she continued quietly. 'He may not have known how to show his affection properly but he did give you the opportunity of a great education, and just look at what you've been able to achieve.'

He lifted his head and nodded slowly. 'You make a valid case, Dr Washington. I've always resented my father for sending me off, for making me feel as though I wasn't worthy of his time or attention, but perhaps he really didn't have any clue how to relate to me.'

'Exactly. It's completely different with you and Simone. That little girl adores her daddy. Everyone can see it and with you she really is the apple of your eye. You relate to her, you're the most important person in her life and you love her completely, Daniel. You're a good father.' The last words were imploring.

'Thank you, Melora. That does mean a lot and maybe you're right. Boarding school for Simone would be very different because she would know I was doing it so she could have a brilliant future.'

'And as such it also proves that you are nothing like your father. Your motives are different, your sincerity is real. Also, I wouldn't doubt that your father's sincerity in ensuring you had a good education was also real.'

'He just didn't know how to express it.' As Daniel said the words, he breathed in deeply and exhaled slowly, as though he was letting go of heavy animosity that had been gathering deep within him for almost four decades. 'He wanted the best for me.'

'It's what every parent wants for their child but some express it better than others and, besides, it's quite clear that *you've* turned out just fine.'

He quirked an eyebrow at her, his expression changing from one of confusion about his daughter's education to awareness of the woman before him. The instant she saw that look in his eyes she knew he was changing the subject, and because she felt more comfortable with him now, she let him. He captured her hand in both of his and thankfully she didn't try to pull away. 'Just fine?' he fished, the corner of his mouth twitching upwards.

'Well…better than fine.' Melora felt the proverbial ground, which had just started to settle beneath her feet, shift again. Daniel was flirting with her…and she was liking it.

'You know, you've agreed to a date with my daughter,' he said softly. 'So does that mean you'll agree to a date with me?'

'Uh…' Her throat went instantly dry at his words.

'After all, it's only right that I get to know the woman who's going to be spending time with Simone. I'm a very protective father.'

'I have no doubt about that.'

'So what do you say?'

'To what?' She was actually getting quite confused.

'To having a date with me?'

'People out here date? Where do they go? What do they do?'

'Of course they date. How else do you think marriages eventuate?'

'M-marriage?' Her eyes widened with shock. 'You want to get *married*?'

CHAPTER SIX

DANIEL'S heartbeat stopped for what felt like an eternity but in reality it was just a moment.

'No! No. Did you think I was…?' He shook his head. *'No.'* He quickly stood from the bench seat and crossed his arms over his chest. He didn't want to get married again. He already had too much on his plate. Work. Simone. Feelings for Melora he didn't want to have. No. Marriage didn't figure in his future plans at all.

'You scared me.'

'You misunderstood me.' They spoke in unison, stared at each other and then both laughed, Melora placing a hand over her heart as though she was relieved.

Why was she relieved? Didn't she want to get married? Not necessarily to him but to anyone? She'd already been through so much, with her cancer and the treatments that went with it, so it was understandable, but how had she jumped the conclusion that he'd been asking her to marry him?

Was she lonely? He would have thought someone as gorgeous as Melora would have had someone waiting for her in Australia but she hadn't mentioned anyone. Maybe it had been the way he'd asked her for the date? Had he said it wrong? She was the first woman he'd asked since B'lana and maybe he'd done it wrong.

It was another example that they came from completely different worlds. His life was here in Tarparnii and *if* he ever decided to head down the path of matrimony again, it would be with someone who understood this land, who understood its customs and who loved the people.

Still, he had to admit that the prospect of getting to know Melora better, of perhaps seeing where this attraction he felt towards her might lead, was rather appealing. He looked at her, the pink tinge on her cheeks, the expressiveness of her honey-coloured eyes, the way she bit her lower lip. She was very beautiful, there was no denying that.

'Daniel?' Melora's sweet voice brought his mind back to the present and he realised he was still staring at her.

'Sorry.'

'I think we'd better head to clinic—or at least I do. The more I familiarise myself with the place, the better.' As she spoke, she carried her empty plate to the washbasin, pleased that her legs were able to support her as she cleaned up after herself. The way Daniel had looked at her when he'd first entered the food hut, the way he'd been staring at her only a moment ago, all of it—the attention, the banter, the flirting, the laughter—made her feel… pretty. And she hadn't felt pretty in a very long time.

He knew about her surgery and yet it didn't seem to bother him. He saw her as a woman, as a colleague and, hopefully, a friend. The attention, though, or even the thought that a man—an extremely good-looking man at that—found her attractive was enough to give her self-confidence a much-needed boost.

Of course, it could never mean anything. She could come here to Tarparnii, work, meet new people and flirt with Daniel Tarvon and still return to Australia with her heart firmly in place. Nothing serious could ever happen. Daniel had big decisions to make on his own and she had test results that were still waiting to be confirmed.

She knew she was already attached to Simone and wondered if she shouldn't pull back a little. She'd only been there for two days and already bonds had formed. That was one thing she hadn't expected at all. It was easy to see that Daniel and Simone were genuine, the real deal, and sharing accommodation with them had afforded her the rare opportunity to see what a real, loving family was like. The family she'd never be able to have. It was a bitter-sweet pill to swallow.

Within a few hours Melora had had her first taste of packing up and moving out for a medical clinic. A large transport truck was loaded with medical supplies as well as canvas tents and other equipment such as poles, ropes and food.

'What happens to Simone when you head out on these clinics?' Melora asked Daniel as she hefted a crate from the hut where they slept and carried it to the transport vehicle.

'She'll spend the day with Nandi—Belhara's wife. Whenever I head out on days away, she barely misses me.' He chuckled but behind his words Melora could see the wheels still turning.

'If you do decide to send her to boarding school, who do you think will take longer to adjust—her or you?' she asked softly, after he'd placed the crate into the truck.

He shrugged. 'More than likely me.' Daniel shook his head and headed back to the supply hut for another crate, and the subject dropped. Soon the PMA team bundled into the rear of another transport truck, which had a canvas roof with a large red cross painted on the side, and the large vehicles rumbled their way out of the village.

'How long will it take to get there?' Melora asked Sue, who was seated next to her on the transport, but it was Daniel who answered. He was sitting opposite her, along with the other members of the team, and yet she seemed to be acutely aware of every move he made. It was wrong. She shouldn't be so aware of him and the fact that she was only brought more consternation and confusion into her life.

'Depending on the number of stops we have to make along the way, about an hour. We need to unpack, set up, do the clinic, pack up and head back to the village all by the time the sun goes down.'

Melora nodded, unable to really look at him except for the odd glance in his direction while he'd been speaking. She'd decided to try and keep her distance from him but was finding it nigh on impossible, especially when the entire medical team consisted of a total of eight people and Daniel was their leader. Professional. She simply needed to be professional and polite, but now that their gaffe about marriage was out in the open it was as though both of them felt self-conscious around the other.

'OK. Thanks,' Melora replied, nodding slowly. 'Just so long as I know.'

'It certainly makes for one very long day,' Sue remarked. 'But so worth it when you see the smile of happiness on a patient's face.'

'This way you'll also get to experience what it's like holding jungle clinics, as we've now come to call them,' Daniel continued, his tone laced with a hint of teasing. 'As opposed to the ones we can do in the clinic building.'

Melora's smile was instant. 'The clinic building with the running water that you love so much?' She couldn't help but meet his gaze, noting that his rich, deep eyes were twinkling with delight.

'Oh, yes, Daniel does love that building.' Sue chuckled. 'We all do.'

'He was stroking the bricks the other day,' Melora felt compelled to point out, teasing him a little. She didn't usually say things like that but in this group of wonderful people she was more relaxed and in teasing Daniel, she hoped it also hid her burgeoning feelings for him…feelings she realised it was going to be difficult to fight, but fight she must.

'I don't blame him,' Sue responded, and as the truck rumbled through the jungle, the entire team joined in the conversation, sharing stories and anecdotes of different scenarios from their pasts. They talked over each other, they laughed, they shared experiences, and Melora couldn't believe how wonderful she felt.

For years she'd been a surgeon attached to the general surgical department, working day in, day out with much the same people, but never had she felt such an instant camaraderie as she did now. Even the brief stopping now and then to go through the necessary checkpoints, Daniel showing their papers before they continued on their way, didn't diminish the level of conversational enjoyment eight medical professionals, all with very different backgrounds, could share.

By the time they arrived at their destination, Melora was filled with an energetic excitement. She followed the necessary directions in helping set up the tents and getting ready for what Daniel called the busiest medical experience of her life.

He leaned in close, his scent tantalising her in that mesmerising way. 'And this is only the beginning.' He flashed her that enigmatic smile of his and then headed off to the well to draw water.

Melora closed her eyes and breathed out. How was she supposed to keep her distance from him when he was so easy to be around?

As she was unpacking the last of the supplies, there was a loud rumbling sound, as though there was thunder above them. The last time she'd checked, there hadn't been a single cloud in the sky.

'What's that noise?' she asked, coming out of the large canvas tent and looking up at the sky.

'It's not thunder, Melora.' Daniel directed her gaze to the surrounding trees and as she watched, several people materialised seemingly from nowhere. 'It's your patients.'

'Sounds like a lot of patients.'

Daniel's answer was to laugh, the rich sound washing over her. 'You said it. Saddle up. It's time to ride the wild clinic,' he called with a joviality Melora found highly infectious. It was clear he loved his work and as the clinic progressed, all of the staff dealing with patient after patient after patient, Melora couldn't believe how much *she* was enjoying herself.

Daniel had arranged for one of the women in the village who had helped them in the past to act as the receptionist-cum-triage nurse while P'Ko-lat worked with Melora in a nursing and translator capacity. It certainly made things easier.

Melora gave injections, checked ears, noses and throats, relocated a shoulder, treated and bandaged sore limbs and even sutured a head wound. Although when a woman was brought to her with severe abdominal pains, it was the first time Melora really wished for state-of-the-art medical equipment to be available at her fingertips. For all of the cases she'd already seen, she'd been able to adapt, to make do or rely on her colleagues to introduce her to an alternate way of doing things. Now, as she felt the woman's abdomen, she knew it could be several different diagnoses and wished she had X-ray facilities.

'Ask Daniel to come through if he's free,' Melora instructed P'Ko-lat. A moment later Daniel came around the cotton sheet partition, erected to afford a certain amount of privacy to their patients. Melora sensed him before she saw him but pushed the thought to the back of her mind.

'Problem?' he asked.

'Just need a second opinion.' She explained her patient's symptoms to him and he, in turn, asked questions in the woman's native language.

'What do you think it is?' he asked.

'Appendicitis, but her symptoms of vomiting, diarrhoea and massive abdominal cramping could be early signs of hernia, bowel obstruction, gastroenteritis, just to name a few.'

'What do you want to do?' Daniel asked.

'Given the lack of means to test and rule things out, and also the fact that she hasn't been able to eat anything for days, I want to open her up. It's the only logical conclusion.'

'Agreed.' Daniel turned to P'Ko-lat. 'Get Belhara in here to give this woman an anaesthetic. Sue can be the surgical nurse and I'll assist Melora.' P'Ko-lat headed off to do his bidding.

'Just like that?' Melora asked. 'Right here, right now, we're going to open her up?' There were no waiting lists. There were no protocols or red tape. There was no theatre!

'*You're* going to open her up. You're the surgeon.'

She glanced at her surroundings, which seemed fine for treating patients but for some strange reason she'd thought they'd take their patient somewhere else to operate. She'd known she'd be doing rough-and-ready medicine when she'd started her research about Tarparnii, but she hadn't fully comprehended the lack of sterile environment. It wasn't the physical act of doing the surgery that was bothering her but the location.

'Daniel! Where's the theatre?'

'Here. There *is* nowhere else to do the surgery. This is the most sterile environment we have and as you can tell by Meimii's blood pressure, we can't wait to take her back to the village.'

'So I operate here?' She trusted Daniel to guide her in what she should do. He'd worked here for so long, he knew the conditions, he knew the risks of infection, but he also knew the risks of not performing the surgery at all.

'You operate. Right here, right now. It's your job to save Meimii's life.'

Melora looked into his eyes, his gorgeous eyes, eyes that she could look into for an exceedingly long time and not get tired of. Eyes that were now reaching out to her, giving her confidence and strength to do the job she'd come there to do. She accepted his strength and squared her shoulders, nodding once in affirmation.

'Then that's exactly what I'll do.'

Daniel had watched the different emotions cross her face and when he saw the one of acceptance, it gave him confidence that she was the right person for the job. She'd fitted into life as a jungle doctor with relative ease, and he felt as though he was watching a butterfly begin to emerge from its cocoon.

Within next to no time Belhara had Meimii anaesthetised. Daniel had ordered someone to draw fresh water from the well, Sue had helped Melora set out the equipment they'd need and to position the operating stretcher for easier access. P'Ko-lat was erecting another set of sheets to provide them with an enclosed environment and then assisted in removing Meimii's clothes.

The ground was dirt, the operating table was a canvas stretcher, the light came from that great big ball of burning gas in the sky called the sun, assisted by a torch one of her colleagues would hold.

Melora had never operated like this before.

After she'd washed and dried her hands, pulled on some gloves and a paper apron to protect her clothes and allowed P'Ko-lat to tie her mask in place, she was physically ready. Mentally, she had reservations but wishing for an X-ray machine or an ultrasound was pointless. She looked directly across her patient to where Daniel stood.

'Ready?' he asked.

Melora swallowed and tried to ignore the flies and other insects that were also in the tent with them. It wasn't her job to shoo them away. It wasn't her job to worry about the conditions. It was her job to save Meimii's life. Daniel had faith in her to perform under such circumstances—she could see it in his brown eyes. This man trusted her, believed in her and, taking strength from him, she nodded.

'Ready.' Holding out her hand to Sue, who was standing beside her, she ordered, 'Scalpel.'

After making a careful and neat incision, Melora started a methodical exploration, deciding to rule out appendicitis first and foremost before checking on other possible reasons for Meimii's pain.

'Looks as though you were right,' Daniel remarked as they looked at the enlarged appendix. 'Good call, Dr Washington.'

'Thank you. Retract, please.'

As she continued to operate, completely in the zone, Daniel admired her skill. Although he was quite content to be a GP, to be able to assist with surgery and to treat his patients to the best of his ability, he appreciated Melora's skills. She was clear and precise in her instructions so that both he and Sue knew what she needed and when.

At one point she chuckled and he could hear the smile in her words as she spoke. 'I'm used to doing this operation through keyhole surgery. Amazing how dependant we become on technology.'

'Agreed, but we work with what we have and you are doing a mighty fine job, Mel.'

She glanced at him and her eyes twinkled with happiness. 'Thank you.'

Daniel had a receptacle ready to accept the excised organ and once it was out, he checked it as best he could. 'No perforation. How does the site look?'

'Looking good. I think if we'd left Meimii any longer, we'd be dealing with peritonitis.' As the surgery progressed, Melora felt more alive and more invigorated at performing this type of surgery than she had in years. Out here, she could really see how her skills, her knowledge and her expertise really made a difference to people's lives.

After doing a quick exploratory, she was ready to

close, content in the belief that if Meimii followed doctor's orders and took the full course of antibiotics prescribed, she would make a full recovery.

'OK, Belhara. I'm done and you can do your thing,' she finally said once the wound had been sutured closed in layers and then bandaged. As she peeled off her gloves, mask and protective gown, she turned to Daniel, who was doing the same. 'What happens with Meimii's after-care? Does she come back to the clinic with us or—?'

'She'll come back with us.' He nodded. 'Given that you weren't able to perform keyhole surgery and that a laparotomy was required, she's going to need constant care for at least the next two weeks, not to mention ensuring that her wound site stays clear of infection. We can also administer the antibiotics. People in Western society are used to going to the doctor, getting a prescription, having it filled at the pharmacy and then taking a course of antibiotics, knowing the dos and don'ts associated with them.'

'But out here that's not the case?'

'Natural remedies are often used to help with healing and while I am a complete advocate for these, they also have a time and a place. Wherever I can use natural means, I do, but sometimes, such as with Meimii's situation where we've needed to operate in an unsterile environment, it's imperative that she not run the risk of infection.'

'What are some of the natural remedies used? Should I have a crash course in them so I know what to look out for or, alternatively, what treatment to prescribe?'

Daniel couldn't help but be impressed with this woman's attitude and on a whim enveloped her in a big hug. He knew he shouldn't because holding her close was like playing with fire—dangerous—but he hadn't been able to resist. He heard her breathe in sharply at the impromptu contact and quickly eased back before her sweet scent penetrated his defences.

'Thank you, Melora. Thank you for understanding that life here is different. We have so many doctors who come here to help, who hand out Western medicines and think their job is done and dusted. Then we have the doctors who come here, who embrace the wonderful people of Tarparnii, who are interested in the culture, in the festivals, in the beliefs and in the natural medicines that have seen this country through a lot of good and bad times.' Daniel nodded, trying to ignore the way the atmosphere between them had instantly thickened.

He shouldn't have touched her because now he was completely aware of her and itched to haul her close once more. He cleared his throat and took a step back 'I *knew* you were the latter and you've just proved me right.'

'Well...thank you, Daniel.' Feeling self-conscious, Melora found it difficult to meet his gaze. She was still trying to come to terms with the fact that Daniel had just hugged her, held her close, pressed his body to hers. He'd felt warm and solid and given that they'd been out here for quite some time, in hot and humid conditions, her senses had still been teased with that earthy-spicy scent she was coming to equate with him.

'I might just...go and get a drink. A little breather before I jump back into treating the rest of the patients.' And a little breather from being so close to him and having him create absolute havoc with her equilibrium.

'Good idea.' He was about to offer to go with her, to talk about some of the different methods they used in

Tarparnii to promote healing, but as she pushed aside the hanging sheet she glanced back at him and the look in her eyes told him she needed some distance.

Had she been aware of the sensations released when he'd hugged her? Was she as affected by him as he was by her? If so, then it would be best for him not to follow her, to respect that she wanted some distance between them.

He knew she was right to keep him at arm's length but he knew himself too well. He was a gung-ho sort of man. When he did something, whether it was driving on mud-slides, seeing more patients than he could poke a stick at, or wrestling with a deadly snake, he usually jumped in with both feet, safe in the knowledge that if there were any repercussions, he could think quite quickly on his feet and come through with flying colours.

However, he was starting to question whether that was the case with regard to Melora. She was an amazing surgeon, an incredible woman whose vibrancy had been stripped from her due to cancer, and yet here she was, fighting back, determined to find a new life.

His admiration for her was increasing with every moment he spent in her company and where, in the past, he might have jumped right in to figure out where this admiration might lead him, he now wasn't so sure he'd be able to think quickly enough on his feet.

Putting some distance between them was no doubt a good thing. Working hard to keep their relationship strictly professional was another area where he needed work. After the brief hug he'd just given her, Daniel could clearly acknowledge that he was attracted to Melora Washington.

He'd held her in his arms before, he'd talked to her, he'd offered her comfort, and those memories had played often through his mind during the past few nights since he'd met her. He didn't mind mild flirtations, he didn't mind sharing special moments with incredible women, but the more he got to know Melora, the more he *wanted* to spend more time with her, and it was those sensations that made her very dangerous to be around.

He hadn't planned on meeting Melora. He hadn't planned on being attracted to her. He hadn't planned on his daughter bonding with her so instantly. Melora would be gone soon, back to her world of laparoscopes and X-ray machines. Back to work in a large, impersonal hospital, and he would be here, with Simone.

He hadn't really contemplated remarrying before, his world feeling as though it was already full with work and family and Simone. Now, though, after the silly mix-up with Melora that morning, Daniel wondered if he would indeed get married again. He'd always thought he'd been super-lucky with B'lana. Was it possible for it to happen again?

He and B'lana had been friends for a long time, having had much in common, given they'd both been raised in two cultures, but he'd also been cautious. Having seen his own parents' marriage break down and dwindle to nothing due to cultural differences, he and B'lana had been careful how much time they spent in both England and Tarparnii.

However, if he were to even think about marrying a non-Tarparniian, would she have the same outlook? Would she be willing to spend time in both countries, more in Tarparnii?

He thought about Melora, the woman whose life had changed, the woman who was reaching out for a new life, a new and improved version of herself, and even in the short time she'd been there, he'd started to notice subtle differences.

She no longer tugged and pulled on her oversized shirts, which showed him she wasn't feel as self-conscious as when she'd arrived. She'd embraced the culture with open arms, as though appreciating it for the rare gift it was, and a smile seemed to be on her lips ninety per cent of the time.

Whilst she might love this place now, Australia was her home. His home was here, in Tarparnii, and he knew it was impossible to try and live in two places at the same time. His parents had tried and it hadn't worked, ending in pain for all involved. He and Melora came from different worlds...and never the twain should meet.

CHAPTER SEVEN

FOR the next few nights they were able to establish a loose routine, where Melora would read a story to Simone at bedtime before Daniel gave his daughter a cuddle. Usually, after that, Simone would drop straight off to sleep, content in the knowledge that she was loved but leaving the two adults to face each other…alone… with no one to act as a buffer.

Tonight, however, as Melora lay next to the child, cuddling her close, Daniel sitting a little further away, listening to her read, Melora couldn't help but be aware of every move he made. She was half concentrating on the story and half on the man who seemed to fill her thoughts during the day and her dreams at night.

When she finished the story, she closed the book and was pleased when Simone snuggled in a bit more. Her arms instantly came around the child, loving the way it felt to hold her close, to offer comfort and love. It was true that this child meant the world to her and Melora had no idea how she was going to leave Simone when her time there was up.

She was breathing in the sweet scent of the four-year-old when Simone spoke her name, tiredness evident in the girl's voice.

'Yes, darling?' Melora answered.

'Why do you feel all different up here?' She eased back and pointed to Melora's chest. 'It's all soft but different on that side. Why?'

Melora couldn't help but tense at the child's words, mortification replacing mellowness. Heat suffused through her and her mouth went dry. Simone had noticed the difference? Melora's heart pounded wildly against her ribs.

'Simone.' There was censure in Daniel's tone as he said the girl's name. 'You shouldn't ask questions like that.'

'But…why?' Simone shifted slightly away from Melora and looked worriedly at her father, completely perplexed by the adults.

'No. No. It's all right, Daniel. It's fine.' Melora reached out for Simone, soothing the child's apprehension and at the same time started to let go of her own. 'You're not to know, sweetheart, and it's a very good question.' Simone went back into Melora's arms, still a little uncertain.

'A while ago I had an operation there. I had a bad lump in my breast and so the doctors needed to take my breast away so that I could live, but I'm fine now.' Even as Melora spoke the words she felt tears prick at her eyes, but this time round they were more as though she was saying goodbye to her old life, rather than for the way her life had been forced to change.

'A bad lump?' Simone asked, yawning and relaxing further.

'That's right, but now that they've removed the bad lump, I'm fine. I'm healthy but it means I need to wear a fake breast—or prosthesis, as they're called—to help me.'

'Oh.' Another yawn. 'So that's why they feel different.'

'Yes.'

'Melora?'

'Mmm?'

'I'm glad they took the bad lump away and that you're fine.'

Melora smiled and dropped a kiss to the little girl's head. 'Me, too.' And she was. For the first time since her surgery Melora was truly pleased that she was indeed fine. If she hadn't found the lump in time, her prognosis could have been a lot worse. As that wasn't the case, she'd been able to receive treatment, to pick up the pieces of her shattered life and to come here, to meet such amazing people and to feel loved by the little girl sleeping in her arms.

Daniel came over and pressed a kiss to Simone's cheek. 'Goodnight, my *Separ*,' he said quietly, before looking across at Melora. 'You handled that very well. I should try to remember to teach my daughter not to ask such difficult questions.'

'I think you'll be fighting a losing battle,' Melora remarked as she shifted the sleeping Simone so the child lay on her frilly pink pillow.

'Probably.' Daniel knelt on the opposite side of Simone, the sleeping child between the two of them as Melora sat up. 'Seriously, though. Are you all right?'

'Medically? Mentally? Physically?'

He smiled. 'All of the above.'

She nodded. 'I'm doing quite well and just now...well, that's the first time I've really been able to articulate, in the simplest way, what happened to me, and do you know what?'

'What?'

'It didn't sound all that scary. I've survived this far.' She smiled and nodded. 'It's nice to be able to say those words out loud and not feel as though my life is crumbling. Finally, I feel as though my feet are on solid ground.' She straightened her shoulders and lifted her head just a little bit higher.

'Mel, that's very good news.'

She swallowed and sighed. 'It is.'

'Well done. That's quite an achievement.'

'Thanks, Daniel. It means a lot to hear you say that.'

The atmosphere between them started to intensify, the awareness building as they sat there, looking at each other, in the diminishing light. She didn't need light, however, to know every contour of Daniel's face, as she'd already memorised each and every one. Being around him, being close to him, being a part of his life, even if it was just for a short period of time, was definitely enough to make her forget the pressures of the past few years and to look forward to whatever her future held.

She licked her lips as she sat there and looked at him, wondering if he was ever going to lose his strong sense of self-control and drag her close, his mouth hungry on hers as they gave into the overwhelming attraction they—

Daniel cleared his throat. 'Excuse me,' he said and without another word he stood and headed out of the shack. Melora closed her eyes as he left, wondering if he'd been able to read the direction of her thoughts. How was she supposed to hide the fact that she was attracted to him when he was so incredible?

The awkwardness between them seemed to stretch even tighter after that night but both of them did their best to ignore it. After the way they'd shared that long and heated look the other morning, plus her gaffe about thinking he'd been proposing marriage to her, something that still caused her cheeks to suffuse with colour every time she thought about it, the atmosphere between them seemed to have shifted.

She'd noticed that while Daniel was still attentive in a professional capacity, he seemed to be putting a bit of distance between them personally. For the first few nights she'd been in Tarparnii they'd both been in the hut at night-time, chatting quietly before dropping off to sleep, Melora, usually exhausted beyond belief. Now, though, after he'd said goodnight to Simone, he would head out of the hut and wouldn't return until much later.

At first she thought he was just giving her some space, as well as seeing to his duties with the few patients who were in the clinic building, but last night, when he'd come into the hut, she'd asked him if everything was all right.

'Everything's fine, Mel. Sorry. Didn't mean to disturb you.' And with that he'd headed back out of the hut, having barely finished taking his shoes off.

When she'd woken early this morning, he'd been sleeping, facing away from her, his breathing even. Simone had already been awake and about to pounce on her father so Melora had suggested they both tiptoe, albeit not as quietly as Melora had hoped, out of the hut together. If she could entertain Simone in the mornings, thereby giving Daniel a chance to sleep in, she would.

Besides, spending one-on-one time with Simone was like she was being granted a special gift. Knowing the chances of her becoming a mother were quite slim given her increasing age, her lack of husband and all of the health problems she might still need to face...

She stopped her thoughts there, pushing aside the fact that any day now she should be hearing from her specialists to find out whether or not her cancer count was within normal parameters or whether she'd be needing another course of chemotherapy. She'd always known there was a slim possibility of having to cut her trip to Tarparnii short and she'd accepted that fact, but now that she was here, helping out and making a real difference, plus being treated to gorgeous girl cuddles from Simone, Melora really didn't want to leave just yet.

And Daniel? A little voice inside her heart asked the question. If she had to leave tomorrow, wouldn't she miss Daniel? Well, of course she would. He was her colleague and her friend. He'd saved her from a mudslide and a deadly snake, as well as sharing his home with her. Of course she would miss him. She'd miss the way his brown eyes seemed to wash over her, the way his deep rich voice made her body tingle with delight, especially if he was standing close to her...

'Hey, Melora!' Daniel's strong voice cut cross the village clearing and her thoughts. She turned to face him. 'We're all heading down to the waterhole. Come. It'll be great fun.' His smile was warm and sexy and highly inviting and she felt a wave of delight wash over her. Never, in all of her forty-one years, had a man been able to make her blush simply by smiling at her across a village clearing. He could make the butterflies in her stomach take flight with a simple word, his deep tones resonating through her body and leaving a mass of goose-bumps in their wake.

It was their first day off after days of hectic clinics and all the staff were eager for a bit of rest and relaxation, but at the thought of going to the waterhole Melora swallowed, apprehension and anxiety building within her. While she might be coming to terms with her situation, feeling a little bit more confident in not hiding the fact that she'd had surgery, she also wasn't ready to flaunt her body. She hadn't packed a bathing suit, which had been a deliberate move as she was highly self-conscious about her body at the moment.

Melora nodded and quickly headed into the hut…the hut she shared with Daniel and his daughter. She stood there and closed her eyes, wondering how best to deal with this new turn of events.

'You don't need to swim.'

Melora couldn't help the slightly startled gasp that escaped her lips at the sound of his voice, goose-bumps spreading over her as she opened her eyes and turned to face him.

'Daniel! I…er…didn't hear you come in.'

He smiled at her and her knees started to buckle from beneath her. She quickly bent down and put her hand on her bag, which was situated next to her bedroll. Looking at him was dangerous. Hearing his sexy voice was dangerous. Standing too close to him was dangerous, and right now, as she was doing all three, she realised she was slap-bang in the middle of a minefield.

'We're almost ready to head to the waterhole but I just wanted to let you know that you don't have to swim if you don't want to.'

'You mean if I feel uncomfortable?'

'Exactly.' He shoved his hands into his pockets and took a step away from her. The woman was kneeling beside her bag, looking up at him with those big honey-coloured eyes of hers as though he'd just granted her the moon. The sun was shining in from behind her, creating a golden, ethereal glow around her. The sight was glorious and intoxicating and he had to force himself to stand firm, not to give in to the need to gently help her to her feet before pulling her into his arms and pressing his mouth firmly to her own.

'Thank you for your concern.'

'I just didn't want you to feel as though there was any pressure. There isn't.'

Melora stood and Daniel took another step back, almost knocking over a stack of crates filled with medical supplies. He quickly stopped them from toppling over, annoyed with himself for letting this gorgeous woman get to him.

He'd tried over the last few days to put a bit more distance between them, making sure they weren't left alone in the same room or area. Night-times were the worst, especially once Simone dropped off to sleep. The atmosphere between them, particularly as they were both lying down getting ready to sleep, usually became very personal. He would be highly attuned to every breath she breathed, every move she made, every little sigh she uttered as she dropped off to sleep, as though she was sighing out the tension of her day.

He'd often thought about going to her, massaging her shoulders, helping her to unwind, but even the thought of placing his hands onto her skin, of feeling the softness beneath his roughened palms, had been enough to keep him awake most of the night.

So for the past few nights he'd tried his best to remove the temptation and had left the hut, going to the clinic and monitoring the patients, while he'd waited for Melora to fall asleep. Then he'd crept in and eventually settled down enough to drift off into a light sleep.

'I would like to go to the waterhole. We've been so busy since I arrived that I haven't had a chance to see it yet.'

'It's got great style. Amazing shapes and colours,' he said, relaxing a little as he talked of his wonderful land.

'And snakes?'

He paused. 'There *may* be some in the surrounding rocks and trees but they'll keep to themselves. That's their home and we are the intruders. The village policy is to only kill them when they venture too close. A green-belly ringed snake, like the boa constrictor, can kill a small child quite quickly. The children must be protected at all costs.'

'Oh, I completely understand and agree. They are important little cherubs and speaking of that, where is your darling cherub? I thought she'd be in here, getting ready to head to the waterhole?'

'She's already there.'

'I would have thought she'd need to change first?'

Daniel laughed. 'No. She usually swims in her clothes, most of the kids do. Gives the clothes and the kids a bit of bath and within fifteen minutes of getting out they're all dry. It's only you city slickers who feel the need to don a completely different set of clothing in order to enjoy the water.'

Melora smiled at the teasing glint she saw in his eyes before looking down at her khaki shorts and baggy shirt. Instead of allowing it to hang limply at her waist, she'd pulled the edges to one side and tied them into a knot. It meant the shirt was still baggy on top but accentuated her curves. 'Well, I'm going to stay dressed as I am but I will take my sketch pad with me. How's that for different?'

Daniel straightened from where he'd been leaning against the crates. 'I didn't know you could draw. Are you any good?'

'Fair to medium.'

There was a shout outside their hut door from Belhara.

'Are you both ready? We are all leaving.'

'Coming,' Daniel called back, and held the screen door to the hut open for Melora. 'Shall we?'

'Sure.' She picked up her sketch pad and a pencil and headed to the door, determined, as she passed him, not to accidentally touch him. Being that close to Daniel, feeling the warmth radiating out from his body, his breath fanning her cheek… She glanced up at him, just for a split second, and was surprised to find him looking intently back at her.

'Melora.' Her name was a caress upon his lips.

'Daniel?' she breathed, cautious and confused by the veiled desire she saw in his eyes.

'I can't stop thinking about you.' The words were out of his mouth before he could stop them, causing her to gasp in shock before slowly shaking her head.

'Don't. We can't.'

'I know we can't go down that path. I don't want to be attracted to you but…' He stopped and tried again. 'I've tried to fight it but it's there, Melora. Between us. More than friendship.' Neither of them moved, caught in time.

'Daniel.' There was pain in her eyes. 'We can't. *I* can't.'

'I know. We live in different countries, different times, different circumstances.'

'It's not only that…' Melora took a step forward, away from him, heading down the stairs, glad she'd finally managed to get her legs to obey the signals from her brain. 'I'm…uh…waiting.'

Daniel closed the screen door and fell into step beside

her as they started walking through the village. 'Waiting for what?'

'Results.'

He stopped short, his eyes wide with concern. He put both hands on her shoulders, turning her to face him. 'You're not OK? The cancer? I thought you'd been given the all-clear? You said the PMA doctors were—'

'Satisfied,' she interrupted. 'The majority of my tests came back before I left but there were a few pathology results that wouldn't be in until later.'

'How much later? When?' There was real concern in his voice and she couldn't believe he cared that much for her. It was odd, especially after Leighton, who had been *supposed* to care about what happened to her, hadn't bothered a jot.

'I'm not sure. Maybe today. Maybe tomorrow. Soon. I'm completely confused as to what day of the week it is.'

'It's Monday.'

'Oh. Then hopefully today.'

'The whole time you've been here, you've had this sort of news hanging over your head?' He gave her a little shake and then dropped his arms, his frustration evident.

'I guess. But—'

'And you didn't think to tell me?'

'I didn't think it was that concerning. Besides, there's nothing you could have done about it. You can't wave a magic wand and hurry the results through.' She paused. 'Or did you need to know because you're the PMA team leader?'

'No. Not because of that. I'm your friend. Friends help and support each other. I could have...'

'What?'

'Been there for you.'

She visibly relaxed, pleased to know that he really cared about her. 'You have been.'

'Not knowing the results must be incredibly stressful.'

'Yes and no. The results will be in when they're in, and while I'd like to know, I've learned the hard way that stressing about it, fixating on it, obsessing about what it might or might not tell me, isn't any way for me to live, hence why I'm here.' She spread one arm wide, encompassing their present surroundings. 'Tarparnii is full of brilliant distractions.' Such as standing still and losing herself in his eyes. 'I can't even contemplate looking into the future when I'm not all that sure whether I'll need more surgery.' It was why she couldn't get involved with him and Simone.

'Mel.' Daniel shook his head in awe. 'You're an incredible woman. You're much stronger than I think you realise, to speak so calmly, in such a controlled way, when referring to all these things that have happened to you.'

'Believe me. I have enough bad days that sometimes outweigh the good ones.' They started walking again, Melora glad to be on the move. She found it much easier to resist Daniel, to keep her head focused, when she wasn't looking directly at him and when he wasn't looking directly at her.

Thankfully, as they walked along, they discussed their surroundings, passing the tree with three trunks that Daniel had shown her on her very first day here. It seemed so long ago. It felt as though she'd been in Tarparnii for so much longer and she had to admit that in less than a week she felt very different. Her love of medicine, of seeing patients, of helping them had definitely returned, along with the delight at finding so many new friends.

Simone, of course, had been an enormous highlight, the little girl so generous with her affection. Just like her father. Daniel was such a good man and he deserved only the best, which, as far as she was concerned, wasn't her. She would finish up her stint in Tarparnii then return to Australia, where she would do whatever it was the surgeons told her to. If she needed more invasive surgery then that's what she would do. If she didn't, her reconstructive surgery could commence. There was too much going on in her life and she really didn't have any time for her handsome colleague and his daughter...as much as she wished otherwise.

When they arrived at the waterhole, Melora sat on a rock and started to draw, but that was only after she'd recovered from watching Daniel take off his cotton shirt and shoes before jumping into the water to join his friends. Simone laughed and giggled, instantly swimming over to him and placing her arms about his neck so she didn't need to tread water in order to stay afloat. Melora was surprised at what good swimmers the children were, especially Simone.

When, after a while, Daniel clambered onto the rocks before heading in her direction, she tried so hard not to notice his incredible body, so firm and dark and gorgeous. She was a doctor, a surgeon, for heaven's sake. She'd seen naked chests before but...never like this!

Small, fine droplets of water clung to his dark skin and the smattering of dark, curly hair that spread down towards his shorts, which he wore low on his hips, glistened in the sunlight. She licked her lips, idly wondering what it would be like to brush her fingers across his skin, to feel the heat radiating from those perfectly sculpted arms of his, to have his mouth pressed to hers, robbing her of breath as he took her to new heights, to kiss—

'You shouldn't look at me like that, Melora.' His tone was deep and intimate so that only she could hear. He settled himself on a rock next to her and propped himself up on one elbow as their gazes met. She saw the intensity in his eyes and felt a mass of tingles flood her body.

'Sorry.' She immediately looked away, swallowing over her embarrassment.

'Don't be. I'm not saying I don't like it—I do, I *really* do—but we're friends and colleagues. I'd hate there to be animosity between us.'

He had to admit that he was still a little hurt that she hadn't told him about her situation sooner. Perhaps not at first but over the past few days they'd most certainly become closer.

Then again, he'd already gathered that Melora was a very private person and as he'd been raised in and now lived in a small Tarparniian community, where everybody knew everyone's business, he often forgot that new PMA doctors tended not to live by those same values.

'Festering is not good for the soul,' his mother had often said, and he'd heard Meeree say the same sort of thing. Right now, though, Daniel was definitely trying to keep the way Melora made him feel close to his chest. It wasn't festering, per se, but it also wasn't his usual modus operandi. Then again, he'd never been attracted to another woman since B'lana's death so he was definitely in uncharted territory.

The fact that he could still sense that Melora was uncomfortable with the discussion they'd just had was evident so he decided to change the subject. 'Do you mind if I take a look at your drawings?'

Melora still held her sketch pad in her hands and although she was hesitant to show him, she decided it was better to focus on her sketches rather than how close his body was to her own. She flicked over a page and showed him the brief drawings she'd made of him and his friends in the waterhole.

'Wow. These are really good, Melora.' He sat up and gave them his full attention. 'How long have you been drawing?'

'Not long. I started as a means of relieving boredom when I was stuck in hospital. I went from being a hectic surgeon with waiting lists here and there to having a lot of free time. I'd always enjoyed art back in high school so decided to give it another go. The psychologist I saw also said it would be very therapeutic.'

'And has it been?'

'Yes. When my engagement ended, I started to paint a lot of dark, night scenes. Angry clouds, lightning, a lot of destruction.'

'You were engaged?' Daniel tried to make the question sound as disinterested as he could but he knew he'd failed. Again it only reiterated just how much he didn't know about her.

'Yes.' Melora sighed. 'Leighton was Head of Surgery. When we became engaged it was touted as being the marriage of the hospital…only the marriage part never eventuated.'

'Why not?' He pushed aside any feelings of jealous and instant dislike he felt for the unknown Leighton, telling himself he needed to be a supportive friend, for Melora's sake.

'We were both so busy. Our schedules regularly

conflicted and whenever Leighton tried to pin me down to a date, something always cropped up. A conference, a research programme, a journal article deadline.'

'You're published?'

'A bit.'

'You're lying. That much I can tell,' Daniel said turning his head to look at her for a moment before deciding it was too dangerous to gaze at her soft, supple skin not too far away from him.

'A few articles over the years. I've done a lot of research and publishing those findings is part and parcel of the whole thing. My dance card, as they say, was completely full.' She sighed. 'So, as it turns out, was Leighton's. He'd been having multiple affairs with different women behind my back.'

Daniel growled at this news, furious with the disgusting Leighton for treating a woman such as Melora with so much contempt. 'When did you find out?'

'When he told me.'

'He confessed?'

'In a way.' Her voice had thickened with emotion and he could hear the pain in her words. 'Two days after my mastectomy surgery. He said it would be best if we called off the engagement, that I'd no doubt want to concentrate on my recovery rather than having to worry about planning a wedding. He then went on to say that he'd met someone else and it would be better for the entire general surgical department if we simply stayed colleagues.'

'He said that? Two days after you'd had major surgery?'

'Among other things.'

Daniel propped himself up on his elbow and looked down into her face. She had her eyes closed, tiny tears trembling on her lashes as she worked hard to control her emotions. No wonder she had self-confidence issues. This Leighton chap, along with the cancer, had destroyed her.

'Once our engagement was officially over, all the stories about his affairs came pouring out, everyone telling me I was too good for him.'

'You are. You *are* too good for him.' Daniel's tone was filled with vehemence. 'A woman like you deserves to be loved with honour, to be cherished with heart-felt desire and to be protected with firm strength.' He reached out and tenderly brushed the tears from her eyes with his thumb.

Melora opened her eyes and stared into Daniel's face. His hand caressed her cheek, the touch soft and tender. She swallowed, her breathing intensifying again, but this time it was due to desire rather than anger at her past.

He was close, his breath mixing with hers. Her heart pounded wildly against her chest and she wondered if he could hear it, it was so loud.

'You're a strong, independent woman, Melora Washington.' His words were barely a whisper, touching her deep down inside. 'I wonder if *you* know just how strong you really are.' He brushed his thumb across her lips and they parted with anticipatory longing. Her breathing was erratic, her mind puzzled at hearing a man speak so highly of her. No man had *ever* upheld her, hence why she'd always fought for what she'd wanted.

'Daniel.' His name came from her lips mixed with re-pressed passion and confusion. 'What's happening?'

'I don't know,' he answered truthfully. 'Our lives have collided, Mel. Slammed into each other with a resound-ing *thwack*.' His words were whispered as he edged closer. 'I have no idea what it means but it's becoming more and more difficult for me to deny how you make me feel.'

'Oh…' The word was released on a trembling breath and she swallowed again as Daniel continued to move nearer, her gaze flicking between his mouth and his eyes, her mind spinning so fast as she tried to make some sort of sense out of what was happening.

He was going to kiss her! She could sense it. She could feel it and she wasn't at all sure what she should do about it—if anything. The fact that Daniel admitted to finding her attractive, that he was interested in her, that he thought her a strong, intelligent woman was already more than she'd ever dreamed of…but the truth of the matter was they came from different worlds and really shouldn't…follow through…on…

Her mind stopped working, stopped processing, stopped trying to make any sort of sense of what was happening between them, simply because all she could think about was his mouth finally touching hers.

CHAPTER EIGHT

'DAD-DYY. Mel-ora.' Simone's voice penetrated Daniel's mind and without shifting his body, still remaining close to Melora's delicious mouth, his thoughts still firmly directed towards following through on his desire to kiss her, he slightly turned his head to the side. Melora did the same, their cheekbones resting together as they looked over to where Simone was trying to get their attention.

The child had climbed onto a rock and was about to jump into the water, her friends waiting below, encouraging her. The rock, however, was one of the higher ones and Daniel's parental alarm instantly started ringing in loud warning tones.

'It's too high,' Melora whispered, both of them moving, rising to their feet.

'It's too high,' Daniel called a moment later. 'Simone. Get down.' Daniel looked around them, realising that Belhara was already out of the water and was heading around on the rocks to get to the little girl.

Simone wiggled her hips and clapped her hands, her wet blonde hair swishing from side to side. The shorts and T-shirt she wore were wet and dripping down onto her bare feet, causing the rock she was standing on to become dangerously slippery. 'I'm nearly five,' she told her father.

'It's too high,' Melora called, her heart—where it had been pounding wildly in sensual anticipation—now thumping wildly with fear and trepidation.

'*Separ*,' Daniel coaxed in a firm but gentle tone. 'It's too high. Turn around and climb back down. When you're ten, then you will be old enough to—'

'I'm old enough now,' she protested illogically, and shifted closer to the edge.

Melora stood, her hands clasped tightly to her chest, feeling helpless and inadequate, willing the child to be sensible, to listen to her father.

'Simone.' There was now a stern warning in Daniel's tone and Simone stopped and looked at him, realising she was making her beloved daddy angry. Melora watched as the visual stand-off between father and headstrong daughter continued as they held each other's gaze. There was nothing she could do and she felt so useless.

She wasn't the little girl's mother but she most certainly felt like it. The love, the need to protect, the powerful surges of wanting to keep the gorgeous girl close to her for the rest of her life—it was all there, and where she'd been telling herself not to become too involved in these people's lives, she was starting to realise that it might actually be too late.

Belhara had climbed the rocks and was now within reaching distance of Simone. Within another moment he would be able to snake out his arm and put it around her little waist, hauling the child back to safety. Melora's throat was dry, her eyes wide with concern, her heart filled with a silent prayer.

The children in the water below, the ones who had been encouraging Simone, probably daring Simone to jump, were now silent, being told by one of the other parents to come out of the water.

Belhara was almost there. His arm almost touching her but the last thing any of them wanted was to spook the child, who was now crying.

'I'm sorry, Daddy.' Where there had been courage in her tone before, it had now changed to trembling fear and it was as though she was glued to the spot, unable to move.

'It's all right, *Separ.*' Daniel, who was now standing at the edge of the waterhole, looking pleadingly up at his daughter, made sure his tone held no censure. 'Turn around slowly. Carefully. Go with Belhara.'

As Daniel spoke, Belhara's arm touched Simone, startling the child. She screamed in fright and shifted away but as she did so, her little feet slipped on the rock and within another second there was a sickening thud—the sound of bone connecting with something hard—before the child dropped into the water. Had she just hit her head? Had that sound been her head hitting against the slippery rock?

'No!' Melora hadn't realised the scream had come from her and she made her way towards the water's edge, heart pounding fiercely against her chest, tears welling in her eyes. She looked around for Daniel but couldn't see him, realising a split second later that he'd already dived into the water to rescue his daughter.

'Oh, God. Please let her be OK,' Melora prayed, clutching her hands to her chest, realising belatedly that she was trembling in fear. She'd never been this frightened, this concerned, this worried before. Not when she'd been diagnosed with breast cancer, not when she'd had surgery, not even when Leighton had broken their engagement, leaving her to face her recovery all alone.

No. Nothing compared with the pain a parent would

feel if *anything* bad happened to their child, and her heart ached for Daniel. It seemed like hours ticked by while she waited for the two of them to surface, even though it was only a matter of seconds.

The instant they broke through the water's surface, Simone's loud, wailing cries filled the air, and Melora couldn't believe the relief which flooded over her. Her knees buckled beneath her and she landed in the shallows of the water, unable to move, watching as Daniel swam towards her, Simone crying loudly.

When they were closer, she held out her hands and Daniel instantly passed Simone to her. Melora pressed kisses to the child's head, cradling her close. Simone was still crying, hopefully more through fear than pain.

'It's OK. It's OK,' she soothed, rocking back and forth, her arms secure around the child. Daniel had pulled himself next to them and leaned over Simone.

'Let me take a look. Does it hurt? Where does it hurt, baby? Show Daddy.'

Simone nodded her little head and pointed to her arm which, now that they had the opportunity to look at her properly, Melora realised, was hanging limply at a very wrong angle. Daniel was touching it gently but even then Simone was whimpering.

'Feels fractured. We need to get her back to the clinic and have Keith take a look at it,' he murmured close to her ear, and although his words were clinical, Melora could hear the veiled panic.

'She'll be fine, Daniel,' she reassured him. 'You had her out of the water so fast, even though it felt like an eternity. You were there. You were looking after her.'

'I should have done more. I should have been watching her. Playing with her in the water. Protecting her, rather than thinking only of myself. She's my child.

My responsibility,' he returned, his words crisp as he stood and lifted Simone from Melora's arms. The child whimpered again and Daniel cradled her close. 'Shh. It's fine. Daddy's got you. Daddy's going to fix you and make it all better.'

Melora looked at him as she managed to stand up, reaching out a hand to brush some hair back from Simone's face. His face was an emotionless mask, his eyes dull yet filled with pain. 'I should have been with her.' Daniel edged away, putting some distance between them, and Melora dropped her hand back to her side, feeling as though she'd just been slapped.

'I need to get her to the clinic,' he said, and without another word turned and started to make his way expertly over the rocks, his daughter held protectively in his arms. Melora knew he was concerned, she understood that he was worried about Simone—so was she—but she hadn't missed the way Daniel was blaming himself for the accident. If he hadn't been paying attention to her, if he'd been watching his daughter more closely, the accident might never have happened.

She stood in the shallows of the water, watching them walk away, feeling lonely and bereft. She wasn't Simone's mother, she wasn't even a member of Daniel's extended Tarparniian family. She was just a doctor who had come to help out for a while. Someone who would leave soon, who would return to Australia and probably never see either one of them again.

At that thought, at the realisation that she could face the rest of her life without either Daniel or Simone, Melora's heart contracted with a new sort of pain. It was powerful and intense and one she'd never felt before. She'd survived cancer, she'd survived the messy break-up with Leighton, but the thought of surviving the rest of her life without Simone and Daniel made her heart break.

She needed to do something. She couldn't just stand there and watch two people that she cared about most in this world just walk away from her, especially when one of them was hurt! She'd felt helpless and alone when she'd made the decision to come to Tarparnii and on her arrival here she'd learned that the main thing about these villages was a sense of community. J'tana had been cared for by her sister and her mother during the delivery of her first child. Meeree and Jalak offered friendship and family to all of the people who came to their village, whether to receive treatment from the doctors, or the doctors coming from overseas to help out.

Friendship. Family. Community.

That's what *she* had found, that's what Daniel and Simone had helped her to feel, and after quickly scooping up her sketch pad she hurried after them, eager to offer her services and support in any way she could. Daniel might brush her aside, might hold her at arm's length because he was mad at himself, but that wouldn't stop her from giving to him, from caring for him, from showing him that he was important to her.

Although she didn't have her final tests results in yet, although she would be leaving this glorious place soon to return to Australia, although she wasn't sure how her affections would be received, she had to take this chance. She had to show Daniel that she cared.

Even though she hurried, picking her way through the jungle, on the path, past the three-trunked tree, Melora still didn't manage to catch up with them, and when she entered the clinic, the sounds of Simone crying tore at her heart. She entered the examination area where Keith was having a look at Simone's arm. Daniel was sitting on the examination bed holding Simone in his arms, his emotionless mask still in place.

Daniel didn't even glance her way when she came in, his attention focused on what was happening to his little girl. It was as though the doctor in him had disappeared, leaving a nervous and worried father behind.

'We'll get you some medicine, Simone,' Keith was saying to the little girl. 'That will make you feel better and take away that nasty pain.' Keith looked at Daniel. 'She's not allergic to anything is she? Tarvon?'

Daniel didn't answer and Keith looked over at Melora, concern on his face. Melora nodded and instantly went to Daniel's side.

'Hey.' She put her hand on his shoulder, reassuring and comforting this man who had come to mean so much to her in such a small amount of time. Slowly he turned his head to look at her and Melora smiled. 'Everything's going to be just fine, Daniel.'

Simone whimpered in his arms and he winced as though he was the one who was in agony. 'Daniel, is she allergic to anything?'

He shrugged. 'I don't know. She's never had anything wrong with her before.'

Keith nodded and crossed to the cupboard, drawing up an injection of Midazolam. Melora looked down at the little girl, still held safely in her father's loving arms. 'Hi, sweetie.'

Simone sniffed and her words were full of misery. 'I hurt my arm, Melora.'

'I know, but Keith is going to make it all better. You'll be just fine.' While Melora spoke, she dropped her hand from Daniel's shoulder, as it would be all too easy to leave it there. Given the emergency, he hadn't had time to don his shirt, and being this close to his torso, to his smooth warm flesh wasn't helping her to keep focused.

Right now, Daniel needed friends around him and she wanted to tell him that she was there for him, in whatever capacity he required. She wanted to tell him that it wasn't his fault that his daughter had had the accident, that it had been circumstantial. She wanted to tell him just how much he'd come to mean to her and how it was becoming increasingly difficult for her to stop wanting to be close to him.

But she didn't. Now was neither the time nor the place.

Keith administered the anaesthetic and Simone soon became sleepy, dozing off. 'You can put her down now, Tarvon. From what I can see, it appears to be a clean break, nothing a quick re-set and a cast won't fix.'

There was no movement. Daniel still sat there, his sleeping daughter in his arms. Keith once more looked at Melora. 'Here, Daniel.' She gently put her hands at his waist and urged him to stand up. 'Pop Simone on the bed and you and I can head out for some fresh air.'

Daniel lifted his gaze from his daughter and once more looked at Melora before nodding. 'Yes. Yes. OK. Good.' Tenderly, he placed his daughter on the examination table. Keith put his hand onto Daniel's shoulder.

'Trust me, buddy. I'll be looking after her as though she were one of my own.'

'Thank you.' Daniel allowed Melora to lead him from the room and once they were outside the clinic building, he leaned against the warm bricks and raked his hands through his now dry hair. 'I shouldn't have taken my eyes off her. How could I have been so selfish?'

'It was an accident, Daniel. They do happen and she's going to be fine. Keith is a brilliant orthopaedic surgeon. We both know that and he'll fix her up as good as new.'

Daniel looked at her. 'I know. I trust Keith. I was just so…caught up…in…you and how you make me feel and…' He stopped and shook his head. Melora could see sadness in his eyes and her heart went out to him. 'Anything could have happened to her. She could have hit her head or fallen into the water at a bad angle and split her skin, she could have really done some damage and—'

'Shh.' Melora couldn't bear his words, his anguish any more, and put her finger over his mouth to stop him talking. He put his hand around her wrist and held it. 'She didn't, Daniel. You can't watch her twenty-four hours a day. We head off on clinics to other villages and she's always safe here in the village with the rest of your people.'

'But I promised B'lana I'd keep her safe.'

'And you do. You're a good father, Daniel.' Her words were earnest, imploring, desperate to get through to him. 'Don't go beating yourself up because that's just a waste of energy and right now you're better off expending that energy in being with Simone. She needs her happy, big, strong, protective daddy, which is exactly what you are.'

He was still holding her wrist, his thumb gently caressing the lower part of her palm as she spoke. It was difficult to concentrate, difficult to remember she was supposed to be helping him when all she wanted was to kiss him.

'You're right.'

She smiled at that. 'Words every woman wants to hear.'

Daniel gave a little tug on her wrist, drawing her closer. She went.

'I apologise if I snapped at you earlier.'

'Don't worry about it. You were concerned for Simone. I understand.'

'Mel…' He brought her hand to his lips and pressed a long and tender kiss to her soft skin. Melora closed her eyes for a second, committing the touch to memory because when she looked at him again, there was sorrow in his beautiful brown eyes.

'We can't do this.' The words were soft, sweet and sad. 'Simone is my world. She's my everything.'

'As she should be.'

'I've never been this interested in a woman since B'lana's death and I want you to know that you are important to me but right now I have to put Simone first.'

'Of course you do.' Melora swallowed over the dryness in her throat and gently eased back from him. Daniel reluctantly let go of her hand and as he did she was astonished to find there were tears pricking behind her eyes. She forced a smile and ignored the pain around her heart. 'I'm, uh…going to go and get a drink.'

Biting her lip in an effort to control the trembling sadness wrenching out from her, she knew the sooner she had some space from him, the sooner she'd be able to get herself under control. Hearing him say that he was interested in her had been incredible and then to hear, in the same breath, that he couldn't do anything about it, was playing over and over in her mind.

'Sure.' Daniel pushed his hands through his hair and nodded, feeling hollow as he watched her go. When he'd asked her to come to the waterhole with them, he'd had no idea that things would escalate so quickly. He'd been sidetracked from watching Simone by the stunningly beautiful Melora, her golden hair shining brightly in the sun. He'd been looking at her drawings, wanting to get close to her, wanting to touch her, wanting to kiss her.

The fact that he was even interested in another woman, had wanted to pursue her, was a miracle in itself because after B'lana's death, although she'd told him to find someone else, he'd never thought he'd ever again meet anyone who he connected with so completely. Meeting Melora had proved him wrong and he'd allowed himself to be sidetracked from his main responsibility—his daughter.

Simone was his world and he'd been right to put the brakes on anything else that might have happened between Melora and himself. Simone needed him now and it would be selfish of him to focus on himself, on the rapidly increasing feelings he felt for his newest colleague.

'Tarvon?'

Daniel looked around as someone called his name, to see Jalak headed in his direction. 'She's fine,' Daniel said quickly. 'Broken arm. Keith's fixing her up now.'

Jalak nodded and smiled. 'Simone will be running around sooner than you realise.' Jalak tapped the side of his head. 'It is the father who will have the lasting image. Children bounce and forget. As parents we do not.'

'True.'

'I am also wanting Melora. You have seen her? There is a call on the satellite phone for her.'

'That must be about her results,' Daniel said, more to himself than to Jalak. 'She's in the food hut. I'll get her.' He knew she wouldn't want to be alone when she found out the results. It must have been nerve-racking for her to come here without knowing the outcome of her final tests and yet, like the strong, independent woman she was, she'd still come.

He sincerely hoped it was good news and just as he headed off to the food hut, Keith came out of the clinic. 'Ah…just the man I was looking for. Break's set, Cast's in place and she's about to wake up.'

Daniel looked from Keith to the food hut where he knew Melora was, and back again.

'Go to your child,' Jalak encouraged. 'I will tell Melora of the call.'

And once more Daniel realised that now was not the right time in his life to be moving on, to be trying something new with an amazing woman. He nodded and headed into the clinic. It was time for him to look after his baby girl.

Later, after night had fallen, Melora stopped by the clinic to check on Simone. The child was sitting up in one of the hospital beds, chatting brightly to anyone who would listen. Her plastered arm was resting on a large blanket in front of her as though it was her pride and joy.

'Hello, gorgeous girl.' Melora knelt down beside the bed and was treated to a huge one-armed hug from Simone.

'Look at this, Melora. Look at my cast. I have a cast and Daddy says that he'll find me a big pen and people can write their names on it and it has to stay on for three weeks and Keith said I was very lucky and that 'cos my arm is only four-and-three-quarters, nearly five years old it will be all better really soon and Sue brought me some fresh fruit from the tree and Bel comes and checks on me and takes my temperature and I get to sleep here tonight!'

Melora laughed at the run of constant chatter. 'Wow. That's…really a lot of things happening.'

'And Daddy's going to sleep here too but he's not allowed to use one of the beds because they're for the sick people so he's gone to get his sleeping mat from our hut and…ooh, you could get your sleeping mat and come on the other side and we can *all* sleep in the clinic.' Her eyes were wide and she scrunched her shoulders up with delighted excitement. 'I've *never* slept in here before. I wanted to but Daddy said no and that only sick people got to sleep here but I'm sick now and so I get to stay here but Daddy said just for tonight.'

'Yes. He's quite right. One night should be just the right amount to help make you better.' Before Melora had finished speaking, Daniel walked in, his sleeping mat and blankets rolled up beneath his arm. He'd also donned a shirt so his naked chest wasn't causing her as much havoc as it had before. He still looked incredible, though.

'Daddy! Melora's going to sleep here, too. You on one side and Melora on the other and me in the middle. Just like all the time in our hut,' Simone informed him before Melora could say anything.

'Actually, I don't know if there would be enough room,' Daniel said quickly. 'We need to make sure that Bel can get close to your clinic bed to take your temperature and look after you during the night.'

Melora frowned. She'd already been going to refuse the little girl's offer but to have Daniel do it for her felt like another slap in the face. 'Daddy's right and, besides, it will be a great adventure for the two of you to have.'

Simone's bottom lip came out, her brown eyes mimicking those of a sad puppy. 'But I want you to be here.

You're like the mummy and Daddy's like the daddy and then we can all stay together. Family.'

Tears of delight instantly sprang into Melora's eyes at Simone's words. *You're like the mummy.* She smiled but her sadness was evident. 'You and Daddy stay here tonight and then you'll have lots of exciting news to tell me in the morning. OK?'

She couldn't look at Daniel. Couldn't even bring herself to glance in his direction. She had no idea how he'd coped with Simone's declaration at how she saw the three of them but as he'd said outside not a few hours before, he needed to focus on Simone. It was true and right and after she kissed the child, she headed out of the clinic.

She'd not made it halfway across the village clearing when she heard Daniel call her name. She turned and clasped her hands together in front of her.

'Uh…sorry to bother you, but Jalak mentioned earlier that you'd received a call on the satellite phone.'

'Yes.'

'Was it your results?'

'Yes.'

She wasn't making this easy for him but then again why should she? He'd all but pushed her aside, telling her that he had feelings for her but wasn't going to do anything about it. In a few more days she would be back in Australia and out of his life. Even though he didn't like it, it was the only way for things to be.

'Good news?'

'Yes.' Her smile was watery but she swallowed over the lump in her throat. 'Everything's fine. I am now officially cancer free. My oncologist doesn't want to see me for another twelve months.'

'Oh, Mel, that's brilliant.' He wanted to rush towards her, take her in his arms, swing her around in a large circle before hauling her close and showing her just how happy he was by kissing her deeply, passionately, completely. Instead, he clenched his jaw and crossed his arms firmly over his chest. 'Congratulations.'

'Thanks.'

Both of them stood there. Silent. Uncomfortable. Painfully aware of each other but unable to do anything about it.

What she really wanted was for him to close the distance between them, tell her that he was wildly ecstatic at her good news and now that she no longer had an axe swinging over her head, he wanted her to stay permanently in Tarparnii, to be with him and Simone, and that she really should go and get her sleeping mat so they could all bunk down in the clinic and have a fantastic time together…as a family.

He didn't.

What he really wanted was for her to run towards him and throw herself into his wide-open arms, telling him that she wanted to stay in Tarparnii, that she loved it here and that her life had become meaningless without him and Simone.

She didn't.

Silence reigned.

'Well…goodnight,' she finally ventured.

'Have a good sleep.'

'You, too. I hope Simone settles down, she's still very hyped.'

'Side-effect of the pain medication Keith has her on.'

'Or is it more the fact that she's super-excited to sleep in the clinic?'

He nodded slowly. 'Good point.'

Silence. Insects chirruped around them.

'Goodnight,' she said again and before anything else was said or done she turned her back to him and walked calmly to the hut—*his* hut—where she unrolled her sleeping mat, prepared for bed and lay down.

All alone.

Again.

CHAPTER NINE

THE next morning Melora woke early. When she opened her eyes she saw no Simone and no Daniel. Just crates of supplies.

It was ridiculous to feel so alone, given that in Australia she lived on her own. Every morning she would wake to the décor of her apartment, alone in her bed, and not have any problems getting on with her day. Now, though, even though the birds were chirping outside, she missed Simone, missed spending those early morning hours with the gorgeous girl. She missed hearing Daniel's steady breathing as he caught up on his sleep.

Was this what it was going to be like when she returned home? When she flew back to Australia in a week's time? She'd come to Tarparnii to stretch her wings, to try new experiences, and she had. However, she hadn't expected to leave feeling more alone than when she'd arrived.

She rolled over onto her stomach and closed her eyes, not wanting to think about it. Daniel and Simone. Having them around, sharing this hut with them had only succeeded in showing her how wonderful it would be to become part of their family.

The three of them. A family. Together. Supporting. Loving.

'No.' She couldn't think like that. Daniel had made it clear yesterday that there was no place in his life for her and she needed to respect his decision. Even when he'd come to the hut last night to collect Simone's frilly, pink pillow for her to sleep with, Melora's hopes had skyrocketed, hoping, for one brief instant, that he'd come to the hut to tell her he was wrong and that she really should come and join them in the clinic rather than being here by herself.

He'd come into the hut, politely apologised for disturbing her, collected the pillow and called a quick goodnight before leaving, and her hopes had plummeted into the pit of despair.

He wasn't a part of her life. He was just a colleague she was working with for one more week and most of that week would be spent in a different village. They were due to leave in a couple of days' time to head further south to spend the rest of the week in the village of Daniel's mother. From there, Melora, Sue and Keith were to leave, their time in Tarparnii coming to an end. While Melora was intrigued to meet Daniel's mother, she wasn't looking forward to leaving Meeree and Jalak. Everyone here had been so incredibly welcoming and so incredibly supportive.

She sighed. Lying there, doing nothing except working herself up into a tizz, wasn't going to accomplish anything. She needed to get up and go and see Simone, to check on how the child had slept and how she was feeling. Of course, Melora had other patients to check on, such as Meimii and J'tana—who had decided to head back to her village—but it was the thought of seeing Simone that prompted Melora to actually get up and get her day started.

Before she even stepped foot inside the clinic, she heard Simone laughing and her heart instantly relaxed. The girl was happy. That meant a lot.

'Melora!' Simone almost squealed her name as Melora walked into the room, the little girl running over. Melora picked the child up and held her close.

'J'tana let me have a careful hold of J'torek and I put my frilly pink pillow over my cast arm and then Bel put J'torek in my arms and I had a cuddle but then he started to cry and so now J'tana has to give him mother's milk but I was very careful with him, wasn't I, J'tana?' Simone switched between Tarparnese and English with fluidity, depending on who she was talking to.

'I'm sure you were.' Melora smiled at J'tana and Meimii, both of whom were in their beds, talking to each other while J'tana fed her son. However, there was no sign of Daniel. 'Where's your dad?' Melora asked, trying to make the question sound as natural as possible.

'He's sleeping,' came the deep, muffled reply from somewhere on the floor beside Simone's bed. Melora smiled at the grumpy, exhausted tone of his voice. She looked at Bel, who was getting ready to do Meimii's observations.

'Simone took a while to settle last night. Lots of excitement,' the Tarparniian nurse informed her.

'Ahh. Well, how about we give Daddy the chance to have a bit of a rest? We can go to the food hut, have breakfast and read a book,' Melora suggested to the little girl.

'Like we do *every* morning?' Simone's excitement was boundless.

'Yes.'

'Can we still do that with my arm all broken?'

'Of course we can.'

'Yay!' Simone hugged Melora close with her good arm.

'We'll leave you in peace,' Melora said, and with great delight she and Simone went to the food hut. She would miss this little girl so much, holding her, cuddling her, sharing with her. She decided it was very important that she make as many memories as she could, to store all of these special moments away, because she knew that on her return to Australia she would experience an emptiness such as she'd never felt before. That would be when she'd need these memories, of Simone, of the whole village, but mostly of Daniel, to keep her warm on the long lonely nights.

As the day progressed, Simone bounced back to her normal self and apart from the cast on her arm it was as though nothing bad had ever happened. Daniel, however, was another story. He remained polite and professional towards her but she also noticed that he seemed preoccupied.

Over the next couple of days he became even more withdrawn, not only from her but from everyone. He spent every free moment he wasn't working with Simone, monitoring her, watching her, caring for her. Melora was becoming increasingly concerned and on the morning when they were due to travel to his mother's village she noted that he didn't even bother sleeping.

With Simone sound asleep beside her, Melora tossed and turned but her concern for Daniel, from the way he was only focusing on work and his daughter, was robbing her of sleep. Sighing, she flicked back her covers and pulled on a long cardigan, which covered her summer pyjamas. With bare feet she padded through the hut and on opening the screen door found Daniel sitting on the top step of the hut, looking up at the sky.

'Hi,' she said, coming to sit beside him.

'Mel? What's wrong? Is it Simone? Is she all right?' He stood and was about to head into the hut when she stopped him.

'She's fine, Daniel. She's sleeping…snoring, actually.'

Daniel opened the door of the hut to check for himself and returned a second later, coming down the stairs, needing some distance from where Melora sat. 'Did she wake you? She can snore pretty loud sometimes, especially for someone so small.'

'No. She didn't wake me. I was…uh…concerned about you.'

'Me?' His eyebrows hit his hairline.

'Yes, you. Am I not allowed to be concerned about you?'

'Er…I don't know.' He shoved his hands into the pockets of his shorts to stop himself from touching her, hauling her close into his arms.

'Why don't you come and sit down and we can talk?'

Daniel remained where he was, at the bottom of the steps, looking at her. So close, yet so far. 'I don't know if that's a good idea. No offence, Melora, but being around you is difficult. You're beautiful and caring and wonderful and you smell so good all the time.' He took a hand from his pocket and raked it through his long hair. He hadn't shaved for a few days so his rugged stubble back in place, making him look just as he had when they'd first met—dangerously sexy.

'Oh!' Melora's eyes widened at his frank and honest words. 'Uh…sorry…but, hey, you're one to talk. Don't you think I have trouble being around you? Don't you realise that when you stand there with your hair loose and your arm muscles almost bursting out of your mis-buttoned shirt and…and that sexy look in your eyes, as it is right now, that *I* have trouble resisting you?'

'Oh. I…uh…didn't realise.'

'This isn't all one-sided, you know. I know you told me that you couldn't get involved and I understand that. I appreciate that fact and I also know it doesn't change the way we may feel about each other, but that's not why I wanted to talk to you.'

'It isn't?'

'No. I wanted to ask you if you'd come to any decisions about Simone's education.'

'Why would you ask that?'

'Because you've been very preoccupied of late, almost to the point of being withdrawn, and I wondered if Simone's accident had triggered your deeper thought processes.'

'That's very perceptive of you. Have you been taking lessons from Meeree?'

She smiled. 'No. It's actually more like a lucky guess.'

'Well, it's a good one.' He exhaled harshly then shook his head. 'I feel as though my head is going to explode. My thoughts keep going round and round.'

'About whether to send her to boarding school?'

'No. I've come to a decision on that front. She's not going.' His words were vehement. 'After her accident, I realised that I couldn't parcel her off, send her overseas to another country far, far away while I stay here to help out with my people. I will not leave my daughter to be raised by strangers and it's better for both of us if she stays here.'

Melora nodded. 'Decision reached.'

'Yes.' He frowned when she remained silent. 'You're not going to talk me out of it?'

'Why should I? She's your daughter, your responsibility, and you know what's best for her. You know she'll get a different education here but perhaps that's all she needs. Her community is here, she's happy, you're happy. Academic excellence isn't the be-all and end-all in life.'

'Yes. Exactly.'

'So why aren't you happy with your decision?'

'What makes you think that?'

'Daniel, for the past few days you've been so preoccupied, so withdrawn, always with that same concerned look on your face that you have right now, that if you had truly made the right decision, you'd be feeling a lot more at peace.'

He breathed in deep and shook his head slowly. 'How do you do that?'

'Do what?'

'Appear to know me better than I know myself.'

Melora shrugged. 'I don't know.'

'You're right. You're right. If it was the right decision to keep her here, it would feel better. Her education *is* important but I can't send her away. I need her with me, near me. I will not let her have the same disjointed childhood I was forced to endure.'

'Understood. I do, however, have one other question.'

'Uh-huh? What's that?'

'Why do *you* need to stay here in Tarparnii?'

He gave her a blank look. 'I work here.'

'I know. Why do you need to stay, though?'

'Because this is my home.' He spread his arms wide. 'PMA needs good doctors. They've agreed to support

Tarparnii, to send medical personal and supplies, and all of it is vital to my country.'

'Agreed, but you haven't answered the question. Why do *you* need to be here? People have changed jobs in the past.'

'Are you saying I should leave PMA? Leave Tarparnii?' His tone was getting angry now and she hadn't meant to upset him.

Melora shrugged. 'I'm not trying to tell you what to do, Daniel. I'm merely asking why you're limiting yourself. Why can't Simone receive a good education in another country *with you there*?'

'You mean, move back to England? Take Simone to England with me? Leave Tarparnii?'

'I don't think you could ever really *leave* Tarparnii, Daniel. It's such an intrinsic part of you, but it was just a thought.' She shrugged. 'Over the years I devoted so much of my life to my career. Working hard, securing the right placements, writing articles, undertaking research, doing what needed to be done in order to gain the job I'd always wanted, and when I finally reached my goals, when I thought I was where I wanted to be— great prospects, marriage on the horizon, time to start a family—it was all taken away with one simple lump I found in my breast.

'In a matter of weeks my entire world came crumbling down. I had scans, tests, appointments, concern, worry, decisions. My operating lists were handed on to another surgeon, my clinic lists divided up among my colleagues, my research finished off by my assistant, my engagement broken. For the first time in my life I wasn't in control. I wasn't the one driving my life forward, the cancer was.

'Coming here, to this incredible country, meeting the

most accepting and loving people I've ever met in my entire life…it's changed me. It's helped me. You said on my very first day here that you hoped I would find healing here and I have.'

'I'm glad.' His words were deep, personal and full of true meaning.

'But the point I'm trying to make is that I discovered the hard way that work is not the be-all and end-all of my existence. Neither should it be for you. Simone is much more important than your job with PMA.'

'I've been spending more time with her. I've been focusing on her and—'

'And has it worked? Daniel, you need balance in your life. Everyone does. We need to make room for work and play and family and friends and happiness…and love.' Her voice broke on the last word because she knew within that very moment, and with perfect clarity, that she loved him. She loved him and his daughter.

She watched him, standing there, his hands in his pockets as though to keep himself from touching her, and her heart pounded with love for him. She knew he had other concerns, namely Simone, to deal with, and she would never dream of asking him to forgo that, but being here with him, being close to him day in, day out, would become increasingly difficult.

'I'd compartmentalised my life so neatly that before coming here I hadn't realised that one part of my life links with the others. If it doesn't, I end up in a big old mess rather than becoming whole.' She pulled the cardigan closer around her. Watching him, wanting him, loving him and not being able to have him would be the next challenge she would face.

'Don't look at me like that, Mel.'

'Like what, Daniel?'

'Like you want me to hold you, to kiss you.'

'I do,' she whispered. 'I *really* do…but I understand why you can't and I respect that, but it doesn't stop me from wanting it.'

'I know.' His hands came out of his pockets and just for an instant she thought he was going to cross to her side and haul her close, pressing her body to his as they gave in to the yearning and need and desperation that seemed to be surrounding them…but he quickly crossed his arms over his chest and took a small step away. Decision reached.

The sun's rays were starting to peek through the clouds and the humidity of the day was starting to increase. The birds were starting to sing and within another few minutes Simone would wake up. Daniel would become engrossed in his daughter and his work once more and Melora would work hard to keep her distance and deal with this latest twist in her life.

She was in love with a man who couldn't love her back.

Later that morning everyone assisted in packing the transport trucks. Sue, Keith and Melora said their goodbyes to all their friends.

'Thank you so much for having me to stay,' Melora said as she hugged Meeree.

'You have learned much, Melora Washington, and we will see you soon.'

'But I won't be coming back here. We're leaving from the other village to go straight to the airport.'

Meeree's smile was indulgent. 'That is not what I meant. Your heart has been changed.' She touched a hand to Melora's cheek. 'Until we next meet, *Separ.*'

Melora had been shocked to realise that Meeree could

see that she was in love with Daniel. Could everyone? Was it that obvious? Before she could ask any more questions, Simone came bounding over.

'I'm so excited, Melora. I get to go with you and I get to see Nahkala. I'm getting on the truck now. Come on.' She took Melora's hand in hers and tugged her along.

'Nahkala, the mother of Daniel, will be as happy to welcome you to her village as I was here. Go. Enjoy. Be safe,' Meeree called, and Melora allowed herself to be led away.

As the trucks rumbled along, Melora pulled out her small sketch pad and a pencil and began to doodle.

'What are you drawing?' a little voice asked, and Melora looked up to see Simone watching her closely. The child was sitting next to her father on the opposite side of the large transport truck.

'Just some of the trees you have here. We don't have them back in Australia.'

'Really? That's funny. Do you have that tree?' Simone pointed to one far in the distance as they drove by.

'No.'

'What about the red bushes?'

'Red bushes?' Melora asked.

'She means the *kapordhe* bushes. I believe you were sketching them yesterday, around the back of the clinic building,' Daniel offered as he placed a protective arm about his daughter, keeping her close to him as the truck bumped up and down.

She was surprised that he'd seen her. As far as she'd known, he'd been giving her a wide berth. Since their talk that morning he'd again withdrawn into his shell, keeping busy, organising everything for the next few days. Now, sitting on the truck, there was a slight tension between them but both were determined to ignore it—if only for Simone's sake. 'Oh. No. We don't have them in Australia.'

'Well, what do you have?' Simone asked.

'We have gum trees and we have bottle-brush trees and flowers with funny names like kangaroo paw.'

Simone giggled. 'That is funny. I thought a kangaroo was a hoppy animal.'

'It is. Here.' Melora turned a page in her sketch pad and quickly sketched a picture of a kangaroo and then a kangaroo paw flower. Simone was impressed.

'Can you draw me?' she asked.

'I'm not very good with portraits but I can try. You'll need to sit as still as possible, which might be a bit difficult at the moment.'

'And draw Daddy, too,' Simone instructed.

Melora met Daniel's gaze to see if he objected but he merely shrugged one shoulder so she began to draw. It felt strange being able to have an excuse to stare at Daniel, especially when she was usually trying to sneak glances. Now, though, she had the opportunity to capture him, to absorb the angular lines that made his face perfect, his nose, his stubble-covered jaw, his incredibly expressive eyes.

When she had finished, she held out the sketch pad so they could view her handiwork.

'Not good at drawing portraits,' Daniel scoffed ironically, clearly impressed with what he saw. 'You understated your talent, Melora. That looks just like us, doesn't it, Simone?'

The little girl was stunned as she looked at the picture of herself. 'Wow!' The word was breathed with awe and Melora felt a warm and fuzzy glow spread through her at the combination of father and daughter showing her their appreciation. Daniel looked over at her above

Simone's head. The child was still exclaiming about the drawing. There, in his rich brown gaze, she saw a gentle caress, as though he was not only appreciating her talent but also thanking her for making his daughter happy.

When she smiled back at him, the look turned from one of thanks to one of need and Melora felt as though a burning hot sensation of desire had shot from him, penetrating the defences she was still scrambling to erect. How could he make her entire body tremble, make her breathing escalate and her heart pound wildly with just one look?

She was unable to look away, even though he was creating havoc with her equilibrium.

'Daniel…' she began when the loud screeching of truck brakes pierced the air. The PMA transport truck was braking rapidly, the action jolting them all around and onto each other. Daniel automatically reached out for Melora while his other arm stayed firmly around Simone's waist. Eventually, when they came to a stop, for a split second no one moved.

'What was that?' The question was out of her mouth before she could stop it. Obviously something was wrong or they wouldn't have stopped.

'I don't know. I'll need to check it out.' He looked down at Simone then back at Melora. He had no idea what danger might be around them and how he was going to protect them from it. Simone was his baby girl, his world, and he'd vowed to B'lana that he would take care of her. Melora, however, was the woman he simply could not stop thinking about. The fact that she'd become so very important to him in such a very short time was undeniable, and he wanted to keep her safe as well.

Melora and Simone. He had to protect them.

'Are you hurt, *Separ*?' he asked his daughter, his hands quickly running over her to make sure she didn't have any bumps or bruises and that her cast was still intact.

'I'm fine, Daddy.'

'Good. Melora?'

'I'm fine.'

Daniel looked around at the rest of his crew. 'Everyone OK?'

'Yes,' they all replied.

'We go and look,' Belhara said to Daniel, who nodded in agreement.

'Melora, would you mind holding Simone?'

'Sure.' Melora quickly held out her arms and Simone needed no more coaxing than that, leaving her father's arms to go to the safety of Melora's. He stood and started making his way through the truck, and just before he was about to jump off the end, Melora couldn't help but call, 'Be careful.' Goodness only knew what they would find. Would it be soldiers? Soldiers with guns? Friend or foe?

Daniel's answer was to look at her over his shoulder, grin and wink, sending a rioting shock wave of goose-bumps through her.

'Always.'

CHAPTER TEN

'IT's an emergency,' Daniel said, appearing at the rear of the truck a minute later. 'Simone, come and sit up front in the truck with Perry, the driver. You remember Perry,' he said as he lifted her from the truck and carried her round to the driver's door.

'Hi, Perry,' Simone said cheerfully. 'Look at my arm.'

'How on earth did you do that?' Perry asked, and Simone started to tell him the whole story.

'That should keep her busy,' Melora remarked from behind Daniel, and it was only then he realised that she'd climbed out of the truck. 'What's the situation?' she asked as they headed back to the rear of the truck to collect supplies.

'An old car has crashed. Wrapped around the tree.'

'How many people on board?' Sue asked as she quickly pulled a few of the portable medi-kits from the containers they'd packed in the rear of the truck.

'I did a brief head count. Made at least five. Could be more. Perry's calling it in.'

'At *least* five?' Melora's eyebrows hit her hairline. 'But doesn't the car only seat four?'

'Not many people have transport,' Daniel replied. 'So if a car is headed in a specific direction, people just hop on board. Everybody ready?' he asked as the team assembled. 'Good. Let's go.' Daniel quickly blew a kiss to Simone before leading his team forward.

By now, as they'd been working together for some time, they all shifted into their specific areas. Bel and P'Ko-lat did a sort of triage, Richard called for Keith to come and take a look at a patient who had multiple fractures, Belhara was working with Sue to help stabilise and talk to one of the young teenagers who had been thrown clear of the wreckage to find out exactly what had happened.

Daniel had walked over to the wreckage, calling for Melora to grab a medi-kit and follow him. She gasped when she saw the vehicle. It wasn't a sturdy Jeep like the one she'd travelled in with Daniel but a small old car, circa 1950s, which appeared to be held together by string and tape, the rust doing its best to break it all apart. The roof of the car had been cut away a long time ago, no doubt in order to hold more people. The large, firm tree trunk, however, had penetrated the bonnet, smashing through the engine and ending up almost in the driver's seat.

'Most of the hangers-on would have been knocked clear when the vehicle hit the tree but not these guys.' Daniel's words were direct but filled with compassion as they carefully went closer to see to the people most affected by the crash. The smell of petrol was in the air and both of them recognised this fact.

It was clear that the driver was dead, impaled through the heart by a large branch, but Daniel still pressed his fingers to the man's carotid pulse to confirm it. There were two people and a lot of baggage, items wrapped in large blankets all crammed into the back seat, and one person in the front passenger seat. Melora went round to the passenger side, stepping carefully through the debris of bits of car panelling, leaves, twigs and other things in order to get to where she needed to be. All the time she was mentally going through what she needed to do.

She was finding it difficult to come to terms with the fact that this MVA was just like the ones she'd assisted with back in Australia. For some silly reason she'd thought that out here in the jungle she wouldn't see this sort of accident. There were no six-lane highways here, no freeways, no cement flyovers, and yet here she was, assisting at an MVA that was just as intense as the ones she'd attended back home.

While she wanted to look and watch and understand how this could have happened, to grasp the fact that there had been so many people in such a small vehicle, to compare this country with her own, she had a job to do. Nothing mattered except doing what she did best.

She put the medi-kit on the ground at her feet and pressed her fingers to the neck of the woman in the front passenger seat. 'Pulse is weak.' She called to the woman but received no answer. She shifted to help Daniel check the people in the back. 'This young man is dead,' she reported of the teenager closest to her, noting how even if he'd somehow managed to survive the enormous visible damage to his skull, he would have suffered from massive brain damage.

'The girl has a pulse but still not as strong as I'd hoped,' Daniel told her after checking the other passenger in the back. 'These blankets crammed around her no doubt cushioned her from much of the impact.' He shook his head at the image before him. It wasn't the first time he'd come across such an accident and this one was nowhere near as bad as others as it appeared there had been a total of about eight or nine people involved. Sometimes the roads out here, especially after rains, could be as treacherous as any of the roads back in England.

'Right,' he said to Melora. 'Let's get them out so we can treat them.'

'We just shift them out?'

'There's no time for stabilising before moving. This car is volatile and even if we cause more injuries along the way, it's better than getting blown up.'

'Blown up!' This country was so different from her own. Coming here, she'd expected to be treating gunshot wounds, or giving immunisations, or doing minor surgical operations, and even then she'd had her eyes opened, especially after performing emergency surgery on Meimii, but attending an accident where the car might blow up?

Again, she realised there was no fire brigade coming to douse the area with foam to protect against such an event. There were no ambulances on their way to help out with the casualties. *They* were the help and if she didn't get her thought processes back in focus, she wouldn't be able to provide much of that.

Daniel came around to her side and together they managed to shift the woman in the front passenger seat, carrying her to a safer area. Melora collected her medi-kit and checked the woman while Daniel called for Richard and Belhara to help him pull out the front seat of the car to give them better access to the people in the back.

'The petrol leak is not too large,' Melora heard Belhara remark, and within another moment she was joined by Sue, who helped her to stabilise the patient as best they could.

'What will happen to all these people? The ones who are still alive?' Melora asked. 'They need more treatment, they need more care. We don't have any facilities out here, only the medical supplies we've brought with us. What do we do?'

Daniel could hear the heartbreak in Melora's voice as he and Belhara carried over the young girl from the back seat. They placed her on the ground near where Melora knelt.

'I've had our driver radio for another transport. We'll shift as many as we can to my mother's village. They have a clinic building there with supplies. Apart from that...' he met her gaze and she could see the pain and suffering he felt '...we do whatever we can.'

And that was the entire reason why she'd come here, not only to find some peace within her own life but to give to others. In looking outwards, she'd been able to heal inwards, and as her gaze held Daniel's for a split second, she could see that he was as much affected by what was happening around them as she was. This great man loved his country, loved giving help and support on a daily basis. He was truly amazing.

'OK.' Melora nodded and returned her thoughts back to her patients. As the older woman was as stable as possible, she shifted to work on the young girl, running her hands over limbs and bones and feeling her way to some sort of diagnosis. She used her penlight torch to check the girl's eyes and then hooked a stethoscope into her ears, listening to the heart, the lungs and the abdomen.

'Pupils equal and reacting to light, fracture to right arm as there is no radial pulse on that side, distended abdomen, possible bladder rupture due to patient voiding, and head injury. High probability of internal bleeding.'

Keith came over and rechecked the girl's bones. 'Fractured pelvis, or so it feels.'

'That could account for the internal inju—'

'Melora!' Daniel's tone was insistent and she immediately stood and headed over to where he was. He was kneeling on the ground next to a child of about eight who had been thrown from the car. The child had a large slash across the abdomen as well as having an arm and leg twisted at odd angles.

'I thought it seemed odd that the woman in the front seat was all alone. She had no paraphernalia around her, which meant she'd no doubt been holding someone. The orthopaedic fractures are clean breaks but...' he pointed to the child's red-stained abdomen '...take a look.'

Melora pulled on a fresh pair of gloves and felt gingerly around. 'I need light. Have we got a torch?'

Daniel pulled one from his pocket and shined it in the area.

'Right, I'll need gauze, packing, a clamp and double-zero Vicryl. As the child is still unconscious, let's get to work.'

Daniel arranged for one of the less injured passengers to come and hold the torch while he pulled on some gloves to assist Melora in this impromptu surgery. She debrided the wound as best she could before finding the offending arteries and suturing them closed.

Bel had come over and inserted a saline drip, which would help replace fluids. Melora was almost finished when the child started to regain consciousness but Belhara was on hand to administer a sedative in order to keep the child still while Melora finished what she was doing.

After suturing the wound closed, Bel applied a sterile bandage while Daniel took a look at the boy's arm, carefully manipulating the bones back into a more stable alignment before splinting them into place.

'His blood pressure is more improved,' Bel announced, and Melora gave a little sigh of satisfaction.

Daniel was kneeling beside her, finishing off his bandaging, and looked at her with a mixture of pride and happiness. She was such a remarkable woman. Life here in Tarparnii was very different from her own world in Australia, and yet whenever a different situation was presented to her, she took a moment to readjust and then dived right in. 'Good work,' he said softly.

She swallowed. 'Thanks.' The word was but a whisper. They looked into each other's eyes for a moment longer before both of them jolted back into their professional personas. 'What's the status on the other patients?' she asked, rising to her feet and pulling off her gloves. She headed in one direction, Daniel headed in the other, but even as they worked, continuing to provide medical care to the people who needed it, she was acutely aware of his whereabouts at any given moment.

When the second transport truck arrived, bringing extra bamboo stretchers and supplies, they were able to load the most critical patients into that truck. The people who had either jumped or been thrown clear of the impact and had, therefore, only suffered less extensive injuries boarded the medical transport along with Simone, Sue and Bel.

As they were packing up, some of the soldiers arrived at the scene and Melora recognised one of them as Daniel's cousin, Paul. The two men spoke gravely for about five minutes, Daniel explaining as much as he knew. They walked to the front of the vehicle and were looking at it when Melora climbed into the truck to monitor the more critical patients.

Out of the four people they'd found in the car, only two had survived and neither of them had regained consciousness as yet. The total number of people involved in the accident had been nine and as Melora checked on the eight-year-old boy, pleased he seemed to be doing much better, she knew there was still much to be done.

Daniel climbed into the truck just as she'd finished doing observations on the two unconscious women from the car. Keith was monitoring the two other critical patients and Belhara was keeping a close eye on the boy.

'Reports?' he asked as the truck rumbled to life, taking them to their destination. They all filled him in on the status of the patients and by the time they arrived in the village where Daniel's mother lived, Melora was positive the young girl with the pelvic fracture would require immediate surgery to stabilise her.

Their arrival at the village of his mother was not what Daniel had initially planned, the trucks basically pulling up and carting their patients directly to the clinic, where another three PMA staff were in residence. Melora and Keith along with Belhara as anaesthetist went directly into the 'operating room' with the young girl.

It was three hours later that they finally came out, Melora looking weary and ready for a sleep.

'How is she?' Daniel could see how exhausted Melora was and wanted to haul her into his arms, hold her close, support her weight, tell her to rest her head. He wanted to take her tension and make it disappear like a magic trick. He wanted to massage her shoulders to relieve her anxiety and when he realised his palms were itching to touch her, to help her, he quickly clasped them together.

'She's stable. Any other news on the rest of the patients?' She closed her eyes, listening to his report, and was pleased to hear that the other woman from the car had regained consciousness and was improving.

'They are mother and daughter. The driver was her *par'machkai* and the other teenage boy in the car was her son. At least we have managed to save two of her children.'

'Oh, the poor woman. To lose so much!'

Daniel heard the crack in her voice, her words so heartfelt and filled with compassion. She cared. Melora *really* cared about these people and he couldn't take it any longer. Without a word he stepped forward, placing his arms about her, urging her closer, and by some miracle, instead of pushing him away, especially after he'd already told her he needed to focus his attention on Simone, she drew close to him…needing him as much as he needed her.

Her arms came instantly around him, both of them offering and receiving comfort in the wake of the devastation they'd witnessed. Such loss, such heartache, such pain.

'Along with Keith, you have saved her daughter. That will mean a lot.' He spoke softly near her ear, breathing in the intoxicating scent of the woman he found difficult to resist.

'I hate MVAs,' she murmured against his chest, breathing him in, desperate to make a memory, to recall every tiny detail about this man who she knew she could never be with. Worlds apart. 'I guess I hadn't thought I'd come across them here.'

'Sort of jolts you back into reality. One minute you're sketching and the next you're suturing.' And it *had* jolted him back to reality because even though he knew on a logical level that there really couldn't be any future for himself and Melora together, he was desperate to keep her safe, to protect her, to be near her—for ever.

He'd tried to deny such feelings, he'd tried to push them to the rear of his mind and to focus on keeping his daughter safe, doing his job, doing what was expected of him, but surely he could find some room in his life to keep this woman close?

Melora eased back, knowing if she didn't make some sort of move to put distance between them she might just want to stay in the secure embrace of his arms for the rest of her life. She looked up at him and noticed that although his brows were drawn together in confusion, there was also repressed desire in his eyes.

'When I'm in your arms,' she whispered, 'I feel as though I can cope with such situations as we've just come through. You give me...' But she shouldn't. She couldn't tell Daniel that he gave her strength, that ever since he'd come into her life her world had become enriched. Where there had been pain, he'd brought healing. Where there had been lack of self-confidence, he'd boosted her up. Where there had been hopelessness, he'd shown her how to hope.

She didn't want to put any extra pressure on him, let him know that she'd come to rely on him. He had big decisions to face because if he *did* decide to take Simone out of the country in the pursuit of her education, it would mean that *he* would have to leave Tarparnii. His work, his friends, his family...his life. There was no place for her in such a decision. This was something he needed to figure out and although she wanted nothing more than to suggest he come and live in Australia for a while, to investigate the schooling system in a country that was much closer to Tarparnii than England, and that he think about *his* needs as well as those of his daughter, she didn't feel she had the right to put so much pressure on him.

As she continued to look into his eyes, her own heart radiating love for him, Melora knew she was moving deeper and deeper into the fire, wanting to be with him, to be close to him, wanting to have what she couldn't have.

She didn't care where they were, who was around them or what else was happening in the world. Right now, at this point in her life, she was accepting the fact that being in Daniel's arms, feeling that same surge of longing and need pass through both of them, only succeeded in enhancing the intense emotions she already felt for him.

'I give you…what?' he prompted quietly.

She paused before answering, breathing in and out, allowing his scent to wash over her, to relax her. 'You give me strength, Daniel.' The words were barely a whisper. 'And I thank you for that.'

'Oh, Melora.' He exhaled and tightened his hold on her as though he never wanted to let her go. 'You are important to me. Please don't think you're not. But—'

'I know. I know,' she interjected. 'We come from different worlds. We have different circumstances to face. Me with reconstructive surgery, and you with Simone's education.'

'Our lives are on separate paths,' he confirmed. 'And I wish that it could be different. I wish we'd met each other at a different point in our lives, when these issues weren't so relevant.'

'It just wasn't meant to be.'

There was such sadness in her eyes, such desolation and despair in her voice, and Daniel's heart turned over with yearning. He wanted this woman. He was through denying it and even though he knew he shouldn't, he urged her closer, tightening his arms around her, the need to kiss her, even if it was just once, was something he desperately desired. It wasn't often he gave in to his own desires but right here, right now, in this one brief moment, he needed to.

Neither of them spoke, both of them caught up in the sensations that surrounded them. She was only there for a few more days. After that she would be gone from his life for ever. He wanted to hold her, to touch her, to kiss her, and this might be his one and only opportunity to do that.

He knew it was wrong. He knew he shouldn't allow them to traverse this path, knowing that it could lead to even stronger heartache, but the longing, the need, the overwhelming desire to press his lips to hers were becoming too hard to fight.

'Mel...' She was looking at his mouth, watching the way his lips formed her name. When her tongue came out to lick the plump, pink lips, as though she was just waiting for him and him alone, something deep within him snapped and he edged closer.

He had never felt this strongly about any woman since B'lana and that in itself spoke volumes. Melora was intelligent, she was honest and she was absolutely divine. She loved Simone, he could see it whenever the two of them were together. The 'bright' girls, their hair shining in the sunlight. Melora was important to him and the sensations whirring around them, their pheromones, mixing and combining together, were becoming too intoxicating to ignore.

'Daniel,' she whispered, the distance between their mouths now barely millimetres. 'Please?' There was a slight pleading, a slight question and a lot of need radiating from her. She wanted this. He wanted this.

With their hearts beating wildly in unison, the rest of the world disappearing from around them, their mouths finally came into contact with each other.

Melora sighed into the kiss, unable to believe that Daniel was actually kissing her but at the same time enjoying every passing second. His mouth was soft and sensual, not hot and demanding, as she'd thought it might have been. He wasn't pressuring her, he wasn't forcing her into anything she didn't want and instead was taking his time, as though he was savouring every new sensation.

Cherished.

That was the way his touch, his hold made her feel. It was as though now that they were here, he wanted to take his time, to make it last and to burn it into his memory. His hand at her back was warm and firm, his thumb moving in little circles, each tiny motion causing a new flood of tingling awareness to course through her.

Never had any man kissed her in such a way. He not only made her feel safe and secure but he made her feel cherished and treasured. She was important…to him. And when he opened his mouth a little wider, his tongue gently caressing her lower lip, she gave up any remnants of control. She wanted to get lost in the passion and the pleasure that was Daniel Tarvon.

As though by mutual consent, they deepened the kiss, the flavours of her mouth, the sweetness of her scent, the delight of her body so close to his a memory he would hold close for ever. This woman, this most special, most precious woman who had been through so much, who was far stronger than she realised, was building a response in him he'd never felt before.

The fact that he wanted to hold her close and protect her for as long as he possibly could was something he could rationalise and come to terms with, but the way she was setting his body alight, with the way her response to him was firing up a furnace that he doubted would ever burn out, was something he hadn't expected at all.

The woman was intoxicating. Melora Washington's luscious lips, opened to his own, accepting his touch, her body as close to his as she dared get, was enough to show him how incredible she was. The scent of freshness, the scent he equated with her was mingling with his own scent and the pheromones they were creating between them became a heady concoction, driving them both forward.

He'd wanted this moment—the one he now realised had been inevitable from about five seconds after he'd been made aware of her presence at the airport—to last far longer than he knew it could, but oxygen, or the lack there of, was starting to become a necessary factor for him to consider...soon.

When she sighed and leaned into him, he brought her nearer, the need to have her as close as possible becoming almost too much to bear.

The sound of someone else clearing their throat behind them made Melora freeze, her eyes snapping opening to look intently into his.

'Daniel?' The female voice was accented but rich and mature in its tones.

Daniel slowly relaxed his hold on Melora but didn't let her go even as she swivelled in his arms.

'Melora.' His voice was deep, personal and very close to her ear, as he held out a hand to the woman before them. 'May I introduce you to Nahkala. My mother.'

CHAPTER ELEVEN

His *mother*!

Melora was quick to disengage herself from Daniel and, trying not to blush at having been caught in such a compromising position by his *mother*, she stepped forward and took the woman's outstretched hands, pleased she knew enough Tarparnese now to greet his mother properly.

'You are very welcome,' Nahkala said in her perfectly modulated English. 'I am sorry that your arrival in my village was not all it should have been but we all appreciate your gifts in saving the lives of our people.'

'Thank you. I am honoured to be here and to be so warmly welcomed by you,' Melora replied, and then was surprised when Nahkala let go of her hands, only to place a warm hand against her cheek.

'How could I not welcome the woman who has rescued my Daniel?' After a brief moment Nahkala stepped back. 'Please, excuse me. I can hear my grandchild calling my name. I do miss her.'

Melora watched Daniel's mother go, admiring the way she seemed to glide with authority and grace. She turned to face Daniel. 'Rescued?'

Daniel shook his head. 'Sometimes she mixes up the translation of English words. Don't worry about it.

Right now we need to check on the rest of our patients and then have something to eat.'

Melora was too tired to argue and allowed him to lead the way. She still couldn't believe that he'd kissed her, that it had been completely amazing and that all she wanted was more, more, more. Pleasure was mixed with pain as she worked hard to put mental distance between them. They both knew that this attraction, which only seemed to grow more intense every moment they spent together, couldn't lead anywhere permanent.

They'd only be fooling themselves if they thought otherwise and Melora prided herself on not being a fool. Focusing on work, on the people around them, seemed to be the order for the rest of the day. Nahkala and the people of her village were holding their own version of a welcoming banquet for all the new and familiar people who had come to help out.

The banquet involved some of the younger women doing a native dance and some of the young men showing off their hunting skills as they pretended to hunt the shadows cast by the fire. Melora enjoyed it all immensely but as the evening progressed, she made sure there was distance between herself and Daniel.

He'd kissed her. It had been one of the most incredible events in her life. It had shown her that even though she may consider her body unattractive and maybe even deformed, Daniel most certainly didn't see her that way at all. When he'd held her, he'd made her feel soft and gentle and pretty and highly feminine.

It went a long way to boosting her self-confidence, which had been seriously damaged. Now, though, if she looked at herself through his eyes, she saw a woman who was a survivor. Not only had she survived breast cancer and the incapacitating treatments that went along with it, but that she'd survived Leighton's dismissal of her. Through Daniel's eyes, she saw herself as strong, desirable, a woman of substance…a woman who was more than capable of facing her uncertain future.

After the celebrations and before she turned in for the night, she checked on their patients once more, talking to Bel and Keith, who were doing the first night shift. When she was satisfied with the statuses, she headed to the hut where she'd been told she was sleeping. Richard, Sue and Belhara were already lying down on their mats, half-asleep as they chatted to the three other staff members who resided permanently in this village.

'Where's Daniel?' she asked as she unpacked her bag, hoping the question came out sounding nonchalant, even though she felt as though she was drawing attention to herself simply by asking.

'He's sleeping in his mother's hut,' Sue told her. 'Apparently, Simone fell asleep on Nahkala's shoulder at the end of the celebrations. The little darling looked so gorgeous.' Sue yawned as she'd finished speaking.

Melora nodded, feeling lost and sad and bereft at the fact that she hadn't been able to say goodnight to Simone. Her throat started to ache and her eyes started to itch as she worked valiantly to hold back tears.

She knew she had no cause to complain. Nahkala was Simone's grandmother and of course she and Daniel would be staying in his mother's hut, rather than bunking down with the rest of the PMA crew. It was silly to feel so upset about that, about feeling as though she'd been shut out once again from Daniel's life.

He'd kissed her.

She had known at the time that it couldn't change anything, had warred with herself about going through with it, but, of course, she'd been unable to resist him, especially when he had been the one to reach for her as she'd exited the hospital. He'd been the one to touch her, comfort her, hold her close.

He'd kissed her…and nothing had changed. He still had his life. She still had hers. The world would keep turning and time would continue to pass. Simone would be cared for by those around her and Daniel would come to an arrangement about the importance of her education. She would return to Australia, focus on her reconstructive surgery and then decide what to do with the rest of her life.

Coming here to Tarparnii had shown her that there was much more to life than what she'd settled for over the years. She'd always thought that having had cancer was a bad thing, but surviving cancer had forced her to look outside her normal bonds, to see the world through different eyes and to realise there was more to her life than the inside of a hospital.

Loving Daniel, though, had certainly put a spanner in the works. She hadn't expected that to happen at all but accepting it was part of the new process she was learning to follow. The people of Tarparnii had a way of accepting things beyond their control. They would contemplate, absorb and then move on with their lives.

Melora thought about Daniel, sleeping in his mother's hut beside his daughter, who would no doubt be quietly slumbering, her head resting on her frilly, pink, pillow as she nuzzled close to her father. Simone was as much a part of her as Daniel was, and as she lay there and closed her eyes, she knew that she would not trade her time here in Tarparnii for anything in the world. Never had she thought she would feel as though her life was back on track and never had she thought she'd be able to open her heart and love another.

She only hoped that when she left, returning to her world in Australia, her heart would be able to continue to move forward, that her love for Daniel would diminish over time and that she would be able to think of her wonderful time here in Tarparnii without the pang of regret that pierced her heart even now. Silently, though, she doubted she would ever stop loving him or his gorgeous daughter.

'I wish we'd met each other at a different point in our lives.'

Daniel's words ran around her head and as she closed her eyes tighter, clutching her hands to her chest, she wished it could be that way, too.

'Goodnight, my loves,' she whispered quietly into the dark.

Over the next days they ran several clinics, which usually started before the sun came up and ended long after it had set. Simone was as bubbly and as bright as usual, getting nearly everyone she met to sign her cast.

'There's no more room left,' she told Melora one day, showing off her cast. The little girl was still very generous with her cuddles and kisses and had insisted on having Melora read the bedtime story every night.

Nahkala was a quietly spoken woman who tended to observe more than she talked.

'When you stop and you listen to people,' Nahkala said, the night before Melora was due to leave Tarparnii, 'that is when their hearts tell you what they are really feeling.'

Melora had just finished reading Simone a bedtime story, and the two women were sitting and watching the child sleep. 'That's how I feel with Simone. I love spending time with her. She is a wonderful girl. Daniel has done an amazing job so far and will no doubt continue to do so.'

'You hold my son in high esteem.' Nahkala's words were a statement and Melora knew there was no getting around it. Honesty was valued with these people and she respected that.

'Yes. Very.'

'Your heart, when you look at him, is filled with love.'

Melora looked over at Simone, then back at Nahkala. 'Yes.'

'It is right,' Nahkala said with a bright smile. 'You are a woman of great integrity, *Separ*. I am thankful that my son has chosen well.'

'Oh, no.' Melora quickly shook her head, instantly pushing back the tears that sprang to her eyes. 'Daniel and I are not together. I'm leaving to return to Australia tomorrow and Daniel has some big decisions to make. There is very little chance we'll see each other again.'

Nahkala reached over and took one of Melora's hands in hers. 'There are many paths that love can take, Melora. Some are straight, some are winding, some are of great surprise, and some have mountains that need to be patiently traversed.'

Melora smiled. 'I think Daniel and I must have the last three combined.'

'What seems impossible is not. The two of you still have some work to accomplish.' She brushed her free hand down Melora's cheek with motherly concern. It was touching. 'You must have the faith, *Separ*.'

Melora nodded and looked over at Simone, swallowing and trying to get her emotions back under control. 'Faith?'

'Faith in yourself and in Daniel.' After a short

pause Nahkala let Melora go before rising gracefully to her feet. 'It is time for you to rest. Tomorrow will be eventful.'

'Yes.' Melora leaned over Simone and pressed one last kiss to the sleeping child's forehead before standing. 'Thank you, Nahkala.'

'You are most welcome, *Separ*.'

As Melora left Nahkala's hut, she headed across the now deserted village clearing just as Daniel was coming out of the clinic. Her heart leapt with delight when she saw him but it was swiftly followed by a deep and powerful ache. Within a matter of hours she would be leaving him.

Ever since their kiss the other day, both of them had worked hard at maintaining a professional distance, knowing that any acceleration of what they might be feeling towards each other couldn't be. She had her life in Australia and he had his life here with Simone. To deepen the feelings they had for each other, to give in and touch and kiss and simply enjoy spending whatever free time they had together, would have only made their inevitable parting that much worse.

Daniel stopped walking the instant he saw her but after a moment shoved his hands into his pockets and came in her direction. 'Simone asleep?' he asked.

Melora's smile was always easy when they talked of his daughter. He could see quite clearly just how much she loved Simone and also how much Simone loved Melora. Never before had his daughter bonded so completely with another woman. Never before had Daniel bonded so instantly with a woman as he had with Melora. He dug his hands deeper into his pockets.

'Yes. She's an angel.'

He chuckled. 'When she sleeps? I'd agree with that. A perfect angel.'

'I didn't mean it like that. She's an angel all the time, in my eyes.'

'Yes, but you seem to see the best in people, Melora.' His words had softened and with the way he was looking at her, as though she were the most incredible woman in the world, Melora was having a difficult time coping being so close to him.

'Thank you, Daniel. That's a nice thing to say.'

'It's the truth.'

They were both silent, both intensely aware of the other, but they still kept their distance.

'Everything all right at the clinic?' she asked.

'No complications. Patients all sleeping. Sue and Richard are taking the night shift.'

She nodded, pleased to hear that everyone in the clinic was fine. She'd also planned on heading to the clinic, knowing she wouldn't sleep much at all tonight. Every time she thought about leaving here, about returning to her bleak Daniel-and-Simone-less life back in Australia, her throat would close over with sorrow and her eyes would sting with tears. She'd hoped that keeping busy at the clinic tonight might help keep her thoughts at bay.

'Well…' Daniel sidestepped her. 'I'd better get some sleep. Big day tomorrow. Pack up here and then two trucks headed in very different directions.'

Was he talking about them?

'Anyway, I hope you get some rest tonight, Mel.'

'Mmm-hmm.' She nodded, wanting to reach for him, her heart begging for him to reach for her, to hold her, to tell her that he loved her, that he never wanted her to leave him. She bit her tongue in order to keep herself somewhat under control. He turned and had taken two steps away from her when she called his name. He stopped and turned eagerly to look at her.

'I've been meaning to ask you...'

'Yes?' His eagerness increased.

'What does *Separ* mean?'

'*Separ.*'

'Yes. I've heard you call Simone that a lot of times. I've always meant to ask you what it means and as I leave here in about seven hours' time, I thought now might be the last chance I get.'

He wished she wouldn't talk about leaving because it only caused his heart to ache. '*Separ* is a precious gemstone. They are very rare in Tarparnii now, the government having mined the land many years ago for these exquisitely beautiful stones. They are red and green, blue and purple, pink and orange, with flecks of silver and gold.' He frowned for a moment. 'They are difficult to describe but they are more beautiful than any opal, they are brighter than any diamond. The only time I saw a stone was when I was about eight years old and even then I remember being captivated by the colours when holding it to the light. It was a defining day for me. It was the day when I felt an emotional connection to beauty, when I appreciated it.' He paused then asked, 'Why do you ask now?'

Melora shrugged. 'Your mother...called me *Separ* tonight.'

Daniel processed this information then stepped forward, crossing the distance between them. He knew if he pulled her into his arms he would never let her go and let her go he must so instead he took both of her hands in his and held them tightly.

'She is right to call you that, Melora. You are radiant,

you are stunning, and you are incredibly open and honest and beautiful.' Daniel couldn't believe how his voice cracked at the last few words. 'You are a precious gem-stone, priceless and greatly appreciated.' And loved.

He swallowed over the dryness in his throat as the words penetrated his mind. He loved Melora? No. He couldn't possibly have fallen in love with her...could he?

Melora put her key into the lock and opened the door to her Sydney apartment, pushing it wearily as her carry bag fell from her shoulder, jolting her elbow. The instant she was inside, she left the bag on the floor by the door, tossed her keys onto the side table and shuffled through the place, not even bothering to turn on any lights.

In her bedroom she slumped down across the bed, not even bothering to take off the coat she'd had to put on at Sydney airport due to the coolness of the evening breeze. Closing her eyes, she pulled a pillow close, hugging it to her before letting the pent-up emotions she felt like she'd been holding onto for an eternity to come to the surface.

Everything was wrong.

Her world was wrong. The plane she'd disembarked from had been large and impersonal. There had been no one waiting for her and she'd come home to a dark and depressing apartment. Even the bed felt far too soft after two weeks of sleeping on a mat on the ground.

She missed the bright cheerful faces of the people from the villages, she missed the native Tarparniian birds singing their songs to wake her in the morning, she missed the thatched, peaked roofline of the huts, she missed...everything.

And everyone.

She missed Simone.

But most of all she missed Daniel.

Daniel. The man she'd fallen in love with.

She had never expected to meet a man who was so incredibly wonderful, who made her feel special and loved and cherished. A man who was such an amazing father to his little girl, determined to do everything he could to give her the best possible upbringing. A man who gave to other people like the heavens gave sunshine and rain. A man who, when he held her close, his lips wreaking havoc with her insides as his mouth moved tenderly over hers, made her feel as though her life had true meaning again.

The phone by her bed started ringing but she ignored it, pulling the pillow tighter, hugging it closer. She didn't want to speak to anyone, didn't want to see anyone, didn't want to do anything. From the moment he'd dropped her hands and walked away from her last night, Melora had felt her heart start to slowly break. When the transport trucks had come to take them to the airport, Daniel had had to forcibly peel a crying Simone from Melora's arms, the child declaring that she wasn't going to let 'her Melora' go.

Daniel had held his sobbing daughter, the tears in his eyes mirroring the devastation in Melora's as he'd stood there and watched as her truck had rumbled away, the distance between them increasing, emulating the pain in her heart.

The two people she loved the most were not with her and that alone was enough to cause her immeasurable pain.

She pulled the other side of the duvet over her, not even bothering to take off her shoes or get changed. Curling into the foetal position, she realised that nothing else mattered in this world. Not her job, not her apartment, not even her impending surgery.

Daniel and Simone.

She'd gone looking for her life and she'd found it, but without Daniel and Simone it was as meaningless as it had been before…perhaps even more so. With tears streaming silently down her face, pains in her chest due to the heart that really did feel as though it was breaking, Melora allowed herself to wallow in sorrow.

'Right, that's it. I'm officially worried about you.' Emmy sat down opposite Melora at her dining-room table. 'You've been back in Australia for three days and you've hardly said a word about Tarparnii other than it was "good". What is that supposed to mean?' Emerson Freeman pushed her long auburn hair back from her shoulders, picked up her coffee cup and glared at her friend.

'It means it was just what I needed. Sort of.'

'Why didn't you call us to come and pick you up from the airport? You've been hibernating here in your apartment ever since you got back, except for seeing your surgeon, and you're not answering any of your calls.' Emmy put her cup down, coffee forgotten, and looked at her friend with concern. 'What happened, Mel?' she asked softly, and it was that soft, caring tone that was Melora's undoing.

As she looked at her friend, she felt her eyes blur with tears and her bottom lip start to quiver. 'So much,' she whispered, and sniffed. 'I went to Tarparnii to try and figure out what had happened to my life and…I got more than I bargained for.'

She swallowed over the lump in her throat and stood, heading to the tissue box on the coffee table, only to find the box was empty. She went to the box on the kitchen counter but it was empty as well. She pulled off a piece of kitchen paper towel and blew her nose.

Melora leaned against the kitchen bench for a moment, trying to gather her strength to talk to her friend so that Emmy wouldn't continue to be worried about her. After a few deep breaths she headed back to the dining room and sat down, feeling more composed.

'Tell me about your time. What you did? Which villages you stayed at? Did you like the clinic buildings?'

Melora smiled, her mind instantly jumping to the memory of Daniel stroking the bricks. 'The clinic buildings are brilliant, although I have to say I didn't really appreciate them until we travelled to a different village and I had to perform an appendectomy in a tent.'

Emmy smiled and nodded. 'Good times.'

'I helped deliver a baby not long after I arrived. That was…' she thought back to Daniel, delivering the baby, of J'tana holding her baby for the first time and thanking them both so much for stopping to help her '…miraculous.' She sighed with reflected happiness. 'They called me the "bright" doctor because of my blonde hair.'

'Ah, of course.'

'Simone and I were instant friends, mainly because of our hair.'

'Hair colour is very important to almost five-year-old girls.'

'Yes.' Even saying Simone's name was enough to cause pain in Melora's heart. 'Meeree and Jalak are in excellent health, as always, and Daniel introduced me to his mother, Nahkala.'

'She's an incredible woman, in charge of a very large village and all on her own. That's pioneering stuff in Tarparnii but Nahkala is wise and just. Tarvon definitely takes after her. Caring and protecting people. Just like his mother.'

'Yes. He is good at that.' Melora sipped her coffee, not tasting a thing as she tried to steer her thoughts away from Daniel. She missed him far too much to think about him because when she did, when she allowed herself to contemplate all that she had lost, how her life had changed completely from black to white, her overactive tear ducts started to do their thing again.

'Sue was there.' Melora informed her friend. 'Along with Keith and Richard. They were great and, of course, Bel and Belhara and P'Ko-lat.'

'Sounds as though you were working with a great team.'

'I was.'

'And Tarvon is an excellent leader.'

'The best,' she said with a heartfelt sigh.

'He's quite a guy.'

'You have no idea.' The words were out of her mouth before she could stop them and she quickly put her cup down and closed her eyes.

'Was that a slip of the tongue, my friend? I know something happened in Tarparnii, something big.'

'How can you know that?' she asked, opening her eyes and standing, needing some space.

'You've shut yourself away, Melora.' Emmy spread her arms wide. 'It doesn't take rocket science to figure out that something was wrong. What *really* happened?'

Melora bit her lip then shrugged, deciding she needed someone to talk to.

'I fell in love.' The words came out on rush and the instant they were out she wished them back. Their love could never be. Different worlds. Daniel needed to focus on Simone, to make sure he provided the best education

and care for his child, while she had multiple reconstructive surgeries to undergo. Their lives were just too
different…but that wouldn't always be the case, a little
voice deep inside her heart whispered.

Perhaps once the surgeries were over, after she'd made
a complete recovery, she could go back to Tarparnii, or
to England, to wherever Daniel and his gorgeous girl
were. At that thought a small sliver of hope started to
grow. Could it be possible? Did he care for her in that
way? Did he love her?

'Love?' Emmy's eyebrows hit her hairline. 'With
Tarvon?'

Melora's eyes widened. 'How do you know?'

'I don't know anything. I'm just guessing, but given
the fact that he's taken to calling Dart via the satellite
phone on a daily basis since you returned to Australia,
simply to find out how you are, well, that sort of gave
us a clue.' Emmy clasped her hands to her chest. 'You
really fell in love with him?'

'Yes. He's been calling?' She couldn't believe it.

'Yes.'

'Why didn't he call me?' Perhaps he simply wanted
to know that she was all right and hadn't really wanted
to talk.

'Hmm…let me think…have you been answering your
phone since you returned?'

'Oh, no.' Melora closed her eyes and shook her head.
How could she have been so stupid? She'd been so
wrapped up in her own misery that she hadn't wanted
to talk to anyone. Daniel had tried to call her? Could
that be true?

'The man's been beside himself with worry for you
and when neither Dart nor I could get hold of you, it
was time to take action.'

'I'm sorry.'

'You should be. We were all worried. Poor Tarvon has been crazy with concern.'

There was a knock at her front door and Melora frowned. She wasn't expecting anyone. She looked at Emmy and found her friend grinning like the Cheshire cat. 'Crazy and desperate,' Emmy finished.

Melora's eyes widened with surprise. 'Desperate?'

Emmy didn't answer as she was already on her way to the door, Melora hard on her friend's heels. 'Is that Daniel? Is he here?' Even as the words came out, her entire body started to tremble with fear and uncertainty. Daniel? Here? At her place?

'He wanted to make sure you were home when he arrived. Dart and the twins went to pick them up from his hotel and dropped me here beforehand.'

Melora was astonished.

'It's only because we love you. We would never have interfered otherwise.'

'Well…you could have warned me a bit sooner.' Melora stood in front of her door, brushing down the jeans and pale pink shirt she was wearing. She checked her hair and looked at her bare feet. She was trying not to tremble, trying to remain calm and controlled, but it was becoming increasingly difficult. 'Do I look OK?'

'You look great,' Emmy encouraged. 'Open the door.'

'What if it's not him?' Melora whispered, her heart pounding wildly against her chest, her words drying up in her throat.

'Open the door and find out.' Emmy pointed to the door.

'Right. Right. I know you're right.' She breathed in,

then out, before putting her hand on the handle and opening the door.

And there he stood. Simone was in his arms, and he looked as though he'd aged a year in just a few days. His gaze met hers before quickly taking in the rest of her, lingering briefly on her lips before meeting her eyes once more.

'You're a sight for sore eyes,' he murmured softly.

'My eyes are sore, too, Daddy,' Simone piped up, wriggling from her father's grasp and almost throwing herself at Melora. Melora instantly enveloped the child, holding her close to her heart, breathing her in, kissing her cheeks.

'I've been missing you, Melora. I've cried at night and everything and then we flew on a plane because Daddy said we had to come and get you and tell you that we love you and think you're brilliant and— Ooh, Aunty Emmy!' Now that Simone had 'her Melora' back, it didn't take much to divert her attention. She scrambled from Melora's arms and ran to hug Emmy.

Melora was still stunned, still trying to take it all in. Daniel was here. He was here in Australia. He was in Sydney, in her apartment, standing before her. Daniel was here!

'Why don't Dart and I take Simone and the girls out for some ice cream? Give you two a bit of privacy,' Emmy suggested, and as Simone was more than happy to go with them, they all left.

Melora and Daniel didn't move for a split second before rational thought finally kicked in and Melora stepped back.

'Sorry. Please, come in,' she offered belatedly.

'Thanks.' Daniel came into her apartment, his hands in his pockets, feeling nervous yet determined. She led him past the kitchen and dining room into the lounge room and indicated a chair.

'Have a seat.'

'Thanks,' he said again, looking at the floor-to-ceiling bookshelves filled with all sorts of books, journals and magazines. A computer was set up on a small desk in the corner where the natural light shone in. The two-seater lounge was accompanied by two wingback chairs, a patterned rug in the middle of the floor with a coffee table on top. 'This is just the sort of room I imagined you'd have,' he murmured, not sitting down but rather looking slowly around the room.

'It is?'

'Yes.'

She was feeling highly self-conscious at him being in her home, his size and presence so commanding that he dwarfed the place. It was odd. Standing here. Behaving like polite strangers. Him in his usual attire of shorts, shirt and boots, hair tied back, three-day growth on his face. He looked as wild and as rugged and as incredibly handsome as the first day they'd met.

He took his hands out of his pockets and rubbed them together before returning them to his pockets. 'It's a little cooler here than in Tarparnii.'

She nodded. 'You should have packed warmer clothes.'

'I don't own any.' He smiled then, that gorgeous, heart-melting smile, and Melora reached out a hand to one of the chairs in order to stop herself from falling over. 'Guess I should go buy some, given Simone and I are going to be staying for a while.'

Melora blinked twice. 'Staying?'

His smile was gorgeous and sexy and he was starting to slowly walk towards her and she wasn't sure what to do. Her knees would definitely give way if she tried to move. Her limbs were filled with tingles of anticipation as she watched him close the gap between them.

'Yes. Staying here. In Australia.'

'For Simone's education?'

He shrugged. 'Perhaps…but that's not why I'm here.'

'It's not?' She frowned, her mind unable to compute things due to his nearness.

'No.' He continued to advance slowly towards her, his gaze filled with need and longing and desire.

'Then…why?'

'For you.' He stood before her and put his hands onto her shoulders, looking down into her upturned face with a look of utter adoration in his eyes. 'I'm here for you. After watching you being taken away by that truck, watching as you disappeared from view, watching until the transport was out of sight and still being unable to move due to the constricting pain in my heart, proved to me that letting you go was completely the wrong thing to do.'

'It was?' The words were barely a whisper, her heart melting at what he was saying, her body capitulating at the way he was touching her.

'Simone said it all when you first opened the door, Melora. Neither of us have been able to sleep, both of us—more particularly me—have been so concerned and worried about you. I didn't hear anything from you after you'd left Tarparnii. I had no idea whether you'd arrived home safely, how you were feeling, whether or not your reconstructive surgery was still going ahead, how you were feeling about it all. I knew nothing and I was so beside myself that I took indefinite leave from

PMA and flew here earlier this morning, desperate to be with you.'

'You took leave?'

'Yes. For you. So that I can be here for you when you go through your surgery.'

'You…you *want* to be here?'

'Of course I do, you silly, gorgeous woman.' With that, Daniel pulled her into his arms and Melora leaned against him, feeling the strength he exuded seeping deep into her body. Daniel was here. He'd come for her. He'd come specifically to be with her, to help her, to support her.

He looked down into her upturned face. 'I love you, Melora. I should have said it earlier but I didn't think you wanted to hear it.'

'You crazy man.' She smiled at him. 'How could you not think I would want to hear that when I love you so completely?'

'You do?' He seemed genuinely surprised at that.

'Yes. I've been miserable since I arrived home, not wanting to do anything except return to Tarparnii to be with you and Simone.'

'You want to go back to Tarparnii?'

'Of course I do. I loved it there.'

'But your surgery?'

'Needs to happen. You said that our timing was off and I believed you.'

'I was wrong. Watching you go the other day proved that to me. Without you there, in my life, being an integral part of it…nothing else made any more sense. Not my job with PMA. Not Simone's education. None of it mattered at all if you weren't there by my side. My Melora. My *Separ.*'

'Oh, Daniel.'

After that, there was no more talking as he lowered his mouth to hers, claiming her lips in a kiss of promise…a promise that would last them a lifetime. This time, now that they'd declared their love for each other, there was no holding back.

'Ah…Melora, I think both of us have been a little crazy. Love seeped into us and we were too stunned to think clearly. At least, that's the way you make me feel.' He kissed her again. 'I have missed you so much. These past few days felt like for ever, especially when I couldn't contact you. I'd been notified by PMA that you'd been through your debriefing but apart from that—nothing. That's why I contacted Dart and Emmy, why I enlisted their help, because I simply had to know that you were all right.'

'I'm sorry I wasn't answering the phone. I was… upset. I didn't want to see anyone, talk to anyone… I just wanted you and Simone, and as I couldn't have you…I just shut myself off.'

'Oh, Mel.' He pressed another reassuring kiss to her lips. 'We're here now and we're never going to let you go again. After you left, my life was empty. I had everything I'd always had but until you arrived, I hadn't realised anything was missing. I know that probably doesn't make much sense but the way I feel about you, the deep abiding friendship as well as the intellectual link we share, not to mention that I find you incredibly sexy,' he added, brushing a quick kiss to her lips, 'is what I need to make my life complete. I've loved and lost once in my life and it was painful.' He slowly shook his head. 'But I lived through it. I have Simone and she is a constant blessing on my life. However, there is a void within both of us, a hole that only you can fill.'

Daniel released her but only so he could take her

hands in his as he knelt. Melora's eyes widened in astonishment.

'I apologise if this seems sudden but I know what I want—and that's you. Please, Melora, I humbly beg that you would do me the honour of becoming my *par'machkai*—my partner for life, my wife.'

'Daniel!' There were tears in her eyes, happy tears as she looked down at him. 'Are you sure? I have a few surgeries ahead of me and I don't want to be a burden to you.'

'Yes my beautiful *Separ*. Do you think that because that simpleton you were previously engaged to didn't want you because you've had cancer, I wouldn't?'

'I don't know, Daniel,' she answered honestly. 'My body is…well, it's deformed.'

He shook his head. 'That is only physical. To me, you are perfect.' When he realised she didn't quite believe him, he tried again. 'In Tarparnii we have a saying that roughly translates to mean even a goat with three legs is still a goat.'

'I'm a goat in this scenario?' She wasn't sure whether to be pleased or indignant. Her mind was whirring, trying to compute everything he'd told her.

'You're missing the point. Goats are very valuable in Tarparnii. They provide mohair and milk as well as companionship and warmth in the cooler months, but a goat with three legs can still do what it was designed for. You may have been unfortunate to contract cancer but simply because a part of you has been removed, it doesn't mean you are not beautiful.' His words held power and meaning and she knew he meant every single word.

'It doesn't mean you are less "Melora Washington" than you were when you were first born and named. It doesn't mean that the endearment *Separ* doesn't fit you because it most certainly does. I want to be there, to support you, to protect you and keep you safe.' He rose to his feet, his words firm and direct. 'From that first day when I showed you the tree, split in two, with the new growth coming up through the middle, and you ended up in my arms—I've wanted you to stay there.'

Melora smiled, unable to believe she could really be this happy. Daniel was here. In Australia. Declaring his love and wanting her to marry him, to be with him, to become a family with him and Simone. 'And I wanted to stay. I want to support you, too, Daniel. Simone's education is important and I'll be with you whatever you decide.'

'Whatever *we* decide,' he corrected. 'You're already like a mother to her, Melora. She loves you completely.'

'As I love her. I want to be with you and Simone for ever because, quite simply, you make me so very happy…and before I met you, I didn't think I'd ever find the one place in this world where I truly belonged.'

'It's here,' he said, enfolding her in his arms.

Melora rested her head against his chest, listening to his heart beating, sure and steadfast. Her own heart, which had been so empty and so lost not too long ago, was now filled to overflowing with love, hope and happiness simply because Daniel loved her.

EPILOGUE

LATER in the year, when they returned to Tarparnii, they were greeted warmly by their old friends. Simone had run off in search of her friends the instant the Jeep had come to a stop and as Emmy and Dart helped to unpack their bags, Jalak and Meeree came to greet them all.

Nahkala had come to visit Jalak and Meeree, as well as to attend a very special occasion.

'Melora. I am pleased to know that you have been able to keep the faith in you and Daniel and gain your happy ending. I am honoured to be accepting you into my family,' she said as she kissed both of Melora's cheeks. 'I did not think my Daniel would be blessed to find love twice in his lifetime but then you came and it was clear straight away that the two of you would one day be joined for ever, and now that day is here.'

The village itself was a hub of excited activity as people prepared for the annual *par'Mach* festival, the ceremony where two people were joined together, pledging their undying love and having their hands bound together in a symbol of unity, to thereafter be known as each other's *par'machkai*.

'Thank you for agreeing to have two weddings,' Daniel had murmured near her ear as he'd held her close and kissed her neck. They'd been married in Australia in a private ceremony with Emmy and Dart as their witnesses and Simone as their flower girl. This was to be their proper wedding, with all of their family and friends.

'I'll marry you as many times as I'm allowed to,' Melora replied, unable to believe how incredible it felt to be held by Daniel. She'd come through her recent surgery without any complications. Her surgeons were astounded at her rate of healing and Melora had put it all down to being ecstatically happy. 'That way I definitely know you're mine.'

'You, me, Simone and any other little blessings that come our way.' Daniel slipped his arms around his wife's waist. 'We are a family, my beautiful, intelligent Melora, and that's the way it's going to stay.'

Melora's sigh was filled with contentment as she slightly turned her head to kiss her husband's lips. 'I love our life,' she whispered against his mouth.

'So do I, *Separ*. So do I.'

Medical Romance™

SUMMER SEASIDE WEDDING
by Abigail Gordon

Dr Amelie Benoir plans to spend the summer healing her bruised heart—not falling for the impossibly handsome Dr Leo Fenchurch!

REUNITED: A MIRACLE MARRIAGE
by Judy Campbell

GP Sally Lawson is shocked that her ex, Dr Jack McLennan, still make her pulse race… But Jack is a changed man and he's fighting for a second chance. It might take a miracle, but he wants Sally as his bride

THE MAN WITH THE LOCKED AWAY HEART
by Melanie Milburne

There's definitely chemistry between the mysterious new cop Marc Di Angelo and local doctor Gemma Kendall. But can Gemma release his tightly guarded emotions before he leaves town for good…?

SOCIALITE…OR NURSE IN A MILLION?
by Molly Evans

Spanish doctor Miguel Torres isn't convinced new nurse Vicky has what it takes. Vicky is determined to show him that behind her socialite reputation lies a heart of gold—a heart that's rapidly falling for her gorgeous new boss!

**On sale from 4th March 2011
Don't miss out!**

*Available at WHSmith, Tesco, ASDA, Eason and all good bookshops
www.millsandboon.co.uk*

ST PIRAN'S: THE BROODING HEART SURGEON
bY Alison Roberts

Everyone at St Piran's hospital has fallen under Dr Luke Davenport's spell, except Anna Bartlett, who is certain the ex-army medic is hiding something. She should remain professional, but Anna's longing to be the one to save Luke from his nightmares—if only she can reach out to the man behind the brooding mask…

PLAYBOY DOCTOR TO DOTING DAD
by Sue MacKay

Arriving in Nelson to run the A&E department temporarily, gorgeous Kieran Flynn is greeted with a few life-changing bombshells—including Abby Brown, the woman he spent a magical night with two years ago…

On sale from 4th March 2011
Don't miss out!

Available at WHSmith, Tesco, ASDA, Eason and all good bookshops
www.millsandboon.co.uk